Requiescat

RICHARD B. STEINBERG
AND
GLORIA USISKIN STEINBERG

Northwest Publishing, Inc.
Salt Lake City, Utah

Requiescat

This is a work of fiction.
All characters and events portrayed in this book are fictional,
and any resemblance to real people or incidents is purely coincidental.

For information address: Northwest Publishing, Inc.
6906 South 300 West, Salt Lake City, Utah 84047
SCM 05 12 94

PRINTING HISTORY
First Printing 1994

ISBN: 1-56901-263-6

NPI books are published by Northwest Publishing, Incorporated,
6906 South 300 West, Salt Lake City, Utah 84047.

The name "NPI" and the "NPI" logo are trademarks belonging to
Northwest Publishing, Incorporated.

PRINTED IN THE UNITED STATES OF AMERICA.
10 9 8 7 6 5 4 3 2 1

PART ONE

ROBBY'S WORLD

CHAPTER ONE

SMALL WORLD

From childhood's hour I have not been
As others were—I have not seen
as others saw
Then, in the dawn of a most stormy life,
Was drawn from ev'ry depth of good and ill
The Mystery which binds me still
From the thunder and the storm,
And the cloud that took the form
of a demon in my view.

—Excerpts from Alone
by Edgar Allan Poe

The helicopter raced through the twilight sky, its navigation lights bouncing back at it from the heavily laden clouds of the storm. The air was charged with the electricity from the gathering storm and from the tension in the back of the Medi-Vac chopper.

The medics worked feverishly on their patient just trying to hold their own, trying to keep him alive until they reached the hospital. It was a losing battle. Only the man's will kept him going.

3

The chopper banked and came in on the helispot in the Medical Center's parking lot.

As the door slid open, a large cobalt blue ball of static electricity generated by the helicopter's blades, drawn from the storm, struck at the dying man. It hit the stokes stretcher he lay on, knocking down two of the medics and sending the man crashing to the wet pavement. It was as if the Gods themselves were trying to take the dying man.

Stubbornly, he clung to life.

≥

"What's the prognosis?"

"Dismal."

"Any special instructions?"

"Try and keep him comfortable...until the end."

"What's his name?"

"Robert Moss."

The nurse adjusted Robby's I.V. and checked his pulse. The gunshot wounds to the chest and head had been devastating. He'd had almost his entire blood volume replaced and he was still bleeding internally. He was in a deep coma and, the nurse thought, not long for this world.

Somehow he fought his way back. It was like swimming against the tide in an ocean of molasses but slowly, methodically, he gained ground. He had no time sense, but the fight seemed to last for hours. He felt himself dying but he never gave up, never quit.

He didn't know how.

≥

Images began to flood in on him. The chase, the shots, the searing pain. Suleimein, his family, their bodies.

As Robby struggled to find his way out of the miasma of coma, he remembered the conversation when it was discovered that Suleimein had been blown.

"Is there any direct connection between him and us?"

"No."

"Any way at all that the Iranians can link him to any of our people?"

"No."

"Good, no problem then. Just get another source."

"What about Suleimein? We can't just leave him there! He put his ass on the line for us!"

"I never heard of Suleimein...and neither have you."

≥♣

The desert air had been still and unusually cold. The full moon lit up the stark landscape brightly. Uncomfortably so.

In the distance, Robby watched as the headlights steadily approached. The car stopped at what he knew was the last road block between them and him. He held his breath and prayed, and hoped that God still listened to unredeemable sinners.

His answer came a moment later as he saw the car suddenly lurch forward, shots fired at it from the road block. The car careened wildly ahead, finally slamming into a sand bank. Robby raced forward.

Someone had fired a star shell into the night and the scene was even more brightly illuminated. He could see the body of Suleimein slumped over the steering wheel. He could see the security forces closing in.

He couldn't reach them until it was too late. The soldiers were standing around the car laughing as he opened fire. He cut down three of them with his first burst before they began to return fire. Although he was outnumbered, his anger and pain made the difference. After three minutes, it was over.

He limped to the car, not even aware of his wounds. He steadied himself on the car door and looked in. They were all dead. Suleimein had been shot at least twice in the head, his wife, his son, his baby girl, all dead, their features distorted from the impact of the heavy Kalishnikov shells.

"I'm sorry," he wept softly before turning away. He began walking back into the desert. He got about ten feet before he collapsed from blood loss. He never saw the mercenary's chopper come in for a landing. He briefly opened his eyes as the big man called 'Barker' lifted him into the bubble of the helicopter.

≥♣

He remembered snippets of the trip back. Nameless faces, odd snatches of conversations.

"You can't move him again, he'll die!"

"Then he dies."

"What in hell was he doing out there?"

"Breaking the rules."

As he fought his way out of the coma, he remembered what his favorite professor had once said about his bosses. "They are soulless people whose only rule is win. Not doing what's best or even what's moral, just win."

❧

"Get that tube out stat!"

"Bag him!"

Robby started to cough and then settled into an easy rhythm of breathing.

"You're going to be all right, God knows how, but you'll be all right." The nurse smiled down at him. He tried to speak but succeeded only in getting out a soft croaking sound. She put some ice flakes in his mouth. "The director will be delighted. He's checked on you almost every day."

A minute later, with the nurse leaning very close to hear, Robby said his piece.

"Tell him, I don't work for him anymore."

❧

The kids hurried to get to their classes. Giggling, screeching, whispering, they stopped at their lockers to talk to their friends. Anything to make the most of the six minutes between classes. Their Madonnaesque clothes, their aping of presumed sexiness, contrasted with the innocence of the setting. The bell rang and the corridor emptied, leaving the man standing alone, inhaling the fragrances of youth and dreading the meeting to come.

He made his way to the school office slowly, enjoying the sounds of reluctant learning he heard as he passed each classroom.

"Can I help you?" The sixteen-year-old girl behind the counter eyed him suspiciously. He was used to it.

"I have an appointment with Principal Garner. My name is Robby Moss." He smiled and the young girl smiled back as she went to a telephone. She looked Robby over as she waited for the Principal to answer.

He was just over six feet tall with brown wavy hair, full

mustache and beard. He wore an expensive three piece suit which oddly, did not seem to clash with his longish ponytail.

After a few moments of uncomfortable waiting, the girl showed him into the office.

Garner settled in behind his desk, and he too looked over the stranger.

He saw the hardened expression, the edge of a scar just visible at his collar, the thick callus on the outside edge of Robby's right palm, and he could sense more than see the toughness of the body beneath the expensive clothes. Overall, he felt a danger beneath the smiling blue eyes.

"Thank you for coming, Mr. Moss. Can I get you a cup of coffee?"

"No, thank you, sir. I'm glad you were able to make the time to see me."

The pleasantries were over. "When a Congressman and two former White House Aides sign a letter of recommendation, I make the time. Did you bring your résumé?"

Robby took the Xeroxed sheets from his inside pocket and handed them across the desk. Garner frowned as he smoothed out the sheets. "Let's see what we have." As he read, his forehead furrowed and his concerns deepened.

Robby was born and raised in Los Angeles, graduating high school second in his class with a grade point average of 3.94. From high school, he had gone into the Army Special Forces (the Green Beret). Throughout his service, he studied part-time at local colleges near wherever he was based.

After four years, he transferred to the Defense Intelligence Agency where he stayed for two years. His job description at DIA was simply 'Operator'.

Then he retired from the Army and went to work for the Central Intelligence Agency. His job description at CIA, 'Field Analyst'.

He worked for the CIA for six years during which time he received a B.A. in history from the University of Virginia, and an M.A. in education from George Washington University.

Later, he resigned from the Agency for "personal and philosophical reasons." Since then, Robby had been working at a string of jobs ranging from substitute teaching, researcher for a network news show, bodyguard work, and the more exotic jobs which would never find their way to his résumé.

Garner briefly looked up. "You have a most...interesting background."

Robby knew what was coming, but he smiled.

Garner continued reading. Robby spoke several languages fluently including French, German, Spanish, Hebrew, and Russian. He was a licensed pilot for many types of aircraft. Under special skills he listed Expert: Explosives, Marksmanship, Edged Weapons, Hand to Hand Combat, Intelligence, Survival Evasion Resistance and Escape (SERE, he was listed as an instructor).

Garner inwardly flinched. Christ, he thought, Rambo with a degree!

Two pages of the résumé listed Robby's decorations and special citations including the Congressional Medal of Honor, the Distinguished Service Cross, the Silver and Bronze Stars, and the Civilian National Security Medal.

Garner put down the résumé, adjusted his glasses, shuffled the résumé sheets and tried to put off the moment of decision. How could he hire this kind of person to teach tenth grade history? The man was violence personified. He could go off any time. What would the school board say? He looked over at Robby.

"That's uh, quite a résumé, Mr. Moss. Very impressive. I've never seen one quite like it before."

Robby sat quietly and waited for the 'but' hanging in the air.

"I have to be candid. As impressive as your résumé and recommendations are, I have to wonder why you would choose to teach. You seem qualified for so many...other things."

Robby conceded the point. "I just decided that at this point in my life I could use a little less excitement than those 'other things', as you call them, provide. Also, I think I have something to say to the next generation of leaders. And what better place to say it than in high school when they're most receptive."

Garner noticeably flinched at the prospect of what Robby might have to say.

Robby had heard it all before and knew what was coming next.

"To be honest, Mr. Moss, your actual experience is somewhat limited as far as teaching goes; and there are others I have to see before filling this opening."

Garner seemed to tense for an outburst, but it never came. Instead, Robby stood, smiled, and extended his hand. "Thank you very much for your time, sir." Garner felt the callus as they shook. "I hope to be hearing from you soon." Garner sighed deeply as Robby left his office.

Robby smiled as well as he walked to the parking lot. Well he thought, I tried. He climbed into his 1969 powder blue Mustang Hardtop, threw a Temptations disc into the player and sped off towards the freeway.

He drove aimlessly at first, allowing the traffic to guide him. He left Los Angeles behind him and found himself on the road to Las Vegas.

The road home.

He pulled into the left hand lane, switched discs to Ray Charles, accelerated to seventy-five and allowed his mind to wander as the countryside sped past.

He thought about the interview. He wasn't upset about not getting the job. He'd been fairly certain of the result. However, something deep within him wondered what if this one had gone differently? What if I'd gotten the job? He started to contemplate a conventional life. He disliked routine and convention but he regularly reached out for it. He partly blamed his grandmother.

Every now and then, he tried to respond to a little twinge of conscience, a recessive gene inherited from his Russian grandmother that whispered "have a proper traditional life."

Every time he tried, he failed. Joyfully! Because he knew that the million odd other genes compelled him to choose a different life. One he was really good at.

He had lived, he felt, many lives. Inevitably, however, he would run up against the same "traditional" mandates of greed, corruption, and irresponsibility.

So, he had constructed a world of his own; where he was the sole arbiter of right and wrong. He liked to think that he remained open to new ideas and the sensitivities of others, but when it came right down to it, Robby did what he had to do. It was the only way he could keep from blowing his brains out.

But still, occasionally, he stepped back into "the world" to see if it had changed or improved.

Well, once again he was sure that Grandma would understand.

He pulled off to a gas station near the Nevada border. After filling up and buying some burgers, he parked beneath the one shade tree of note and changed his clothes.

The suit was put away carefully in a garment bag in the back seat and he quickly dressed in jeans and his favorite T-shirt. The one with the double zero on the front.

He drove for several hours in an automatic mode, feeling loose. As the sun slowly set behind him, he could see Vegas begin to rise before him and he felt safe. Home.

An hour later, he was parked in the lot of the Empress Hotel and Casino, in his reserved space, and was moving through the lobby towards the elevator. As usual, he didn't make it.

From the corner of his eye, he saw a flash of red hair and he heard the voice he thought of as musical, saying, "Place your bets, please." He wandered over to the roulette table.

Jenna smiled and nodded at him. The croupier was in her late twenties, pretty and intelligent. She and Robby had been a sort of couple on and off for the last two years.

"Welcome back, stranger."

Robby smiled. "Hi. How's your dad? Give me a hundred."

"He's fine. Being a pain to all of his students. By the way, I'm fine too."

Robby accepted the rebuke with good humor as he signed the credit pad she slid across to him. She gave him five green twenty dollar chips. An elderly lady sat down next to him and bought ten two dollar chips.

"Place your bets, please." Jenna spun the wheel. The lady played two dollars on the red. The safest bet on the table. Robby played forty dollars on the double zero, the toughest bet on the table. Jenna spun the ball and it came up seven red.

The woman smiled and clapped as Jenna placed two more chips on her pile. She swept away Robby's bet. "Place your bets." She spun the wheel.

The woman bet a number, a color, and a row. At the last moment, she added a bet on even. Robby put sixty on the double zero.

"Twenty-eight black. Pay black and even."

The woman happily counted her money and watched sympathetically as Robby's bet was again swept away.

"Thanks, Jenna." He stood to leave.

"You going to be around later?" Jenna asked as he started to turn.

"I guess."

The woman turned to Robby as she placed her next bets. "If you want to win at this game, young man, you shouldn't keep playing the double zero. It's next to impossible to win that way."

Jenna covered her mouth and coughed to hide a giggle. Robby smiled at the woman. "Story of my life, ma'am." He turned and melted into the casino crowd.

Robby went up to his suite. He had lived at the Empress for just over three years, making him its longest staying guest. His suite was a sitting room and a bedroom, with a view of downtown through a wall length floor to ceiling window. He pulled the curtains and let the neon spill into the room.

He undressed, put some Charlie Parker on the stereo and climbed into a cool bath. Soon, caressed by the soft tones of Bird's sax, he was deeply asleep and oblivious to all.

He had been sleeping for an hour. The disc had played through and restarted, and the last sunlight had disappeared, flooding his room with neon pinks and greens from the signs on the street.

The door to his suite was noiselessly opened and a man entered. He stood for a moment, allowing his eyes to adjust to the combined gloom and glare. Without moving, he scanned the living room. He saw the light from the bathroom, and moved quietly to the bar and sat down facing the bedroom door.

A few minutes later, something woke Robby. He lay in the tub and listened. He heard nothing except the sax. He sensed more than heard something which set off alarm bells in him. He moved slowly, silently out of the tub, and to the bathroom door.

The bedroom was empty. He moved to the bedroom door

and stood just inside it for a full minute. He was sure, although he couldn't have told you how, that he was not alone. He carefully stepped into the living room when the lights came on and momentarily stunned him.

"Michaelangelo's David you're not." Danny Gale, son of the hotel's owner, and casino manager in his own right, laughed.

"Great. I've got a pervert as a best friend," Robby groaned as he went into the bedroom to dress.

"So, you gonna get the job?" Danny called to him from the living room.

"Do I ever?"

While Robby dressed, Danny made an ice cream soda for him to match the one that he was already working on. Amongst the hotel's staff, Robby and Danny were known as the ice cream junkies. A chocolate ice cream soda with strawberry ice cream was finer to them than the most magnificent dry martini. Robby came back into the living room and picked up his soda.

"What're you going to do now?" Danny asked as he added more soda to the mix.

"Damned if I know."

"No action?"

Robby shrugged. "Yeah, but nothing that grabs me."

They drank their sodas quietly for a few minutes. It had been over two months since the thing in San Juan with the FBI and the missing icons. The investigation, the chase, and mostly the rescue and, of course, the payoff had kept Robby energized for six weeks. But now, money was running low and boredom high.

"Well," Danny began softly, "my father might have something for you."

Robby looked up from his soda. "Yeah?"

"Come by the office tonight around two."

Robby looked at the clock. Ten minutes after eight. Six hours to kill. He looked over at Danny who was finishing his soda. "You want to go to the game over at Cashman?"

Danny shook his head and stood. "Can't do it." He walked to the door. "See you later, tough guy." He let himself out.

Robby walked to the window and looked out over downtown

Vegas. Six hours, he thought. Six hours...I wonder what Jenna's doing tonight. He picked up the phone and dialed the pit boss.

a.

Seymour Gale was old Vegas. He had arrived when the sleepy layover for traveling servicemen had only one saloon and a whorehouse, and he had carved out his Empress from the sand and the heat and the dust.

Anyway, that's how he liked to tell it.

Tall, thin, and graying, with a salt and pepper mustache, he wore thousand dollar suits, had his hair specially styled daily, manicures twice a week, and was equally comfortable with European Royalty and tourists from Dubuque. He had that rare ability to accept people non-judgmentally and then make up his own mind about them. It was this ability, in the final analysis, that had enabled him to build his desert empire.

The empire was vast indeed. Two hotels in Las Vegas, one in Reno, one in Atlantic City, and controlling interests in several hotels in Europe. But the Empress was his personal jewel. It was his first, and like that first kiss or first love, it would always have a special meaning for him.

He sat behind his circular desk and looked out through the two way mirror that lined one wall, at the casino action spread before him. He smiled as he always did at times like these, and then turned reluctantly back to business.

"I'm sorry, Ernie, go ahead."

Ernie DiNofrio, the aging chief of security, was still more like the New York cop that he had been for thirty years, than like a public relations conscious hotel man. But he was honest, fair, and absolutely trustworthy; and he was Seymour's closest friend for the last ten years. As always, he referred to his little red notebook as he talked.

"Okay, so I check her out, make a couple of phone calls. Most of what she said is true. She is from L.A., she's an associate professor at UCLA like she said. But she's been in some kind of trouble there. I ain't exactly sure what kind, but bad enough for them to ask her to take a leave of absence."

"Professor of what?"

14   **REQUIESCAT**

Ernie checked his book. "Uh, Contemporary American History." Seymour nodded. "Anyway, those two guys she says got whacked," he waited as Seymour checked out something on the casino floor, "did die."

Seymour turned his full attention to Ernie. "Like I said, they did die but officially the L.A. and New York cops are calling them two routine T.A.s."

Seymour frowned. "And what she said happened here?"

"Metro confirmed the accident she says took place at Boulevard and Flamingo, but they say it was a hit and run, drunk jumped the curb and split. They didn't even know about her being there."

Seymour looked hard at the security chief. "And do they now?"

Ernie smiled for the first time. "Don't be insulting."

"Sorry. Get to the main event."

Ernie turned a couple of pages. "She checked in two days ago. Paid cash. Nothing unusual on her room service, except she's been taking all her meals in her room. This afternoon, a girl from housekeeping hears screaming in 2508. A minute and a half later, my boys get there and find this girl lying on the floor of the room, screaming that someone tried to kill her. My guys saw no one in the corridor and neither did the maid."

"What about the adjacent rooms?"

"We checked as discreetly as we could but no one heard nothing but the screaming. We told them it was just an accident. Everybody's cool."

Seymour was quiet for several minutes. He looked out over the casino and then used the intercom to get the light over blackjack table number twelve changed. Finally, he turned back to DiNofrio and signaled him to wrap it up.

"My boys took her down the service elevator to the office. I talked to her for about five minutes. I thought she was a whacko, you know paranoid."

Seymour leaned forward. "Thought? Past tense?"

It was Ernie's turn for silence. He closed his book and picked up his water tumbler of Scotch. After a long pull on it, he turned back to Seymour. "Sy, something weird's going on."

"Tell me."

"I have the doctor come over and look at her. While he's doing that, I figure I'll go up to her room and get her purse and look around. Everything's the way my boys said it was, nothing special, right? So I leave but, you remember 2508 is at the end of the hall, right? I figure, what the hell, I'll check out the fire door while I'm there. I open it and look around the stairwell. Nothing." He looked expectantly at Seymour.

Seymour shrugged. "So?"

Ernie continued, "I didn't get it right away either. But suddenly it hits me. The door alarm should have gone off! It should have rung there and down in Central, but nothing. I checked."

Seymour seemed to lose interest. "So get it fixed."

"That's what I'm coming to. On my way down, I call the techs and send them up to fix it. Twenty minutes later, I'm getting ready to call Metro and turn the girl over to them, when the techs call me back up there."

He took another big swallow. "Sy, that alarm was bypassed just as pretty as you please, a real pro job. You couldn't even tell until you took the damn thing apart."

Now Seymour was listening intently. "No chance of mistake? You're sure?"

"I'm sure. I had all the others checked too. The one on 23 was rigged the same way. That's when I called you."

Seymour took a deep breath. Incidents like this could hurt the image of the hotel, and yet...there was something more here, different from your run-of-the-mill, hysterical girl. Something very odd.

He had gone down to see her right after Ernie called. She had quieted by then, but in all his years he had never seen anyone or anything as terrified as she. The look in her eyes stayed with him even now.

He had ordered her taken to a comfortable room to rest while Ernie investigated. He had also issued strict instructions to Ernie, "I don't know what we have here, but nothing happens to this girl." Ernie's people were with her from then on in the room.

Making decisions had never been difficult for Seymour and he made one now with typical dispatch. "Bring her down a little after one. No later than one-thirty."

Ernie nodded and stood to leave. "What're you going to do, boss?"

Seymour turned back to watch the casino. "I thought I'd have our resident lunatic talk to her."

Ernie left shaking his head. "There go the insurance premiums." He left as Seymour started laughing.

🙵

There are two Las Vegas'. The Strip, which is predominately resort hotels, self-contained pleasure palaces where the visitors never have to leave; then there is downtown. Downtown, the hotels are smaller and closer together. At night, the streets are jammed with people walking from one place to another, always seeking a change of fortune at the next casino's tables.

It was to downtown that Robby had first migrated when he came to Vegas. He loved to walk, to mix and mingle with the tourists, the gamblers, the humanity. So it came as no surprise to Jenna when, after dinner, Robby suggested that they take a walk.

They had eaten at the Empress and then wandered over to the Four Queens for ice cream sundaes, the best in Las Vegas. Now they strolled back towards the Empress, arm in arm.

As they moved through the crowd, the casino barkers on the street all acknowledged them. Downtown, everybody knows everybody. Outside the Lucky Horseshoe Casino, they stopped momentarily to watch Barker do his thing.

He was tall, over six-feet-six, strongly built with a deep voice that echoed across the street like a megaphone rumbling out of a deep hole.

"Hurry, hurry, hurry! Nickel a play, million dollar jackpot, building even as I speak! Hurry, hurry! The pot builds with every play! Five cents can win you over a million dollars! Free drinks and door prizes every hour!"

As people hurry-hurried in, he spotted Robby and Jenna watching him. He smiled broadly and waved them over.

"Hey beautiful! What are you doing out in public with this sorry looking drag-ass loser?" Jenna laughed, as he looked Robby over, head to toe, and then shook his head. "Anytime you feel like trading up baby, you know where I am."

"I'd take you up in a second," Jenna began, "but somebody has to be his…" She paused and turned to Robby. "Just what am I to you?" Jenna and Barker both looked at Robby waiting for an answer.

He seemed to be considering it. Finally, as if arriving at the difficult conclusion, he announced "My keeper?" Jenna slugged him and Barker laughed.

"How you been, Barker?" Robby asked while trying to ignore Jenna's annoyed stare.

"Staying a little ahead, man. You get the job?"

Robby was always surprised at how news traveled in Vegas. Despite the glitz, glitter and neon, it was basically a small town. Almost a company town.

"Same old story."

Barker helped a man on crutches into the casino. While he was gone, Jenna turned to Robby. "Were you serious about getting it this time?"

"I think so. I'm never sure."

Barker returned and they talked between his pitches for a few minutes. If Danny Gale was Robby's best friend, then Barker was his most trusted. More than once he had saved Robby's ass. They didn't socialize, go to each other's homes or anything like that, but both men knew that they would always be there for each other when it counted most and that was enough for them.

Robby and Jenna returned to the Empress around eleven-thirty and went to the lounge for a drink. They sat quietly together for ten minutes before Jenna spoke.

"You're unusually quiet."

"I'm just restless, just thinking."

"About what?"

"Life, death, chocolate ice cream sodas."

She knew Robby too well to be put off by the joke. She knew he had a tendency to slip into melancholy whenever he had long periods of inactivity. She had seen the signs before and recognized them now. "What time do you have to see the boss?"

"Around two."

"What do you want to do until then?"

"Don't know, hang out I guess."

Jenna smiled, took his hand and led him towards the elevators. Robby kissed her as the doors closed behind them and whispered in her ear, "but will you respect me in the morning?" She slugged him again.

&

In the cool dark of Robby's bedroom, Jenna quietly sipped a drink, while Robby slept, his head on her shoulder. It was only in these moments that Jenna allowed herself to think about him in anything other than casual terms.

He could be very tender. His caresses, soft, barely felt kisses exploring her body, never failed to excite her. He was caring, never forgot a birthday or an important date. Did the right things at the right times, and he could be very romantic.

But there was another side to him. A nameless something that was just beneath the surface. And she knew it was this which would one day lead to his end.

She didn't think that Robby could ever completely care about anything. No. That was wrong. It wasn't that he would never care for anything. It was more like there was never any way to tell what he would allow himself to care about.

She had seen him broken and bleeding, limping home from some craziness, some lost cause. Sometimes he would cry out in his sleep and she would watch, amazed, as he would cry deeply and then wake up as if nothing had happened.

She loved him, at least she thought she did, but she knew she couldn't commit to him, any more than he could commit to her. His torment always got in the way.

It was moments like these, soft, quiet, unguarded times, when she hoped, almost prayed, that one day he would care as much about her as he did his 'causes'.

Till then, she would wait. For now.

Robby stirred slightly. "What time is it?" he slurred out.

"Around one-thirty. You have to get up." His response was to roll over and pull the pillow over his head. She'd been through this before too. "Hey! You're going to see Gale in less than half an hour, get up and get dressed." His answer was a groan.

Jenna braced her back against the headboard, drew her knees to her chest, and with both feet, unceremoniously shoved him out of bed and onto the floor.

He stood and slowly walked around the bed and into the bathroom. A minute, later she heard the shower running. When he emerged, he looked at her curiously while he dried his hair.

"Did you kick me out of bed?"

"Yes."

"I mean literally kick me out of bed?"

"Yes."

"Oh."

He dressed quickly in jeans and an Empress sweat shirt. As he pulled his hair back into a ponytail, he studied Jenna's reflection in the mirror. "You really kicked me out of bed, I mean with your feet?"

She smiled her sweetest smile. "I did."

He shook his head, as though now he had seen everything and left the bedroom. At the door, he stopped and turned back. "See you later."

She decided then and there that something would have to change. That she deserved more, needed more. She stayed another twenty minutes before she showered and dressed.

As she brushed her hair, her anger grew and then slowly dissipated. By the time she left the bedroom, the time for serious thinking was gone and she returned to the world of "casual friends."

&

The girl sat slumped in the overstuffed chair in Seymour's office. She seemed attractive but without makeup, and with her eyes red from constant crying, it was hard to tell.

Seymour brought her a drink and she made an effort to sip at it. "Thank you, Mr. Gale." Her voice was barely above a whisper.

Danny tried to comfort her. "Everything's going to be fine. Don't worry. You're safe now." She looked up at his smile and for a moment seemed about to come out of it, but then retreated back into herself.

She began to whimper, "No good. It's no good. They're going to get me. They got the others, now they're going to get me too." Her voice trailed off.

Danny looked to his father for help. Seymour walked over to her. "Miss Palmer, I promise you. We will see to it that you get the help you need. You're my guest. And I don't let bad things happen to my guests." He paused and smiled. "It would be bad for business."

She wiped her eyes and turned to face him. "I'm sorry, Mr. Gale. I get a little," she seemed to be struggling to maintain her composure, "a little out of control sometimes. I'm better now. I really am." She stood a little uncertainly and smoothed back her hair. "Thank you for your patience. I really don't want to bother you any..."

She never finished her sentence. She raced for the door and flung it open. She would have run out into the casino if she had not run smack into the logo of an Empress sweat shirt. She felt the shirt, soft and sweet smelling against her face and looked up into piercing blue eyes as arms closed around her. She collapsed.

Robby easily lifted her into his arms and looked across the room at Seymour. "You wanted to see me?"

≈

In a private dining room adjacent to the office, Seymour and Robby talked, over sandwiches. A doctor had been called and, along with Danny and two security people, was with the girl now.

They talked small talk for a few minutes while they made their sandwiches. Both men ignored what had just happened. Once they were settled, Seymour with a beer, Robby with the ever present ice cream soda, they got down to business.

"How long have you been living here now, Robert? Two, three years?"

Robby put down his sandwich. If Seymour was starting like this, it must be something really miserable he had in mind.

"And you know, I almost think of you as a surrogate son, no disrespect to Danny, but I feel very close to you."

It must be even worse than miserable.

"What is it Sy?"

"A favor, just a favor like you've done for us before, no more." He was smiling his most charming smile.

It must really be something bad.

"Sy, just tell me, no *schmaltz*, no grease. Just tell me what you want. I assume it has to do with that girl?"

They talked for the better part of an hour about everything that had happened to the girl and what everybody thought about it. Robby asked some questions, more to bring out some overlooked details than for real investigation, but basically he remained quiet. He ate his sandwich and listened. Finally, Seymour was finished.

"So, Robert? What do you think?"

Robby thought it over. This mini-mystery showed signs of becoming something interesting. Something he needed. "What do you want?" He knew the answer, but this was how negotiations worked and Seymour loved negotiations.

"Just talk to her. See if you can help her. C'mon. Be a *mensch.*" Seymour smiled, warming to the moment.

"And I get? If this turns into something, who pays expenses?"

"Who always pays your expenses, *schmuck.* I'll pay anything you want for expenses for walking across the hall." He reached into his pocket. "Shoe leather, wear and tear on your clothes, here's a dollar. Now be nice and go talk to the girl. It's a *mitzvah.*"

Robby laughed and took the offered dollar. "Let's go talk to the girl." They stood and walked to the door. "By the way, what's her name?"

CHAPTER TWO

EVE PALMER

"Robby Moss, Eve Palmer."

Robby smiled and walked over to her. She acknowledged him with a bare whisper and a nod. He pulled over an ottoman and sat down directly in front of her. Still smiling, he studied the frightened expression, the trapped look, and immediately felt sympathy for her. He held out his hand.

"It's nice to meet you, Ms. Palmer." She made no effort to move, to take his hand. He turned it slightly palm up but held it steadily out to her. Unwavering. After several long moments, she uncertainly reached out and took it.

He gently closed his fingers around hers and could feel the fear, the trembling. "You can talk to me." He said it flatly, as a statement of fact, not as an offer or an order. She looked from his hand to his eyes and something she either saw or felt or sensed made her grip his hand the way a child grips its parents when in pain. They held hands throughout their conversation.

When she spoke, it was in tones so quiet that everybody in the room had to strain to hear. It was a voice choked with fear and pain.

"Can you help me?"

Again, he spoke with conviction. "Yes."

She looked deeply into his eyes, felt his strength. Later, when she had time to think about it, she couldn't exactly say why she knew, but she did know.

"Where do I start?"

"Who's trying to hurt you?"

"I don't know."

"Why are they trying to hurt you?"

"I don't know." Robby sensed her start to drift back into panic and gently squeezed her hand.

"When did it start?"

It seemed like years ago but she realized it was less. How long ago, God, could it only be two weeks ago! She let her mind drift back to the beginning, to that day when she had first realized something was wrong.

The day had started normally enough…

᠅

In the heart of the concrete jungle of Los Angeles sits a small oasis of green called Westwood, the home of the University of California at Los Angeles. Just below the Sunset Strip and nearby Beverly Hills, it consists of small pretty homes each with a touch of lawn and yard. While not expensive, it isn't cheap either, and an Associate Professor of American Contemporary History, like Eve, could only afford to rent.

She had lived in the two bedroom, ranch style house for a little over a year. It was her sanctuary from students and faculty politics. One bedroom had been converted into an office where she graded papers and worked on her book *Monocles and Mercedes: A History of Nazi Disinformation in America 1933 to 1942*. She loved to spend days sitting at her desk, overlooking the garden, reading and writing. There she felt safe and secure.

That security and safety was shattered when she came home on the Friday before Spring Break to find the front door ajar.

She stood at the foot of the walk, staring at the door which she was sure she had closed and locked. Slowly, the realization crept in that she had been burglarized. She ran to a friend's house and called the police.

Twenty minutes later, they arrived. Only after they had gone through the place and made sure it was empty, did she go in.

The place had been trashed. Every drawer, every cabinet, every closet had been opened and its contents strewn about the floor. She shivered as she walked through it.

After going through it all, she went to her office. It was in similar shape but now, something that had been troubling her came sharply into focus. She turned to the officer writing the report.

"Why didn't they take anything?"

"Ma'am?"

"I know I don't have the best or the fanciest jewelry in the world, but c'mon. They left my computer, my typewriter, heck, even my stereo."

The cop never looked up from his report. "Consider yourself lucky. It was probably just vandals, kids. Would you sign at the bottom, please?"

She signed and agreed to put together a list of anything that turned up missing. After they left, she double locked the door and called her friend Liceth. Liceth came over and the two young college professors spent the night together, cleaning up and commiserating.

The next morning, Eve left for classes while Liceth stayed behind to wait for a locksmith to put a new double deadbolt on the door.

Eve was 'off' all that day. Her morning classes went badly, and over lunch with Liceth, she had cried. She felt violated and angry at the same time. After a "sloppy emotional lunch", she agreed to spend the night at Liceth's and then left for a meeting with her research assistants.

≈

Robby interrupted her story. "Did the police take any fingerprints?"

"They said they would send someone over, but they never came."

He nodded. "And how did the 'vandals' get in? Did they ever find out?"

Eve wiped her eyes. "They said I must have left the door unlocked."

"And did you?"

She sniffled. "I don't know. I don't think so. I'm usually pretty good about those things."

Robby moved to sit beside her on the couch. "You were about to meet with your research assistants."

❧

Stefan Wald and Joseph Mann were about as different as two men could be.

Stefan was a senior history major from the Bronx. Street tough and arrogant, he knew his way around and took no crap from anybody. He was also brilliant. A straight A student throughout school (he told his friends that he averaged high C's) he didn't like being thought of as a "brain." Secretly, he hoped one day to be one of the world's great historians.

Where Stefan was tough, Joseph was thoughtful. Raised in the bedroom communities of the San Fernando Valley, from the time he was a small child he lived for his time in the library. It was his favorite place in the world. A sophomore journalism major, Joey as he was known, had few friends outside of school and fewer outside interests.

Both young men worked as research assistants to faculty members who were writing books. Although it was minimal pay, it looked good on the record and was occasionally interesting. Today was their last meeting with Eve before Spring Break so there was a lot to accomplish.

Eve, having released a lot of what was bothering her at lunch, came into the office smiling and feeling better. After the routine pleasantries, they got down to business.

"Okay guys, what do you have for me?"

As usual, Stefan went first. He handed a sheaf of notes across to Eve. "These are my notes on the Los Angeles press coverage of Hitler's election and first two years in office. It includes commentaries and editorials both for and against him. I also talked to a guy, a friend of a friend of my Uncle's who says he can get me into the New York Times Morgue when I go home."

Eve thumbed through the notes and then looked at Joey. He fumbled for his notes in his briefcase and had to rearrange them before handing them to her.

"Uh, I cross referenced those names you gave me, you know, the list of German diplomats who served in the U.S. before the war?" Eve nodded. "Well, I uh, couldn't find a whole lot on some of them but I went back to the bound copies of every newsmagazine in the U.S. from 1933 to 1935 and extracted these pieces."

Eve read his notes and glanced at his Xeroxes. "Nice work, Joey, Stefan. This is going to be good background material." She put the notes in her briefcase. She smiled at them. "So what are you two guys planning to do during the Break? Terrorize half the girls in Palm Springs?" Stefan laughed and Joey blushed and laughed.

"Well," Joey began, "I'm going up to San Francisco and go through the Historical Society's files. You know the German Consulate was up there back then."

Eve shook her head. "You shouldn't work on your vacation." Joey shrugged. "At least promise me you'll try and have some fun, go to Fisherman's Wharf, check out the clubs in Stinson Beach." Again he shrugged noncommittally.

Stefan looked at him and grinned. "Don't worry, Joey. I'll be doing enough partying for both of us." He looked at Eve. "I'm going home and party for ten days." He started to say something else but stopped himself when he saw Eve's questioning look. He sighed. "I'll also check out the *Times*. Don't worry, Ms. Palmer." They all laughed.

The meeting broke up and they walked out together. On the way, she told them about her break in. They were solicitous but not overly. They parted, agreeing to meet again right after Spring Break.

Joey's body was found the next morning.

After leaving the young men, Eve drove home. Traffic seemed worse then usual, and the short trip home longer than ever. As she came closer to her street, her house, the sense of violation, the fear began to well up in her once again. Fighting the panic, she began to plan the evening's work. She'd go over Joey's and Stefan's notes, work on the book.

Taking refuge in the normalcy of her regular routine, she tried to lose herself in mapping out the next steps in writing. By the time she pulled into her driveway, she had almost succeeded in calming herself. As she walked to her front door, she saw all the lights on, and for a moment was overwhelmed with terror. Then the door opened, and there was Liceth, smiling and wiping her hands on an apron. Liceth stopped and looked at Eve. "My God, what happened? What's the matter?" She put an arm around her, took the books and papers from her, and lead her into the living room.

"I saw the lights on and thought..." Her voice trailed off. Eve sank into a chair, sighing heavily.

Liceth shook her head. "I forgot to have your kitchen door lock changed so I took care of it. Then I figured, as long as I'm here, I'd cook up some dinner for us." She hit herself on the forehead. "I'm an idiot."

Eve began to relax and smiled up at Liceth. "It's just me. Actually, I'm glad you're here. I was really panicked about coming home alone."

Later that evening, the two women did the dishes, continuing their dinner conversation about school, the news, TV, and the trivia of the day. Finally, Liceth said goodnight, and Eve, who had begun to feel much more at ease, reluctantly let her go.

As she turned from watching Liceth go down the walk, Eve spotted her notes on the table. She went into her little office, sat down at the computer, and prepared to work.

At first, she matter-of-factly called up the file she'd worked on last. Nothing happened. Laughing at herself for stupid mistakes, she tried again. Still nothing.

With some trepidation, she tried another file. And another. Still nothing. Everything she'd been working on was wiped out. A creeping fear rose in her. Calm down, she told herself. Those damned vandals probably tried to play with the computer and accidentally wiped it all out. It's a good thing I have backups on everything except the last few notes. I'll just call Joey and reconstruct it with him and Stefan.

Realizing the hour was late and that Joey lived with his parents, Eve decided to wait until morning.

The next morning was sunny, and the radio woke Eve with an upbeat song. She showered, dressed, and felt good for the first time since the break in. Over coffee and a muffin, Eve dialed Joey's number.

Eve hated answering machines, so when she reached his, she left a brief message that she would call again and hung up.

She tried unsuccessfully for a time to resuscitate her files, to no avail. She checked her other discs, those not related to the book and they were equally blank. Damn she thought, I'm having a truly lousy couple of days.

Feeling frustrated and alone, she decided to go out. She double checked her locks, walked around the house to see that all the windows were closed and locked. Finally, she got in her car, put the top down, and headed off for a drive through the canyons of L.A.

Along the Sunset Strip, into Beverly Hills, and finally the relatively straight climb up into Beverly Glen Blvd. she left city traffic behind as she accelerated into the canyon and the increasingly winding road. As she got deeper into the drive, she enjoyed the challenge of guiding her car through the turns.

After the crest, she slowed down and let the car guide itself down the relatively straight north side. She looked out over the San Fernando Valley displayed before her and smiled. For the first time in the drive, she had a destination in mind. At the base of the canyon, she turned right onto Ventura Blvd. and headed for North Hollywood and Joey's home.

As she went past the curio shops and restaurants of the boulevard, she questioned whether or not to call first. Her sensibilities won out over impulses and she pulled into the famous DuPars parking lot at Ventura and Laurel Canyon to use the pay phone. Again, the machine. This time, she left a message that she would drop by later in the afternoon.

Walking back to her car, she turned over in her mind what to do. Impulses won out over sensibilities and she headed for the Mann house.

Ten minutes later, she turned up Denny Ave. and looked for the large apartment building she had visited once before.

She had gone about a block when she was forced to stop by a police and fire department road block. Looking past them, she saw an ambulance and several police cars about half a block ahead, in front of the building she was looking for. She parked and walked up the street.

A body lay on the ground near the curb covered by a gray sheet. She looked quickly away as she saw a pool of blood near the head and a large stain forming on the top of the sheet. She started up the stairs to the apartments. Then something, she wasn't sure just what, made her stop and look back at the scene.

ॐ

Eve was shaking. Robby quickly signaled to Danny who brought over a drink. Robby helped her take a sip and then took away the glass before she could drink too much.

"Just relax," he said. "Take your time and tell it as best you can." She took the glass back and took another drink. Sy gestured Robby over to him.

"We can get the doctor up here," he said quietly. Robby shook his head.

"I don't want her out. If we don't get the story now, we may never get it all." He nodded at her. "She's already starting to block out things."

Sy nodded reluctantly and Robby returned to her side.

He smiled. "Ready to go on?" She nodded but still clung to the glass. "Something made you turn and look back at the body…"

ॐ

She went back down the steps to the edge of the restraining tape. Her unease and tension grew. She didn't know why, but there was something familiar about the shape beneath the sheet. She flagged down an officer nearby.

"Excuse me, can you tell me what happened here?"

The cop looked her over. "Hit and run. Some kid got killed."

The panic began to grow within her. "What was his name? Who was he?"

The cop wasn't going to answer at first, but the look in Eve's eyes made him. "He lived here. His parents said he was out all night and then he was found this morning. I'm sorry I can't say anymore."

Under her breath, she uncertainly said the thing which was becoming increasingly certain to her. "It's Joseph Mann, isn't it?"

"Did you know him?"

Eve went numb with the confirmation.

She felt as if she was in a fog. "He was so sweet. He was going

to give up part of Spring Break just to help me with my project."
Involuntarily, she turned from the scene and walked slowly back to
her car.

She started to drive home but, pulling into her driveway, she
couldn't bear the isolation she felt. She backed up, turned the car
around and went to her office at UCLA.

Walking along the nearly deserted campus and into the too quiet
hall leading to her office, she felt a moment of extreme confusion,
disorientation. She wasn't sure where she was, or what day or time
it was. After a moment, it passed, and she went into her office.

She sat down at her desk and began to cry. She didn't hear when
another professor pushed past the half open door.

"Eve? Are you all right?" Professor Krumholz was her department head. He could usually be found on campus at odd hours.

Eve looked up as the professor pulled a chair up to Eve's desk.
"What's wrong?"

Between sobs, Eve told him about Joey's accident, then about
the break-in at her house. "What am I going to do? I can't handle
this."

Professor Krumholz spoke quietly and steadily. "You're not
expected to handle everything. Why don't you take advantage of the
break and get away for a while? I've never known you to break down
before. You'll be fine."

She stopped crying. More to reassure the professor, he looked
so uncomfortable, than really believing it, she agreed she'd be fine.
"I don't need to go anywhere. I'll work on my book at home. That'll
get me back on track." The professor nodded, relieved, and, after a
word or two, escaped to his own office.

Eve gathered some papers from her desk and decided to take her
own advice. She'd go home and work on the book. In a couple of
days, she'd call on Joey's parents. Poor Joey. The tears started again
but she quickly regained control and left the office.

The next three days were spent reorganizing the material for the
book, checking the computer backups. The normal rhythms of life
were healing, and the book was progressing.

Thursday came and brought with it a note from Stefan. He was
partying away in New York but had managed to squeeze in enough

time to arrange an appointment for this Friday at the offices of the *New York Times.*

With a start, Eve realized that Stefan didn't know of Joey's accident. She thought about it for a minute and then decided to not tell him until he returned. Why spoil his vacation? Like hers already was.

It was a pretty, clear, cool day, so she packed her backpack and jogged over to the campus. Always aware of possible threats, attacks happened around the campus uncomfortably often, she stayed on busy public streets all the way. Still, despite her comfort with the route, she felt as if she were being watched. Several times she stopped, or turned around and jogged backwards for a few paces just to see if she was being followed. She never saw anything. But still the feeling lingered.

Once on campus, she headed directly for the Powell Library tent and spent the rest of the morning blissfully submerged in the intricacies of the Treaty of Versailles and the German perspective on it.

In the afternoon, she and Liceth met at a French sidewalk cafe on Westwood Blvd. Although her feeling of being watched had lifted at the library, she had been sitting at the table with Liceth for less than five minutes when it returned.

"I'm going to say something weird," she told her friend.

"I'm always up for that." When Eve didn't smile, Liceth took her hand. "What's wrong?"

Eve hesitated and then plunged ahead. "I think I'm being followed."

"By whom?"

"I can't tell you why, but I think the people who broke into my place."

Liceth looked patiently across the table. "Listen, girlfriend, you've had a lousy week. First your house, then your T.A. I'm surprised you're functioning at all." She laughed. "Me, I'd be a complete wreck. You know, curled up in the fetal position, thumb firmly planted in my mouth and the electric blanket turned up to nine!"

Just then, a black sedan pulled up to a space across the street from the cafe. The two occupants stayed inside. Liceth and Eve looked at each other. Liceth picked up the check. "Let me give you a ride home." They left quickly.

Turning left on Wilshire Blvd., Liceth headed into the heavy mid afternoon traffic. She drove through Westwood and kept heading east. Eve looked over at her when she realized they weren't headed home. "Where are you going?"

"That black car is about three cars back." They drove on in silence for about five minutes when Liceth turned north on Rossmore Drive and headed for the heart of Beverly Hills. Eve looked at her. "What are you doing?"

"I'm going to lose them." Liceth said it flatly but with conviction. Eve thought her friend had lost her mind but one look at Liceth's whitened knuckles on the steering wheel convinced her to not argue.

Liceth threaded her way through the back streets and alleys of Beverly Hills for the next ten minutes. Three times they thought they had lost the black car, only to have it turn up again in their wake. Suddenly, Eve had an idea. When she told it to Liceth, she nodded grimly and turned the car in the proper direction.

For ten more minutes she drove on, turning occasionally, always making sure that the black car was still behind them. Then suddenly a right followed by a sharp left and they screeched to a stop. As hard as she could, Liceth leaned on her horn and wouldn't stop until the car was surrounded by five officers of the Beverly Hills Police Department who had come out into their parking lot to see what all the commotion was about.

They looked, but the black car had disappeared.

ðŸ”¸

"What did the police say?" Robby was standing by the bar.

The telling of the story had calmed Eve down considerably and now she vented some of her anger.

"Those bastards! They treated us as if we were two helpless females who panicked without reason. They said they looked for the car, but I doubt if they looked very hard. They just seemed to think it was funny!"

"Did you manage to get the car's license plate?"

"They said it was not in file or some trash like that." She wrote it down for Robby. He took it and gave it to Danny. "See if DiNofrio can run this." Danny nodded and left the room. "Go on. What did you do next?"

She paused to take a sip of her drink, this one, ice tea. "I spent the night at Liceth's house. We locked the doors and put furniture in front of them, the whole thing." She blushed slightly. "I suppose that does sound like a couple of panicked women."

Robby smiled again and shook his head. "Sounds prudent at the least."

"Thank you for that." She was quiet for a long time and then she stood and walked over to the bar, sitting on one of the overstuffed barstools. In a quiet, controlled voice she turned to look Robby in the eyes. "So you believe me?"

Robby thought it over. All of his instincts sided with her, and Robby trusted his instincts. Still…

"Sure, why not?" She seemed surprised at his answer. Before she could ask another question, he motioned for her to be quiet.

"I don't have any reason not to believe you because what you've told me so far could just be an unfortunate series of coincidences." Danny came back in and handed a piece of paper to Robby who scanned it and pocketed it. "Maybe not a coincidence."

She looked at him, puzzled. "What was that?"

"Never mind. What happened next?"

❧

The next morning Eve and Liceth had breakfast together. Still shaken, Eve went home to shower and dress, feeling more secure with Liceth in the living room. As she finished dressing, a neighborhood cat knocked down a trash can lid with the accompanying din. Eve reacted to the noise by dropping her compact on the tile floor in the bathroom.

She swept up the broken pieces of mirror and tossed them in the waste basket. Picking up her jacket and purse, she determinedly walked through the living room, past Liceth. At the door, she paused. "C'mon, Liceth. I've got to get out of here. Everything sets me on edge."

They parted, each to her own car. Back on campus, there were signs of life as some local students arrived back early. She waved to a couple of faculty members on their way to their offices.

Somehow, being around people made her feel better.

As usual, Professor Krumholz was wandering the halls. He greeted her enthusiastically. "You're looking better, Palmer. Everything squared away?"

Eve smiled feebly and nodded. She was not about to relive the events of the past few days. She spent the morning in her office, going over some material she was considering for next term.

At lunch, she joined some colleagues discussing their weekend plans. Eve sat quietly, picking at her salad. "So what do you think, Eve? Want to go up to Santa Barbara with us?"

"Huh?" She realized, with a start, that she'd been zoning out. She stood up, made some excuse about having some work to do, and left.

The rest of that day, she made a point of staying on the main paths and busy campus areas. She didn't want to be alone, but she didn't feel up to socializing.

Driving home, she looked in her rear view mirror more than necessary. Several times, she thought she saw the black car again, but she couldn't be sure. By the time she arrived home, she was taking no chances. She locked the car and ran to the house, slamming and locking the door behind her.

Dinner was a microwave quickie and then to the computer. The rest of the evening was spent immersing herself in work on her book. She finally achieved some calm and went to bed, leaving most of the lights on.

The next day was Saturday. Liceth had gone off with her boyfriend so Eve was faced with getting through the weekend alone. Just as well she thought. It's time I pulled myself together. The house could use a good cleaning and later I'll get more time in on the book. As she ordinarily did, Eve approached the problem methodically. She checked the cupboards, made a list, and went to the supermarket.

As she wheeled the cart through the aisles, she thought she saw someone following her. Paying for her purchases, she hurried to the parking lot. She thought she saw the same man approach her. She threw her packages into the car, jumped in, and locked the door. As she left, she looked back, but there was no one in the lot.

❧

Eve looked up at Robby. "I really did see someone."

"What did he look like?" Robby asked.

"I...I don't remember. Except he wore a business suit. Nobody wears a business suit in Westwood. Certainly not on the weekend. And he had short, dark hair, very neat. I don't remember much else. I was in a hurry to get away."

"Why?"

"I don't know. It just felt wrong. Like the black car. He scared me."

"Okay, then what?"

"I went home and stayed there, keeping busy all weekend. By Monday morning, I had convinced myself that my imagination had been working overtime. After all, why would anyone want to follow me? The whole thing was ridiculous.

"I was actually cheerful going to work. Then it happened. The last straw." There were tears in her eyes again but she continued.

❧

There was a staff meeting for the History Department that morning. After it was over, some people stood around, drinking coffee and discussing the news. The big subject was the upcoming confirmation hearings for the new CIA Director. That, and the Lakers' chances at another championship. UCLA staffers had a natural bias in that direction.

Eve moved from group to group, occasionally making a comment. In one corner, Professor Krumholz and another instructor were in serious conversation. She couldn't help overhearing the loud "Oh, no, how awful!" from the instructor. Not wanting to hear any bad news, she, nevertheless, found herself drawn to them, asking, "What's so awful?"

The instructor turned to Eve and said, "One of my students was in an accident. The boy had gone back to New York to see his family and was hit by a car." Eve barely heard the instructor explain that Professor Krumholz had been notified by the boy's family, and that he told her about Eve's student who had also died in a similar accident.

Eve turned ashen and would have fallen if the instructor hadn't caught her. She heard the woman saying something about drunk drivers deserving to have the book thrown at them, and on, and on. She heard herself, as if from afar, saying "Who was it?" and the confirmation of her worst fears. "His name was Stefan Wald, a very good student. It's such a shame."

Almost as an observer, Eve heard the low moan which became a shriek. It was coming from her, but she was somehow separated from it.

Her world was crashing around her. The break-in, Joseph, now Stefan! What's happening? Why? A dull roar filled her ears as she stumbled backwards against the wall.

She was vaguely aware of people looking at her, moving to help, to comfort her, but it was all background to the terror, that now came boiling to the surface. As her colleagues reached out to her, she shrank away, mumbling.

"Get away! All of you! Get away from me. Don't you see what's happening?" The rest was a blur of people, paramedics, and doctors.

She regained her senses the next day.

She was in a hospital room. Her arms were held in leather restraints and her legs were pinned to the bed somehow. First, her fear came flooding back. They, whoever they were, had gotten her! Then slowly the realization that she was safe. Relatively speaking.

Periodically, nurses came in to check on her. She tried to convince them that she was okay, but they just smiled benevolently. She would have to talk to the doctor, she was told over and over again. Finally, she just grit her teeth and waited for the doctor to appear.

He came in the early afternoon. Young, clean cut, he was the classic type, plastic smile and all. They talked about what she had been through. The doctor explained about grief and delayed stress syndrome.

Her session with the doctor lasted about a half hour. When he left, he took off the restraints. "If you want, you can get dressed and go out into the day room."

She dressed and wandered out into the day room. Trying not to look at anyone around her, she found a chair in a corner and tried to become invisible. After about an hour, she heard her name being called on the P.A. She went over to the nurses' station.

"I'm Eve Palmer." The nurse checked her bracelet ID and nodded at the orderly.

"The doctor wants some tests. Please go with this orderly." Seeing the fear in Eve's face, the nurse smiled. "It's all routine."

The orderly led her through the two locked doors and out into the hospital proper. They went down one long corridor and through a series of interconnecting rooms to an elevator bank. The orderly pressed the button and they waited, Eve becoming more nervous by the minute. The elevator doors opened.

Standing just inside were the two men from the black car. Before she could scream, the orderly threw her into the arms of one of the men, and the doors closed. She was trapped!

The man next to her spoke quietly as the elevator moved slowly down. "Don't fight us. Just do as you're told, and everything will be fine." He pulled a syringe from his pocket. "Don't struggle or this will hurt more than it has to." He pushed up her sleeve.

She kicked, she squirmed, everything she could think of to do. The men cursed and readjusted their hold on her, just as the elevator stopped.

They paused, distracted by the elevator doors, and she kicked out blindly. She felt her left foot bury itself deep in something soft and she heard the man with the syringe cry out in pain and double over. His companion momentarily seemed not to know what to do. He relaxed slightly and she threw back her right elbow for all it was worth.

She must have hit something important, because he released his hold and grabbed his stomach. All of this had taken place in the time it took for the elevator doors to open and she bolted through them just before they closed.

She ran blindly through the parking structure she had been let out in. She ran out into the street. What should she do? She paused to catch her breath and to think. Call Liceth. No. Joey and Stefan were enough. She wouldn't add her friend to the list. Call the police. No. She was an escaped mental patient as far as they were concerned. She realized that she was all alone. She took her bearings.

She was on Wilshire Blvd. Apparently, she had been taken to Cyprus Medical Center near the campus. She had to get away, far away and then figure out what to do. She started jogging down the street as a plan began to form.

She easily covered the mile and a half between the hospital and the school in fifteen minutes. But she didn't go onto the campus itself. Instead, she headed for her bank on Westwood Blvd. where, after explaining several times why she had no ID with her, and after spotting an old friend who was the assistant manager, she withdrew two thousand dollars from her account.

Down the street to a travel agent, another acquaintance. She was thinking more clearly now than she had thought in days. She booked a rental car and had it delivered to his office. She didn't even remember the explanation. Once in the car, she drove as fast as she could out of the city.

She had no exact destination in mind, but as the city faded behind her, the way began to be clear. She quickly found herself on the way to Las Vegas. She wasn't certain why, only the belief that, among its thousands of anonymous tourists, she would be safe.

She had been driving several hours. It was starting to get dark. The adrenaline rush that had kept her going had begun to subside. She was hungry and cold.

Catching a glimpse of herself in the rear view mirror, she decided she'd better stop and make herself more presentable. She turned into the main shopping center in Barstow and pulled into a parking space near a small department store. It was more like a Thrifty Drug Store with an attitude, but it would do. She went in, bought a few cosmetics, tooth brush, comb, and some basic necessities. She added an inexpensive wallet and purse to the pile in the cart, and a cheap sweater/jacket.

Outside the store, she put on the jacket and placed the smaller items in the purse. The rest she locked in the car trunk. Looking around, she spotted a fast food shop nearby (ironically, the same place Robby would stop the next day). She bought a couple of burgers and a coke to go, and returned to the car. With the jacket buttoned, and the food inside her, she felt better and decided to push through to Vegas.

After a stop for gas and a trip to the rest room where she applied some makeup, she was ready to go on. The gas station was giving away cheap vinyl "luggage" with a full service fill up. She stuffed the bag with her earlier purchases from the car trunk. Now she was ready. Just another tourist making a quick weekend trip to Las Vegas.

By the time she arrived in Las Vegas, the sky was darkening, but the world around her was exploding with neon and laughing, noisy, happy people. She drove along the Strip but decided against the resort hotels. She continued on to downtown and randomly selected the Empress. She checked in for "two or three days," and paid cash. Now she was grateful that she had chosen the gambling Mecca. Where else could she spend cash without it being noticed? She went up to her room and slept for the first time in days.

The next morning, she ordered breakfast from room service, again paying cash, and tried to figure her next move. She was safe, at least for the moment. She was sure of that. But for how long? Exhaustion overcame worries and she went back to sleep.

She awoke in the late afternoon. After a room service lunch, she reached her first decision. The FBI. She remembered reading that the FBI office in Las Vegas was considered one of the best in the country. She would go to them. She wasn't sure they would believe her, but just on the chance that they might, she had to go. She got directions from the concierge and left the hotel an hour later. Not knowing the streets, and filled with tension, she quickly became lost. She drove on, finally spotting the strip, Las Vegas Blvd. There she decided she would get directions. She was so intent on her driving, that she failed to notice the black sedan pull in behind her. A block from the Strip, it happened.

The sedan suddenly accelerated, pulled alongside her and forced her car off the side of the road, over the curb where it came to rest with a jolt, against a chain link fence. The cars were only two hundred yards from the Strip, on an access road but they might have been miles away. Nobody saw anything or did anything.

Momentarily stunned, Eve recovered just in time to see the black car circle around and come to a stop in front of her car. The men from the elevator got out with murderous looks on their faces.

After almost forty-eight hours of being a victim, Eve's anger overcame her fear. She acted without thinking. She threw the car into reverse and, throwing dirt and gravel everywhere, she sped backwards for about fifty yards. The men were caught off guard but quickly recovered and raced to their car.

She thought of Stefan, Joey, and of her own harassment. She jammed the car into gear and aimed it right at the men and their car. The one who had held the syringe just managed to leap across the hood of his car as Eve's car tore the open driver's door off its hinges. She sped away, her courage waning as the possibilities of what might have happened poured in on her. She returned to the Empress more convinced than ever that no one could help her. Thoughts of the FBI were driven away by panic. She barricaded herself in her room.

She sat for hours, in a chair facing the door to her room. She knew they would come, and she knew somehow, that she had run out the string.

Why they were after her, why they had killed Joey and Stefan, all the questions continued to plague her. The one thing she knew for sure was that the men would come and that this time it would be all over, and she would never know why.

They came early that evening.

She saw the knob turn, the lock slowly rotating from an unseen pick. Oddly, an icy calm descended upon her. As the door opened against the chair she had placed there, she began to scream.

All right, she thought, They're going to get me, but people are going to know I've been gotten!

The door flew open and there they were. With large guns drawn. They stepped into the room and then, suddenly, they were gone. Replaced by a scared looking housekeeper looking in on her. She managed to think about what providence it was that kept protecting her. She thought in clear, concise images…But she couldn't stop screaming.

❧

When Eve finished her story, everybody remained quiet for some time. It was as if they were paying silent respect for all that she had been through, or thought she had been through. Each in the room had his own opinion, but the only opinion that counted was Robby's and all eyes were on him.

He sat on the ottoman, facing her. "Nothing's going to happen to you while you're here." He nodded at Sy. "Believe me. He'll protect you." Sy pressed a button on his desk and a moment later Ernie DiNofrio entered.

"I want you to go with him." Eve hesitated. He helped her up and walked her over to Ernie. "Don't worry. You'll be all right. I'll see you in a couple of hours. Get some rest." He turned to Ernie. "Nothing happens to her." Ernie studied the flat expression, the eyes which had gone from deep blue to battleship gray, and the anger which seemed to come off of Robby in waves. Ernie had seen the look before. He put his arm around Eve.

"I'll take care of you. Me and my boys."

As they started to leave the room, Eve turned back to Robby and silently pleaded with him. He smiled at her and softly said, "Trust me."

CHAPTER THREE

RUDY EHRENCOLES

It was as if a heavy cloud had lifted with Eve's departure from the room. Danny poured JB on the rocks for his father and himself. The silence lasted for almost five minutes. Finally, Seymour spoke.

"Well?"

Robby looked up and smiled. "What do you think?"

Danny looked grim. "I don't know. I think maybe we ought to call Metro and turn her over to them."

Seymour shook his head. "If she were my daughter, far from home and in trouble, I'd hope that someone would help her. And she is our guest."

"Dad, you can take that too far."

Before Seymour could respond, Robby held up his hand. "I believe her." Both men turned to him. "I think she's legitimately in danger and that the cops can't help her."

Danny started to say something, but Seymour interrupted. "Make your point, Robert."

Robby began to pace. "First, we've got the tampered with fire alarms, then the accidents, three of them in three different parts of the country. And finally, we have this." He pulled out the paper

Danny had brought him earlier. "The plate of the car that she said the bad guys were using."

Danny nodded. "Ernie ran it. It was 'not in file' just like the cops said."

Robby smiled. "Not just 'not in file'," he paused, "but not in sequence." He looked triumphantly at them and they returned his look with confused expressions.

"Don't you get it?" he asked. They were blank. Just then Ernie walked back into the room.

"She's safe. I put her in a tower suite with two guards and one of the women concierges."

Robby turned to him. "Ernie, if you wanted to pull a job using a car, and you didn't want any connection with that car, but you also wanted to slow down any police search for the car, what would you do?"

"Simple. Alter a plate. Use some reflective tape to turn an E into a B or something like that."

"And if the cops ran it, what would they get?"

Ernie thought for a minute. "If I put some thought into it probably…" he said the words slowly "not in sequence or not in file. In other words, a plate number that hadn't even been stamped out yet." He realized the numbers he had just run for Robby and uttered a low "Jeeez…"

Robby turned back to Seymour and Danny. "Ernie knows about that trick, I know about it. But I'd be willing to bet you whatever I'm down at the casino that only about a thousand people nationwide know about it and that none of them are in the Tower Suite right now."

Realization spread across Seymour's face. "So what do we do now? Call the FBI?"

Robby was quiet for a long time. He walked over to the mirror overlooking the casino and looked down at the action. "I need some time. There's something about this that stinks of organization, big time! Before we do anything, I'd like to get into it, at least a little bit."

Seymour's expression was grim. "Do what you think you have to. I'll foot the bill, for now. She's our guest so she gets our help."

Danny started to say something but his father's look made him think better of it. "But I can't risk exposure to this hotel. We'll help her, but only so far. Understand, Robert?" Robby nodded. "Work fast."

Ernie sighed. Seymour indicated the meeting was over. Ernie and Robby left the office together. He turned to Robby, "What are you going to do?"

"I'd like to bring Barker in to look after the girl."

Ernie sighed again. "Yeah, okay." He began remembering how long the reconstruction of the golf clubhouse had taken after Robby and Barker had 'looked after a problem' there for Seymour.

Robby, seeming to read the older man's mind, smiled. "I'll tell him to watch the bric-a-brac."

"Where are you going?"

"To find a problem solver."

❧

To say that Rudy Ehrencoles had a limp was to say that Quasimodo had a posture problem. He loved his limp, luxuriated in it, he made it his own personal billboard to the world. His world of escalators.

"All of life is a series of escalators," he was fond of saying with little or no provocation. "We are constantly traveling up or down, in constant pursuit or retreat. Seeking our destiny or running away from it."

When he was truly in his element, half drunk and addressing his sometimes dull but adoring students, he would expound on his theory of life for hours until his voice would slur, and he would slowly drop off to sleep. In the morning, he would awaken to find himself covered by the throw placed lovingly around him by those same students.

His life was a constant. A reassuringly slow, upward moving escalator that would leave him one day Chairman of the History Department. Probably a year or two before his retirement. Till then, he would enjoy talking bullshit philosophy to pleasantly stupid students and he would ride his escalator...like all before him.

As he walked to his first class of the day, increasing or decreasing his limp depending on how many students were around, his mind wandered to the only person he had ever known who had deliberately stepped off that escalator.

Rudy was forced from his thought by the approach of the "hamster."

"The hamster," Associate Professor Jules Douglas was the timid, myopic, close minded little thing that had been assigned as Rudy's project for the term. Every year the Chairman, in his wisdom, assigned Rudy a lump of clay generously called an Associate Professor, to make over in his image, and every year, Rudy would find the teacher in the clay and sculpt it into being.

But in Douglas' case, maybe all that was there was the lump.

"Professor Ehrencoles?" Reluctantly, Rudy stopped and turned to face the onrushing Douglas.

"Professor, I'm so glad I caught you. I've been looking all over."

"Not possible, hamster."

Douglas ignored the sarcasm. As usual. "There's a man waiting for you in your office. He said it was important that he speak to you."

"Define your terms, hamster."

"The man is in his thirties, well dressed, polite…"

Rudy just stared at him. Finally, he spoke. "How am I supposed to turn you into a first class historian if you are constantly being vague about the present? Come on man! Expand, expound, explain!"

Douglas thought for a moment. This was an old trick of Rudy's. A lesson created out of a situation.

"The man seems the blue collar type, with polish. He appears to know you, but not well, or he would have known you are never in this early. There also seems to be a wariness about him."

Rudy's ears pricked up. "Wariness?"

"Yes, sir. It's hard to explain, but I get the definite impression that he's not only aware of his surroundings but is doing a constant set of, of…" He struggled for the phrase.

Rudy picked it up. "Threat evaluations. He looks you in the eye but also looks past you?"

"Yes, sir."

Rudy smiled. "Anything else? About the way he looked, anything?"

Douglas thought long and hard. "A scar. He has a scar at the base of his neck. I could just see the edge of it."

Inwardly, Rudy smiled. Perhaps there was an image hidden beneath the clay after all. He started for his office.

"Out of my way, hamster! I loathe keeping interesting visitors waiting." He pounded off into the building.

As he approached his office, he increased his limp to truly pathetic levels, and dragging his leg behind him, he opened the door.

"*Guten morgen*, Herr Professor." Robby stood and walked across the office to embrace Rudy.

Rudy pried himself loose and maneuvered behind his desk. He threw his bad leg up on an open drawer as he looked across at his old student, the proverbial bad penny.

"Hello, *Momzer*."

Robby nodded.

"Sit, sit." Rudy settled back in his chair. "How's my gorgeous daughter? And when are you going to make an honest woman of her?"

Robby drew a chair up to the desk. "Jenna's fine, as you'd know if you drove across town to see her. And she doesn't want to make an honest man of me."

"To address the first item, *Momzer*, I call her regularly. Whenever I visit, she fusses over me too much. I only like beautiful young women to fuss over me when they're not related. As for the second, despite my inquiry, the thought of you as my son-in-law is too horrible to contemplate. But I love you, anyway. So what are you doing here?"

"It's a long, weird story." Robby began to tell Rudy about Eve's strange tale. Rudy pulled out a yellow legal pad and began making notes. Occasionally, there'd be a terse question to clarify or verify. Finally, it was done.

"I have one question only. Do you believe her story, Robby?" Rudy watched his face intently.

"Yeah, I do. Everything checks. Alone, she doesn't stand a chance." He paused and looked out the window. "And I don't like inequities."

Rudy reviewed his notes. The question wasn't whether or not he should help, but rather, whether or not he wanted to help. He turned the pages and silently balanced possibilities. He looked up.

"I'll need to see her research."

Robby nodded. "Her backups were left behind in L.A."

Rudy opened the small refrigerator he kept behind his desk and took out two cold sodas. He gave one to Robby and held the other up to his forehead. It was going to be another hot, boring, day. He picked up the phone and put the unopened can of soda back in the refrigerator. Then he dialed a number. "Hello, Thomas? Ehrencoles. Can you cover my classes for the next few days? Yes, the hamster has my notes. What?" He looked directly at Robby. "Off chasing windmills I expect." He hung up.

Robby got up. "Our plane leaves in an hour." Rudy stood, grabbed the bag he kept packed and stored in the office closet for exactly this eventuality, and limped out beside Robby.

In the Tower Suite of the Empress, two security guards sat watching television while Eve picked at her lunch. A knock at the door brought them all to attention.

One of the guards drew his gun and stood next to Eve, who was moved behind the bar. The other guard checked the peep hole, nodded, and opened the door.

Ernie and Barker walked in. Barker carried a gym bag in one hand and a briefcase in the other. Ernie nodded at the guards.

"This is Barker. He's in charge now. As long as our guest remains at the Empress, follow his instructions." He walked over to Eve. "Are you okay? Do you need anything?"

Eve never took her eyes from the bulk of Barker. "I'm fine." In a whisper, she said to Ernie, "Who is that?"

Barker came over to them, and Ernie stepped away. "My name is Barker. Robby sent me to look after you."

Eve reached out and tentatively shook his hand. Something about him exuded danger. Eve could see that even the men in the room were nervous. Barker seemed to sense her concern.

"Don't worry. I promised our mutual friend that nothing would happen to you." He opened the briefcase and pulled out a sawed off 12 gauge shot gun in a leather shoulder holster. "And I always keep my promises."

They sat in the car for ten minutes before Robby nodded that it was okay to approach the house. Robby went first, followed closely by Rudy. Just as they reached the door, Rudy pretended to be reaching into his briefcase, making a big show of it and effectively screening Robby from the street as he picked the door locks. They were inside in seconds.

With the door closed behind them, they stood in the foyer for several minutes, listening. Robby drew his gun, a Mauser .380 H.S.C. automatic. Satisfied that they were alone, Robby nodded off to the left. "The office's in there." Rudy went there immediately.

While Rudy went through the files, Robby silently toured the house. He went room by room, quietly examining everything. Finally, he went to the office to find Rudy happily at work.

Robby glanced at the computer monitor and then moved to the window. "So?"

Rudy smiled. "Like she said. Everything's gone, wiped clean."

"So why are you so happy?"

"Because my computer phobic friend, they have been wiped clean, but not formatted." He seemed thrilled with his discovery and sat grinning at Robby.

"In English, Professor."

Rudy sighed. "You never did learn anything did you? If the discs have not been formatted, then the information on them is quite recoverable."

Robby nodded. "Take them and anything else you need. We're not alone. Time to leave."

Rudy quickly gathered everything together in his briefcase including the contents of two drawers. They walked to the front door together. When Robby spoke, his voice was cold, devoid of all emotion. Rudy had seen him like this before and braced himself for the inevitable.

"Go straight to the car. Get in on the driver's side and start it up. Pull it around to this side of the street and open the passenger door." Robby reached out and took the briefcase. Count five and then go." He disappeared back into the house. Slowly, Rudy counted. Not once did he look back for Robby. He did as he was told. That's how you stayed alive with Robby.

At the count of five, Rudy casually opened the door, paused, and waved back into the house. "No, no. I'll get the door. Don't get up." He closed the door and walked across the street.

He got in and started the car. Still he didn't look for Robby. The street seemed empty, but he trusted Robby. He pulled the car around front and leaned over to open the passenger door. That's when it happened.

From out of nowhere, a green van appeared and began racing down the street toward Rudy. Shots rang out. Three in all and suddenly the van went veering off to its right, out of control. It crashed into a fire hydrant, causing an urban geyser to erupt.

In the time it took Rudy to see all of this, no more than five or ten seconds, Robby materialized, leaping into the passenger seat. "Go!"

Rudy needed no encouragement. He floored the gas pedal, sending a cloud of smoke into the suburban air to mix with the vapor of the gushing hydrant. Five minutes later, he pulled over and they changed seats. Half an hour later, they were back at LAX and an hour after that they were walking through the maze of slot machines that made up the passenger lobby of McCarran Airport in Las Vegas.

ﻌ

Rudy and Eve sat together on the couch in the living room of the Tower Suite. Spread out, all over the coffee table and spilling onto the floor around them, were folders, printouts, and legal pads with scribbled notes. Rudy was asking questions and writing notes as Eve answered. They discussed, they argued, they explained.

Eve felt more rested and relaxed than at any time since the beginning of what she had come to refer to as "the nightmare." She knew from the moment that she met Rudy, that he was a kindred spirit, albeit a generation older. They spoke in the same shorthand, and shared enthusiasms.

Rudy, for his part, was having a party. Ever since he had restored the lost computer files, he had jumped into the fray with both feet. He was exhilarated. He had a few thousand ideas that he wanted to explore with Eve.

The two academics were so immersed in Eve's project that they barely noticed Robby enter the room. Barker noticed and nodded to him from his seat by the door.

Robby nodded with his head towards the bedroom and Barker joined him there, leaving the door open for a clear view of the front door.

"We've been here too long," Robby began. "It's time to go."

Barker nodded. "About fucking time. How do you want to do it?"

The two men discussed the plan for the next few minutes, making minor changes in Robby's original idea. When they were both satisfied, they returned to the living room. Robby walked over to the coffee table and touched Rudy on the shoulder.

"Sorry to interrupt."

Rudy grudgingly put down his pad. "No, you're not." Even before Robby could say another word, Rudy began to pack up the material. Robby came around and sat next to Eve.

"We have to leave now. Get your coat." He spoke matter-of-factly.

Eve looked at him with concern. "Is something wrong? Has something happened?"

Robby shook his head. "Everything's fine. The time to go is before anything happens. Right now." He stood up.

"I'll be ready to leave in a few minutes. I just have to pack," Eve said as she stood up.

"No." Barker stood between her and the bedroom where she was heading. "We go now." Eve stopped dead and looked at Robby, fear beginning to reassert itself. Rudy saw it and came over to her.

"Don't worry, dear. If they say you leave now, you leave now. Trust them." He smiled. "I'll make sure your things catch up with you."

She looked around the room. Barker already had his coat on and Robby was at the door. With a sigh, she gave in and walked over to Robby. Why she kept putting her trust in these strangers she wasn't sure; but she would continue to do so. What other choice did she have?

"Stay behind me and to the right of Barker. Don't talk to anyone while we're in the hotel. If anything happens, just do what Barker tells you. Understand?" She nodded. "Let's go."

Robby opened the door and went out. Barker slammed it shut behind him. They waited in silence. One minute, two minutes, three…Finally there was a single knock on the door. Barker unholstered his shotgun and held it loosely beneath his coat in his left hand. He opened the door and they stepped out.

They walked down the corridor to the private Tower elevator. Robby was waiting for them there. A sheet had been hung over the glass of the elevator so that they could not be seen from the outside. They rode down in silence, Eve's tension building by the minute. Finally, the elevator stopped.

Robby was holding the button to keep the door closed and looking at Barker. Barker pressed Eve into the corner of the elevator and pointed the big gun at the door, then he nodded. Robby released the button and the door opened.

Not five feet from the door, Danny and Ernie were standing by an aging Cadillac with all four doors open. Ernie had his gun out and was looking anxiously around. Without warning, Eve was grabbed by Robby and thrown into the car. Barker jumped in beside her, while Robby slid behind the wheel. Before she could realize what was happening, they were off, the forward momentum of the car slamming the doors closed.

They drove in silence for twenty minutes. They turned often and never stayed on the same street for more than two minutes. Just as Eve was regaining her sensibilities, the car made a sudden turn and pulled to a stop in front of a warehouse-looking building about the size of a large garage.

Barker turned to her. "Stay in the car." Before he finished talking, he was out of the car and into the building. Now Robby turned to her. "Slide over to the passenger side." She did as she was told. They sat silently for over five minutes. Finally, Barker emerged from the building and returned to the car.

Robby got out with his gun drawn. Barker opened the door and helped her out. She could see that they were both tight with tension. Talking seemed somehow wrong. Barker turned away from her but commanded, "Follow me."

As they walked to the building, she could see the neighborhood for the first time. It seemed deserted, part of an industrial area with lots of little warehouses like the one into which they were going. As she got to the door, she heard the car door slam and tires squeal as Robby peeled away. Barker slammed the door shut behind her.

She was in the safe house. It was far nicer than she had expected. After going through a small office, Eve found herself in a comfortably furnished living area complete with entertainment center, dining area and a partitioned off area in the rear which contained a mini bedroom. After her brief tour of the place, Barker took her aside.

"There are three rules you need to follow," he began softly. All of the tension was gone from his face and the ever present shotgun was holstered. "You never leave this area. Not even to go into the office. Anything you want or need, ask me. There are no telephones except for the cellular in my case. And I won't give you access to that."

Eve was puzzled. "Why not?"

"You're a non pro," he said. "You're going to be tempted to call someone. To tell them you're all right or whatever. That creates a risk. I don't take risks."

"I wouldn't do something like that," Eve huffed, although deep down she had wanted to call Liceth for the last couple of days.

Barker smiled as if reading her thoughts. "Just relax. Jenna's bringing some food by later." He turned and went into the office. She heard the door lock behind him.

For a moment, she felt trapped. But over the coming hours she would gradually feel more and more secure.

Prison it might be, but it was certainly a comfortable one; and with Barker out front, she was convinced, a safe one.

≈≈

Jenna stood at the door, one hand on the knob. "Remember guys, this is my apartment, not a bear pit. I don't want to see empty pretzel bowls and bottles all over the floor when I get home. And Dad, don't stay up too late. You need your rest."

Rudy grimaced. "If it were up to you, I'd be in bed by eight and spend my days in a rocker with a shawl around my shoulders."

Robby laughed at the concept. "Don't worry, Jenna. The worst we'll do is finish off your strawberry cheesecake. I'll take good care of the wizened decrepit one."

Rudy looked at Robby. "Quiet, *Momzer*." Then, to Jenna, "Go to work. I won't let the muscle-bound cretin turn your place into a demilitarized zone."

When Jenna left, Robby turned to Rudy. "What've you got for me?"

"Well," Rudy began, "in our profession, you have to publish or perish."

"So?"

"So, Eve's a solid researcher." Rudy picked up some printouts and gestured with them. "It's not a book you'd rush right out to buy but for what it is...some good information, systematically presented...I think it'll make a good supplemental text for some classes." He tossed the papers aside.

"Are you telling me that a rival professor is just trying to keep her from publishing her book? That's a little thin."

"Don't be an idiot." Rudy leaned back in his chair, one arm hanging over the back. He propped his leg on the table, and smiled expansively.

Robby recognized the pose. This was 'the professor at home'.

Rudy continued. "I don't have any idea why someone's trying to kill her. But...in going over her research, a couple of things jumped out at me. First, she talked a lot about one particular guy, Franz Konigsmann. It reminded me," Rudy paused reflectively, "I was living in San Francisco then. Just a young buck starting out. This man, I think he was," he skimmed through the printouts, "a German officer. Tall, handsome, wore a monocle, always dressed to kill. He was the darling of high society. You couldn't open a newspaper without seeing his picture at some important party or the races, or just having lunch with a celebrity.

"There was a whole group in Hollywood that hung on his every word. There they were, idolizing one of Hitler's closest advisors, doting on him. Just because he was a good looking, well-dressed, smooth talker. You want to know about disinformation? This guy was the master of it."

Robby sat quietly. As Rudy talked, Robby almost unconsciously pulled out his pocket watch and started polishing it, unseeingly, concentrating on Rudy's face and words.

Rudy went on. "Secondly, There was a woman, a Countess no less." Once again Rudy referred to the printouts. "Countess Lisl von Hostetter. The tabloids of the time called her 'the mystery woman of Europe'. She seemed to be all over the place...here, South America, everywhere. She was close to Hitler, and, incidentally, to Konigsmann. Also very big in social circles in the States."

"She seemed to be spending most of her time sympathetically explaining the Nazi point of view. It was pretty hard to suspect someone of duplicity when she seemed like a little middle-aged woman who reminisced of her youth."

Robby stopped polishing. "Okay, but how does that relate to our problem?"

Rudy sat back. "I don't know. But one thing's certain. Most of the material in the book has been covered in a dozen or so different books with just as many points of view. This stuff on Konigsmann and the Countess is, if not new, at least not well known. Eve's a damn good researcher, there's an interesting slant here.

"Those are the only things that make her computer data different. And if we make the safe assumption that Professor Palmer's troubles are related to the book," he looked at Robby who nodded, "then our next logical assumption is that the attacks must be related to any new material in the book."

Robby responded. "If I understand correctly, all those people have been dead and buried for years. That all happened over fifty years ago, and they were not kids then."

Rudy laughed. "I don't know if they're dead or not. What I do know is that if there is anything else in the book that could be considered 'new'," he picked up the large stack of printouts again, "it's not here. And frankly, these two people were so trivial in the overall scheme of things as to confound me as to why they'd be so important today."

Robby thought for a moment. "Can you find out more about them?"

"Given time," Rudy stood and limped to the window, "and the resources."

Robby also stood and moved to the window. Both men looked

up at the sky, ink black except where the neon of Las Vegas intruded.

"I'll talk to Seymour."

☙

It was a dark room. No light penetrated from even a crack beneath the door. The man liked it that way. There were some things best left to the dark. He spoke quietly, forcing the others in the room to lean forward to hear. It was a technique he had used for many years. He thought it gave him authority. As if he needed any.

"Begin."

A slide was projected across the room from him. It was a picture, taken several hours earlier, of Robby and Rudy standing in a window. No one spoke until he did.

"Talk to me."

A young briefer stood and turned on the small light on his lectern. It slightly illuminated the room. Five men sat around the conference table, all middle aged or older, all in suits. The light didn't reach the man. He remained semi-hidden in a kind of quarter light.

The briefer was to the point. "This picture was taken two hours ago in Las Vegas. Since that time, we have lost contact with them."

The man in the dark spoke. "How did that happen?"

One of the other men at the table spoke after clearing his throat. "Well...uh...he is very good. Former Company man, former Beret." The answer was silence. "Be assured, we'll have them back under our surveillance shortly." More silence filled the room.

The man in the shadows shook his head. "Do they have the information?"

The briefer nodded. "It seems that they were able to recover or reassemble the information."

"That is unfortunate." The man waved the briefer away. After he had left the room, "Discussion, gentlemen?"

For the next fifteen minutes, they discussed and debated the best ways to find and to maintain surveillance on Robby and Rudy. Considering the resources represented by the men in the room, it was not a difficult problem. After a time, the man in the shadows spoke again.

"My friends, time is running short. When they are found they must be…dealt with. Thoroughly."

Slowly, one by one, each of the men in the room nodded his agreement and left. At last, the man in the shadows was left alone.

He stood and walked over to the screen and carefully examined the image of Robby. "A shame really." He walked from the room quietly and out into the light of day.

ès

Robby didn't like New York. He didn't like the people and he didn't like the smell. As a result, as he drove to the Bronx, his mood turned sour.

He had left Rudy in Washington to continue his research and then taken the shuttle to Kennedy. From there, in a rented Camaro, he had driven to the scene of Stefan's 'accident'.

When he got out of his car, he immediately went into his 'alert mode'. All senses keenly attuned, walking in measured paces, arms hanging loosely at his sides. The neighborhood resembled Beirut and Robby prepared himself for whatever.

In the alley where Stefan's body had been found, it was hard to distinguish signs of an accident from the decay of the city that had accumulated there. A homeless man lay against a dumpster and Robby tried to talk to him but he ran off, obviously afraid. It didn't surprise him. He examined the alley futilely for the better part of ten minutes and then turned to leave.

"Gimme your money, asshole!"

A tall teenager stood between the alley's entrance and Robby. He held a knife in his right hand and had a look of hatred on his face. Momentarily, Robby wondered what could have happened to create such anger in a boy so young. Instantly, he answered his own question. 'God I hate New York'.

The mugger raised his knife and stepped towards Robby. "Didn't you hear me, asshole, give me your mon…" He never finished the word.

As he got within arm's length of Robby, Robby lashed out with his left hand, grabbing the boy's right wrist and forcing it high above his head. Simultaneously, he grabbed the boy's throat in his own right hand and pressed the teen back against the alley wall. This all happened in seconds.

Instantly, the boy's expression changed from menacing to shock, and then to fear as Robby began gently applying pressure to the young man's windpipe.

Robby smiled. "Not really good at this, are you?" More pressure. "Drop the knife." It clattered to the ground. As he was deciding what to do with the boy, a thought suddenly occurred to Robby. "You hang around this alley a lot, do you?" No answer until the pressure on this throat was slightly increased and he began to cough for air. The boy nodded furiously.

Robby released some of the pressure. "A few days ago, about a week, a body was found here. Remember?" The boy nodded.

"Good. The cops say it was an accident, hit and run. What do you think?" He released the pressure on the throat but kept his hand there. When the boy tried to raise his free arm, Robby quickly reapplied the pressure. The boy understood the rules. Robby released the pressure again.

He coughed three or four times getting his breath back. "Shit. Don't kill me, man. I don't hardly know nothin'."

Robby smiled. "Tell me what you do know."

The boy looked into the cold eyes that didn't match the smile and decided then and there that honesty, in this case, was the best policy.

"Wasn't no accident. Cat was worked over real good. I seen the body." He didn't mention that he had seen the body while he was robbing it.

"You see how it got here?"

"Three suits. Pull up in a flash car, look all around, open the trunk and pull him out. Cat was still alive, I think. He made a kinda sound so they whack him out, lay him down behind the ride and then back over him a couple times. Cat was serious dead then, man." He waited for Robby's reaction.

Robby released him and backed away. The boy thought of running but he was becoming intrigued by Robby. He chose to stand there and rub his throat.

"You see anything else? A plate number, recognize any of the suits, anything?"

The boy stood up straight. "What's it worth to you?" Robby took a menacing look at the boy who quickly stepped back. "Okay,

okay! It's cool!" Robby stepped back but kept his eyes locked on the boy's eyes.

"The car, man," the boy began. "It was a big old LTD, vinyl hardtop, look like it just come off the lot. Big old blue LTD, vinyl hardtop with some kind of funny sticker on the back bumper."

Robby had looked away, but now he turned back to the boy so sharply that it made the boy jump back. "What kind of sticker?"

The boy laughed nervously. "Funny looking thing. Like a parachute with a star on top of it and uh, uh…"

Robby interrupted. "Feathered wings coming out of the sides?"

"Yeah. You know it?" Robby didn't answer. Instead, he reached into his pocket and gave the boy a twenty. He took it hesitatingly and started to walk out of the alley. When he reached the street, he turned and looked back at Robby and called over to him. "Hey man, who are you anyway?"

"Just a bill collector," Robby called back as he turned and walked back deeper into the alley.

The boy pocketed the twenty and started to walk off. "I'd sure hate to owe that sucker."

&

Deep within the microfilm stacks of the national archives, Rudy threaded a tape into the machine.

For the last eight hours, he had ceaselessly read old reports, analysis, and communications regarding Konigsmann and von Hostetter. For the most part, he had run across only mildly interesting information. Until now, that is.

He advanced the tape to the document number he wanted. It was a report of an interrogation of Konigsmann immediately after the end of the war. He had read it earlier, but something had bothered him, and until he figured out what it was, he would get no rest. He read the report for the third time when suddenly it struck him.

In the middle of the interrogation he found the passage and read it to himself.

&

| Interrogating Officer: | What was the purpose of your trip to Amsterdam in Christmas of 1944? |
| Konigsmann: | It was related to routine matters regarding |

Planning Group Crystal Movement.

Interrogating Officer: And what was Planning Group Crystal Movement?

Observing Officer: Let's go off the record for a moment.

(Code name Cloudburst 414)

ஃ

The next three pages were heavily censored. Rudy could read a word here and a phrase there, but not enough to figure out the meaning. This was common enough in declassified documents but one thing still niggled at Rudy.

What was Crystal Movement?

He spent the next two days virtually living at the archives. He read everything he could both in American and captured German documents, but he could find no Crystal Movement. For that matter, he couldn't say for sure that Crystal Movement was important. But it felt right so he plunged ahead.

With his frustration growing, he turned for help to an old colleague of his, Yohannon Berg.

Berg was a professor of history at American University. An old friend and occasional chess partner of Rudy's, he was also an expert on most things related to World War Two as far as they concerned Germany. They met in Berg's office.

"So Rudolph, come to get your comeuppance in a vicious game of chess?"

Rudy laughed. "Not this time." He cleared some books off of a chair and sat down. "What do you know about a German Operation or Planning Group called Crystal Movement?"

Berg rubbed his forehead. "That's a new one on me." He pulled several bulging cardboard files down from a shelf. "Let's see what we can find."

For the next two hours they worked at the files. While they worked, they talked about old times, family, and campus politics. They didn't find much but they had a good time. That afternoon, they took a break and walked across the campus to a coffee shop. They settled down to their coffee. "What are you doing out in the desert still? An old guy like you, you could dry up and blow away out there."

Rudy laughed. "Some Sabra you are. I thought you Israelis

loved the desert."

Berg shook his head. "Not true. Why do you think we keep planting trees and irrigating? We're trying to get rid of the damned thing."

They laughed. "Seriously," Rudy said, "are there any decent opportunities open here?" Rudy was constantly indulging in fantasies of leaving UNLV.

"Only one I know of I don't think you're qualified for."

Rudy tried to look serious. "How would you know? Despite my carefully styled reputation, I am a truly gifted individual."

"Gifted enough to become a university president? That's the only opening here I know of."

Now Rudy remembered. E. George Williams the president of American University had just been nominated to be the new CIA Director.

For the rest of the hour, they talked about the nomination of Williams and its effect on the college. Suddenly, in the middle of a sentence, Berg slapped himself in the forehead. "Such a *schmuck!*"

Rudy looked at him amusedly. "You, me or Williams?"

"Me. I just remembered. There's an archival source we haven't tried yet. If anybody has something on this Crystal Movement, I bet they will."

"Who?"

"The Williams Archives and Special Collections over at Maynard Library."

"Expand, expound, explain." Rudy leaned forward.

"Williams has put together a great research archives right here and it has a lot of obscure World War Two references. We can go by right now and try it."

They paid the check and headed off to the library. It was closed, but using Berg's influence they got in and worked for an hour. They didn't find much but what they found provided, as Rudy put it, "A direction."

The next day, Rudy returned to the National Archives, requested an entirely different series of microfilms and nine hours later, smiling broadly, he met Berg for dinner and a game of chess. He didn't mind losing. He didn't mind paying for the meal. Well,

not a lot. Nothing could bother Rudy that night.
He had unearthed 'Crystal Movement'.

≈

Rudy sat at the computer in Yohannan Berg's office, grateful for a friend who asked no questions, just acquiesced to his urgent request. Earlier, he had called Robby, who had only just arrived back in Vegas, on the secure line in the CC800 Communication Control Center, that lightweight sturdy little attaché case they both carried whenever Robby decided to fight inequity with his help. Fortunately, a lot of those fights were lucrative. Those attaché cases were expensive.

Now, some seven hours later, Rudy prepared to transmit his new found enlightenment to the secure computer in the Las Vegas safe house.

Robby sat down in front of the computer and checked his watch. Eve pulled up a chair alongside. Barker, having made his rounds, and positioned his two 'associates' for security, sat down behind them, trusty shotgun close at his side.

Robby opened his attaché case, checked the telephone monitor, tap alert, and balance voltage meter. He punched in the code on the phone scrambler, and placed the receiver on the computer modem. He nodded to Eve, and they all watched the screen expectantly.

Then it was there. Rudy was on line.

"Greetings, my children. Get comfortable, sit back, and let me tell you a story."

PART TWO

CRYSTAL MOVEMENT

"The two most fragile things, fine crystal, and conspiracies."

—*Winston Churchill*

CHAPTER FOUR

THE BEGINNING

1938...The forces of darkness swirl and cling. They engulf some, bypass others, and consume from within. Their influence is subtle and cunning. Men who succumb to the seductive whisperings often find themselves thrust to the forefront of events and the world becomes a cistern for their bloodletting.

Such was Adolf Hitler.

In the deprivation and hardship following World War I in Germany, he found a fertile ground for his ambitions.

The cauldron had begun to boil; and as the Czechs died alone, as the British and the French slept uneasily, as the Americans tried to look away, and as the world tried to deny the obvious, "Peace for our time" seemed to be a remarkably fragile thing.

¿&

Sir Ernest Oppenheimer's whole life was marked by a search for new fields to conquer. Aware of the potential of the diamond fields of Southwest Africa, he bought up the mines formerly owned by the Germans. He amalgamated them under the name of Consolidated Diamond Mines of Southwest Africa Ltd.

In time, Sir Ernest became one of the most important figures in the diamond producing world, controlling most of the world's diamonds.

A man who knew and loved the manipulation of businesses, Oppenheimer also had within him a sense of humanity. In a country where apartheid was the rule, he was the exception. As a result, he involved himself in politics. By 1938, he had been a member of the South African Parliament for fourteen years.

He treated all his employees with fairness and caring concern. Respected by them, he was rewarded with tremendous loyalty.

Now he sat and fumed.

His assessment of the world situation differed radically from Chamberlain. There was no question in his mind that, left unchecked, Hitler would systematically go about gobbling up whatever territories he desired. And Oppenheimer was painfully aware that a considerable portion of Consolidated's diamond holdings were in the former colony, German Southwest Africa. He had an obligation to stockholders and employees alike.

In all his decisions, he always proceeded cautiously, with carefully thought out judgments. Now it seemed to him that precautions needed to be taken to safeguard the workers and the mines. He didn't know how long it would be before Hitler turned his eyes toward Southwest Africa.

Still in deep thought, he reached for the intercom on his desk. "Miss Henley, please bring in your pad." Oppenheimer selected a cigar from the hand carved humidor in front of him, held the flame just beneath it, warming the tobacco in preparation for lighting. This familiar ritual cleared his head as he prepared to dictate.

∂⅄

To: **Fontein Site Manager Kleeman**
From: **Consolidated Diamond Mines of Southwest Africa Ltd.**

Message: I believe European conflict now inevitable stop If it spreads it could endanger Fontein holdings stop I highly recommend that you make plans to spike holdings and transship stocks to Pretoria stop Use your own judgment as to date of implementation stop Advise upon commencement stop As always you have my complete confidence stop

Sir Ernest Endit

∂⅄

Max Kleeman looked deep into the mirror and studied his face. He felt cheated. He deserved a better face.

Forty years in the bush, forty years spent picking at dead rock under a harsh and unrelenting sun, forty years trying to pry loose the diamonds from their hiding places had left his skin dark and leathery, his features craggy, his expression permanently sour. He spat the tobacco juice into the spittoon expertly and turned away to more important issues.

Max was the site manager of CDM's most prosperous mine in Southwest Africa. As such, he worked twenty hour days overseeing the digging, the sorting, the rough grading, and the many daily catastrophes that only he could solve.

Personally picked for the job by Sir Ernest and answerable only to him, Max took enormous pride in the job he did. He ran his mine his way. He was fair to everybody, black and white, and friendly with nobody. That was his way and he never compromised on it. For this, he was respected and, perhaps, a little feared.

He had started in the pipe mines of Kimberly. Working miles below the surface in the artificially illuminated bowels of the earth, he could unerringly find the paystreak that would yield the highest quality stones. His instincts never failed him and he trusted them implicitly.

When Sir Ernest had asked him to leave his beloved Kimberly, Max had laughed. He was as much a part of that pipe as any of the diamonds they dug out of it. To leave was unthinkable. But he could refuse Sir Ernest nothing and within a fortnight he was off to the dried riverbeds south of Black Reef.

To this day, some seventeen years later, he remembered Kimberly more as the home where he had grown up rather than the job he had before this one; but twenty years of driving a drift (the mining term for digging through alluvial stone) had developed in him a love of the place and respect for the work.

The thrown together rock and gravel of an alluvial mine had gotten into his blood and he knew, however much he dreamed, that he would never return to the pipes.

He might well die someday, here in Southwest Africa, in the narrow, shallow tunnels of Fontein SW 2, but his heart would always be miles further down, deep within the greater heart of the Kimberly pipes.

He sighed and returned to the business that had initially caused this momentary reflection. For the third time, he read the cable from Sir Ernest. He looked out over the moonscape that was Fontein SW 2 and thought about the prehistoric forces that had come to bear to create this place, and about the forces that were beginning to bear down around him.

Standing in the doorway of the Admin. shack, Max looked out at the busy scene before him.

Working across the shoreline, the small dredger swept slowly back and forth in precisely planned rows checking the sands, draining the water and the silt, searching for the diamonds.

At the moment all was quiet over the alluvial cone, the area at the seaward side of the prehistoric delta. This area was basically a pit. As wide as several football fields and twice as long, throughout the day workers would dig the sand, shoveling it into hand cars that would be pushed on tracks to the sluices both mechanical and hand. Here it would be washed and the small diamonds plucked by hand from the muck.

Rising from the edge of the pit, dark and ugly, was the fan, the former delta.

Boulders piled upon boulders. That would be your first impression. Closer examination would show you the tons of sand, silt and gravel wedged between the boulders. It rose twelve feet above the ground and was two hundred feet across. Moving around it, away from the ocean, you were confronted by the second pit.

This pit was actually an excavation. It showed that the fan went down some forty-five feet to the original river bed. However, the pit was only wide enough and deep enough to show the true dimensions of the fan. A rope fence went around the pit with warning signs keeping people out. It was the second most dangerous place at the mine. If the fan were to shift, it would shift in this direction, collapsing into the pit, saving the lives and sadly more importantly, the equipment working on the seaward side of the fan.

The most dangerous place at the site was inside the fan itself.

Two tunnels diagonally cut into the ancient pile and met in the middle. An airshaft went up the ten feet or so from there to break through at the top. The tunnels were narrow and heavily shored with the hopefully strong oversized drift slabs. Hopefully strong, for the fan could shift or settle at any time and the slabs were all that stood between the diggers and instant death by crushing.

The fan itself was crisscrossed inside with even smaller interconnecting tunnels, some as small as four feet across. Dimly lit, these tunnels were potentially deadly. At any time while crawling through, you could come across a mole hole, that is a hole dug straight down from any given point in the tunnel to explore for diamonds.

Throughout the larger tunnels, cars on tracks were constantly carrying the gravel to the outside to be sluiced. People were constantly moving around inside the great pile and all that activity forced you to raise caution to the highest level possible.

If disaster did happen, if the low rumble of a fan shift was heard, your best chance for salvation was to try and get to one of the cross cuts, openings in the shafts that led directly to the surface. Used primarily to ease the transport of the gravel from the richest paystreaks, every man inside the fan constantly checked where the nearest one was. To not know could mean death.

As Max walked toward shaft number one, he looked for the tunnel boss. The tunnel boss was the man who had complete control of what went on in each of the shafts. First there was God, then the site manager Max Kleeman, then there was the tunnel boss.

Freddy Reineke, tunnel boss of shaft number one, had just come up and was leaning against a wheel barrow.

"Shit, Reineke! You come up for air already?" Kleeman's standard greeting brought a grin to the younger man.

"It'd be a lot easier if we'd get some of those machines we were promised. More profitable too," Freddy waited for the inevitable reaction.

Kleeman screwed up his face in mock rage. "Shit, boy! When I was a lad, every boy wanted to get in to the rocks faster than they could be held back. You didn't see any of them complainin' for a little air," he paused "of course we were a tougher breed back then."

Freddy laughed. "I know, you dug the shafts with your hands

and ate the rocks for meals. Care to try that on this beast?"

Kleeman laughed loud and hard. "We also shit diamonds, boy. Do not be forgetting that!" He looked into the tunnel. "How's she comin'?"

For the first time, Freddy frowned. "She's a bitch, boss. But I think we're beginning to worry her."

Kleeman slapped Freddy on the back and walked into the tunnel.

Over the next six months, Max Kleeman read the newspapers and listened to radio reports. Ordinarily, he was not a man who worried about world affairs. His world was bounded by prospecting trenches and drift mines.

Ever since that cable from Sir Ernest though, he had grown extremely worried. He followed the foreign news closely, and even made an effort at friendly conversation with the Germans at the local bar in Conception. After all, he had a responsibility and he would discharge it properly.

In general, he hadn't been too upset by the news but lately the word from the 'outside' was getting troublesome. Hitler was going to do whatever he wanted to, no matter what he said. It made him nervous. Sir Ernest was always correct in his assessments and Max trusted that.

The situation had even affected the people working at the mine, not only SW 2, but also the neighboring ones. From time to time, fights would break out among the crews. It wasn't just the heat or the hard work. The men were beginning to take sides, and it was disrupting everything.

The final nail in the coffin was last night. He felt his aching jaw as he remembered.

He had stood at the bar, having one last drink before calling it a night. The two Felder brothers showed up so drunk it didn't seem possible they could swallow anything more. Karl, the younger one, elbowed his way through the crowd, pushing Max aside and spilling his drink.

"Watch it, boy. There's plenty for everyone." Max blotted his shirt as the bartender refilled his drink. It was hard to keep the peace in a mining town.

Karl looked up at him drunkenly. "Oh, it's you, Kleeman. The fancy CDM boss. Well, I got news for you. You think you're better than us. Well, your time's coming."

Max just wanted to finish his drink and leave. But then Karl's brother came up from behind and slugged Max.

It was a little confused after that. Not that Max minded a little brawl now and then, but things really got out of hand. Almost everybody in the bar that night was German, or so it seemed. And they were holding Max personally responsible for the Germans losing Southwest Africa after World War I.

There were shouts of *"Der Fuhrer"* and *"Deutschland Uber Alles."*

It got downright ugly when they started shouting about taking the mines back.

Max was outnumbered but he cracked more than his rightful share of skulls before escaping. He smiled to himself. Sir Ernest would have been proud.

Thinking of Sir Ernest brought him back to the reason he'd stayed up all night. He'd found it impossible to sleep. The sun rose on a bleak day for Max. He had thought it through and come to the conclusion that it was time to follow Sir Ernest's instructions. Better to spike the mines now than let that wild crowd destroy everything. There'd be a time to take it all back and shape things up again.

He found it very difficult to give the order. Nevertheless, he pulled himself together and called in the tunnel bosses and other supervisors one last time.

As they crowded in, the small office buzzed with excitement and questions. Kleeman rarely called them all together unless it was something momentous. Either a gigantic screw-up, or the opening up of a new drift. When they saw the site manager's face though, quiet suddenly blanketed the room.

"Men, I don't know any easy way to tell you this," Kleeman paused. He was finding it increasingly difficult to get the words out, though he had gone over and over it in his mind for hours. "You all know what's been going on. I don't really give a shit which side you're on. The important thing is that Hitler's moves in the rest of the world have begun to touch our world here." He paused again, wiping his forehead with his sleeve. "It's not just a problem. It's not just dangerous for us working here. It's become totally impossible, so," he looked at each of the faces of his men in turn. "I'll just say it straight out..."

❧

April 10, 1939

To: Consolidated Diamond Mines of Southwest Africa LTD.
From: Fontein Site Manager Kleeman

Message: Reference cable 1 October 1938 stop Have begun recommended operations stop Will advise further developments stop

Kleeman endit

❧

J.D. Hoynsten, special courier for CDM was an immense individual. Six foot three and over two hundred forty pounds, his barrel chest and bulging biceps gave mute evidence of the man's power.

Many was the bar that possessed proof of his strength and his willingness to display it. In Kimberly, J'oberg, Pretoria, and Windhoek, broken bar stools and shattered glassware were routinely left in his path. All gratefully paid for by CDM. For Hoynsten's reputation, always enhanced by these brawls, helped to make him the most successful courier in Southwest Africa.

Four to six times a month, he would make the rounds of CDM's mines, take the loose stones, and deliver them to the graders and cutters in South Africa. It was rumored that he was among the highest paid employees of CDM; a rumor that was close to the mark.

This morning he rose from a drunken sleep in his home at Pelican Point just south of Walvis Bay. He sat naked on the side of his bed, already feeling the effects of the growing heat, and threw up into the stoneware pot that had been left there by his driver Bwabwata.

Bwabwata was his driver, his house boy, his bodyguard, and his only friend. He took care of Hoynsten like a devoted son and was rewarded for it with a standard of living totally impossible for him to achieve on his own.

Bwabwata was a Bindu, the smallest of all the tribal groups in Southwest Africa, and hated by all the rest. Routinely, the Bindu were given the best jobs and the best pay. Of all the tribes, theirs was the best educated and the most comfortable with western ways.

As he heard Hoynsten retching into the pot, Bwabwata began to cook. In an hour Hoynsten would emerge from his bedroom, stumble out to the beach and swim one mile out and back. When he was done, Bwabwata would meet him with a towel and a meal. This was always their routine on days when they would be traveling.

An hour later Hoynsten was cutting through the water, stretching himself to the limit. On these swims, he allowed his mind to wander.

As he moved smoothly through the choppy water he thought about the message from Kleeman. A pickup today at Fontein SW 2. Extra caution urged.

He knew Max Kleeman well. Kleeman was not the type to "urge caution," to panic over trifles. Knowing this was an unscheduled pickup, and the need to be careful, he prepared himself mentally for whatever would come his way in the next few days.

After the meal, he returned to his bedroom to dress for the trip.

First he stood naked in front of a full length mirror, his prized possession. He examined himself critically, not happy until he sucked in his stomach an extra inch.

He had many scars on his chest and back, some from bar fights, but most from attempts of dead men to rob him. For each scar, he could account for at least one and sometimes two or three men who had been unwise enough to challenge him. He began to dress.

First shorts and a T-shirt. Then he strapped a British Enfield Multitool knife to his right ankle and an American Bowie to his left. He pulled his pants over these and fastened them with a thick leather belt with a flap holster on the left. Into the holster, he placed a Webley Arms .308 automatic.

A loose safari shirt was next. He put three extra clips for the Webley into the left breast pocket. In the right pocket his government passes, acquired at great expense, that allowed him to use any roads, at any time.

Over the shirt, he placed an American shoulder holster, a new acquisition. Its black leather shone as he placed the Colt .45 revolver into its soft leather place.

Since it would soon be over one hundred fifteen degrees in the shade, he grabbed a lightweight poncho (in case of morning rains) the kind favored by the Americans and of course, his old battered hat. As he walked out to the jeep, he gathered some money, a watch, and some extra ammunition for the Colt and stuffed these into his trouser pockets.

As he reached the jeep, Bwabwata started the engine and gunned it for a moment. Hoynsten climbed in and grunted.

"Fontein SW 2." They pulled away and were soon swallowed up by the shimmering waves of heat that were common to the few paved roads in the country.

The sun was barely up when the two men met inside the Admin. shack. In the pale light of dawn, they seemed cut from the same piece of granite. Kleeman and Hoynsten. The same side of the same coin.

No pleasantries were exchanged. None were needed. They simply shook hands and got down to business.

As Hoynsten read over the manifest, he showed no outward sign of the shock that was running through him.

"Big shipment."

"Yeah."

He put down the manifest and looked Max in the eye. "Is there something special you need to tell me?" He intentionally placed the emphasis on Kleeman.

"One thing only. This is our last shipment for awhile. J'oberg thinks things are going to get a little messy around here. We're shutting down in two weeks."

Hoynsten walked to the door and stared out around the compound. Even at this early hour, the work was proceeding. All appeared normal. He turned back to Kleeman and arched an eyebrow.

Kleeman smiled. "All show, old son. When we leave, it will be in the middle of the night accompanied by the loudest bang you ever heard."

Hoynsten nodded and walked back to Kleeman's desk. "You going with them, Max?" It was the first time in years he had used Kleeman's first name, and was an indication of the emotion he felt.

Kleeman nodded, eyes downcast. "This has been my home most of my life, but, yes, I have to go too. How about you?"

"It's still my home. I guess I'll just hang around till you get back." They shook hands solemnly and silently.

"I'll try not to make it too long, Jan. Take good care."

"Always do. You too."

"Have a cup of coffee and come on over to the sorting room in about fifteen minutes. Your package will be ready then." He left Hoynsten standing alone, dwarfing the doorway and seeming to take a last look around the site.

"Charlie boy. Is everything ready?" Kleeman looked around as he entered the small, well-lit room. It was the cleanest, neatest of all the buildings in the mine complex. Charlie Marshall, who was in charge of the grading at the mines was a meticulous young man.

"All ready to go, Sir. A sad day."

"I know, son, but hopefully it's only for a little while." Kleeman still found it hard to believe the world was on the brink of catastrophe. His own world was though, and that was enough. He patted the young man on the shoulder and spoke uncharacteristically gently. "Let's go over it once more. That way we'll make sure it's all correct. After all, it's the last shipment for some time. We don't want to make any mistakes, do we?"

Charlie nodded and Kleeman pulled out the manifest that he planned to forward to Sir Ernest. He took a seat at a table near one of the windows. Charlie brought out the packet of diamonds and joined Kleeman at the table. As he spoke, he moved the diamonds into individual piles with a tweezers and occasionally offered Kleeman a ten power loupe for his inspection.

"Well, for starters, we have a total of three hundred and one diamonds, three hundred and one units of close goods."

"Are you sure?"

"Yes, Sir. I know there'll be a more exacting grading when it gets to Pretoria, but you said you wanted it really accurate for this manifest.

"All the stones are close goods, that is, good color and symmetry. They're free from all blemishes, spots, flaws and fractures observable in a rough."

Kleeman checked a few stones at random and nodded for Charlie to continue. "I broke it down for you. As you can see, there are twenty ten carat size rough stones, twenty-six nine carat stones, fifteen five carat stones, twenty-two stones in the four carat size, and two hundred and nine stones ranging from $1/2$ to $3^1/2$ carats each."

Kleeman smiled grimly. "I guess we're going out in style." He stood up as there was a knock at the door. "That's Hoynsten. He has to sign off for the shipment, you know."

Charlie stood, pushed his chair up against the table carefully and "stood guard" as Kleeman opened the door for the courier.

ðŸ•

April 12, 1939

To: **Consolidated Diamond Mines of Southwest Africa LTD.**
From: **Fontein Site Manager Kleeman**

Message: **Reference cable 10 April stop Pretoria shipment in transit as of 0600 stop courier JAE DEE Hoynsten may be expected 13 April stop 301 Units close goods stop Will advise further developments stop**

Kleeman endit

ðŸ•

It had been a long wait. The sun beat down upon the man relentlessly, but he waited quietly on the small group of boulders overlooking the road.

His shoulders ached from the work just completed and his head throbbed with the expectation of the work just ahead.

Through the scope of the rifle, he watched as a distant dust plume slowly resolved into a jeep slowly bumping its way down the rock-strewn pot-holed semi-road. The heat mirage obscured the occupants, but that was no matter. These roads were lightly traveled and only one jeep would be here now. The man smiled slightly as he pictured how his hard work would soon pay off.

He had spent hours, earlier, in the sweltering heat, removing every rock, filling every pothole, working feverishly to undo the ravages of heat and wind that the Namib Desert, one of the hottest in Africa, had wrought in the fifty meter stretch of road beneath him. All for a smoother ride for the oncoming jeep. A smoother ride and a cleaner shot.

As the jeep approached the clear area, the man raised himself to one knee and used the dried branches of a scraggly Musanga tree that somehow clung to life, despite temperatures in excess of one hundred thirty degrees, as cover. He sighted in on his target as it bounced towards him.

The jeep reached the cleared path and abruptly ceased its bone rattling motion. A moment later the high powered rifle spoke and the left front tire of the jeep exploded, sending the jeep into a spin, nearly throwing the two men in it flying. The Bindu driver fought the wheel and somehow kept the machine from turning over. It came to a stop, teetering precariously on the edge of the sea wall.

Through the scope, the man watched as the two occupants, Hoynsten and a Bindu boy, slowly steadied themselves. He could hear Hoynsten curse as he straightened his hat. He watched as the Bindu leaned out and looked at the tire.

The cross hairs settled on the massive chest of Hoynsten and the rifle spoke its message again.

Hoynsten stiffened as if coming to attention. His huge body straightened and he took a half step out of the jeep before plunging face down into the sand. The bullet had ripped through his body, leaving a rapidly growing stain of gore on the back of his shirt.

The Bindu looked around wildly. In a panic, he started to run towards the sea. The gunman, now disdaining his hiding place, stood up, took deliberate aim at the fleeing tribesman and spoke his final message. The Bindu fell and crawled his way into the foam at the sea's edge, disappearing beneath a wave.

The gunman watched for several minutes before being convinced of the Bindu's death. Only then did he come off the hummock and walk to the jeep.

Walking around the jeep, he stood before the fallen courier. He put his rifle in the jeep, bent down and turned the corpse over. Tearing open the shirt, a momentary panic struck him when he failed to find the pouch. Then he saw the leather cord around the man's waist.

He pulled up on the cord and slowly a long thin leather pouch, about four inches wide and two feet long came out of Hoynsten's pants leg. Now the work was easier as he pulled a second pouch from the other leg. His work completed, he walked back to his hidden jeep behind the boulders. Not once looking back.

If he had, he would have seen the Bindu's body, not yet dead, wash up on the shore.

ᶻ᰼

April 20, 1939

To: **Fontein Site Manager Kleeman**
From: **Consolidated Diamond Mines of Southwest Africa LTD**

Message: I regret to inform you that your man Hoynsten killed on or about 13 April stop Bindu driver reports ambush by unknown assailants stop Foreign Office believes British Citizens endangered stop I implore you to take precautions stop God hasten your safe return to these shores stop

Sir Ernest endit

ᶻ᰼

Depression had settled over the camp area of Fontein SW 2. The news of Hoynsten's violent death, coming as it did on the heels of German nationals rallying against British and South African rule, hit the mine workers hard.

Kleeman was drinking heavier than usual, and even Freddy Reineke seemed distracted. Reineke would often be seen wandering around the fan late at night, walking nowhere in particular. He usually returned covered with dirt. The workers assumed that he was trying to work off his tensions with some private prospecting, a common practice.

CHAPTER FIVE

HONORABLE SERVICE

Bernhard von Streck stood on a balcony overlooking the reviewing grounds of his base camp in Luanda, Angola. As was his custom, he watched the sun set slowly over the Atlantic and allowed his mind to wander. As the Commander of the Advanced Knife Edge Force, the Wehrmacht's top Commando unit, it was the only time of day that he could truly call his own.

Born only fifty miles from the Dutch border, his early life had been middle class cosmopolitan. His family, distantly related to some count or other, had enough money to provide a good private education for their only son.

Always a bright student, Bernhard pleased his parents by enrolling in University. His college days were filled with a joyous journey of discovery of history, poetry, and literature. He graduated near the top of his class in 1901.

A bright young man in search of his destiny in Germany at the turn of the century, naturally was drawn to the patriotic lure of the military, and so, when he was conscripted less than a year after graduation, he happily engulfed himself in the experience.

Unfortunately, it was not what he had hoped it would be. He

found himself stifled by the rigidity of the command structure, and by the inflexibility of its leaders. Most men would have left when their term of service was over, but Bernhard felt a need to try and change the system. Like most who had tried before him, he failed, rising only to the rank of 1st Lieutenant at the outbreak of the First World War.

In its own terrible way, the war turned out to be a godsend for the frustrated young officer.

Early on, the senior officers in his company were killed and young Bernhard found himself in command. Remaking the unit into his own image, "Company Streck" as they came to be known, developed a reputation for boldness, courage, and success. Bernhard's methods challenged conventionalities and were always vindicated.

By the end of the war he was one of the most decorated officers in the Army, holding the Legion of Honor and the Iron Cross. He had also been promoted over older officers and ended up a full colonel.

The years immediately after the war were hard on him, as they were on all Germans. He married, and tried unsuccessfully to become a gentleman farmer. After a little over a year, he sold the farm for what he could get and accepted a position as an instructor at the General Staff College in Berlin.

An early advocate of the blitzkrieg, lightning war, that would later change all warfare, he taught commando tactics and principles of airborne operations for eight years. He was among the first in the world to argue that large groups of men and materiel could be airdropped effectively deep behind enemy lines and fight successfully. His superiors viewed him as brilliant, but a dreamer. One of the few who took him seriously was another staff instructor, Karl Albrecht.

Not particularly political, Bernhard watched the rise of the National Socialists with the same hope that his countrymen had. Perhaps Adolf Hitler could restore Germany's place in the world. True, Hitler was extreme, but historically extremists favored a strong military. Bernhard made friends where he could.

In the late thirties, he was given a chance to address the High Command on his theories of airborne assaults. The generals listened patiently and then dismissed him as unrealistic. So Bernhard was shocked when three days later he was ordered to report to the Chief of Staff, Keitel himself, to make his case again.

At the meeting, he spoke eloquently and with passion of the possibilities.

"Drop by parachute five hundred or a thousand men, deep behind the lines of the enemy, equip them to provide for themselves for a period of time and they will so torment the enemy and force him to commit troops to their destruction as to make a landing so much easier by conventional ground forces, who would easily break through and relieve the airborne commandos."

Keitel, not very bright, was helped to understand the finer points by his aide, Karl Albrecht, Bernhard's old friend. Within a month, the 17th Codo was created and the command given to the recently promoted Colonel General Bernhard von Streck. (He had taken to using the distant relation's 'von' as it seemed to impress the Nazi Officers.)

From the 17th Codo, the Advanced Knife Edge Force soon sprang. The most fully independent, self-sufficient commando unit in the world. One thousand three hundred men, hardened by months of training in all aspects of airborne and commando operations.

They now stood below this balcony, or waited on ships in the harbor, tightened like a well-wound watch spring, waiting for the moment when they would go forward and reclaim for the Fatherland what had been taken years before.

The sun set, and Bernhard remained on the balcony for a while. He stood and looked out over the sea, and over his life, and smiled. He was in the right place, at the right time, with precisely the right tool.

Soon, he would make history.

ᔓ

The general staff had worked hard and long on the plan known as Jaguar. The distances involved, the problems of supply and reinforcement, the problems of command and control seemed insoluble. Insoluble that is, until von Streck remembered Thermopylae.

The battle of Thermopylae stood in military annals as the

perfect example of the usage of men and terrain and Bernhard immediately saw the parallels. He tried to explain it to the sometimes dense generals who made up the planning team.

"In 480 B.C. Leonidas, King of Sparta, sent six thousand men to the mountain pass of Thermopylae to prevent the Persian Army, led by Xerxes from conquering all of Greece. The pass was narrow and made for a natural choke point. Even when Xerxes went around the pass, by sea, forcing Leonidas to send almost all of his troops away from the pass, the Spartans were able to hold the pass with only one hundred men against a Persian force of many thousands."

Jodl, more well read than the rest, interrupted. "Yes, and all of his forces at Thermopylae were massacred except for one Theban boy. Hardly an example to use for a successful operation." There was laughter around the table.

Bernhard let the laughter die down and then continued in a calm assured voice.

"That is true, my general, however Leonidas was unable to reinforce his men. In our case, that will be no problem. Von Runstadt has assured me of this."

Jodl paused to consider and then nodded for Bernhard to continue.

"Let us examine the realities." He walked to the large map that dominated one end of the room. "Of a population of over two hundred fifty thousand, only six percent or about fifteen thousand are White. The rest, uneducated natives. Of this fifteen thousand most are loyal Germans longing for a return to the Fatherland. The rest, British or Afrikaner. Over eighty percent of the White population lives in the capital, Windhoek. The rest are scattered about the country at mines or in the three other towns, Swakopmund and Walvis Bay in the North, and Luderitz in the South.

"My plan is simple and direct. I propose a combined seaborne and airborne assault on the ports of Walvis Bay and Swakopmund. Elements of the AKEF will air assault these two targets in the predawn hours, cutting off outside communications and securing the harbors for freighters which will then come in, bringing the rest of the force and artillery.

"We will divide into two Task Forces. The first will march on

Windhoek and cut it off from either communications or contact with the outside world. The second will march south and seize the port and road at Luderitz and the rail junction at Seeheim.

"From these positions, we in effect control the entire country. We will not enter Windhoek or attempt to move farther south than Luderitz. We will leave those honors to von Runstadt's OB West troops which will arrive after we have pacified the countryside, in four to six weeks."

An older general scoffed noisily at the plan. "And I suppose," he began sarcastically, "that the South Africans and the British will run cowering from your paltry force?"

Bernhard was ready for this.

"No, my general, they will not run, because they will not know we are there until it is too late to stop us.

"Advance units of the AKEF will cut the telegraph in each city and town as we approach it. Intelligence reliably tells us that it is not out of the ordinary for the telegraphs to go down for as long as ten days at a time. The lines are through mountainous jungle and a most formidable desert and are quite isolated. When they go silent, it will be days before anyone becomes suspicious, and once our artillery is in place at Seeheim and Luderitz..."

He allowed his voice to trail off as he lit a match and held it for long seconds before lighting his pipe. They all looked at the flickering flame and understood.

"And the forces already inside the country?" This was Jodl again.

"A constabulary that is lightly armed and poorly trained." Bernhard smiled.

"In essence, what I propose is to seize the country with only one thousand three hundred men. By seizing the only deep water harbors, at Swakopmund, Walvis Bay, and Luderitz, by controlling the only rail line into the country at Seeheim, by cutting off Windhoek completely, my men and I will recreate history. As at Thermopylae, a small force will completely control a larger force, and unlike Thermopylae when we are reinforced and relieved, we will control the entire South African Peninsula within days."

He inhaled deeply on his pipe and waited for the inevitable questions. To his surprise, none came. After several moments of silence, General von Bock, the eldest in the room and the former chief of staff during the First World War, spoke softly.

"Streck, what if the worst happens? What if you are cut off from re-supply and reinforcement? What then?"

Before he could answer, Keitel who had remained silent throughout, stood up and turned to von Bock. "That will not happen!" He said defiantly. "We are not the same as we were," he paused for effect, "under your regime. If we say he will be reinforced, he will be. Enough, I will submit the plan to the *Fuhrer* for approval. Good day, gentlemen."

As the generals left, Streck gathered together his briefing materials. As he prepared to leave, he noticed von Bock still sitting at the end of the table studying him curiously. Bernhard turned to him. "Another question, my general?"

"Do you remember what message the Theban survivor carried to Sparta?"

Bernhard thought for a moment. "My master bade me go tell the Spartans that our stand was well made and we have died for the glory of Sparta."

Von Bock rose and wearily walked to the door, where he stopped and faced Bernhard.

"They also were promised reinforcements." He turned and left the room.

&

To: Commander AKEF Luanda
From: CG OB West
Date: 25 April 1939
Subject: Jaguar

1. *You are hereby to begin operations no later than 1 May.*
2. *Landing site Swakopmund approved.*
3. *You are hereby ordered to take Windhoek by I+25 days.*
4. *You are hereby ordered to take Luderitz by I+30 days.*
5. *You are hereby ordered to hold these targets until relieved 18 June.*
6. *British and Crown Colony citizens are to be treated fairly, pending repatriation.*

Authorized by my hand,
Von Runstadt from Keitel

&

'Begin operations'. Bernhard laughed out loud as he contemplated the efficiency of the Wehrmacht. The ships had been at sea for over a week, heading under radio silence for their targets and just now they get around to authorizing the operation. Typical.

He sat on a bench lining the side of his transport aircraft, and looked up and down at the paratroopers around him. These were good boys. Under other circumstances he would give them a good laugh and tell them about the 'authorization' but not now. Now their minds were too closely attuned to the business ahead and he would disturb that for nothing.

The six planes that made up C flight continued to move quietly through the night sky in a tight formation. They had just made their last course adjustment and were descending for the jump; but only Bernhard's body was there.

His mind was fourteen minutes ahead with A and B flights as their men from the AKEF stepped into the still night air and drifted down onto the sleeping towns of Swakopmund and Walvis Bay. Their jobs were to cut the telegraph lines and secure the ports. Simple in concept, dangerous in execution. If they were successful, when C flight disgorged its Commandos into the night over Walvis Bay most of the mission would have been accomplished, at least the initial phase. If they encountered unexpected resistance on the ground...Bernhard returned his mind to the jump at hand, and along with his men stepped out into the sky.

As he floated silently towards the drop zone, he looked quickly at the darkened town below. He could see no flashes of light or fires. That was good. So far he could hear no gun fire. That was better. He landed and assumed his position in the heart of his men as they moved towards the port.

The rest of the AKEF also moved towards their targets.

As the sun slowly broke above the horizon, the first sounds of Jaguar were heard as an old man, out early for some fishing, was cut down. In Swakopmund, three other Afrikaners died quickly in the dawn as the commandos efficiently went about their jobs.

By six-thirty it was all over, and the people of Walvis Bay and Swakopmund awoke to find themselves under occupation. Some, recovering from the shock of the discovery, first tried to fight or get help. It was pointless. They were simply and completely over-whelmed by the Germans.

By seven o'clock, the people had been rounded up and were being held until reinforcements from the freighters docked. There were no more incidents as the stunned citizens watched as the three freighters docked and unloaded the rest of the AKEF and its supplies.

Bernhard ran through the town. He checked each watch point, and in a quickly confiscated truck, drove to a point between Walvis Bay and Swakopmund to meet with his senior commanders.

Colonel Erich Krasna, was waiting for him. The youngest senior commander in the unit, Krasna smiled broadly as he reported to his general.

"Walvis Bay is completely under our control and the harbor facility is already unloading the Bremen Maiden. The task force will be ready to move within the hour. It is a glorious day!"

Bernhard remembered once feeling the exultation the young officer felt and he smiled. Before he could respond Colonel Ernst von Schumacher arrived in a jeep that had been unloaded from one of the ships.

"My apologies, my general, but things became a bit uncoordinated a few minutes ago and required my attention."

Von Streck nodded curtly. He knew von Schumacher's reputation for understatement and assumed that he would hear in time of some disaster narrowly averted.

"Task Force Brandy will be ready to move by 1100 hours. There was an inspection unit from the South African Defence Forces in the port, and they caused the delay; but we will make up the time. Otherwise, all is in order."

Bernhard gave a few terse orders and the men left to form their task forces. In a few minutes, Bernhard and his headquarters company would link up with Krasna's task force and begin moving south towards Luderitz.

For now, he would allow his subordinate officers to do their jobs, long a policy of his.

He walked to a spot from which he could see the ocean and took a long deep breath. He smelled the salt spray, he smelled the fish, and he smelled his first true victory since the first World War. A victory that he was sure would not be his last.

ે๑

It was a surprisingly hot April and Friederich Reineke, tunnel boss at CDM's SW 2 site was feeling more uncomfortable than usual. The hot, arid, flat land looked more desolate than ever, and once more Friederich asked himself the old question 'What the hell am I doing here?'

The son of an honored general in the OKW, and grandson of Count Josef Reineke, he had almost always found life pleasant and easy. Then, as graduation from college neared, his father began pushing more and more for Friederich to follow him into the Army. With the rise of Adolf Hitler and Germany's continued devastation, Friederich could no longer remain a dilettante.

At school, he had been friends with Jan van der Keer, the son of a British family living in South Africa. Jan had filled him with stories of adventure in the diamond fields. Now Friederich felt this was his way out.

Against his father's wishes, he had left school just before graduation, and headed for South Africa. With his education, and the help of the van der Keer family, he soon found a job with Consolidated Diamond Mines.

The work was a great deal more taxing than he had expected, but there was also a kind of exhilaration about it. So he had stayed and been promoted along the way. He was trusted by his boss, Max Kleeman, and headed for the number two position at the mine. Everything was going well.

But he felt a strange restlessness. The German Army was marching through Europe. There were all kinds of wild rumors; and he didn't really want to spend the rest of his life bossing around a bunch of kaffirs. Maybe it was time to call it quits, but what did he have to show for it, for all the time and effort? His father, the great man, would expect answers. All he understood was the military life, service to one's country and on and on and on.

Well, Friederich would have to think about it. In the meantime, the boss wanted to see him.

Kleeman was waiting for him outside the explosives shed. "It's time to be getting started." Friederich nodded. Kleeman unlocked the door and they walked inside.

This room always made Friederich nervous. There were enough explosives in here to move a mountain, which in fact was its intended use. Kleeman stood over a box of detonators. "We'll use the six minute fuses with stacks of seven sticks. That ought to do the job sound enough."

They carried the dynamite, fuses and detonators to a hand car which Kleeman had brought close to the shed. For fifteen minutes, they carefully loaded the material. When they were finished, they slowly pushed the car to the mouth of shaft number one.

"I'll go up top with the stacks," Kleeman said as he loaded some of the stuff into a lift designed to bring materials to the top of the fan. "Go and get some of the old stuff, the stuff that's started to sweat, and don't bloody well trip on your way back with it."

Friederich returned to the shed and after taking a deep breath, went in and over to the shallow pit dug in the floor.

Old dynamite sweats. Beads of moisture form on the outer skin, beads of pure nitroglycerin. One of the miners had once shown Friederich by taking his finger and gently stroking a sweaty stick, gathering some of the deadly liquid on his finger tip. He had then flicked his finger, sending the moisture flying against a rock. It had sounded like a gunshot. Friederich had never forgotten that.

Now he stood before over two dozen such sticks and both he and they were sweating. He took a pail filled with sawdust and slowly loaded five sticks into it. When he was done, he carefully stood and slowly walked back to the fan.

Kleeman watched from the top of the fan. The boy has balls, he thought to himself. Freddy reached the foot of the fan and Kleeman climbed down to meet him. "You'll never have to do anything else to prove yourself to me, boy. I'll take it from here. Go up top to cut one six and get the stacks ready."

Friederich slowly handed Kleeman the pail. "You be very steady, Mr. Kleeman." He started to climb the ladder. "Or it could ruin my whole day."

Kleeman laughed. It always amazed Friederich how Kleeman could laugh with a pail of death in his hands. "Aye boy, both our days." Laughing, he disappeared into the shaft.

Once on top of the fan, Friederich stopped to catch his breath. Through the many crosscuts, he could hear Kleeman's laborious progress along the shaft. He moved to cut sixteen and began to tape the dynamite into stacks of seven, placing a detonator and a six minute fuse in each stack.

Kleeman called up to him from twelve feet below. "You almost ready, Freddy?" Laying on his stomach with his face over the cut, Friederich could just see Max standing beneath him.

"Ready old man."

"'Bout bloody time too! I've placed an old stick every ten feet or so in both shafts. When we blow the junction, it'll set them off. It'll shut down the works for a bloody long time I expect. Wait till you see me out past the barrier before you light them and drop 'em in the shafts. Then run like bloody hell! You got that, man?"

"I got that, Max. Now get the hell out of there; and mind your step on the way out."

From below him, Friederich could hear loud laughter. "I'll be careful not to step in anything!" The voice trailed away.

Friederich stood and walked back to the stacks of dynamite. He took two stacks and placed them by a cut over shaft number one and then he placed two more by a cut over shaft two. He looked out towards the Admin. shack and saw Max standing behind the drift slab that was used as a blast barrier.

"Fire in the hole! Fire in the hole!" Friederich yelled as he lit the stacks and dropped them into the cut. He ran lightly over the top of the fan to the other stacks and repeated the process.

Now he ran to the edge of the fan. Ignoring the ladder, he leapt to the ground and ran. Stumbling, he threw himself behind the drift slab barrier.

Max looked down at him, shaking his head. "In a bit of a hurry, mate? Six minutes is a lifetime." He laughed at his unintended joke.

Friederich stood and dusted himself off and looked out at the fan. "It's a shame. A stupid shame. How much do you think is left in there?"

"Too bloody much."

They both stood for another two minutes and watched the

prehistoric rock. They both were picturing the fuses burning furiously away. They both were gripped by the waste of it. Suddenly, they heard the first explosion. They ducked behind the barrier as more explosions echoed dully through the fan and spat corrupt black and gray smoke up through all the crosscuts.

After a full minute, they stood. The fan seemed as it always had been. Smoke poured from every opening, but it seemed intact. Then the rumbling began.

Low and menacing, it spread like an earthquake and it was quickly accompanied by a shaking in the ground, but Kleeman and Reineke stood and watched the final act in the death throes of the fan.

It shook and shimmied for over two minutes and then, like some monstrous balloon, it seemed to deflate and collapse on itself. The rumbling stopped and the fan was dead.

Kleeman remained rooted to his spot and Friederich felt compelled to bow his head.

"It'll take a full crew years to reopen that monster." Kleeman looked at Friederich and continued, "Young Mr. Reineke, let's you and me go over to my tent and get roaring drunk."

Friederich smiled. "A wake?"

Kleeman began walking and said under his breath, "Bloody right."

Two days later, the Germans came to Black Reef and Charlie Marshall died.

He was out walking. Taking a last stroll around before he was scheduled to leave. By the afternoon, he would be well on his way to Johannesburg, and the sorting rooms of Consolidated.

He would miss the bush. His time out here was the most exciting in his life and from a purely professional standpoint he didn't doubt for a minute that it would help him advance more quickly in the office. After all, Oppenheimer had started out in the mines.

Something flashing in the distance caught Charlie's attention. He shielded his eyes against the rising sun and squinted.

There seemed to be a convoy of cars moving down the road towards the mine. Odd. Petrol was in short enough supply so that so many cars and trucks moving together must have government sanction. He hadn't heard anything, but then the wire was down again, and that wasn't surprising. He walked toward the road.

He stopped dead in his tracks. From out of nowhere, a soldier appeared. They stood twenty feet apart, maybe less. Charlie had time to notice how young the soldier appeared before the man fired.

The round caught Charlie in the right shoulder and spun him around but not down. Before the man could fire again, Charlie started to run.

In front of him, he could see the fan and to the right he saw Kleeman and Reineke come rushing out of the Admin. shack. He yelled to them as the second shot tore through his back and knocked him against the fan. He slid slowly down to the ground, coming to rest half on and half off of it. Somehow, he turned his head.

There were many more soldiers in the compound now. Charlie saw Kleeman knock one down with a shovel before he was clubbed to his knees. Reineke stood with his hands in the air, shouting something Charlie thought was German. He turned his head away from the scene as he saw several of the black workers gunned down.

When he opened his eyes minutes later, he realized that there were German soldiers standing around him, talking. He couldn't move so he tried to listen.

"Wie ist sein zustand?"

"Er ist am sterben."

"Machen sie was sie konnen fur ihn. Schneller ihn nicht meinen zu scheiben ihm. Es geht bei ihm um leben und tod."

"Der Oberst ist wutend"

Charlie turned back to the fan. He didn't understand the words but he knew the tone. He was dying. Here amongst the rocks of…he couldn't believe his eyes. He tried to focus with his last strength on the shining stone inches from his face.

"Two carat, Top Cape at least," were his last words as he stared at the diamond laying half buried beside him.

Later that day, the day he would have gone home, Charlie Marshall was laid to rest by Max Kleeman under the close supervision of a squad of AKEF soldiers.

The occupation of Southwest Africa had just begun to claim its victims.

ô

May 3, 1939

To: Consolidated Diamond Mines of Southwest Africa LTD
From: Fontein Site Manager Kleeman

Message: No previous communication due to occupation
stop Advised citizens of Crown must leave stop Tunnel Boss
allowed to stay being German born stop Future communications to F G Reineke stop An honor to have served stop

Kleeman endit

&

The concession to allow Friederich to stay at the mine had been
hard won. Max was not about to abandon CDM's holdings to the
Germans blindly. Someone had to stay behind to look after it. To see
that the Germans didn't wreck even the possibilities for the future.

The Colonel remained adamant, to a point. Reineke's being
German helped, the Colonel's legitimate regret at Charlie's death
helped and seemingly the name of Friederich's father helped. Finally
the Colonel agreed, providing that Friederich's relationship to General
Reineke could be confirmed at Headquarters Company at Walvis Bay.

Now Max was trying to pack half a lifetime into the one bag that
the Germans would allow him to take. He tried not to dwell on the
memories attached to the things, and the people, that he would be
forced to leave behind. He tried to think only of his eventual return, and
of the reopening of the drift.

Satisfied with his packing, Max walked out to the compound and
threw his bag into the truck that would carry him and the six other
European workers to Swakopmund for the trip home. He looked
around for Friederich. One of the Europeans muttered something about
Friederich's complaining about having to go to Walvis Bay, but didn't
know if he had left yet.

Just in case, Max went looking. He hadn't gotten twenty feet
when a German soldier stopped him.

"Halt!"

Max didn't care anymore and continued walking towards
Friederich's tent.

"Halt oder ich werde feuern!"

Max turned his depression to rage and whirled on the young
soldier.

"Listen closely, laddie, I'll say it just once. I've one more job to do and if you try and keep me from doing it, I'll take that rifle of yours and shove it so far up your arse that you'll have to hiccough to shoot the blasted thing!"

The soldier spoke no English but understood Kleeman well enough. He took a step back and released the safety on his rifle.

"Korporal!"

The lieutenant in charge came running up. *"Nehmen sie die waffe herunter!"* The soldier lowered his rifle. The Lieutenant turned to Kleeman. "And Mr. Kleeman I would appreciate your not threatening my men. Now what is the problem?"

As much as he didn't want to, Max liked this young lieutenant. "No problem. I've some last minute instructions to give my man and your toy soldier here was trying to stop me."

"You may not leave the group without an escort. The rules were clearly explained to you."

"What am I going to do, sneak off into the jungle and start a bloody revolt! I'm going. Do whatever you bloody well like." With that, he turned and continued his walk towards Friederich's tent.

The lieutenant called after him, "Very well. You have five minutes, but you will not find him in his tent. He is behind your precious pile of stones."

Max turned towards the fan and gave the lieutenant a grunt for a reply.

Walking around the fan, he made mental notes of where the damage from the spiking was the worst and where he would open the new drift shafts. He found Friederich kneeling beside the shift pit almost concealed from view by the drift and some broken drift slabs.

Something was odd. Very odd. Max watched silently while Friederich dug in some loose earth next to the slabs. Oblivious to all around him, he dug silently until he had unearthed his prize.

As Max watched, a black bile rose in his throat. An anger unlike anything he felt for the Germans rose in him until he almost vibrated from it as he watched Friederich Reineke brush the dirt from the leg pouches that he himself had given to Hoynsten. Dead Hoynsten. Murdered Hoynsten! He stepped forward and Friederich looked up.

The rage, anger and pain were written across Kleeman's face as he towered over the younger man. "You filthy bastard," he whispered between clenched teeth. "You bloody, murdering coward."

Friederich's younger, faster reactions were all that saved him from the two handed blow from Kleeman. He caught the blow across his upraised right forearm and rolled with the force of it. He scrambled to his feet just in time to avoid the onrush of Kleeman.

Max had underestimated the young man's quickness and sailed past him. He quickly turned and advanced on Friederich again. This time slower but with death his intention.

"Let me explain. I found some Germans burying this. If you don't believe me, look there. In the hole." Friederich's gambit worked and Kleeman paused and stared at the shallow hole.

It was all the break Friederich needed. His hands gripped the pick that was leaning against the slabs and he swung it without hesitation.

The end of the pick buried itself deep in the big man's chest, making him stagger back. Friederich lost his grip on it and stared in horror as Kleeman, still standing, gripped the pick handle in his two hands and pulled it out.

Blood poured from the wound. Max took a faltering step forward, and then another one. Friederich recoiled from the dead man who was trying to kill him as Kleeman tried to raise the pick over his head; but even Kleeman's strength had its limits and the weight of the pick caused the mortally wounded man to topple over backwards over the edge of the pit.

The lieutenant and the corporal came running around the corner of the fan just as Friederich finished re-burying the pouches.

Friederich stood and faced them. "There has been an accident." They walked to the edge of the pit and looked down upon the broken, dead body of Max Kleeman.

ઢ

May 5, 1939

To: Consolidated Diamond Mines of Southwest Africa LTD
From: Fontein Site Manager F G Reineke

Message: Max Kleeman died yesterday stop Regrettable accident stop Report to follow stop

Reineke endit

ﻚ

Jaguar spread silently and methodically out across the country. The people of Windhoek were cut off from the world in the first week and yet it was another three days before they knew it. When the weekly train didn't come, they sent out some men. None came back. Gradually, they realized they were trapped.

Their reaction came slowly. They tried to fight but had no chance. As long as they stayed in Windhoek they were not attacked, but whenever they tried to leave, in whatever numbers, they were attacked and driven back. It was maddeningly frustrating.

In the South, it was worse.

Within ten days of the invasion, the South African Defence Forces had been alerted and moved out. They moved up the one road along the coast and were stopped by mines and blown bridges. As they tried to clear a way through and repair the bridges, they came under a crushing artillery barrage from Luderitz. Unable to bring up their own big guns on the narrow road, they were forced to fall back again and again.

The Defence Forces tried the rail lines.

They loaded their big guns onto flatbed rail cars and hauled them up towards Southwest Africa on the one linking line; but when they came within range of the guns at Seeheim they were flattened without ever getting a shot off.

Throughout May, the standoff continued. The South Africans pushed and the Germans repelled. Just as Streck had predicted it would happen. With the prospect for relief imminent, the AKEF confidently continued their plan for the rewriting of Thermopylae.

ﻚ

To: **Commander AKEF Walvis Bay**
From: **CG OB West**
Date: **3 June 1939**
Subject: **Relief**

1. *You are hereby commended on your unit's performance to date.*
2. *The High Command awards the AKEF a unit commendation.*
3. *Political situation dictates a delay in relief troops reaching your positions.*
4. *You are hereby ordered to hold your positions until relief 20 August.*

Authorized by my hand,
Von Runstadt from Keitel

Streck crumbled the message in his fist. A small voice in his memory was reminding him of the day he had laid out his invasion plans to the High Command. He remembered all too well General Von Bock's "What if the worst happens?"

As the June 18th deadline for relief of his command approached, that small voice had begun to haunt him. Now he was being told he'd have to wait an additional two months.

Damn Keitel. That fool had no idea of the damage that would be inflicted on his men. Crack troops, sure. Well-trained, certainly. But stores were beginning to run low, and the enemy was starting to regroup from the initial shock. If relief troops came in as planned, there'd be no problem. But now...Bernhard was not sure.

He'd have to put his men on short rations. And ammunition wasn't plentiful either. Did the High Command think his men could eat or shoot unit citations?

Well, he wasn't going to panic. Unclenching his fist, he called in his aide. "Leibrandt, I need to send a message to Krasna and von Schumacher. OB West tells me that our reinforcements will arrive in August, so effective immediately they are to cut back use of supplies. I leave it to their own judgment as to what is available."

He rose from his desk and began to pace. "Set up a meeting for three days from now. I think some strategy changes are in order."

He began to study the tactical map before him. As his aide turned to leave, Streck called over his shoulder, "and Leibrandt, don't look so despairing. This is only temporary, a precaution at that."

The young aide attempted a smile, saluted his commander and left. It looked to him like things were beginning to fall apart all over the place. But he would take strength from his general.

Three days later, they met and poured over the map table on which von Streck had reworked their battle plan. He took a drink of cool water. "Any questions, gentlemen?"

Krasna hesitated, then jumped in. "Our intelligence has all proved out, to this point, but..."

Von Schumacher finished his sentence, "but now that the British and South Africans have gotten their troops into some semblance of order, well, I'd be happier if we had a little insurance."

Streck laughed. "You have perhaps a policy in your other uniform?" They all laughed. "I know it hasn't been easy with everything in short supply. It shouldn't be much longer though. Do you have any specific suggestions?"

As they thought about it, von Streck went on. "One of the few positives in this campaign is that so many of the inhabitants of this God awful place are really on our side. They're Germans who want to see us win. I can tell you, it's not always this way. We even have that young fellow from the mines, what's his name, Erich?"

"Reineke, Friederich Reineke."

Streck remembered. "Yes, of course. The son of General Kurt Reineke of Army Group III. The patron saint of all airborne commandos. And he is doing what for us?"

"He is at the mines, sir. Supervising the workers at several of the mines in an attempt to reopen them. I've met him. He's really quite anxious to be of help to us."

કે▲.

At Fontein SW 2, Friederich Reineke was being affable, friendly, and making himself useful.

"Lieutenant, if I may suggest, those three Kaffirs in shack #2. They're really good workers."

"Kaffirs, Reineke?"

"Blacks. Instead of shipping them out of the mines, I'm sure you could use their strong backs to be of some service. They can be trusted."

"Thank you, Reineke. Good idea. By the way, Colonel Krasna is returning today from Walvis Bay. You asked to be informed."

Friederich spent the night planning his strategy. He had to get out of here. Had to be sure that when it became possible, he could get home, this time home to Germany.

The next morning, Friederich headed for Colonel Krasna's office. Inside, he was greeted warmly. After a few pleasantries, Friederich came to the point. "Colonel, I have heard that this Company is due to go home soon and..."

Krasna interrupted. "Well, that was the original plan but…"

Friederich broke in "Forgive me, sir, but I'd really like to put in a little time with them before going home myself, you know, just to feel I've done my part for the Fatherland. Is there anything you could do? I'm sure my father would be grateful, as I would."

Krasna thought for a minute. This Reineke was a sharp one. He was looking for a ticket home. Still, his father was influential.

"We're going to be leaving a token force here before moving on, but not just yet. In the meantime, if you're really serious, I could talk with Colonel von Schumacher. He is looking for somebody who knows the hills around Windhoek. Perhaps you could be of help."

Friederich was a happy man. His seat on the flight home had just been arranged.

୬

First the desert and now, the jungle.

Blood, filth, heat, and bodies disappearing along the way. There's a certain irony in all this, Friederich thought, and he laughed to himself. His father had wanted him to be a career officer. If he'd gone along, he was sure he could've found himself some posh, easy posting. After all, the sons of generals weren't usually sent to the front lines. Hell, he thought, I got myself into this.

Oh well, he'd just have to continue to be very careful. He was too smart to play hero. Just put up with it a little longer. According to von Streck, they were to be relieved soon. And he'd be going home a rich man with no questions asked. That's the only reason he'd asked to go along with the troop as an advisor. Nobody would check a soldier's baggage too thoroughly.

He studied the terrain. He remembered that CDM had a mine fairly close by. Things were quieter now. Von Schumacher was having them set up headquarters here. Peaceful enough. Not a lot of resistance. Maybe he could do a little reconnoitering on his own. The mine was certainly closed, but for a man who knew his way around, there just might be a little something to add to his stash.

As night closed in and soldiers headed for various posts, Friederich strolled across the compound. The trick is to be confidant. Look like you know where you're going.

At the edge of the compound, he left the path. It was shorter through the lightly forested jungle with less chance of being seen. The mine should only be about a half hour's easy walk.

About five minutes later, it happened.

He never saw the listening post or the commandos lying in ambush for Afrikaner patrols. He did hear a shot and had time to think I'm in the wrong place. He never knew what hit him.

∂●

August 4, 1939

**To: General Karl Albrecht
          OPS Deputy OKW HQ
Berlin**

Message: Please advise General Kurt Reineke believe posted Army Group III that his son Friederich has died stop Unfortunate accident while advisor AKEF stop Will forward effects and full report stop

Von Streck endit

CHAPTER SIX

THE CHARNEL HOUSE

Karl Albrecht was feeling satisfied with himself. Here he was, at age forty-four, a colonel in the Wehrmacht Fuhrungstaab, but more importantly one of the *Fuhrer's* most trusted officers, and definitely due for promotion. He and Lubnitz preparing the reorganization memo had been a master stroke.

The recommendation for the reorganization of the armed forces under one staff and one supreme commander, the *Fuhrer*, was exactly what Hitler was looking for. Like Hitler, Albrecht had no love for the old Prussian military caste, except of course, his beloved teacher Kurt Reineke.

Generally, these aristocrats were all too stiff and self-important. No flexibility. And that, Albrecht felt, was essential in a planner and leader. The Albrecht Papers, as they had come to be known, had gotten him his present post as deputy chief of the armed forces operational staff under General Alfred Jodl. Albrecht had always chafed with bitterness over Germany's losing the Rhineland, his homeland, after World War I. The Rhine belonged to the Germans and Germany was taking it and everything else back. Hitler knew what he was doing.

And he, Albrecht, was an important part of it.

It had been a busy and productive day. The war was going well. Albrecht, a naturally cheerful man, felt life was good and getting better.

His happy ruminating was disturbed by a knock at his office door.

Colonel Franz Konigsmann hesitated, took a deep breath, and walked through the door. He hated to be the bearer of bad news, but…

Konigsmann handed Albrecht the cable. "I know how close you are to General Reineke. I thought I'd bring this to you personally instead of going through channels."

Albrecht looked at the cable, frowned and shook his head. After dismissing Konigsmann, he sat for a while staring at the paper. His thoughts wandered back to when he had first met Kurt Reineke.

He had been sent to the war college; the best teachers and the best students. General Reineke was a brilliant teacher and a compassionate man. He understood the pressures and fears of the young men he was preparing for what he hoped would be illustrious careers. This was a man who loved his country and his work. Albrecht came to think of him as a role model.

A son of the aristocracy, Reineke was given every advantage. Educated at the University of Heidelberg and later the College of War. His father Count Josef Reineke was assistant foreign minister, and young Kurt was brought up believing in service to country. In time, he became a member of the Officer Corps, rising swiftly through the ranks with honors along the way. He married and had a son, Friederich.

Albrecht frowned again. He was remembering when he had been posted to the War College as a junior instructor. General Reineke had taken him under his wing, teaching, helping, treating him as a younger brother or son. Now Albrecht had to be the one to inform the General of Friederich's death.

In the years after the War College, Albrecht and Reineke had kept in close touch, as much as was possible considering their assorted postings and the world upheaval.

Although a loyal German, Reineke had made it clear, in private conversations, that he was less than enamored of Hitler. A man of educated and sophisticated tastes, and clarity of mind, Reineke didn't approve of much of what was happening in Germany and elsewhere. Nevertheless, if it would help Germany rise out of the ashes of defeat, General Reineke would do whatever was ordered, whatever was necessary, putting aside his own distaste, and move on.

Albrecht knew instinctively the General would deal with this personal tragedy the same way, but he wished he could be there to help.

(*)

August 6, 1939

To: HQ Army Group III
           Personal For General Kurt Reineke

      Message: It is with sincere sorrow that I report to you that your son Friederich had given his life for the Fatherland stop The Fuhrer has asked me to communicate his personal sense of grief stop As you have said we must bear the burden of the living stop Comfort yourself that Friederich returned to us in the end stop I remain your devoted student stop

      Albrecht endit

(*)

Leibrandt, General Streck's aide held the cumbersome package in his arms and shifted his weight awkwardly. "Sir, Colonel von Schumacher's company clerk sent this package from the lines. It's the effects of the civilian aide Friederich Reineke."

Streck nodded. "I've been expecting it." He motioned to a relatively clear table in the corner. "Just leave it there."

"Yes, sir. The colonel thought you might want to go through it and send it on personally, since you know Reineke's father." He put the package down. "The clerk apologized for the jumble, but said things were getting pretty hot there, and there just wasn't time to do anything but throw it together and tie it up."

Streck sighed. "I know, Leibrandt, I know." He got up and went over to the package. "I see too many of these every day, all of our best, our finest young men, reduced to a few shirts and a couple of letters." He sighed again and waved a dismissal at the young aide, who continued to linger nearby.

"I was wondering, sir. Would you like me to help? I'd be happy…"

Streck smiled in spite of himself. "Leibrandt, how would I ever get through this war without you? Yes. Make a list as I direct and fold everything neatly. Then we'll ship it home. If we find anything inappropriate, we will forget that it existed. We will send back to the father the son he remembers."

"I understand, sir."

Together, they began.

Streck would pull an item out of the jumble, and Leibrandt would catalog and fold it neatly. They quickly went through more than half the pile when Streck found two elongated leather pouches held together by a leather cord.

He shrugged and was about to toss the pouches to Leibrandt, when he felt something through the leather.

He glanced at the front of each pouch and saw the letters JDH burned into each. Something made him put it aside as Leibrandt was busily folding something else. When Leibrandt looked up, the pouches had disappeared under some papers and Streck had gone on to the next item. Afterwards, Bernhard never really knew why he had done it, even before looking inside.

Soon they were finished and Leibrandt took the now neat and tidy package with the list of contents with him to ship out as soon as possible.

Before Bernhard could turn back to the pouches, he was called away on some urgent matter. He pushed the pouches aside and went out.

It was two days later, while going through some reports, that he ran across the pouches again. This time, he opened them carefully and allowed their contents to spill slowly on to the table.

They were rough and unpolished but there was no mistaking the brilliant stones. He slowly counted them. Three hundred and one rough cut diamonds, quite literally a fortune.

"Mein Gott!"

His mind raced. How did Reineke get his hands on this? More to the point, what do I do now, he thought to himself.

After checking that he was alone, he began to go over the possibilities.

1.   Reineke was really working for the Reich in some

intelligence role, perhaps as a paymaster. (It was well known that German intelligence used diamonds as its currency.) Still, this seemed unlikely. Streck had control of all intelligence in this theater and would have known had young Reineke been an agent.

2. Reineke was working as an agent for the British or the South Africans. This, Bernhard dismissed at once. It was not possible for the son of a great General to be a traitor.

3. Reineke had mined these himself. After all, he had access to the mines, all of them in what was called Diamond Area One. No, not possible. From the little he had learned about the mining operations here, it would have taken years for one man to have accumulated this many large and obviously fine quality stones. This left only one other possibility. Maybe he didn't come by this fortune, for a fortune it was, honorably. Maybe he had "liberated" it. The word had come to mean stolen but it was preferred by those officers who engaged in the practice.

Now, however Friederich had come into its possession, the problem was Streck's. Should it be sent to General Reineke? How to explain it? Should it go to OB West? And for one brief moment only Should I keep it? The thought was banished as quickly as it was formed. Bernhard's honor was not merely a word, nor even a way of life. It was life's blood.

Finally, he decided. It was as if a great burden had been lifted from him. He gathered up the small stones and prepared to package them.

He would send them to Albrecht, recently promoted to colonel general, and an old friend. He could trust him to figure out what to do. Bernhard had enough on his mind without these distractions.

❧

August 9, 1939

To: **General Karl Albrecht**
        OPS Deputy OKW HQ
        Berlin

Message: Am sending package code named Crystal Movement stop Crystal Movement found among effects Friederich Reineke stop Request assistance in disposition stop Notifications left to you stop

Streck endit

Streck stood on the beach, looking out at the horizon. Standing with him was Task Force Brandy Commander von Schumacher. They stared in silence for long minutes at the waves lapping at the shore, at the seagulls circling on unseen thermals, and far out, every once in a while, some jumping fish. The two men stood together, oblivious of the sounds and movement of war just off in the distance.

At last, von Schumacher broke the silence. Taking the liberties only an old friend could, he was blunt. "My General, they are good men. They are doing the impossible with little or nothing. How long can this go on?"

Streck just continued to look out at the setting sun.

"My General," he paused, "Bernhard, we were promised relief on June 18th, then they said August 20th. Will they come this time?"

Streck gestured at the empty ocean before them. "Will they come? This week? Next week? Didn't you know, Ernst? We are invincible. We can hold out indefinitely. When we are out of ammunition, our mere visages will frighten the British and South Africans back across the border." He laughed. "Or so the High Command has assured me."

He laughed again, broader but somewhat bitterly. "Think of it, Ernst. We accomplished all of our goals. We proved the plan works; and now we are left to wither and die because of political considerations. The mentality of the High Command boggles the mind!"

This was as close to an admission of defeat as Von Schumacher had ever heard von Streck make. He tried not to make his uneasiness show but von Streck noticed and turned to him with a smile.

"I make you despair, old friend?"

Von Schumacher nodded at the sea. "I also see no ships."

Bernhard stepped between von Schumacher and the water and faced him. "Do not look out there Ernst, look here at my face. I will find a way to save them, all of them. Our salvation is not somewhere out there; it is here, with us, in our hands."

They started back towards the command trailer. As the sky darkened, the sounds of mortar fire echoed in the distance. They stopped and listened for a moment.

"I must get back. It starts again," von Schumacher said, his voice showing the exhaustion he felt.

Von Streck slapped him on the back. "They will come, my friend. I will make them come. In the meantime, we must depend on our men as I depend on you."

They saluted and separated. As he watched von Schumacher disappear in the early night, he thought to himself, I must make them come!

ॐ

19 August 1939 0325

Urgent message for Commanding General OB West
Sending Authority: Commander AKEF Walvis Bay
URGENT

> I look to the sea and observe whitecaps and the occasional jumping fish. I look to the jungle and I see the remains of the finest forward unit the Fatherland had ever had being slowly disemboweled. Nowhere do I see relief troops or supplies. Perhaps the fish have fended off your valiant efforts to relieve us. It is a sad thing to face defeat at the fins of jumping fish.

> **von Streck**

ॐ

Leibrandt ran out of the command trailer and right into the arms of Sgt. Braun. "I wouldn't go in there right now if I were you," he cautioned the sergeant.

"Why not? Nothing else is going right. I might as well get chewed out by the General too." Nevertheless, Braun decided to execute a strategic retreat.

The reason for all this apprehension was stomping about the trailer, uncharacteristically bellowing at anyone or thing in his line of sight. "Bad enough to have to hold out until August, but October!" Streck bellowed, "That's insane!" He looked at the paper in his hand for the eighth time and snorted.

ॐ

To: Commander AKEF Walvis Bay
From: CG OB West

Date: 24 August 1939
Subject: Relief

1.   *You are hereby reprimanded for tone of communication of 19 August.*
2.   *You are hereby ordered to hold your positions until relief 8 October.*

Authorized by my hand
Von Runstadt from Keitel

ॐ

"No food, no supplies, but they didn't like the tone of my message! I wonder if they are fighting the same war we are."

Streck fell into a chair. He was emotionally drained. All morning he had been receiving communiqués from both north and south. All those lives lost. For the first time, he began to wonder if it was worth it. There'd been so much hope when he first submitted his plan. Keitel himself had sworn that they'd have everything they'd need. No problems with supplies or relief troops.

Bernhard now saw himself as a fool to have believed in those promises. Von Bock had tried to warn him but he'd been too full of himself to listen, too much in a hurry to prove himself.

Well, he'd have time now. Till October 8th at least, if he and his men could survive that long. Maybe longer. Somehow Headquarters must be made to understand. In the meantime, the war still had to be fought.

Nobody had to remind the men of the forward artillery at Seeheim that a war still had to be fought. They lived with it twenty-four hours a day; and died with it.

At the moment, there was a lull in the action. Gun crews stared vacantly out across the plain and tried to capture a few moments of peace and rest. This last time had been thirty-six hours of non-stop fighting and it had taken its toll.

The shortage of shells had been critical for some time. No rapid fire was allowed. No walking the rounds in to the target was allowed.

To Colonel Krasna, this was insane. He had ordered special spotters to creep within meters of the enemy tanks and call in the artillery virtually upon themselves, all the while calling back instructions to the gun crews for adjustments in their firing angle.

This had worked, to a degree, but Krasna was getting desperately short of men to use as spotters.

The South Africans and the British had been cautious, and that had helped, but now they were becoming emboldened as the rate of German fire decreased. Soon they would probe and then follow that probe with a full scale advance and then it would be over.

Already the British guns were close enough to see. Their accuracy was not as great as the Germans but they didn't need to be. They could fire five shells to the Germans' one. Krasna needed a miracle. He thought perhaps he had one.

His gun chiefs assembled in the underground bunker that had once been an exploratory mine shaft.

Krasna walked into the meeting in a freshly laundered uniform. He felt that he must convince the men that all was not as bad as they knew it was, and by looking as fresh as the day that they had landed he hoped to accomplish the feat.

He strode purposefully to the tactical map. "The British have encamped just beyond Gawobab with the South Africans attempting to advance on their left near the Goageb River. If they continue their push, they will successfully split us off from any re-supply from Luderitz and will encircle us and eventually the entire task force. Tonight, we prevent this and drive the enemy back."

"Lieutenant Beeler," Krasna barked.

Beeler, covered head to toe in grime and soot snapped to attention. "Sir!"

"Beeler, can you maintain a rapid rate of fire for fifteen minutes?"

Beeler thought for a moment. "Yes sir. If I dip into reserves."

"You have my authority to do so. Schroeder, is the rail line to Luderitz still operable?"

Schroeder was too tired to stand. "Yes sir. As of one hour ago."

"Very good. Gentlemen, I want half of the guns loaded back on the rail cars at once. Do this under cover of darkness. Then, when Lieutenant Beeler's guns begin to fire, you will move them forty miles down the line to the west. To the village of Goageb.

"Here we will establish a firebase, and at dawn we will give the South Africans a surprise with their breakfast."

The assembled men were quiet for a long time. Finally Schroeder stood. "Sir, with respect. If we do this, we will go so deeply into our reserves as to put us at extreme risk when they counter attack."

"They will not counter attack, Schroeder. They will fall back."

"Sir?"

"The British believe, rightly, that we are unrelieved. So, following long standing British military traditions, they wait until we are at our weakest and then they will attack. But if they believe we have been reinforced or re-supplied, they will also follow tradition and fall back to regroup. The British are nothing if not traditional."

Some men laughed, but not Schroeder. "And if they do not fall back, if they counter attack?"

The room was still as Krasna looked directly at Schroeder. "Then my friend we shall all surely die." The men looked shocked, and Krasna allowed it to sink in before continuing. "We shall all die, which is surely what will happen if we do nothing. But be of good heart. Have I ever been wrong?"

Slowly, the men began to cheer, "NO! NO!"

Krasna looked the men over and especially Schroeder. He had been honest, but he had also lied. This strategy would not stop the enemy, only delay him. He knew it, and Schroeder knew it. Hell, everybody in the room knew it. But only he and Schroeder were facing it.

With the briefing ended, the room emptied rapidly leaving Krasna and Schroeder alone.

Schroeder walked up to the colonel.

"Did I play my role well, my Colonel?"

"Perfectly, my friend. We have drawn them together more tightly than ever before. Thank you, Josef."

Schroeder pulled himself erect and snapped off the sharpest salute he ever had. Krasna straightened his tunic and returned the salute with equal panache. Schroeder left Krasna standing alone.

Schroeder has played his part well, thought Krasna. Now if only the British and South Africans will play their parts to form.

❧

Dawn briefing at South African Forces Headquarters on the Goageb river.

Brigadier MacMillan, a transplanted Scot, stood in front of his officers calmly and with an air of aloof professionalism.

"There was some activity last night in the vicinity of Gawobab. We have received reports of sustained and heavy artillery bombardment on all British positions in the area. Intelligence believes that the Germans in this area have been newly re-supplied. As a result, we are reordering our plan of attack.

"Our allies will now proceed with a retrograde movement beyond the range of the German guns at Seeheim and will wait for us to continue our flanking action. As we are still beyond the range of their guns, we will continue up the river and..."

His next words were drowned out by the shriek of an incoming artillery round and the subsequent explosion. The explosions came steadily, if not swiftly. The German gunners, directed by scouts less than one hundred meters from the South African camp, were deadly accurate.

The first round of volleys took out three tents, the forward supply dump, and two large mortars. The three tents were blazing hells from which wounded poured like water.

MacMillan, miraculously unhurt, stood in the middle of the devastated camp and shouted orders like the drill instructor he once was. When the shooting stopped, he surveyed the damage and muttered to himself "My God, they've been reinforced!"

Krasna had bought precious time.

Time had been running out for some time in the north.

In his headquarters just west of Windhoek, von Schumacher once again went over the lists of the dead.

The fighting had been less intense here, but the toll was rising. Steadily and inexorably. Von Schumacher's forces still cut off Windhoek from the north, west, and south, but the hastily organized local militia had been getting markedly better. So much so, that after a supply drop from South African aircraft, they had been able to break through to the east along the rail line to Gobabis.

Siege was foreign to von Schumacher, a man trained in commando lightning actions, and it didn't sit well with his men.

Not having the strength to enter Windhoek, and the people of Windhoek not having the arms to break out to the north or south, it was an uneasy standoff punctuated by mortar exchanges and sniping. Von Streck had ordered him not to use precious ammunition in an attempt to take the city or even its outskirts, so von Schumacher sat, idly wondering who was laying siege to whom.

The small patrols that ventured out of Windhoek were getting bolder and more deadly. Knowing the terrain far better than the Germans, they moved almost unnoticed until they struck. The patrols had killed enough of the task force to cause uneasiness among the men, and had captured enough weaponry to constitute a legitimate threat.

As long as Krasna could hold the enemy's movements to south of Seeheim, von Schumacher was certain that he could hold out. Hold out or hold on? That was the question foremost in his mind. If Seeheim fell, then the task force's position would be untenable. And if relief was delayed again…the thought chilled the grizzled veteran.

Even von Streck was beginning to show the signs of fatigue and concern. When he visited the task force headquarters at the former pipe mine at Haris, he had been strangely silent. His only words of note had come just before leaving when he and von Schumacher stood alone by the general's command car.

"Ernst, begin making plans for a phased pullback. Not too much, not too soon, but plan it nonetheless. It may become," his voice trailed off.

"I understand, my General."

"Ernst," Bernhard's voice was choked with emotion. "Ernst, it has been so wasted. All of the lives. All for nothing."

It shook von Schumacher to see Streck in this state. "My General," his voice softened, "my friend, you have triumphed. You have proved the plan and led the unit without flaw. It is those," he spit out the word, "politicians in the High Command who have caused our…" He couldn't bring himself to say 'defeat' but it rose in the air between the two men.

Bernhard managed a smile. "Hold firm, Ernst. I will find a way out of this, this, morass. I promise you."

Von Schumacher smiled and saluted. As the General drove off, von Schumacher turned his back and briskly walked to the communications tent. Halfway there, a round from a captured mortar, fired by a patrol from Windhoek, exploded in his path. He died instantly.

ᴥ

Seeheim had to be abandoned. Krasna, using every trick he knew, slowly pulled his men back towards Luderitz in overlapping moves. The enemy was beginning to advance cautiously and the end in the south was drawing near. The task force had lost almost half their men and equipment. They moved at night and fought in the day. When they moved, they brought with them whatever could be salvaged to try and repair and reuse. Morale disappeared.

ᴥ

9 September 1939 0911

Urgent Message for Commanding General OB West
Sending Authority: Commander AKEF Walvis Bay

Urgent

> **For God's sake. Declare victory and let us leave this charnel house.**

von Streck

ᴥ

General Jodl had long ago learned his way through the treacherous maze of life in the High Command. He may have disagreed on various issues but he was too smart to ever go on record with anything but what was expected of him.

Now he finished reading the latest urgent plea from Streck. Something had to be done! He called in Albrecht. "Tell me, Karl. You know General von Streck very well, don't you?"

"Yes, we were at the War College together and we've stayed in touch."

"You've seen the message." It was a statement rather than a question. "Give me your assessment."

Albrecht hesitated for a moment. "I've followed the campaign with great interest, of course." Again he hesitated, and Jodl impatiently motioned him to continue. "We have continued to delay relief long past any reasonable expectation of their ability to hold. I think the general has done a remarkable job."

"Thank you, Karl. That's all for now."

When Albrecht left, Jodl knew he had his work cut out for him.

He had to convince the *Fuhrer* that the campaign had been a success, and that it was time to bring Streck and his men back.

He was finally able to meet with Hitler the next afternoon. Keitel was present, acting as an audience of one until Jodl entered. Hitler had been expounding on how well the war was going. Jodl took advantage of it. "I've been checking on the Southwest Africa campaign and…"

Hitler interrupted. "Yes, yes. It's all going wonderfully well." Hitler continued his conversation with himself as if with another person. "The generals don't appreciate your military genius."

"True, but now they have no choice but to accept it. Every strategy has proved itself." Every now and then, he'd become aware of Keitel who would emphatically agree with whatever was being said.

After a while, as Hitler grew more rational, Jodl would say something about the success of the Southwest Africa campaign. It took several hours of interjecting the right phrase or comment at the right time. Finally, Hitler ordered Keitel to bring home the victorious troops. Keitel passed the order on to Jodl, who left immediately.

ॐ

14 September 1939 2302

Urgent Message for Commander AKEF Walvis Bay
Sending Authority: OKW HQ

Urgent

> **The Fuhrer's congratulations on your sweeping victory. Aircraft are coming to remove you and your valiant men. They will arrive at 0015 on 21 September. You must prepare a lighted strip 1200 meters in length northeast to southwest. Be strong. I will see you soon.**

Albrecht for Jodl

ॐ

"If hell there is, then this be it."

He said it aloud as he stood and watched the scene unfold. It was night, hours after sundown, but the scene was brightly illuminated by floodlights taken from every mine and by wildly colored flares. It was bright enough to work, for the planes to land and take off, and for the enemy's planes to find them and kill them. He cast an anxious glance at the midnight sky.

The general had ordered them out. At last. They had fallen back from Seeheim to Luderitz; from Luderitz to Spencer Bay; and from there to here. As they moved, they abandoned everything that was an encumbrance of any kind, clothes, broken equipment, heavy equipment all left behind, everything but their *kameraden*, their fallen friends.

Now there was nowhere else to go. The coffins stacked like cordwood waited to be loaded. The general ordered that they be loaded last. They would go on his plane. Now there was nothing to do but wait and think, and gaze both hopefully and fearfully at the night sky.

He wandered across the improvised landing field. Moving through patches of white light from the mine floodlights into darkness and then into splashes of red or green light made by the flares, he passed among the sights and smells and emotions of the broken AKEF. He stopped to watch the smoke rise and disappear beyond the artificial halo of the flares. On another night, it would be beautiful.

Suddenly, off in the distance, he could hear engines banking. The electric lights were immediately shut off and the entire field thrown into the semi-darkness of the flares. They waited and watched and then breathed again as they recognized the black cross on the airplane's side.

There was no cheer, no rush forward, just a palpable sense of relief and then silence.

Twenty minutes later as he was loaded on the third plane, he looked out through the door and saw the general standing with the coffins, directing their loading. With head bowed, Leibrandt walked to the area of the cabin floor that would be his seat and the poem came to him again. "If hell there is, then this be it. My friends are twisted and beaten. The stench I smell, the shroud I fit, My life is done, God's beaten."

If the anonymous American poet who had written those lines years before during their Civil War had been beside him, he would have nodded, placed an arm around Leibrandt, and reminded him of the poem's last line which he had forgotten. "Dedicated to the survivors of war."

The plane rose into the night sky. Jaguar was mercifully over.

≷ঌ

21 September 1939 0204

Message for Operations Director OKW HQ
Sending Authority: Commander AKEF in transit

On 27 April, 1,305 men of the AKEF landed in German SW Africa. Today, 1,289 men of the AKEF, 234 of them alive, have left. 16 men are missing. We are returning with our honored dead, the only honor left in this. Expected arrival in Addis Ababa 1645 this date. Hail the Victors.

von Streck

CHAPTER SEVEN

A GATHERING OF EXPEDIENCY

Bernhard sat bolt upright in the darkened room. Bathed in sweat, he was totally disoriented. Slowly, he began to focus and come awake. His left hand reached out and touched something soft. He wanted to look over, to see his sleeping wife lying just beside him, but he was afraid that the looking would cause the dream to end and he would find himself back in the jungle. At last, he forced himself to turn.

He took a deep breath and let it out slowly. She was there sleeping quietly. It was real, not a dream. He was home.

"Home." He said the word aloud just to convince himself that the waking nightmare of Jaguar was far behind him. He was home, in his own bed, beside his wife. The dream that he had had all those months in Africa had finally come true. He smiled and lay back down, but sleep came with difficulty. His mind raced over the events of the last few weeks.

The flight home had been almost as traumatic as the battle. Sitting alone among all those coffins, all those boys who had unquestioningly put their trust and their lives in his hands, had brought home to him the truth of the war.

Germany was being led by men who were morally bankrupt. Men to whom battles were fought strictly for credit and personal enhancement, not for country or honor. The delays in relief had proven that to him, and his reception at home only confirmed it.

The planes carrying him and his remaining men arrived in Berlin at dusk, but it seemed like midday from the klieg lights for the cameras. As he and his men climbed down the ramp, they were met by a blaring band and school children running forward with bouquets of flowers.

They looked at each other in shock. Had they stumbled into a reception for some victorious troops? They were led across the tarmac to a platform that had been specially constructed for the occasion.

As he approached, Bernhard could see the *Fuhrer*, Keitel, Jodl, and the rest of the 'mob' applauding his approach. He was led onto the platform. Instinct alone made him salute. It was no longer a sign of fealty, for he no longer felt a part of them, or of their army. All that had died in Africa.

Speeches. An hour of speeches had gone on before the *Fuhrer* spoke. Bernhard stood at attention throughout. He listened stolidly as Hitler made his point.

"We have sent out a message, that is unmistakably clear. The might of the German people is unchallengeable. The right of our case is unquestionable! No one can stand before us! Let those who would oppose us be warned…" Bernhard looked past the *Fuhrer* to the coffins being unloaded on a corner of the airfield. "…the completeness of this victory is but a small demonstration of what lies ahead for the German nation!"

The words, and their real meaning rang in Bernhard's ears for hours after.

He glanced over at the clock on the night table. Still early. He slipped quietly out of bed so as not to wake Inge, put on his robe, and went into his study.

On his desk was a collection of family photographs. Bernhard, young, not young, and aging. Inge, always beautiful, smiling; Otto in his diapers, school uniforms, and now the uniform of the *Fallschirmtruppen*, a paratrooper like his father.

Looking at the pictures helped Bernhard decompress. They

reminded him of the days before Southwest Africa. The heady, clean days when duty, honor, and country were not political slogans but realities by which every German lived.

He tried to stop his melancholy but it deepened as he looked at a picture of Otto and himself on the day that Otto had made his first free fall. He remembered a talk they'd had.

"Father, what a tremendous feeling. It's indescribable. Is this what you felt? Is this what it will be like?"

Bernhard had laughed. "If you are called to fight, you'll do well. I learned and you'll learn." They were for a moment no longer father and son. They were closer than that. They were fellow paras, the elite of the military machine.

"I hope I get the chance soon," Otto had said.

His father had nodded solemnly then. Patting his son on the back, he had said, "You will, son, you will."

He poured himself a drink and watched the sun rise. The night after he had gotten back from the 'charnel house', Otto arrived home on leave. They had talked then too.

"Is it true, is it true, Father? The *Fuhrer* himself presented you with the Iron Cross?" Otto stammered out the words, choked with the emotion and the excitement of youth.

Bernhard had frowned. "He presented it to me, but I did not win it."

"I don't understand, father."

"And I pray Otto, that you never will."

A wall had existed between them from that moment on. Bernhard stood and moved slowly through the heavily carpeted hallway, and carefully opened the door to Otto's room. Just a crack, enough to see the young man sprawled out asleep.

He walked in and sat down on the edge of the bed. Otto turned in his sleep and Bernhard gently brushed the hair away from his son's eyes. Slowly, Otto woke up.

"Papa?"

"Shh. It's early. Go back to sleep."

"Is everything okay?" Sleep slurred his speech.

Bernhard smiled, but shook his head. "No, my son. But go back to sleep anyway. I love you." Otto rolled over and was quickly sound asleep.

Bernhard sat there for ten minutes. Just looking at his sleeping son, looking and praying.

Praying that some way, somehow, Otto could be spared the coming disaster. He stood and walked to the kitchen where he could hear the hired girl beginning to stir.

No.

Things were definitely not all right.

❧

The morning was cold, crisp and bright. As Inge filled their plates and poured the coffee, they were once again the happy family Streck. Otto read the latest regimental soccer scores while Bernhard read a series of intelligence summaries that had been prepared for him.

Things were going well. Germany had invaded Poland and in retaliation for the Allies' threats and shoot-on-sight orders, the German Navy had effectively blockaded the Allies.

Bernhard nodded and muttered to himself. He wondered about his next assignment, whether they'd reconstitute the AKEF. Then he looked over at Otto. The boy was wolfing down breakfast now, checking his watch, anxious to be back with his company. Where would Otto be assigned? He prayed it would not be another "Jaguar."

After breakfast, Otto prepared to leave. Inge fluttered around, looking for her purse, her keys, her hat.

Then it was time. For a moment before Otto came in, Inge and Bernhard stood looking at each other. Inge's tears almost started. Bernhard took a handkerchief from his pocket and gently daubed at her eyes. "I can't help it," she said, "I almost lost you and now…"

Bernhard held her close, "But you didn't." He smiled. "Take him to the station. I know you'd like to have him all to yourself for a few minutes."

Otto came in. "I'm ready." Father and son shook hands. Then Bernhard impulsively put his arms around his son and hugged him. "I know I puzzle you. Don't worry about it. Just…take care of yourself. Write, when you can." They hugged again. Bernhard stood at the door, watching as the car pulled away.

He continued to stand there, staring into space for a long time.

A staff car pulled onto the tree lined street in front of Bernhard's house. He watched as it slowed to a crawl, and then stopped directly in front of him. A spit and polish General's aide emerged and opened the rear passenger side door, then stood at attention

Bernhard sighed. Even here, the war intruded. He watched as Albrecht got out of the car, spoke a few words to his aide, and then watched as the car pulled away.

Albrecht walked slowly up the drive towards his old friend Bernhard. He was struck at how thin Bernhard looked, his uniform hung on him. Even after several weeks of R & R. There was something else too; a look in his eyes, a pain and an anger that Karl had never seen there before. He raised a hand in mock salute as he drew near.

"Hello, old friend."

Bernhard stared at Albrecht for several moments before extending his hand. They shook, but without the warmth that Karl remembered.

Bernhard led him into his study and got them each a drink. Settling himself behind his desk, he stared silently across at Albrecht. Waiting.

Albrecht shifted uncomfortably. "You're well?"

"Now."

"And Inge and Otto, they also are well?"

Bernhard nodded. "What do you want, Karl?"

"Officially," Albrecht began, "to welcome you home and to tell you that you will be receiving new orders within a fortnight."

"And unofficially?"

Albrecht did indeed have his own personal agenda for this meeting, but first he would have to breach the wall that Streck had erected against him.

"Bernhard, I did everything I could to help you. You must know that?" Bernhard nodded. "It was Keitel and...others who misread the situation."

Streck's face seemed set in granite. "A 'misread'? Is that how they refer to it? Not the phrase I would use."

"Nor I."

Bernhard felt suddenly very tired. "What do you want, Karl? What could not wait until my leave was over?"

Albrecht reached into his briefcase and handed across some internal OKW memoranda. Bernhard started reading through them slowly, became more interested, and began studying them with intensity.

"Gott in Himmel." He couldn't believe what he was reading. Memos written by Albrecht to Jodl, Keitel, even the *Fuhrer*, urging the immediate relief or withdrawal of the AKEF from Southwest Africa. Memos that coincided with the beginning of the end of Jaguar. Memos that, when considered in light of prevailing OKW policy at the time, came dangerously close to treason. After fifteen minutes, he put down the papers and walked over to Albrecht.

They embraced. "I had no idea. None at all." Bernhard said. "I just assumed you were part of," he waved at the memos, "that group. Can you forgive me?"

Albrecht slapped him on the back and sat down again. "It's forgotten. I just thank God that you came through all right."

They both relaxed as Bernhard refilled their drinks. "So you stuffed shirt," Bernhard laughed for the first time, "what can I do for you?"

Albrecht laughed, too, anxious to keep the feeling of camaraderie going. "You already have. I have my old drinking buddy back." He leaned forward. "There is something we need to talk about."

Once more, he reached into his briefcase, this time removing a single sheet which he handed to Bernhard.

Bernhard looked at the message he'd sent to Albrecht about the diamonds. "So?"

"So, did you ever find out anymore about them?"

Bernhard shook his head. "No."

Albrecht sat back. "I couldn't find anything either."

"What does Keitel think about it?"

"Look, Bernhard, you know as well as I do, Keitel and that bunch, they're just 'yes men'. I don't think *lakeitel's* ever had an original thought in his life, and if he did, it probably died of loneliness."

Bernhard smiled at the derogatory term *'lakeitel'*, or lackey, which was generally used behind the Field Marshall's back.

"Besides," Albrecht continued, "we both know the old saying

about power and corruption goes double when it comes to certain groups up there. They'd only find a way to crucify Friederich Reineke in order to 'liberate' the diamonds and line their own pockets. We owe it to his father not to let that happen."

Bernhard agreed. "I owe the old man a lot. I'd never want to see the general and his family hurt."

"What do you think we should do?" Albrecht asked.

Bernhard thought for a minute. "Perhaps we'd better discuss the packet with General Reineke."

Albrecht jumped in eagerly. "My thought exactly. One thing. Right now, we're the only ones who know about the diamonds. I think it's important that until we make a decision, we keep the information just between us. Agreed?"

They talked for the better part of two hours; about the war, about Jaguar, about all the things that close friends who haven't seen each other for a long time talk about. By the time Albrecht's car arrived, the diamonds were long forgotten...by Streck.

Bernhard walked Albrecht to the car. "Take care, Karl. I'll see you again soon."

Albrecht smiled broadly. "I promise that you will." He got in the car and Bernhard watched as it drove away.

In the back seat, Albrecht turned to his chief deputy, Franz Konigsmann and handed him the sheaf of memoranda. "Destroy these."

"They were useful, sir?"

Albrecht nodded. "They were indeed. Most useful." He looked out the window at the passing scenery of a still intact Berlin. "And he never realized they were fakes. My congratulations."

Konigsmann smiled and began slowly tearing the faked memos into small pieces. As they drove through one of the parks that dotted Berlin, he casually let small pieces trail out through the window.

That afternoon, Konigsmann supervised the sending of the message to General Reineke.

à.

October 13, 1939

To: HQ Army Group III
        Personal for General Kurt Reineke

Message: Arrangements have been completed for the disposition of Friederich's remains stop Administrative leave is granted immediately stop Cable your travel arrangements stop Respectfully it is requested that you take time to appear this office stop Your particular knowledge is needed for proposed operation stop Code name Crystal Movement stop I remain your devoted student stop

Albrecht endit

ᐧᐁ

On the right bank of the Weser, in the old section of Bremen, the funeral was held. Representatives from all the services, from the Party, even a personal representative of the *Fuhrer* stood with solemn purpose in the light mist of the afternoon. The military standards of the AKEF stood alongside the flag draped coffin and the honor guard stood erect and true throughout the entire service.

They had come, not to honor the deceased, for in fact very few of them knew him. No, they had come to honor the father, General, soon to be Field Marshall, Kurt Reineke. They all paid their respects in the proper way when it ended and then gossiped about the wayward son quietly as they left.

As the sun went down, the mist turned to rain. The general continued to stand while the coffin was lowered and covered with dirt. He stood there alone, into the early evening until his aide, a young captain named Bertrauer, came to him out of concern.

Reineke seemed not to notice as the younger man put a heavy coat around him and began to lead him away.

"It's all over, all lost," the general mumbled on the way to the car. "At the end, I had a son again. He came back. But for what? Those bastards used him up and killed him. For what? For what?"

"Sir," the aide began reticently, "you cannot blame General von Streck. Most of his force was destroyed."

Reineke turned to the aide and smiled. "I don't blame Bernhard. I know the man, I taught him. No. It is the animals that we have given over to. They took my son from me."

The aide shifted uneasily in the seat beside him. Reineke looked at him understandingly. "You think me a traitor, boy?" The aide shook his head. "I heard nothing, my General."

"Hear this, Bertrauer. I love my country. I've given my life to its service, and I honor those who would bring it back to its former glory." He paused. "But some things are irreconcilable." He motioned for the driver to come over and soon they were on their way back to Berlin.

ðŸ

"But since fate has now nonetheless put us to this test, all of us wish to pledge ourselves with only the greater fanaticism to hold fast to that which was formerly won at the price of the blood of so many of our best men and which today had to be maintained once more through the blood of German fellow countrymen!"

Albrecht rose and walked over to the speaker on the wall of his office. Deliberately, he turned to the entertainment circuit and the strains of Mozart filled the windowless room.

"The corporal will not be satisfied until we are drowning in the blood of our countrymen." Reineke spoke quietly but firmly.

Streck, leaning against a file cabinet, nodded. "The time is fast approaching when our country will be unable to afford his fanaticism."

Albrecht was uneasy. His plan was to get these men together and then convince them to keep the diamonds away from the authorities; but this, this was coming disquietingly close to treason, this time for real. Quickly, he changed the subject.

"General Reineke, Kurt, let's concentrate on the matters at hand." Reineke nodded and took out his portfolio and prepared to take notes.

"So," Reineke said, "what master stroke is this Operation Crystal Movement you need me to consult on?"

Albrecht began slowly. The first moments would decide the thing. He was sure of that. He was also uncomfortably aware that he had not totally won von Streck's support for what he had in mind. They both must be convinced. Taking a deep breath, he began.

"There is no Crystal Movement."

Reineke stopped with his pen halfway to the pad and Streck turned to look directly at Albrecht.

"Kurt, I needed to talk with you, and to you, too, Bernhard. And I needed to ensure that," he gestured at the operations 'pit' beyond his office, "they would not suspect the reason for our meeting."

He let a silence come over the room for a moment before

continuing. "Let me assure you, Kurt, that if it were not for the immediacy and sensitivity of the situation, I never would have taken such an extraordinary action."

From behind and to the side of Reineke, Bernhard suddenly realized what was going on. Silently, he mouthed the word 'Friederich', and Albrecht nodded. Streck pulled over a chair.

Albrecht was talking directly to Reineke now. "Sir, I have known you for a great many years. I admire you as a soldier, as a teacher, but most of all I treasure you as a friend. You cannot begin to know the anguish I felt when informed of Friederich's death."

Reineke nodded curtly.

Streck reached out to Reineke. "If there was anything I could have done, I would have given my life not to have been in command of the operation in which he was killed."

Reineke suppressed his emotions…barely. "The reason for this meeting?"

Albrecht nodded and reached below his desk and pulled out the two leather pouches. "These were found among Friederich's things." He handed them across to the general.

He ran his hand over them and examined them closely. "I don't recognize them, but then…" his voice trailed off. "He was gone for so long." The room fell silent again.

Streck spoke first. "Sir, inside these pouches I found three hundred and one diamonds of varying sizes." Reineke looked up as if shot through with electricity.

"What!"

Albrecht spilled the diamonds from a manila folder. "Diamonds, my friend. A not inconsiderable fortune of diamonds."

Reineke's eyes swept the shining pile. His mind became momentarily numbed. Where could Friederich have acquired such a fortune. The answer was not forthcoming.

"My General?"

Reineke was forced back to his senses. Albrecht was talking to him. Reineke forced himself to listen, but his eyes never left the pile of diamonds.

"Sir," Albrecht was saying, "How, that is, to be delicate…"

Streck finished the sentence. "Kurt, it is hard for us to believe that he acquired these riches," he paused and struggled to find a word that would soften the blow, "conventionally. What we need to know is whether or not you know how he came by them?"

Reineke mumbled, "Could he have been a...what do they call it? A covert paymaster? I have heard that they often use..." He couldn't say the word.

Albrecht shook his head. "I have checked, discreetly of course, and he was not being used by any organ. of state until he volunteered to advise the AKEF."

Streck picked up the thought. "And with us, he was strictly in reconnaissance."

Reineke understood. His friends were trying to tell him gently that Friederich had stolen, or at the least, wrongfully acquired the diamonds. He thought back to a bitter conversation he'd had with Friederich shortly before he had left.

ð

They had been arguing all that week, ever since Friederich had announced his decision to leave school and go to South Africa.

Friederich was leaving in three days but the general was due back on assignment the next day. One last time, they would battle it out, this time in Friederich's room.

"You cannot, cannot do something so thoroughly reprehensible," the general shouted. "You are throwing away your life. I will not allow it."

"I am not one of your tin soldiers. All my life I have followed your orders, but not this time," Friederich shouted back.

"Why? What..."

Friederich interrupted. "Never have I done one thing you were proud of. Not once. And I tried so hard. Your way. Well, I finally realized that your way is not my way."

"I offered you an example of an honorable life. To serve your country. Our family has always served. If I've been hard on you, it's because I care."

"Keep your love, your caring for your little generals in training. It doesn't matter anymore, Father. I'll make my fortune in my own way, and when I return, you'll all sit up and take notice."

ð

Reineke roused himself from his brief reverie. "Gentlemen, we are all men of action. What is past is done. Karl, you did not call me to this formal meeting simply to inform me of my son's deeds or misdeeds, as diplomatically as you may have tried to put it. You could have done that in a quiet chat over coffee." Reineke angrily slammed his hand down on the desk. "I am still touched by the stench of the grave. So why, precisely are we here?"

Streck looked uncomfortable and thought to himself, and I, the stench of many graves.

Albrecht, though, was undaunted. "As always, my dear teacher, you cut right to the heart of things. I wouldn't have dreamed of disturbing you in your grief, or you, Bernhard, after what you've been through but there's some urgency. I think we're all agreed that this," Albrecht gestured to the gems, "has enormous value."

Reineke and Streck nodded.

Albrecht was warming to the subject, growing visibly excited. "Headquarters is no place to keep it. Especially now, as things begin to heat up. I grant you that ownership of the gems is, at best, uncertain."

Albrecht started to rush ahead but Bernhard, looking thoughtful, interrupted. "I've been thinking about that. I know we couldn't find anyone's connection with..."

This time, Albrecht interrupted. "I tried every possible way." Reprovingly, he added. "You know I did, Bernhard."

"Yes, but what if someone we don't know about lays claim?"

Albrecht could see it all slipping away. He'd never felt quite as good as these other officers. Bernhard came from a titled family and had covered himself with glory in the field numerous times. Kurt Reineke was a deeply respected officer of the old school, knowledgeable, honored.

He, on the other hand, was a Rhinelander desk jockey. If he could get them into this project with him, it would bring them down to his level, or raise him to theirs. Even more than the money, this was important to him.

All these thoughts raced through his mind in a moment. They'd been a visceral part of him from the beginning. Now, he had to fight a rising panic. "Someone else? How could that be? No one in this country knows about it. And obviously, with all the turmoil in Southwest Africa, no one tried..."

Once again, Bernhard interjected, "Actually, Karl, Friederich had the diamonds. They really belong to his father, don't you think?"

The deep, measured tones of Kurt Reineke broke in. "For me, this whole discussion is academic." He started to rise from his chair. "Anyway you look at it, it is tainted money. I am not sure I want anything to do with it."

Albrecht jumped up. "Please, please, my General. Hear me out."

General Reineke sat down, and Albrecht took a deep breath. It's now or never, he thought.

"I'll put my points to you simply. Our choices are limited: one, that we give the diamonds to the High Command, or two, that we," he stressed the word, "keep them."

They sat quietly, watching and listening intently.

He continued. "You've both been victims of the cavalier attitudes of some of our most powerful leaders. Their capriciousness cost you a son, Kurt. And you lost some one thousand two hundred good, loyal men, Bernhard, and almost your own life as well.

"If the High Command gets their hands on the diamonds, we could well expect them to finance more lunacy, causing more good, loyal young men to die."

Bernhard leapt to his feet. "You're talking treason, sir, and I will not be a part of that." He turned and started to stride briskly out of the office. To his surprise, it was Reineke's voice he heard call after him. "Bernhard."

Streck turned and looked into the gently smiling face of the one man in the world he completely trusted.

Reineke beckoned Bernhard with his hand, gesturing towards the empty chair. "It is not treason to see things as they are." He laughed for the first time in the meeting. "It is only unwise."

Bernhard returned to his seat as Albrecht tried to suppress a sigh of relief.

Before he could continue, Albrecht was interrupted by a sharp knock on the door of the office. All three men froze as the door was opened. They relaxed when they recognized Franz Konigsmann.

"Forgive the interruption, sirs. The *Fuhrer* requests your presence immediately in the Chancery." Konigsmann saluted and left, leaving the door open. The men looked at each other for a moment and then stood.

As they straightened their coats and put on their hats, Albrecht laughed nervously. "Let's hope that this is not related to our…"

Bernhard finished the sentence. "Conspiracy."

ôê

To get to the *Fuhrer's* private office in the German Chancellery, one first had to proceed down long wide halls that were carefully designed to give the visitor a feeling of inferiority. Forty foot ceilings with floor to ceiling drapings in bold colors, large pretentious depictions of Hitler in various poses, all oversized, bore down upon visitors. As you moved through the checkpoints, the use of color and space changed subtly so that by the time you reached Hitler's office, you were completely subdued.

However, the generals were not casual visitors and they knew the routine well. Each man had long ago developed his own private defenses against this subtle form of mind control.

To Reineke, the hall reminded him of a child's concept of grandeur. He found it amusing that arguably the most powerful man in the world felt a need to resort to stupid mind games and pretension.

To von Streck, the hall always reminded him of a sports arena. Having always been an avid and successful athlete, he rather liked the walk; almost like the walk of a gold medal champion on his way to receive a winner's wreath.

But it was Albrecht who best understood the hall. To him, it was a symbol of unchallengeable power, of a goal, of the dream that he secretly nourished within him. If he had built it himself, it might have been even broader and grander.

After fifteen minutes of going through checkpoints and the oppression of the hall, they arrived at the outer office of Martin Borman, Hitler's appointments secretary. He was known among the High Command simply as 'the ferret'.

Albrecht nodded in greeting. "Hello, Borman."

"General Albrecht, sirs, you are late. You will have to wait," he snapped officiously.

Reineke knew the procedure well and had already taken a seat on the uncomfortable divan kept there. Hitler never saw anybody without keeping them waiting. There was no end to the man's pettiness.

After twenty minutes, Borman picked up the phone and nodded at them. "You may go in now." His smile dripped venom but they ignored it and entered the opulent office.

The office was the size of a small airplane hangar. It could, and did on occasion, hold as many as one hundred people at a time. A tactical map of Europe was the centerpiece of the huge conference table in the middle of the room and to one end, the far end of course, sat Hitler's antique desk with world map covering the forty foot wall behind it.

They stood inside the closed doors of the office and waited. Hitler was at the conference table with a group of generals from the tactical planning board. Keitel stood next to him and Jodl directly across the table from him.

"Fools! You are all fools! Leave Finland to the Bolsheviks. Believe me, they, Stalin, will devour it soon. No! What I want is Denmark! From Denmark, I can operate my forces to the north or the east. Now go back and begin to think like soldiers, not cattle!" He shouted "Get out!"

As the board scrambled to salute and leave, Streck leaned over to Reineke. "At least, he is in a good mood." Reineke's face never changed expression but the glint in his eyes was clear to Bernhard. Hitler turned to them and they snapped perfect fascist salutes. *"Heil Hitler!"*

Hitler casually returned the salute and beckoned them over. They walked at full attention, Albrecht in the lead, flanked by Reineke and von Streck.

"Karl, why is it my planners lack imagination?"

"My Fuhrer?"

"It's true. They lack the ability to see the future as it must be. I must have Denmark. I must!"

They all nodded.

For the next few minutes, Hitler continued his harangue against the planning board, against his planners and against career officers in general. At times like this, it seemed that he was oblivious to all of them. Suddenly, he stopped and turned to Reineke.

"You, my dear Reineke, you are the only one I trust to follow my orders and understand my wishes."

Reineke bowed slightly. "Thank you, my *Fuhrer*."

"Could you give me Denmark?"

Reineke considered the question. There were problems but it could be done. "Yes, my *Fuhrer*."

Hitler was as happy as a small child with a new toy. "Excellent. Excellent. And you, von Streck, could you give me Copenhagen?"

Bernhard knew only one answer was expected. "Yes, my *Fuhrer*."

Hitler clapped his hands together. "Excellent. This is how I see it. Von Streck, your plan of attack in Africa was brilliant but flawed." Hitler bent over the map and did not notice Reineke deliberately step on Bernhard's foot. Bernhard looked at him and Reineke mouthed the word 'careful'.

"My *Fuhrer*," Bernhard began, "perhaps you could show me the ways for improving the plan?"

Hitler seemed to consider the request. It was all a theater of the absurd. The only problem was that the humor had been lost on von Streck.

"I suppose I could. Yes. Yes...see here on the map. The mistake you made was in allowing your troops to become isolated. That should never have happened.

"Your men must have greater support. In the coming operation, I promise you that reinforcement will be provided by von Runstadt's OB West. With that, you should have no problems."

As the familiar words were recalled to him, von Streck felt a desire to vomit. The rest of the Fuhrer's words were lost in a fog of misery. All Bernhard could hear or see was the possibility of a repeat of the agony of Jaguar.

"...and finally there." Hitler was continuing without noticing Bernhard's discomfort. "Also, you made a mistake in allowing civilians to interact with your forces. You must have more discipline. Even German civilians should not be trusted. If they have been living away from the Fatherland for any length of time, they will have picked up the slovenly and untrustworthy habits of the swine we must defeat. I believe you used such untrustworthy types in Southwest Africa?"

Bernhard nodded and sneaked a look at Reineke whose fury was barely contained. *"My Fuhrer,"* Reineke began, "not all of our expatriate countrymen are unreliable. In fact, my own…"

Hitler cut him off. "I said all! And those who served with von Streck were proof of that. It is as I said! Do you understand?"

They saluted and echoed *"Ja Wohl, mein Fuhrer!"*

The briefing continued for another fifteen minutes and then they were dismissed summarily.

Leaving the office, Albrecht stopped to consult Borman on some routine matter. As he talked, he noticed Reineke and von Streck talking quietly in an alcove. When he was finished, he joined them for the walk back to the 'pit'.

The hall was becoming crowded. It seemed there was going to be some official function soon. As they reached the elevator that lead down to Operations, Reineke turned to Albrecht. Although they were around several other officers, Reineke spoke clearly and without concealment.

"I believe you may begin Crystal Movement now."

Albrecht could not believe his ears. He looked at von Streck and then at Reineke. Both men nodded.

"Of course, General," Albrecht said officially, "of course. I will personally see to the equal distribution of the…forces." Again, nods all around. The elevator arrived and Albrecht got in without von Streck or Reineke, who saluted and left another way. On the ride down, Albrecht thought to himself, 'to think, the corporal made the argument for me!'

૨૧

When Kurt Reineke decided to join in the Crystal Movement conspiracy, he did it as he did everything else. Wholeheartedly and efficiently. He realized, and Albrecht and von Streck agreed, that they needed expert help. It was one thing to know the diamonds were worth a great deal. It was quite another to determine how best to get the most value out of them.

Reineke had known General Gerhard Minscel since World War I. He knew him to be a basically honest man but one able to compromise for the right reasons. He also knew that Gerhard had once been one of the richest officers in the OKW. When Hitler had chosen to nationalize the Minscel family holdings in 1936, Gerhard had almost had a nervous breakdown.

Minscel was currently in charge of the Industrial Fiscal Division of the OKW. To Reineke's mind, Gerhard was the ideal man for the job, by reason of temperament, ideology, and profession.

At a meeting at von Streck's, he fit in well, and they settled on a share for him. Minscel, in turn, agreed to look into all necessary arrangements, which Albrecht assured him he could facilitate implementing. There was no hurry. They were planning for the future.

Now, they were all meeting again for a progress report.

The invasion of Denmark had gone flawlessly. Using Jaguar as their model, once again the *Fallschirmtruppen* attacked in a predawn raid followed closely by reinforcement troops on allegedly civilian freighters. With the exception of minor changes necessitated by terrain difference, it was a replay of the early hours of the African adventure.

Bernhard, with a reconstituted AKEF, now known as the 2nd Commandos, parachuted into the brisk Danish morning and by mid afternoon had successfully encircled the capital, Copenhagen. With the arrival of General Reineke's seaborne task force, the victory was assured.

By the end of the first day, the Danes had surrendered and reinforcement troops began arriving, using Danish airports and fields. Resistance was limited at best.

Bernhard was stunned at the ease of the attack and at the lightness of the counterattacks. This wasn't Jaguar. This was the way it should be. He began to believe in himself again, and in the military. Maybe there was hope after all.

For Reineke, he welcomed the distraction of combat, however limited. Kurt threw himself into the job of pacification and quickly his sector of Denmark became known to the High Command as the most peaceful.

Peaceful that is, until the resistance began.

This was not resistance like there had been in Africa, rather it was hit and miss. A bombing here, an assassination there, phone lines cut randomly, a campaign of distraction rather than destruction. But still costly.

The occupying soldiers were not being killed off in appreciable numbers but they were seldom able to fully rest, to fully relax. They were always wary, always cautious, on edge around the clock.

This then was the environment around Reineke's Headquarters in the woods outside of Christiansfeld. It had been slightly over two months since the invasion began and for the first time the four Crystal Movement conspirators all were free enough to try a meeting.

Reineke's Headquarters' seemed logical since both he and von Streck were in the area and Albrecht, as a director of the Operations Staff, could easily travel there. They were now assembled at a table set up outside the Command Trailer waiting for Minscel. He was already a half hour late.

"Accountants," Albrecht mumbled. Bernhard laughed. He was more at ease than Albrecht had seen him in months. Even Reineke seemed more relaxed than at their previous two meetings. *I hope they stay so relaxed,* Albrecht thought to himself as he watched Minscel's staff car arrive.

Everything about Gerhard Minscel was fastidious. From his uniform's crease to his manicured fingernails, from the carefully arranged naturalness of his thinning hair to the practiced smile, he was the picture of a Nazi bureaucrat. Few realized that just beneath the surface raged a torrent of anger against the government that he believed had robbed him and his family of their fortune. He was not in Crystal Movement out of disillusionment, but rather out of revenge.

They shook hands all around and talked small talk as an aide of Reineke's served lemonade and then quietly left. Gerhard produced a flask and offered to "spice up" everyone's drink.

"So," Albrecht began after taking a drink, "give us your report."

Minscel smiled insipidly. "All is in order, my friends." Von

Streck cringed at the reference. "I have made inquiries and reached a preliminary evaluation. First, I'll present our options and their advantages." Gerhard was in his element now. "The fastest way for us to realize a profit would be to sell the rough directly to a cutter. Just a quick transaction. We'd have the money. We'd be liquid right away. Definite advantages there."

Von Streck raised his hand to stop Minscel. "Gem dealer, you say."

Minscel shook his head. "I believe it would be most dangerous to sell it to a German dealer. I was referring to a cutter who could sell the stones on his own."

Albrecht agreed, "And the way things are in the world today, where would we find another European dealer with the money or the ability to do business?"

"And someone we could trust?" von Streck added.

Minscel thought for a moment and smiled. "As for gem dealers, cutters, all of those, I could be helpful in locating the right people without difficulty. Don't let that be a concern."

Minscel continued. "The alternative would be to take it to a cutter. Have him do the work, and return the finished faceted diamonds to us."

Von Streck again. "Same problem."

Minscel responded. "Not at all. Not if you have the 'right people' in your pocket. And we do," he paused, "or we will. In Amsterdam and now in Paris."

"And the advantage?" This from a thoughtful General Reineke.

"The diamonds would become considerably more valuable," Minscel said. "Of course, we'd have to find the right cutter, and then arrange to market the stones ourselves. But, we'd end up with some forty to fifty percent more."

Von Streck spoke up. "This then is your recommendation?"

Minscel preened. "I have some expertise with these...situations. Let me explain. If we're not in a hurry to become liquid," he paused and looked at the other three men, who nodded, "then, yes, I'd have the stones cut. In the world we've created, there are distinct advantages to having finished stones. Diamonds are valuable no matter what happens to the monetary system. In a sense, it's a universal currency. The down side is that a good cutter takes time to cut stones properly, and there are a lot of stones."

"There is another down side, as you put it, my dear Minscel," General Reineke smiled grimly. "The longer we hold the diamonds, the greater the risk of our little conspiracy being uncovered," he paused, "and that would be most unpleasant, most unpleasant indeed."

Albrecht rushed to move past the images that were beginning to form in the minds of the men at the table. "How much time is absolutely necessary?" he asked.

"It's hard to say. I'm guessing, maybe a year, thirteen months."

"Why so long?"

"It's a complicated process." Minscel explained. "For example, you take one ten carat rough diamond. The cutter has to study it carefully to decide on the best possible cut. When the work is done, from the ten carat you might end up with a seven carat and a two carat, or a three and a five, or two threes, or..."

"Does he know what he's talking about?" Karl asked.

Reineke shrugged. "We get the idea. Well gentlemen, which shall it be? We have a war to win, and I, for one, must get back to it. Shall we decide?"

Albrecht said, "I don't feel the situation is really all that grave for us. While the diamonds are at the cutter's and out of our possession, there's no danger at all. The war's going well. It'll be some time before we can make use of any funds we'll be getting anyway. I see no problem in waiting and getting more money for our trouble and patience." Albrecht was feeling very good and lifted his glass. "A toast to our good fortune."

Von Streck lifted his glass, too. "I must admit your argument makes good sense, Karl. I'm willing to wait."

Reineke stood up. "There's another point on which I need to be satisfied."

Minscel looked offended. "I can handle everything."

"Of course, Gerhard. It's just, well, as you know, I am a stickler for detail and planning. For one thing, how do we find the gem dealer or cutter or whatever?"

Minscel relaxed. "I was thinking of Rubschlager, Hugo

Rubschlager. You may remember him, Kurt. He's attached to Headquarters Army Group A at Reims. I've used his services on official business many times before. I can tell him it's official business again, something to do with Crystal Movement. No need to give him any information. Just on a 'need to know' basis."

Albrecht interposed. "What if he becomes suspicious?"

Minscel laughed. "Not Rubschlager. And if he, for some totally unexpected reason, does, well, we could then offer him a small share. No, there's no worry there."

Discussion continued for a few minutes. They finally all agreed, and the project was set in motion.

இ

July 5, 1940

To: **HQ Army Group A**
          Reims
          Personal for Indigenous Industries Officer

Message: Urgent you acquire and deliver to me list of collaborating gem dealers in Paris Amsterdam Lyons areas stop Refer information to case officer Crystal Movement stop OKW Operations stop

Rubschlager endit

CHAPTER EIGHT

FATE'S HAND

The American fighter turned in lazy circles above the French countryside. Like some ancient bird of prey, it seemed to circle on the air currents, its keen eyes searching the ground below looking, ever vigilant, for a lone rabbit to swoop down upon.

Bernhard hated feeling like a rabbit.

Along with his driver and his aide, he was crouched behind his command vehicle that had been rapidly pulled into a thicket at the first sight of the American air patrol. Now they waited silently. Waited for the plane to either pass them by or attack.

It had been four years since the heady days after Denmark. The days of conquests, of Greece, Italy, Northern Africa, Holland, Sicily, most of Russia, Poland and the rest of Europe. It had been four long years where gains had inexorably become reverses, triumph was agonizingly turned to defeat, and the end that he had so clearly predicted on the beaches of Southwest Africa was upon them.

The fighter came in for a low level pass and the men in the thicket involuntarily ducked lower.

The Crystal Movement Conspiracy had moved along leisurely.

The five conspirators, they had been forced by conditions to bring Rubschlager in on the real plans, had met every three months or so to be brought up to date.

An expert of dubious qualifications had examined the diamonds and pronounced them of the highest quality. Unfortunately, the man had neither the skills nor the inclination to try the cutting job.

When it was discovered that the man had tried to take several medium sized stones for himself, it was decided by the group that he must be dealt with. On a seemingly routine visit to inspect more diamonds, the man's car was routed over a bridge due for demolition.

Later, at an urgent meeting of Planning Group Crystal Movement, the Allied invasion at Normandy had been discussed. Perhaps, as Minscel suggested at the time, it was time to become 'liquid'. The diamonds were entrusted to a diamond cutter in Amsterdam who, Minscel assured the group, was completely trustworthy. He had explained.

"The man is a Jew. In exchange for the safe conduct of his family to Sweden, he will cut and polish the gems. If he betrays us or attempts to flee, his family will be liquidated by our agents in Stockholm."

Bernhard, not trusting Minscel, personally saw to the escape of the cutter's family. It was well that he had, for not one week later, Bernhard discovered that Minscel had intended to kill them "for security's sake."

Bernhard was sick of the war.

The plane took a last look around the area, then turned back to the northwest and left. For ten minutes, Bernhard waited to be sure. Finally, he helped push the vehicle out of the thicket and they were on their way again.

Where they would eventually end up, he had no concept.

ঽ৯.

At the end of November 1944, Minscel had received word, which he relayed to Albrecht, that the diamond cutting had been completed. The conspirators collectively breathed a sigh of relief.

Ever since the von Stauffenberg attempt to assassinate Hitler, the entire upper echelon of the Officer Corps, loyal or not, had been feeling increasingly uncomfortable. Everyone looked at everyone else with suspicion. There was a Gestapo presence everywhere, both actual and felt. The normal paranoia at OKW Headquarters had increased a hundred fold.

Albrecht, who had been at the meeting where the attempt was made, had been slightly wounded. It had been a scratch, barely, but he made the most of it. Now was not the time to become a suspect.

This was the time, however, to start making plans for the future. Albrecht could not go to Amsterdam himself. Hitler had moved his headquarters back to Berlin in November. Too many questions would be raised if he tried to leave. The other members of Crystal Movement were actively involved in the fighting in different parts of Europe.

He looked around for someone, a courier who would be beyond reproach as far as the government was concerned, yet loyal to him. Someone he could consider completely trustworthy. In a very real sense, he would be entrusting his life and that of the co-conspirators to the man.

There was no question that the courier would have to know what was going on. It wasn't simply a matter of picking up a package at one location and delivering it to another. It would require a delicate sense of image, a man accustomed to covert, secretive actions while appearing to be totally open.

Albrecht scanned memory, and records, among his friends and close associates. It became clear almost immediately there was only one man for the job. He was perfect.

The man he had in mind had been one of Hitler's superior officers in World War I. When Hitler rose to power, he called on him to be his confidante and personal adjutant. There appeared to be a close attachment between the two men, at least on Hitler's part. Hitler had frequently dispatched him as a special envoy on extraordinary missions to the United States, England, France, and elsewhere. In 1939, Hitler had sent him to the German Consulate in California in the United States.

He had an open, straightforward manner which inspired confidence. He maintain excellent relations with both the Army and the

Chancellery. A diplomat, a military man, charming, very social, he had associated with world leaders and royalty. All in all, he was a man who could give the impression of being just what he appeared, pleasant, intelligent, and a good loyal Nazi. Perhaps occasionally vain and somewhat shallow. Certainly not a man you'd suspect of anything nefarious.

But then not everybody was privy to the confidential file Albrecht had read as his immediate superior. All the years of cultivating the charming persona to mask covert activities which eventually caused the intelligence services of three continents to consider him a master spy, which was why he had now returned to Berlin and worked for Albrecht in Operations.

Even the German people had no idea of the real man behind the engaging mask. There was something else of which most people were unaware. Albrecht knew, that for all of the service to the Fatherland, underneath it all, this man's first and foremost interest was self-interest. Whatever promoted his desires and position, that came first. Albrecht had ample proof of this and recognized a kindred spirit in him. He was satisfied that he had found his man, and was prepared to use his talents in whatever manner became necessary.

Albrecht pressed a button on his desk. A minute later, there was a knock on his door, and Colonel Pieter Franz Konigsmann entered.

≥ઠ

December 17, 1944

To: HQ Army Group B
**   Operations Officer**

Message: Arriving on 24 December will be Colonel Franz Konigsmann stop He will be performing sensitive duties relating to Operation Crystal Movement stop All courtesies to be extended stop No interference with his mission will be tolerated stop Repeat extend all courtesies and assistance stop All information on Konigsmann visit to be restricted stop Inquiries to me stop

Rubschlager endit

≥ઠ

Franz sat in the military transport, staring out at the night sky uneasily. Life was simpler when the Luftwaffe controlled the skies, he thought. Everything's falling apart these days. He had been concerned about the best moves to make for the future. Post-war Germany was not going to be a pleasant place to be. Unfortunately for him, he was now a wanted man in most of the rest of the world. Albrecht's calling him in to help with Crystal Movement had been the miracle he'd been looking for; a treasure in more ways than one.

He adjusted his greatcoat more comfortably. He was, as always, impeccably groomed, every hair in place, every button with a sparkling shine, every crease knife sharp. The only thing he carried with him was his sachet of toiletries. His plan was to pick up some suitable civilian clothes in Amsterdam before going to see the cutter.

The personnel at Group B had instructions to cooperate with him unconditionally. However, he'd probably use his own sources for the clothes. The less others knew, the better. He decided his cover story was a general survey of conditions in Amsterdam for OKW Headquarters. It was, he felt, sufficiently ambiguous, and would avoid questions about Crystal Movement. Most would think he was a Gestapo spy, and the Gestapo spies would think he was an efficiency expert. Either way, he'd encounter no obstacles.

He closed his eyes and tried to sleep. The plane kept banking left and right, climbing and generally making violent maneuvers to avoid night patrols and radar. When at last he dropped off, it seemed only a few minutes before the plane began gliding in and landed at Amsterdam.

Soon he gathered himself together and stepped out into the cold, brisk Amsterdam night.

à.

It was a cold day in Washington, too. A light dusting of snow was the landscape for equally sinister machinations. Two men strolled side by side in Lafayette Park across from the White House. They were alone in the park, except for one tourist family who, having saved for a year, were intent on getting the most out of their visit to the free world's wartime capital.

The men walked silently in a full circle of the pretty little park and waited for the family to leave. After ten minutes, they were completely alone.

"So, why am I freezing my ass off?"

"Masquerade."

The first man stopped and stared at the other man. "Are you nuts? We all decided that it was too crazy, too ill advised, too," he paused and looked around, "dangerous!"

The other man dusted off a nearby bench with his newspaper and they sat down. "It's come up again."

"How?"

"Somebody set off Wild Bill about the Russians. Now that's all he can talk about. He says the war will be over inside a year and we'd better get started preparing to fight the next one...with the Russians."

The first man shook his head. "That's crazy. The Russians are our allies in this war."

The other man nodded. "This war, being the operative phrase. Wild Bill's become convinced we're going to have to fight them sooner or later."

"But Masquerade is going too far."

They sat in silence for a few minutes. Finally, the other man reached inside his jacket and pulled out a single document. "Read this."

For the next ten minutes, the first man read and reread the proposed document. Several times, he shook his head and cursed under his breath. Then he turned back to the other man.

"The man, he'll never sign off on it."

The other man smiled. "Then there's no harm in presenting it, is there? Besides, if it is adopted, you want to have been on the winning side don't you? Handle this and you're covered both ways." He stood to leave.

The first man remained seated. "You can't ask me to argue for this! Christ, I'm Jewish."

"That's why Wild Bill wants you to present it. He figures it'll have more impact that way." He walked away, leaving the first man sitting forlornly on the bench in the park as the snow started again.

 za

Later that evening, in the living room of a senior cabinet official, Masquerade was again discussed.

"Sir, respectfully," an aide began, "at the least this is immoral and at the worst unconstitutional."

The official sighed. "War is immoral by definition. As for unconstitutional, staff counsel informs me that the action conforms to the guidelines set down in the National Security Act."

"Barely," the aide grunted. "And besides, this to me is no different than giving aid and comfort to the enemy."

The old man nodded. "On that, I agree with you. But let's get back to the point, and that is not whether or not the action is right, but rather, whether or not it is warranted."

The discussion raged into the early morning hours. The official mostly listened, content to let his aides argue out all the positions while he absorbed their best points. Finally, at well past three in the morning, he called an end to it. "We have two problems as I see it. First, the moral one. Can we do this abhorrent thing and still call ourselves defenders of truth and freedom around the world without being seen as the hypocrites we would be.

"Second, a political problem." He looked around the room sternly. "What I am about to say goes no further than this room." He paused. "The president is more ill than you have been led to believe. In fact, it is my belief that he will not live another six months."

The men in the room gasped at the revelation. The official waited a minute, then continued. "He is very weak, and has in fact sharply curtailed his work schedule. I think if we make this a knockdown drag out fight, he is likely to enact the blasted thing just to end the argument. Remember also that he and Donovan have become extraordinarily close."

"What do we do then?" his aide asked.

"I want a memo prepared for my review by nine this morning, setting out all the reasons that this," he picked up his copy of the draft, "Masquerade, not be enacted. I believe the president at this time is more susceptible to a strongly written argument than to an oral one. I'll send it over to the White House this afternoon."

He stood and walked out of the room. At the doorway, he turned back to his aides and smiled. "Fear not, gentlemen," he said reassuringly, "he'll never sign it."

Proposed Draft of Presidential Action
Project Masquerade

I

The consensus of the National Security Threat Analysis Board being that the immediate resettlement and granting of amnesties to officers and key personnel of Axis powers is required to maintain national security and whereas;

II

Under the authority granted me by the National Security Act of 1933, the president has the authority to commute unadjudicated indictments and whereas;

III

The Office of Strategic Services has advised me that several qualified individuals have petitioned this office for said services and actions, resolved

IV

I do hereby order the Immigration and Naturalization Service of the Department of Justice to grant permanent resident status to those individuals submitted to them under the terms of this order, and further;

V

I do hereby direct the Department of Justice to grant unrestricted immunity from prosecution to those individuals submitted to them under the terms of this order.

Presented for Presidential Action on December 28, 1944

❧

Official Washington slumbered through the cold nights of late December of 1944, but the man stayed up late reading the two reports.

Both arguments were compelling. Both had their flaws. The overriding consideration, to him, was which would end the war the fastest.

The Justice Department brief spoke of long term consequences, but the man who had sat in the White House for so long no longer cared about the long term. His doctors had already told him that he had no long term. And the O.S.S. brief had spoken directly to that point.

"Despite the possible future repercussions and benefits, it must also be considered that the immediate leap in quality and amount of intelligence we would receive in the short term would unquestionably help to shorten the war markedly."

The short term. That was what was most important. He must end this war now! As quickly as possible. He must see it end.

He made up his mind as the sleeping medications finally kicked in and sent him off to a troubled sleep.

The next morning, the word went out…Masquerade was go.

ح

It was morning in Washington, but late afternoon in German occupied Amsterdam. Konigsmann moved down the narrow roadway in the diamond district, dodging piles of rubble from bombed out buildings. Were anyone to observe him, he was only another civilian bent over against the cold wind, hurrying to reach a warm destination.

He clutched at the collar of his raincoat, picking his steps carefully. In normal times, there would be businessmen rushing around or gawking tourists, but these were not normal times. There were only a couple of older men, like himself using the sides of buildings for protection against the wind. "Just another civilian," he repeated, smiling to himself.

Franz had arrived three nights ago on Christmas Eve. Major Hoffmann had met him at the airport and hurried him to a billet that had been arranged in advance.

"The general asked me to meet you to facilitate any request you have. He'll be pleased to see you in the morning." The major had spoken almost by rote. Clearly, he was not a happy man. It was cold, it was Christmas Eve, and he had to spend it escorting some VIP from Berlin. The war was not going well and this visitor certainly did not bring good news.

Franz asked him to thank the general for his consideration. "I'll only be here a few days, some technical information I need to gather. I don't expect to be requiring much assistance. A map of the city might be helpful. I was thinking also," Franz smiled, "perhaps if there is time, I might pick up a little souvenir for my wife."

Hoffmann was feeling more relaxed. This colonel wasn't such a bad sort, he thought.

Franz added, as if in afterthought, "I'll need to see, among other things, the warehouse where the effects of internees are kept."

Hoffmann nodded. "I'll be glad to take you out there in the morning." Franz assured him he had no intention of keeping the major from his important duties. "Just leave word that I'll be coming by. I prefer to inspect these things alone."

The next morning, Christmas morning, Franz went to the warehouse where he identified himself and was shown inside. He dismissed the young soldier who escorted him. Then he looked around to get his bearings.

With typical German precision, everything had been stacked and labeled with care. There were hundreds upon hundreds of shirts, jackets, trousers, dresses on the shelves. Children's clothing was stacked in a separate section, shoes in another. In a locked cage, there were a multitude of bags, some unsealed with contents visible. These were filled with jewelry, watches, and, of course, thousands of gold fillings. It was obvious this last area had not been sorted, nor had the more valuable pieces been "liberated" as yet.

This was all that was left of thousands of suffering souls, many of them now dead, the rest waiting their turn. None of it affected Franz as he walked purposefully through the aisles. He was looking for specific items with no desire, interest, or time to dwell on their former owners.

Eventually, he found just the items he required, the raincoat, an old suit and shirt. He had to settle for his own Army boots, but that was just as well. As an Army man, he appreciated the importance of comfortable shoes.

He could have gone to the cutter in full uniform but he wanted no obvious connection between them, just in case the Gestapo was getting interested. In all his years in espionage, he had developed a reputation for being careful. Things were no different now.

Along the way, he had cautiously checked but he had not been followed. He had spent the intervening days, in full uniform, inspecting various facilities, and pretending to take copious notes. He also found a deserted building not far from the diamond district and had hidden the clothes there. Today, he judged the time had come to fulfill his real mission.

Facing the street, Franz leaned against the doorway, having confirmed this was the right building. When he was sure there was no one else on the street, he applied pressure and half fell inside the hallway. Brushing himself carefully and smoothing his hair back, he looked for and quickly found the only door with a light showing through a crack.

The man who answered his knock ushered him in quickly while glancing through the hall. When Franz and the cutter had identified themselves to mutual satisfaction, the cutter locked and bolted the door.

Franz looked the man over. He had been given a photograph and thorough description but the ravages of war had taken their toll. The man, van Eyck, was about forty-five years old but the thin grey hair, lined face, and stooped shrunken body on what was once a six foot frame belied this. The eyes, though, remained sharp and alive, and he stared back at Franz. The two men took the measure of each other.

"Your family is well." This was more a statement than a question from Franz.

Van Eyck nodded. "So I understand. You are here for your goods." Van Eyck wanted no pretense at social conversation. He felt only contempt—for the German occupiers, the Germans who obviously planned to use the stolen hoard for themselves, and contempt for himself for dealing with them. But there was no other way to safeguard his family. He kept reminding himself of this during all the long months of planning, and cutting the stones.

Van Eyck moved an old wooden cabinet from the wall and exposed the safe. There was no point in hiding anything. It would be over in a few moments, and he would not be returning here. If I'm still alive, he thought to himself. It doesn't matter. Willa and the children will be all right. He pulled out packet after packet of gems, and placed them on a small table close by.

Franz sat down at the table and watched the process. When it was finished, he pulled a long official looking envelope out of his pocket. He would open a packet, make a notation on the envelope and place the packet inside.

After a few moments of observation, van Eyck had to speak. "You aren't planning to transport the stones like that? There are considerably more than a hundred packets."

"I'm quite aware of that, Herr van Eyck," Franz continued his stuffing and marking, "three hundred and one diamonds. I'm checking it all. From what I've seen so far, you've done an admirable job."

Van Eyck sighed, "There are three hundred fifty-six. You'll note I put the weight and grading on each packet, as well as the number of stones."

"Yes, I noticed," Franz paused, "three hundred fifty-six?"

"I was commissioned to cut the stones to the best advantage. I did it. Sometimes, a rough, to be handled properly, has to be cut into two finished diamonds, sometimes three. Anyway, it's all there. And be careful. I do not want repercussions from your superiors when delivery is made." After that brave speech, van Eyck turned his back and retired to the other side of the room, fully expecting a bullet in the back.

Franz stared at Van Eyck's back, and then broke out laughing. "You're a funny bastard, van Eyck. You hate our guts, but your professionalism forces you to tell me to take care of the parcel. And then you turn away. No, I'm not going to kill you. That's not my job. You'll fend for yourself," Franz stood up, stuffing the envelope into his jacket, and the remainder of the packets into various pockets, "and probably come out of this war better than most of us."

At the door, Franz turned serious. "Van Eyck," he called sharply to the man's back, "you never saw me, heard of me, of the stones, or anyone or anything else connected with this enterprise. Not if you want to live to see your family again."

Franz left the room, stopped at the exit of the building. He checked that he, his pockets, his clothes looked right. Then, pulling up his collar around him, he stepped out into the cold, now rainy night.

ﺯ

Van Eyck waited a full ten minutes before acting. He pulled the dresser across the door frame and pulled up the carpet from where it had once stood.

Glancing at the heavily covered front window, he pushed and pulled on the floor boards until the one he had loosened once before came away in his hand. He reached into the space and pulled out a small notebook bound by thick elastic bands.

He knew he had to work quickly now. He opened the book and began writing feverishly. He wrote from the heart and he wrote from memory. Using the stub of a pencil, he put down all he knew of the strange Germans, of the deal that had been struck, and of the secret that he had hidden in front of their faces.

He rewrapped the notebook and redeposited it in the floor. After pounding the floorboard back into place, he reset the dresser. He smoothed the carpet, and checked for telltale signs that they had been moved. Satisfied, he turned to his last task.

Forty minutes later, the knock on the door that he was expecting came, followed almost immediately by the splintering of wood as the storm trooper's boot kicked in the door.

Van Eyck smiled as he saw the Gestapo thugs. He smiled because he knew that although he was about to die, sometime, somewhere, he would return and lash out at his murderers; he had had time to ensure that.

"Fire!"

The troops, robots that they were, responded immediately and almost cut van Eyck in half. After ten seconds, it was all over and the troops were ordered out. As they left, their leader nodded to the man who had been waiting in the hall, Franz Konigsmann in uniform.

For twenty minutes, he searched the room, finding nothing, finally ordering a Gestapo safe cracker in to open the safe. It was almost empty but the Gestapo man took what few stones were there. Konigsmann didn't care. There had been no documents in the safe, nothing to tie anyone to anything. Happily, he turned to leave.

He stopped at the door. Something was wrong. After a minute, he realized what it was. Van Eyck had died smiling. Smiling! Why? He was forced to leave without the answer by the cold Gestapo hoods on a blood high.

&

It was an hour before his plane was scheduled to leave, and he was taking a chance, but the smile continued to gnaw at Konigsmann. He returned to the house and slipped in unseen.

He wasted no time and began to tear the place apart. As his time to leave came perilously close, he found the floorboard and wrenched it free.

Congratulating himself for listening to his instincts, he threw the contents into his briefcase and raced for the airfield. Only just catching the transport, he settled in, opened the book and began to read.

It was a diary of sorts, and it did in fact contain names, dates, and incriminating evidence. But it was the final entry that chilled him to the bone.

ፉ

From the diary of Abraham van Eyck
December 28, 1944
To My Murderer,
        I made my pact with the devil, yourself, in order to save my family. It worked and they are now far beyond your reach. I never expected to see them again and told them as much when we parted.
        What you hold in your hand is my journal and I give it to you willingly, that is if you are clever enough to find it. I do this so you know exactly what I know. I do this so that you know that I hold death's grip on your throat. I do this because you have found my journal, not my testament! That, you will never find, until one day, you will find it used against you to bring you to justice!
        And so my murderer, think well and long on this. One day, some time, somewhere, I will be avenged!
Abraham van Eyck

ፉ

Konigsmann closed the diary slowly. His mind was working feverishly. It must be a bluff. It must be! he thought. But still the last words stayed with him.

He slept fitfully throughout the trip. The flight was smoother than the last one, thanks in large part to the inclement weather which had grounded the Allied aircraft, and which would have grounded this transport had it not had such a high priority.

Operation Greif (the Battle of the Bulge) was falling apart. Field Marshall Model's brilliant thrust into Allied lines was stalled, and, as of the last report that Konigsmann had seen, the tank divisions had been unable to take the critical crossroads of Bastogne in the southern Ardennes. If Bastogne was not taken, there would be virtually nothing left between the Allies and the Rhine. So weather or no weather, the transports flew for the Luftwaffe on that New Year's Eve.

With the diary safely stored in his satchel along with the diamonds, Konigsmann began to mentally compose his report to Albrecht. He would include the details of his phony inspection trip to show his scrupulousness on matters of maintaining cover and he would exclude the discovery of van Eyck's diary. Who knows? he thought to himself, those pages, with certain deletions, could potentially be worth more than my share of the diamonds. The plane went into a combat glide and shortly landed.

Franz was immediately alert. It was too soon for them to be in Berlin. Far too soon. He asked an orderly where they were but was brusquely put off. All the passengers nervously shifted in their seats, and then silenced as the black-shirted Gestapo men were seen surrounding the plane.

The tension built as Franz watched through his window. They were clearly waiting for something to happen. He could see the pilot of the transport on the ground arguing with the Gestapo commander. Then the convoy arrived.

A truck belonging to the *Fallschirmtruppen* pulled up and the elite of the elite of the paratroopers, the *truppenheit* piled off, slowly, gingerly. The Gestapo man seemed to be trying to stop the men from going towards the plane. The men could now be seen to be wounded and in great need of medical treatment, but still the Gestapo delayed.

In all his time in America, Franz had survived by his uncanny ability to sense a threat and to react boldly to it, many times surviving on the sheer power of bluster and bravado. From what he could see of the situation here, the rest of his flight was in danger, so he acted. He rose and walked off the plane.

The morning was chilled and in the distance to the east a sliver of deep orange light could just be seen. It was going to be a clear dawn, and soon. A beautiful morning without a cloud in the sky, only Allied fighters. He estimated that he had to get the plane moving in the next ten minutes or risk flying into almost certain death.

For a moment he considered taking ground transport, but he could hear artillery in the distance and reasoned that it was equally dangerous. He walked up to the Gestapo officer in charge.

"Where are we and why have we been delayed?" he demanded in his most official voice.

The officer whirled on him, but caught the emblem of the Headquarters Staff on Konigsmann's collar and stopped the epithet that he had been forming.

"Herr Colonel," he began, "you are in Onnasbruck, and we are confiscating this aircraft." He was polite, but barely so.

"Sir," the pilot interrupted, "we were ordered down to pick up these wounded men. They need emergency treatment in Berlin." He seemed to be pleading.

Konigsmann didn't have time for territorial debates. For him the choice was simple, a ride back with the Gestapo or a ride with the wounded. He acted brazenly.

He gestured for the Gestapo officer to walk with him. When they were out of earshot of the others, he turned to him and spoke in quiet, menacing tones.

"Captain, I am Colonel Franz Konigsmann of the *Fuhrer's* personal staff, and upon my return to Berlin I will be reporting directly to him. My report will be simple and concise. Either I will tell him how you and your men bravely gave up your seats on this transport for the greater good of these brave wounded men or," he paused a long time. "Or I will tell him how you left these children of our country to die on a dirty airfield while you and your men saved your asses." He raised his eyebrows. "Which report do you think will be better received?"

The captain carefully studied Konigsmann for a full minute before acting. Then he turned to his men. "Load the wounded aboard the transport. Hurry!" he shouted.

In five minutes, all the wounded were loaded and the plane took off again. The captain stood by a field phone and watched it go, as he waited for his Berlin call to go through.

As the sun came up, the transport dropped to near tree top level and began the violent evasive maneuvers that Franz had become accustomed to. He sat in his seat, now next to a wounded corporal and waited for a safe landing. To pass the time, and much to the surprise of the young corporal, he struck up a conversation.

They talked for about half an hour, about the battles they had been in (although Franz had been in no battles since the First World War) about Germany before the war, and when Germany would finally snatch victory away from the onrushing Allies. As they neared Berlin, Franz smiled at the younger man.

"I hope all goes well with you, young Bertlesein. If you ever need anything, feel free to call on me."

Bertlesein was thrilled. "Thank you, sir." He paused. "Sir, before the war, my father took me to see you race at the Nurburgriing." Franz smiled, recalling his younger days of road and track racing. "Sir, you have always been an idol of mine and now I've met you, and you've saved my life from those..." He couldn't curse the Gestapo, not in front of an officer.

Franz nodded. He smiled broadly and patted the young man's hand as they landed. "You've made an otherwise boring flight most enjoyable. Thank you, corporal." The boy beamed.

As the plane taxied to a stop, Franz rose to leave. Bertlesein reached out, touched him on the arm, causing him to turn back. "I would do anything for you, sir," the young man said. Franz smiled, a look that froze on his face as he saw four black uniformed Gestapo men come up the aisle towards him.

"Colonel Pieter Franz Konigsmann?!"

Franz casually put the satchel behind his back as they approached. As they grabbed him, he felt a gentle tug from behind, and out of the corner of his eye saw Bertlesein hide the satchel underneath his blanket. He wasn't sure but he thought he saw the young man smile slightly and nod as the Gestapo men forced Franz from the plane.

Franz silently prayed that he understood the nod. If not, then he would soon be dead.

&

Albrecht remained close but to one side of Adolf Hitler as the *Fuhrer* strode through the military hospital ward. A staff photographer and an older captain carrying a tray of medals followed behind. From time to time, the *Fuhrer* selected a medal for one of the patients. Frequently these days, Hitler felt the need to get out, to be among the fighting men, if not in the fighting zones. This was the third ward they had visited today.

The routine was simple enough. Albrecht would look at the soldier's chart, whisper something about the young man's achievements to Hitler, who would paternally pat the young man and present a medal. Much of the time, when Hitler was in this restless mood, it was best to make each soldier seem a glorious hero, giving of himself for his *Fuhrer*. Albrecht had long ago learned that this seemed to calm the Supreme Commander considerably.

Hitler had just presented a medal to a young corporal named Bertlesein who had arrived at the hospital that very day. The party started to move on, but stopped when Hitler paused at another bed to talk to the doctor. The corporal sat up and tugged at Albrecht as he passed.

Surprised, Albrecht turned back to the young man. Bertlesein raised himself up and whispered "please forgive my forwardness, General Albrecht, but I thought perhaps you could tell me, Colonel Konigsmann, is he all right?" Albrecht became alert instantly. He noted that Hitler was engaged in animated conversation with the Doctor.

"You know Colonel Konigsmann?" Albrecht moved closer to Bertlesein and spoke just as softly.

"Yes sir. That is, I met him on the plane to Berlin last night. He was very kind to me. It was so kind of him to talk with me, take my mind off the pain."

Albrecht relaxed and thought, so, Franz is back. Good. I'll have to talk to him as soon as I can get away from here.

The young man was still mumbling. "I was concerned when the S.D. took him off the plane. Is everything all right?"

Albrecht blanched. "The Gestapo? Oh yes, yes. He's fine. Just routine." Albrecht could hardly wait to get out of there.

The rest of the day went by in nightmarishly slow motion. There was no chance to check with the other conspirators. At last, it was over and Albrecht went home.

He approached his house with caution. Would the Gestapo be waiting for him? His heart began to pound as he recognized the car and driver waiting in his driveway. It was Gerhard Minscel's. Was the man out of his mind? He'd had a nervous breakdown at one time.

Forcing himself to enter his house, Albrecht was greeted by the family dog, followed by his wife Gerda, who didn't look upset. So far, so good. "We have company, dear. Gerhard Minscel dropped by. Shall I ask him to dinner?"

Albrecht swallowed hard. "I don't think so. He won't be staying long. Just hold dinner a while." He walked into the living room where Gerhard was pacing back and forth. "Well, Gerhard," Albrecht tried to sound jovial, "What brings you here? I was just going to call you."

"Then you've heard?" Gerhard was shaking and looked pale. "About Konigsmann?"

Albrecht nodded and closed the doors to the living room. "Sit down, Gerhard, before you fall down. Do you want a drink?" Albrecht tried to inject a normalcy into his voice that he didn't really feel.

Minscel shook his head but sat down. "One of my men was at the airport this morning. We had heard the Gestapo was going to make a presence there." He stopped.

"Yes?" Albrecht tried to keep the impatience out of his voice.

"My man saw the Gestapo board a plane that just brought in some wounded. They took Franz Konigsmann into custody. What are we going to do, Karl?" He half rose in his chair but Albrecht motioned him back.

"That's all I've heard too, but surely, in your office, you were able to get more information."

"Karl, I had to be careful. You know how they are." Minscel's words began to pour out. "They say they're detaining him to look into an incident in Onnasbruck. For God's sake, that's near the Dutch border. What if they found the diamonds? He could give us all up. What if they know about Crystal Movement? Maybe they've known all along and were waiting. I wouldn't put it past them. Karl, what if…"

"Hold on, man! Get a grip! Franz is a man who can be trusted." Albrecht wished he could be as sure as he sounded. "He's been in pressure situations many times over the years. If they had found the diamonds, if Franz had said anything, do you think we'd be sitting here talking? Come on, now. Think."

Gerhard tried to calm down. "What should we do? Maybe he hasn't said anything yet but you know…after awhile…the longer they have him, well, what should we do?"

"I agree. We should start making serious plans, while there's still time. Find out exactly what they're talking about. In the meantime, my office will be properly indignant over their holding an assistant to the *Stellvertretander Chef des Fuhrungstabes des Oberkommandos der Wehrmacht* during a crucial point in Operation Greif. If he has done something stupid or dangerous, it is still natural for me to make inquiries if I'm guiltless."

"They're going to arrest us. We're going to be executed. I know!" Gerhard's panic had risen again at the word "dangerous."

"Stop it. It won't be Franz who gives us up. It'll be your panic." Albrecht felt everything slipping away. It was a feeling he'd had several times since the beginning of the project. Each time, though, he'd made it through. "Now go about business as usual. You get hold of Rubschlager. I'll contact Reineke and Streck. It's time to make a move. And let me know about that 'incident' as quickly as possible."

Albrecht stood up, as did Minscel. They walked together to the door, Albrecht patting Minscel on the shoulder. When the door closed on Minscel, Albrecht took a deep breath and thought, In every chain, there is a weak link. Well, we knew it when we brought him in. Let's hope he doesn't bring us down.

୬

He had lost all track of time and space. It might as easily have been a week, or a month since he was arrested. He remained in a windowless basement cell with a bare light bulb hanging by a single cord just beyond his reach.

There was no furniture in the cell. He lay naked upon the cold cement, shivering, and tightly clutching the thin, wool blanket around him.

All around him were the signs of the previous occupants. A brownish red stain in one corner, the name "Kleist" scratched in the cement next to the door, the frayed ends of this obviously overused blanket.

They hadn't tried the "heavy hand" yet. He was of too high a profile, too well known by too many powerful people to start in with the goon tactics, but it would come, with time. He steeled himself for it as he heard the lock in his door turning.

Two huge S.D. guards came in and dragged him to his feet. They pulled him from his cell and led him down the narrow, dimly lit hall to the interrogation room.

He was forced to remain standing with his feet placed exactly on the painted outline of two bare feet. If they strayed, even a little, he would be punched under his armpit, violently flinging him back across the wall. Then he would be forced back on the painted spots.

He stood silently, staring straight ahead, for over forty-five minutes. Internally, in his mind's eye, he smiled. These animals had no idea what they were dealing with. He had been trained long ago, by the Abewehr, how to resist these and many other techniques for breaking a man down. In America, he had always been aware that he could be picked up for questioning at any time, so he had practiced resistance often. They would not break him. At least, not yet.

The door opened and in came his chief interrogator, a man he was ordered to refer to only as Herr Buchsenmacher, (Mr. Gunsmith literally, or more precisely, the man who tempers steel) the usual name for AMT III Gestapo interrogators.

"Good day, traitor."

"Good day, Herr Buchsenmacher."

"Are you prepared to answer my questions?"

The prisoner smiled. He knew this would irritate his interrogator but he gambled that he was still off the "Hard List." "Always, sir."

"What were you doing in Onnasbruck? What were your orders?"

"I had no orders. The plane landed, I was aboard the plane, I landed with it." He was hit in his kidneys by a guard behind him.

"Why did you interfere with Captain Leiger?"

"The man is a pig." Again hit from behind, this time by both guards.

"Captain Leiger was engaged in a confidential mission for the Fatherland. Why did you interfere?"

He braced himself for the blows he expected. "Leiger is a coward who placed himself above the safety of wounded combat troops."

"LIAR!!" The prisoner was hit in the stomach with a club like blow from one of the guards and then under the armpit when his feet came off of their spots.

He waited for other blows, but surprisingly they never came. Gradually, he became aware that everyone in the room was looking at the door. He turned to look.

Standing in the doorway was one of the most feared men in Germany, SS Gruppenfuhrer Otto Ohlendorf, Commander of Amt III Internal S.D., the organization responsible for the spying and internal security within the German nation itself. He had *carte blanche* to do whatever he wished; from painting van windows with pictures of happy smiling people so that passersby couldn't see the women and children being gassed inside, to ordering whole city blocks emptied of their residents and all shipped to the death camps. He embodied death.

"Leave us," he said in his usual quite high pitched voice. The guards immediately turned to leave followed quickly by the interrogator.

Ohlendorf walked in front of the prisoner. "So, I don't believe we were ever formally introduced but I have seen you many times, of course." He bowed his head mockingly. "You are an illustrious man, Colonel Konigsmann."

Franz kept silent. Many people who disappeared and were never seen again had seen this round, unthreatening face just before.

"You are quiet today." He smiled. "We will change that." He stamped on the floor twice with his exquisitely polished boots. The interrogator and guards returned.

Ohlendorf sat down in a chair in front of Konigsmann. "Now, my café society friend," he paused and took a long drink of water. "What is Crystal Movement and who is involved?"

It went on for hours. Questions followed by a blow or two followed by the same question. Monotonous, but telling. Slowly, Franz' resistance was being worn away. Now, Ohlendorf was ready to escalate the "procedure."

"You're a strong man, Colonel, but in the end, even the strongest break. I'm sure you agree." Konigsmann just looked at him. Ohlendorf shrugged and turned to the guards. "The next time he refuses to answer, begin working his head, but don't kill him." He turned back to Konigsmann. "We have a long journey ahead."

He returned to his seat, crossed his legs and began again. "You should not have ordered my men around as if they were OKW sheep, Colonel. It is insulting, and if you insult them, you insult me. Now," he smiled that same insipid smile. "What is Crystal Movement and who is involved?"

Before Franz could answer, the door was burst open. A squad of S.A. guards stormed in and pointed their weapons at Ohlendorf and his men. Ohlendorf jumped to his feet. "Who are you? What do you want?" he demanded.

The S.A. men said nothing but the answer was quick in coming. At a leisurely pace, Reichsminister of the Interior and Head of the Gestapo, Heinrich Himmler strolled in.

"Hello, Otto." Ohlendorf snapped a salute, as did his men, but Himmler ignored it and walked deeper into the room, between Ohlendorf and Franz. He raised his riding crop to his forehead to acknowledge the salutes. "You are so predictable, Otto."

Ohlendorf remained at attention as Himmler walked to within inches of him. "This time," Himmler said quietly, "you may have gone too far." Over his shoulder, he ordered his guards to take Konigsmann to the dispensary.

When Konigsmann had been taken from the room, Himmler turned his full fury on Ohlendorf.

"You fool! You excrement! Do you know what you have done? Do you have the vaguest notion?" He didn't wait for an answer. "That man is perhaps the closest man on this earth to the *Fuhrer*! The *Fuhrer* thinks of him as almost a family member! And you arrest him for saving the lives of soldiers that the *Fuhrer* himself decorates!" The riding crop came down viciously into the smaller man's face. "I should let you fry for this!"

Ohlendorf struggled to his feet. "But Herr Reichsminister..."

Himmler spun away from him. He picked up the chair and threw it at Ohlendorf who barely got out of the way. "Recite, my dear Gruppenfuhrer, the first rule of security measures as written by the *Fuhrer* himself!"

Ohlendorf forced himself to attention. "Security Order Number One! No one must have any knowledge of secret affairs which are outside his own province."

Himmler nodded. "When I came in, you were asking him about an ongoing OKW operation that has nothing whatsoever to do with your area. General Albrecht himself has so assured me!"

He walked back to Ohlendorf. "Consider yourself lucky that

Konigsmann's superior chose to intervene with me and not with the *Fuhrer*. Contemplate your fate tonight, and come to my office in the Chancellery in the morning to learn it." He turned and left the room.

Ohlendorf started to relax when he suddenly realized that Himmler's guards had remained behind.

The captain in charge of the detachment turned to him.

"Herr Gruppenfuhrer, the Reichsminister thought you should remain here, on the marks, until you see him in the morning. My detachment was ordered to facilitate this for you."

Ohlendorf looked at the emotionless men, dropped his head and carefully removed his shoes and placed his feet over the painted footprints.

ða

The lot of an enlisted soldier in the German Army is not a good one, particularly when you've been wounded. You lie in an over-crowded hospital ward, with people dying all around you, and you pray that the doctors don't forget you and that Allied planes don't mistake the place for a target.

So Bertlesein was shocked when, after about four days, the doctors prepared him for transfer with a flourish. A special nurse was assigned to him, and after several hours of special attention, he was placed in an ambulance along with his belongings for a three hour ride to the famous "Hospital Six," the luxury hospital of the OKW.

Here he was taken up to an equally crowded but better attended ward, with partitions alongside his bed, giving him the semblance of privacy. He asked questions but was told only that the orders came from "on high."

He had been there for an hour when Konigsmann appeared around the partitions, smiling but walking very stiffly.

"I always remember an act of friendship, Corporal Bertlesein." An hour later, he left with his satchel under his arm, and a decision in his heart.

CHAPTER NINE

FLIGHT

Extract From: Declaration of Status

Date:	9 January 1945	No. 013–4694 ZFLK	
Name:	Kurt Reineke	Service No. K 349	
Rank:	Field Marshall	Date of Rank:	23 January 44

Status

8 January 1945 left Berlin by car for Zone 8 Aerodrome. Reported overdue at 1930. Bridge en route destroyed by Allied bombing raid 1345. Personal investigation leads to conclusion Field Marshall Reineke caught in attack. Clear car crashed into river.

Albrecht
Investigating Officer
Approved
File
Status: **Missing Presumed Killed**
Authorized: **Albrecht for Jodl**

❧

Albrecht stepped off the elevator into OKW Headquarters in the subbasement of the Chancellery. He was greeted by the cacophonous sights and sounds of the situation room. Through the mass of people, he spotted Konigsmann and motioned him to one of the glassed in offices along the wall.

"Anything?" Albrecht asked his aide.

"Nothing so far, sir." Konigsmann was thinner, but already recovering from his brief captivity.

Albrecht was nervous. This phase of Crystal Movement was by far the riskiest to date.

It had been decided by the conspirators to make contact with the Allies. The plan was to obtain an amnesty against a post war prosecution in exchange for information, special intelligence information on the Russians. Albrecht knew of the English and American mistrust of the Russians and hoped to prey on it. If all went as planned, all five conspirators would be out of harm's way long before the war was over.

They would be free, with new names, new papers and all the time they needed to convert the diamonds to cash and divide the spoils, so they had been assured. Albrecht's mind drifted back to the meeting that had set this dangerous path.

They had met at an intelligence post outside Eberswalde. Albrecht, Reineke, Minscel, and the Count. Streck and Rubschlager had been unable to attend due to battlefield difficulties.

The Count was Count Friederich Egon Hermann von Hostetter. Officially, he held no position in the German government, but since the early thirties, he had served as an unofficial conduit for secret communications between the Americans and the Germans. He held a Liechtenstein passport so he was able to travel freely across all borders. More importantly, for years he had been a close, personal friend of the head of the O.S.S. Station in Bern, Switzerland.

Apolitical, and loyal only to his class, it was logical that the Crystal Movement conspirators turned to him to open up negotiations. He asked no questions, the large diamond he was offered as payment was explanation enough. He had taken on the job of making introductions and now he was back to report.

The underground bunker in which he found himself had none of the amenities which the Count considered essential to life, but he'd make the best of it. There were always inconveniences in arranging negotiations. He'd keep it short and simple. Naturally, he sat in the one comfortable chair, and waited for a moment as the others settled themselves, leaning against crates, etc.

Finally, adjusting his cigarette in the monogrammed gold holder, the Count began. "Gentlemen, as requested, I have discussed your situation with *mein parteifreund.* The O.S.S. is definitely interested. However, Mr. Dulles has emphasized repeatedly the importance of dealing with someone of…substance. He will only negotiate with someone of senior rank, not associated with the party's inner circle, someone of unquestioned integrity."

Albrecht shifted uneasily. "What else?"

The Count smiled and exhaled a bluish cloud of Turkish tobacco smoke. "Your emissary must clearly define what Crystal Movement has to offer. He must be in a position to represent all the members of the group and make decisions on their behalf. The O.S.S., and Mr. Dulles in particular, is not of a mind to play games. If you agree, choose someone now and I will delineate next steps." He sat back, closed his eyes and puffed his cigarette.

Albrecht, Reineke, and Minscel huddled at the opposite end of the small room. Reineke took charge.

"There is no time to contact Bernhard or Hugo. We must act for them. And immediately."

Albrecht agreed. "I have no desire to become a guest of the Russians." They all nodded. "It must be you, Kurt. You are the senior man here, and your credentials are impeccable."

Minscel nodded. "Your honor is unquestioned. It has to be you."

Kurt thought for a moment. It would mean desertion under fire. The career officer in him rebelled at the thought but the sense of urgency was strong. "All right. I will go. But you must assure me that you will look after my wife. You must get her out before the end!"

Silently, Albrecht and Minscel nodded.

Reineke turned back to the Count. "I am ready."

&

Konigsmann snapped Albrecht out of his reverie. "Sir!"

Albrecht looked up and saw Keitel entering the operations area with a small squad of enlisted men. They watched as Keitel instructed them on their duties of dusting the rafters and ceiling to try and get rid of the dust that fell and choked the men working in the room every time a bomb fell nearby. Keitel referred to the falling dust as "Allied Rain" and it was becoming more consuming to him than the running of the war.

"Has he," Albrecht indicated the screaming Field Marshall, "seen the report?" Franz nodded. "And?"

"He has accepted it fully." Konigsmann said. "I believe he was actually pleased at the thought of General Reineke's," he paused and smiled, "death."

"You smile too much, Franz. If our deception is discovered, no one will be able to free us from the ministrations of Ohlendorf!"

Franz turned serious at the memory. "Sir, I personally made the General's arrangements. He should arrive at the frontier any time now."

"But still no signal from him?"

"No."

Keitel waved for Albrecht to join him. Karl nodded and as he left the office, he softly called over his shoulder.

"Pray."

ᨠ

The "late" General Reineke felt oddly uncomfortable in his civilian clothes. He kept his head down as he mixed with the crawl of refugees on the road towards the Swiss frontier.

Things had gone wrong almost from the start. He had left Berlin HQ routinely enough and found the car and change of clothes exactly where Konigsmann had said they would be. He changed and set out for the border.

Things had been routine enough at the beginning. He had made the journey to Augsburg without incident. His papers and priority passes got him past all inquiries. In Augsburg, he found the house that had once belonged to Rubschlager and spent the night there. It was the next morning that disaster struck.

During the night, an Allied bombing raid had destroyed the bridge across the Wertach. It was impassable and under irregular but continuing attacks. Kurt was faced with a decision.

If he waited, perhaps a day or two, the bridge might be repaired.

But he was not so sure of Konigsmann's and Albrecht's skills in faking his death so he decided to keep moving south along the riverbank and seek another place to cross. Near Buchloe, he found it. An old stone bridge, possibly dating back to Charles the Great, was miraculously still intact.

As he pulled across it, he started to relax, he would make up for his lost time now. Then the second disaster hit.

The ground on the far side of the bridge was flooded by a broken water main and Reineke's car quickly became mired in the mud. Afraid to call for help, he removed the number plates and set off on foot. Soon he was deep within the crowds that all headed south, all seeking escape to Switzerland.

The going was slow and tortuous, but the old paratrooper trudged on resolutely. Three days later he stood on the northern shore of the Bodensee (Lake of Constance) and stared across at Switzerland.

No ferries were running and the lake was heavily patrolled by German E-Boats, but this he was prepared for. Intelligence reports indicated that several people were doing a bullish business in smuggling. In Friedrichshafen, he found the man he was looking for.

They walked together out to the small hidden harbor.

"You have my fare?" the smuggler asked. Reineke nodded and took off his belt and handed it to the man. The smuggler quickly located the hidden compartment and counted the gold Deutschmarks. He gestured towards a clump of trees. "My boat is there. It's dangerous for us to go together. You go ahead and I'll follow at a distance." Reineke was nervous but had no choice. He started for the trees.

Twice, he looked back. Both times, he was assured at the sight of the smuggler following. He reached the trees and looked around for the boat. It was off to his left, about twenty meters. He turned towards it.

He never saw the young man emerge from the brush and sneak towards him. He never felt the knife strike through his greatcoat and sever his spine. He just stiffened and died, falling face first into the water.

The smuggler walked up to the young man. "Search him, strip

him, and dump him on the Swiss side of the lake." He laughed. "After all, he paid for the trip."

ॐ

It had been almost a week and still no word from General Reineke. The elaborate message relay system that the conspirators had set up when Reineke left yielded nothing. The remaining members of Crystal Movement were panicking and looking to Albrecht as the leader.

Negotiating the now heavily traveled stairway to the subbasement, Minscel grumbled to Rubschlager "I don't see why we can't take the elevator. This is ridiculous."

"I'm told it's totally unreliable now." Rubschlager replied. "What I don't like is meeting downstairs rather than in Albrecht's regular office. I don't mind all the stairs but there's no privacy."

A voice from behind startled them. "Because I prefer living with no privacy than not living at all." Albrecht, coming from the upper floors, had caught up with the two generals. "The bombers are getting much too close for comfort these days. There's a little more protection below."

The dire thoughts implicit in that comment caused them all to finish the downward climb in silence.

Streck and Konigsmann were waiting just inside the entrance to the large room. Dodging broken glass and enlisted men sweeping up, Albrecht led the way to a cubicle in a corner. "Well, Franz, do you have anything new for us?"

Konigsmann frowned. "I checked again just before coming down. There's nothing. We know he made it to your home in Augsburg," he nodded to Rubschlager, "but nothing since then."

Albrecht shook his head. "We should have heard something. Even if he was unable to get across, or was in trouble, there were contingency plans. We'd have received some word, some sign. I don't like this silence."

Streck had just come from the fighting, and there was something about him that made the others uneasy. He spoke softly and slowly. "I fear we may have another casualty to add to the list. Kurt is not young, but he is exceedingly able and resourceful. If there is no word from him, he has either been taken by the Gestapo or…"

His voice trailed off. "Since we are all still here, breathing, and we have no notice of his having been taken," he looked at each man and each shook his head in turn, "we must conclude the worst." He sighed, sadly, and seemed to withdraw within himself.

Minscel pushed forward. "We all have profound respect for the general, and he may yet come through. Of course, we all hope so, but we can't wait around. Karl, you are next senior."

"I'm not rushing off blindly," Albrecht protested. "I agree we can't wait but we need to plan carefully."

"I know I'm the last to join the group," Rubschlager interjected, "and certainly Karl has always planned well. But now, I need to ask some questions."

Albrecht was affronted. "There's no way we could know what's happening. You think you could do better?"

Konigsmann, who had stood by quietly, stepped forward. Smiling and speaking soothingly, he addressed himself to the group. "Gentlemen, I am as aware as any of you of the growing danger. But snapping at each other like a pack of wolves? We are, after all, officers and gentlemen. Let's deal with everyone's questions and make a decision based on fact not speculation." He paused and they nodded. "There is no blame here. Just arrangements to be made. A course correction, as it were."

"I don't intend to sound critical," Rubschlager began. "I just don't understand. Our message system is not invulnerable. Perhaps he did get through and we have yet to hear. Also, what about the diamonds? Why weren't they sent to safety? After so much waiting around, why the rush now?"

Minscel stared at Rubschlager. "You amaze me, Hugo. We all know it's only a matter of time before the war's over. And none of us are likely to be treated as heroes by the Russians, or any of the others for that matter."

Albrecht added. "It's not exactly a rush, but Gerhard is right. It can't be too much longer unless we pull a miracle."

Streck roused himself. "I'm afraid we've used up our quota."

Albrecht continued. "If Kurt did get through, no harm will be done in sending someone else along. Franz and I have checked with Hamburg and all our other relays. Everything is intact. As for the diamonds, we didn't send them because we felt the negotiations would begin quickly and we could all follow with the stones."

Rubschlager nodded. "And now?"

"Now," Albrecht said, "we need to make adjustments in our plans. Someone has to negotiate with the O.S.S. And just in case we don't get out in time, the diamonds must also get to Switzerland. At least, we'll know we have them waiting for us when we finally do get out of our...difficulties."

Minscel put his hand on Albrecht's shoulder. "You must go, and take the stones along. You'll get through and we'll join you as soon as we get the signal."

Albrecht shook off his hand. "No, Gerhard. Kurt's disappearing and then me? It would send out danger signals to the Gestapo. Besides," he grinned, "I hardly think Mr. Dulles would talk to me, no matter what I offered."

Konigsmann had been listening carefully and weighing the possibilities in his mind throughout. This looked like just the opening he'd been hoping for, and he took the step. "You are all far too important to take chances. I may not be senior here, but I do have certain advantages. During my time as the *Fuhrer's* envoy, I came to know a number of world leaders on a personal level. That, and the fact that I have taken tea with the American president. Well, all of that should help my credentials."

Albrecht, who knew the most about Konigsmann, agreed immediately. Also it would let him personally off a dangerous hook. The others took their lead from him and agreed.

Except Streck. "Karl, they made it clear it had to be a senior officer. And anyway, we cannot ask the colonel to take such risks."

"I have spent many years playing this game," Konigsmann said. "Risks are not new to me. After all, I've been carrying the diamonds safely past the Gestapo all this time. Besides, I'm already at risk here."

Streck objected. "I'm afraid it's all falling apart, just like the war."

"Don't be so pessimistic, Bernhard." Albrecht made an attempt at his old joviality. "We'll pull it off. Franz is the answer. We should have thought of that earlier. Be positive. We will work things out."

Agreement was finally reached to everyone's satisfaction. Albrecht did not have to expose himself to further danger, nor did Minscel and Rubschlager who didn't care so long as someone moved things along.

Streck was unable to shake off the feeling of impending doom but could think of no alternative and so tried to hope for the best. The group dispersed, for the most part thinking of better times to come.

Albrecht and Konigsmann stayed behind to go into details of the mission. Albrecht instructed Konigsmann as the count had done with Reineke previously. Most of it dealt with making contact once across the border. Konigsmann preferred to make his own arrangements to that point, and suggested that no "death cover story" be concocted. He was simply going on another confidential mission.

They parted with wishes for good luck on both sides. Konigsmann would leave from home as quickly as possible. His wife and children were accustomed to his leaving on secret diplomatic business. No explanations would be needed. Albrecht suggested that he might look in on Frau Konigsmann and family. Konigsmann shrugged. He exuded a confidence, and especially an arrogance he had not shown in the group. Albrecht had no doubt this one would get through.

❧

Analysis and action.

Franz had lived his life by that creed and now more than ever he was relying on it. Analysis and action. Something had gone horribly wrong with Reineke's escape and that something must be avoided by Franz at all costs.

He spent the night reviewing. The plan had been based on stealth, timing, and secrecy. Reineke was a capable man, the timing had been letter perfect and, as far as Franz could tell, secrecy had been maintained. What then had gone wrong?

Finally, just before dawn, he put away the file and smiled broadly. The answer had sprung whole from his hours of study. If the plan had not succeeded, the answer was not in its refinement but in its abandonment.

Analysis completed, time for action. He left his wife and children sleeping soundly in their beds. They were used to his disappearing for days on end without explanation. His driver opened the car door for him and they were gone.

"Good morning, sir."

"Good morning, Richter. The airfield at Nauen, please."

They drove for about an hour. All the while, Franz kept busy working on routine paperwork just as he did every morning. It was important that all seem as it always was. Just after seven, they were cleared through the gates of the airfield.

Franz dismissed his car and driver with a wave. It was all routine. He often left on secret trips and his driver would be informed when and where to pick him up. Routine.

In the operations office, Franz casually approached the duty officer who snapped to attention. Franz returned his salute and motioned for the young man to relax.

"I need a flight to Schwenningen," he began, "priority routing from the Fuhrungstaabs." He waited while the young man checked the outgoing flight logs. He smiled as the boy began to sweat.

"I am checking, sir." Franz smiled. He knew that there would be no flight, the airfield at Schwenningen had been heavily damaged the night before. Finally, the young officer looked up and sheepishly came over.

"My apologies, Herr Colonel, but Schwenningen is not receiving flights today." He paused and watched as Konigsmann slowly began to fume. It was a carefully designed and played growing anger. When Franz believed the young officer was sufficiently nervous, he spoke up slowly and in deep menacing tones.

"And is that what I am to tell the *Fuhrer*? That you are sorry but you cannot get me to my objective?" He let the thought linger.

The duty officer may have been young but he wasn't stupid. He almost raced to the operations map on the wall and began desperately looking for an open airfield in the vicinity of Schwenningen.

At last he found one. "Tuttlingen. Tuttlingen is open, sir."

Franz grimaced. "And where is Tuttlingen?"

"Approximately thirty miles to the south and east of Schwenningen. I can arrange for a car to take you to your meeting." He took a deep breath and waited.

Franz walked over to the map and pretended to examine it.

Inwardly, he was overjoyed. He had known that he would be rerouted to one of three airfields in the area but Tuttlingen was the absolute best choice. He whirled on the duty officer. "Lay it on! Now!" He stalked out of the office with the duty officer right behind.

"*Ja Wohl*! Right away, sir! It will be the transport in hangar three." Franz strode rapidly across the tarmac and yelled over his shoulder as he went, "and make sure they have a car and driver standing by!" The duty officer saluted again and raced off to make the arrangements.

The sergeant and the staff car were waiting when Franz' transport arrived shortly after ten-thirty that morning. Franz nodded at the man and they left along the heavily potholed road to the northwest.

After they had been driving for about twenty minutes, Franz ordered the driver over to the side of the road. The sergeant nodded and pulled off into a clump of trees. He stopped the car and turned around. His face almost touched the barrel of the Lugar Franz held steadily at eye level. Without a word, Franz pulled the trigger twice, scattering the sergeant's brains along the inside of the windshield.

He worked quickly but methodically. He waited a full minute to see if the shots had roused an alarm. Now fully confident, he got out of the car on the driver's side and pulled out the sergeant's body, hiding it in a nearby bush.

Quickly, he began cleaning the interior of the car, wiping up the blood with his jacket. When he finished, he stripped and changed into a set of clean civilian clothes he had hidden in his briefcase. He took all of his papers, the bloody clothes and his briefcase over to the sergeant's body. He returned to the car and removed a can of petrol from the trunk. Five minutes later, a fire claimed all the evidence including the unlucky sergeant, and Franz was driving south towards the Swiss border.

Now time was the issue and Franz did the sums in his head. In forty-five minutes, he would be missed by the people he had arranged to meet in Schwenningen. They would wait at least an hour before reporting him overdue. Phone calls and uncertainty would use up another half hour. Then another hour before the body of the sergeant would be found, and it would be impossible to be sure whether the body was that of Franz or the sergeant. Three hours fifteen minutes before a general alarm was raised. Three hours and fifteen minutes before the border would routinely be closed.

He estimated that he was no more than two hours from the border, but he pressed down on the accelerator just a little harder. He would still have to ditch the car and walk to the border crossing and that would consume time.

He grit his teeth as he sped south.

             ಶ್ಠ

The S.S. border guard stamped his feet to keep warm. This was the worst duty possible in the S.S. and not for the first time, he realized why.

The traffic that day had been light, but due to strict regulations, he was not allowed to sit or even spend more than ten minutes an hour in the bare shelter that passed for a guard house. So he spent his time stamping his feet, checking occasional visas, and cursing the gods of war.

His attention was taken by a man striding up the barren road with his head bent down against the lightly falling snow. He was tall and well dressed but clearly not well to do. He walked right up to the guard post and would have walked into the guard had he not looked up at the last minute.

"I'm sorry, the snow." He gestured at the sky. The guard grunted. "Papers."

The man reached deep into his coat and pulled out a small leather case, handing it to the guard.

The guard took it to the better light of the guardhouse. There was a *kenkarte* (ID card) and permission to cross all borders in the name of Johann Wenger. It all seemed in order but the guard was in a bad mood. He returned to the man.

"What is your business in Schweiz?" he asked.

"I am a trade representative."

"You don't look like a trade representative." In truth, he had no idea what a trade representative should look like but he wanted to see the man under pressure. What happened next surprised him.

The man pulled himself up to his full height and suddenly displayed an almost military bearing. The guard unknowingly came to attention.

The man reached into another pocket and withdrew a small piece of paper which he handed to the guard.

"This is my business."

The guard unfolded the paper and was stunned to see a *Geleitsbrief* (letter of safe conduct); and the endorsement on the bottom was unmistakable...A. Hitler! He snapped to attention and handed the papers back to the man.

Wenger, trade representative smiled, replaced the papers, and began to walk across the narrow strip of no man's land between Switzerland and Germany.

On the other side, he was two hours in Swiss Customs before he was cleared for entrance. He stepped out into the quickening dusk, stretched, yawned and started the walk to town and a hot meal.

For Franz Konigsmann, the war was over.

For Johann Wenger, it was just beginning.

＊

Founded in 1856, the Schweizerischen Kreditanstalt was the epitome of Swiss banking. Better known as the Credit Suisse, its hallmark is discretion, its style refined, and its customers mostly anonymous.

Down thickly carpeted corridors, the power brokers of the world would softly tread, silently escorted by bank officials, to make their deposits and withdrawals in elegantly furnished offices.

In January of 1945 while the war raged on, Axis and Allies both used the facilities. The bank was as neutral as its country's foreign policy. It was often said in the hushed halls of the bank that "in finance, all are Swiss."

Wenger thought of this phrase as he sat in the plush office waiting the arrival of Dr. Mont, the director of the Bern branch.

The heavy mahogany desk gleamed in the gentle light from the room's lamps. The oils of some of the bank's directors smiled peacefully down on the thick maroon carpet and heavy rust colored curtains. Overall, the room gave off a feeling of safety and security. However, Wenger felt neither safe nor secure.

It had taken him two days to arrange transportation to Bern. Constant fear had been part of that journey for he knew he would not be safe until he had "secured" his package. He flinched as the thick door opened and Dr. Mont walked in, silently closing the door behind him.

Wenger stood and the two men shook hands perfunctorily. Dr. Mont, who was much shorter than Wenger, gestured for him to sit and then took his place behind the desk.

"Welcome to Bern, sir. You wished to see me?" Names were only used if the client wished, and Mont would never be so impolite as to ask if he wished it.

"I was recommended your services by another client of yours."

Mont smiled. "It is always gratifying to be well thought of." He placed a small light green pad in front of Wenger. "If you would not mind to write out your reference." Wenger wrote out some numbers and letters and then pushed the pad across to Mont who studied it. He smiled again. "What can I do for you?" He handed the sheet of paper back to Wenger who folded it and put it in his pocket.

"I wish to open an account and obtain a *bankfach buchse*. And I wish the transactions to remain anonymous."

Mont nodded and pulled a form from the desk's only drawer. "And the amount of the initial deposit?"

In answer, Wenger slowly stood and removed his belt. Politely, Mont looked away as Wenger opened his money belt and deposited several stacks of gold coins on the desk. When he was done, he replaced his belt and cleared his throat.

Mont examined the coins. They were gold Reichsmarks, three ounces each. Mont pressed a button on his desk and waited for the soft knock on the office door. When the aide entered, he handed him five of the coins taken at random. The aide took them and left the office.

The two men sat quietly for five minutes until they were once again interrupted by the aide who returned with the coins and a thin slip of paper. He left silently.

Mont studied the paper. "In what currency would you like your account credited?"

"American dollars and Swiss Francs equally."

"Very wise." Mont finished filling out the form and then placed it before Wenger. "I believe those figures are in order." Wenger read it and nodded. Actually, the figure was lower than he had antici-pated, but he knew enough not to haggle.

"It is acceptable."

It took ten minutes for Mont to instruct his new customer on the proper procedures for administering the account. It was agreed that anybody could have access to the funds in the account or to the safe deposit box if they were to identify themselves by writing down the account number followed by the initials FK and the words *Verstecken Reichtumer.*

'Hidden Treasure' was a bit dramatic for Dr. Mont's taste but he had never questioned a customer's choice before and he was not about to start now. He made the appropriate entry on the form.

"And would you like to place anything in your box today?"

"I would."

Dr. Mont nodded and left the office for a moment. Two minutes later, he was back with a young man who carried a large steel box. The box was placed on the desk and unlocked. Mont gave the key to Wenger. "Please ring when you are through." He and the aide left, closing the door behind them.

Wenger quickly checked that the door was closed and that he could not be seen. Then he quickly removed his shoes and pants.

Draped around his waist by a leather thong were two leather pouches. He untied them from his waist and placed them in the box, locking it and testing the lock. He dressed slowly. The next transaction would be trickier and he calmed himself in preparation for it. He pressed the buzzer.

Mont and the aide returned. Making sure that the box was locked and that Wenger had the key, Mont consigned it to the young man who left the room with it.

"There is one more...transaction I wish to make." Mont's face was blank. "I am led to believe that you can place me in touch with certain people who could be helpful in my business."

"And your business is?" Mont inquired politely.

"Information."

Mont seemed to consider his answer carefully. "And you hope to market your product where?"

"I thought perhaps the Americans."

Mont nodded approvingly. "They are indeed the most consumptive market at the moment." He paused and seemed to be going over several possibilities. "I believe I can arrange an appointment for you. It may take several days, however."

Wenger nodded. "I quite understand."

Mont wrote a name and address on the pad and handed it to his customer. "I look forward to seeing you in the future, sir. Have a nice day." They stood and shook hands and once again the young aide appeared, this time to escort Wenger to the lobby.

ह०

Report on Electronic Surveillance U.S. Embassy
Bern, Switzerland

Subject:	Initial Contact by Agent K
Agent K:	*Guten Tag. Kann ich den konsul sprechen?*
Reception:	*Wie Heiken Sie?*
Agent K:	*Josef Wenger. Hier ist mein pak mitt difum.*
Reception:	*Wo sind sie geboren?*
Agent K:	*Munchen.*
Reception:	*Sind sie Amerifanifcher Staatsangehoriger?*
Agent K:	*Nein.*
Reception:	*Jhr Papiere alle in ordung. Bitte Kommen sie mitt mir zum uufzug.*
Agent K:	*Schon.*

ह०

To:	Paul 701 on 17 February 1945
Subject:	Results Primary Interrogation of Agent K

Summary in 9 Groups

Group 1:	Please advise needed details to confirm subject ID.
Group 2:	Claims proximity to high political officials. No details.
Group 3:	English good.
Group 4:	Claims consular service. No details.
Group 5:	Requests asylum.
Group 6:	Knowledge of German hierarchy convincing.
Group 7:	Suggests Agent K was in upper command structure.
Group 8:	Do not believe it is trap.
Group 9:	Cloudburst 414

ह०

Cloudburst, the code name for E. George Williams, chief of the Human Intelligence Desk at O.S.S. Station Bern, was excited. Young, dedicated and blindly patriotic, he had already developed a reputation as a "natural" in espionage work. He was daring, willing to take chances, and equally willing to take any heat resulting from his actions; but his impulses to charge ahead were usually balanced by a strong survival instinct.

Williams understood that bribery and betrayal were frequently necessary. He lived comfortably with the contradictions between ideals for his country and what had to be done to preserve those ideals.

He was also careful. He got along well with his boss, Allen Dulles. Their meetings were sometimes tempestuous since they were both known to blow up easily while defending their positions, but they also cooled down quickly. Their dedication and their goals were essentially the same.

This afternoon's meeting was no different. They met in a large luxurious second floor apartment at Herrengasse twenty-three above a local business. This floor had been converted for use by the O.S.S. Dulles distrusted the staff at the Embassy where he had originally been posted. Though maintaining two offices there, he had rented this apartment as his main headquarters. No one entered it, or even knew about it, unless he approved.

He sat at his desk, barely moving. It was a cold day and his bad leg was acting up. He stared at the cable on his desk. His face was livid. "You're making a laughing stock out of this station. Every other phrase is 'no details'. If this one is as important as you seem to think, you should have gotten more details to start with. And certainly you should have checked with me."

Williams jumped out of his chair. "Now, wait a God damned minute, Allen. You're always saying 'Trust no one', so I didn't. I gave Washington just enough to get started. And you told me yourself to expect someone sent by the Count."

They shouted back and forth for a time. Then quietly, Dulles said "This is getting us nowhere. Tell me what you do know."

Just as quickly, Williams calmed down and smiled. "You're going to love this." He paused and pulled out his notebook, consulting it as he talked. "Most of it's in the cable. As for the rest, well, first he told me that the Count had arranged for this meeting."

"Hold it," Dulles interrupted. "This is not General Kurt Reineke."

"Apparently," Williams said, "they sent Reineke first but he didn't get through. We don't have a clear read on that yet."

"So, who's sitting in the den?"

Williams sighed. "He claims to be an OKW Headquarters staff officer who's one of six officers involved in Crystal Movement."

"We can't even think about beginning negotiations until we definitely establish this fellow's identity. And just what does he have that he and his associates think we're going to want so badly?" Dulles went back to studying the cable. "What's this about consular service? Where? We should be able to get a good take on him from that."

"He says he's a colonel in planning, and used to be in the German Consulate in California. As for what he has, he claims Crystal Movement can give us valuable necessary data on the Reds. I think he's for real."

Dulles stood up. "Let's take a look at him."

Together, they walked down the hall. They stood outside the den as Dulles opened the door slightly and looked inside. Wenger sat on the couch, sipping a cup of coffee. Dulles looked for several seconds, turned to Williams and, grinning like a Cheshire Cat, slapped him on the back. "M'boy, he's for real all right."

ès

Over his coffee, Wenger observed the young woman who had brought him refreshment. She was quite short, a little plump, but with long, thick red hair, and large green eyes. The small talk she made was in flawless German, perfectly accented, yet there was something clearly American about her. He imagined that she had been an O.S.S. field agent recovering from a wound. If he was to be kept here, he hoped she would remain. She'd be a pleasant companion between what he expected to be long interrogations.

For her part, Constance Marie Cadiz, O.S.S. Coding Clerk and translator liked what she saw. Most of the Embassy staff were, in her estimation, shallow social types. The people in her section were more goal oriented but still fairly social. In fact, the O.S.S. had come to be known as the "Oh, So Social." She never felt quite comfortable with them.

She had been asked to sit with this man while Mr. Dulles and Mr. Williams had their meeting. Even in the light conversation they'd had, she found him well read, obviously educated, and charming without being crude. She hoped he didn't turn out to be some terrible spy and enemy of the Allies.

While they sat drinking coffee, busy with their thoughts, the door opened. Dulles came in, followed by Williams.

Immediately, Wenger put down the coffee and stood up with rigid military bearing. Dulles came forward and shook hands formally, and for a few moments carefully studied the man before him. "Sit down Mr......Wenger. I'm sure you've been wondering about the next steps. Mr. Williams will give you the details. If you have any difficulty with English, Miss Cadiz will assist."

Everyone sat, Wenger ramrod straight.

"I believe," Dulles said, "we met a few years ago at a party in Washington, a dinner given by Count von Hostetter."

Wenger nodded and relaxed a little. Constance looked at him with renewed interest.

Dulles continued. "Naturally, we have our rules and regulations to follow." Dulles looked sternly at Wenger. "Remember three things. One, the fact that you're here and at least temporarily under our protection is indicative of nothing.

"Two, your treatment from this point forward will depend on you; how truthful you are and how completely you answer questions. That also means how complete any information you give us is. No half truths, no omissions."

"Three, although we're in a neutral country, you will remain under our close supervision at all times. Any violation of these terms will be viewed in the harshest possible light. Do you understand?"

Wenger nodded.

Dulles went on. "George, you set up the medical and psychiatric appointments before the next discussions." He turned back to Wenger. "We'll get to your agenda as quickly as possible. Miss Cadiz will help you wherever necessary." He stood up. "It's interesting to see you again. Very interesting indeed."

As Dulles left, Williams began outlining the program.

ॐ

Interrogation of voluntary informant
hereinafter referred to as Agent K

O.S.S. Station Bern

February 1945

Q: State your name.
A: Pieter Franz Konigsmann.
Q: Where were you born?
A: Lunen, North Rhine Westphalia.
Q: When were you born?
A: 22 November 1889
Q: What was your mother's name?
A: Clara.
Q: Have you ever had sexual relations with a woman other than
    your wife?
A: Is it necessary to answer that?
Q: What is your rank?
A: I am a Colonel in OKW Headquarters.

Dulles and Williams sat in the living room of Herrengasse
twenty-three and read over the transcripts. Dulles made meticulous
notes on a pad he kept balanced on the knee of his left leg which he
propped up on a chair.

"He holds up on the stress questions rather well."

Williams nodded. "I'd hate to face those questions myself or
worse, have my wife see my answers." They laughed.

"Do we have confirmation on his rank particulars?" Dulles asked.

"Paul seven hundred and one in Washington confirms. We should
have everything DC has on him within the week."

Dulles nodded as he continued reading. "Check out pages twenty-
one and twenty-two."

Q: What was your assignment in 1929?
A: I was assigned to the consulate in San Francisco, California in
    the United States.
Q: What were your duties there?
A: I assisted in dealing with Germans traveling in the area.
Q: You are lying.
A: Sir, I am an honorable man!
Q: Didn't you have espionage duties there?
A: No!
Q: In the course of your espionage activities in the United States,

did you ever have cause to meet with high government officials?
A: As a representative of the German Government, I frequently
met with officials of the United States Government.

Dulles smiled. "Did you know that the Roosevelts had him to
Hyde Park for tea? Can you imagine!"

"Is he really that well connected?"

Dulles thought for a moment. "We never were able to fully
figure him out. Everyone knew that he was something more than
just an aide in the consulate; we all knew he was close to Hitler."

Williams turned the page on his pad. "I'd sure like to see the FBI
file on him."

"Not a chance," Dulles said, shaking his head, "Hoover would
never part with it. Especially not to us."

"He starts to get to the point on page thirty-five," Williams said
while reading.

Q: Are you here to undermine the efforts of the Allied Intelli-
gence?
A: No, sir.
Q: Are you a traitor?
A: No, sir. I am not!
Q: You deserted under fire and came over to the enemy.
A: That is not exactly true.
Q: What is exactly true?
A: The members of our group are well aware of the impending
cessation of hostilities. We have no desire to become victims of
the Russians. We felt, therefore, that we could offer valuable
documentation to your country in exchange for assurances of
amnesty and resettlement.
Q: What information?
A: Documentation covering the post war intentions of the Communists. I do not have the details readily available.
Q: The Communists are our allies.
A: Sir, we all know how easily and quickly that can change.
Q: So, in effect, we are to take the word of a man who is willing to
commit treason against his country, desert his men under fire,
and give aid and comfort to the enemy, only to save his own skin
from just punishment?
A: The end is imminent. We are not deserting men under fire. We
are merely attempting to (ONE MINUTE PAUSE) to prevent
wholesale meaningless murder.
Q: Your murder, you mean?

A: That is true.

"You can't blame the guy for making up justifications, can you?" Williams said. "He's scared of the Russians, post war trials and who knows what all."

Dulles agreed. "Still, you've got to remember that whatever may drive the men who sent him, our guest is a very different bird. He's a trained intelligence officer who is telling us only what he wants us to know." He put down the transcript and began leafing through another. "Where does he say what's what in this 'Crystal Movement'?"

Williams checked his notes. "Third interrogation, near the end of page one hundred thirteen."

Q: What specifically does Crystal Movement want?
A: Amnesty. We also require assistance in coming over.
Q: Hess said he carried secret information and deals but he was repudiated by your government.
A: Hess was a fool.
Q: And you?
A: I am a representative of some of the most important men in the German High Command. That is considerably different. We are not concerned with so called repudiation. The situation has gone far beyond that.

"If they really have intelligence on the Russians," Dulles said as he stood and stretched, "I want it." Williams nodded. "You and I both know that when this war is over, we're going to have to fight them over every piece of Europe they have their troops on."

Williams took a drink of coffee. "And we have to remember the Nazis have one of the best intelligence organizations in Eastern and Central Europe." He paused. "I think what he's got may be gold."

Dulles picked up the last transcript. "Did you read what he said about the state of the leadership over there? It's in the last transcript page four hundred twenty-nine."

Q: When the Allies reach Berlin, will Hitler stay or flee?
A: The man is irrational. But I do know he has a special bunker prepared. Whether he will use it or not is anybody's guess.
Q: What do you mean irrational?
A: I would say he has become a maniac, at least since the end of 1941. You can understand Hitler's policies only if you accept

the fact that he isn't quite sound in the head. A completely split personality. On the one hand, he can be charming, on the other, he is stark crazy. Even from a medical point of view.

Q: We have been contacted by certain…other leaders in your government about the possibility of their overthrowing Hitler in exchange for a negotiated peace. Can they be trusted?

A: It would depend. There are those who would overthrow him just to take over his position. It would still mean the same thugs running things.

Q: What about Himmler?

A: I think he is one of them.

Q: And Goering?

A: He is a drug addict and a farce.

"That's the real reason they'll make a deal," Dulles said. "They're going to fall one way or the other and they know it. At least your enemy you can trust."

Williams nodded. "Sounds like a real snake pit."

For the first time, Dulles laughed outright. "Been to Washington lately?" He started out of the room. "Draft the cable but leave out all but the essential information. We'll hard package that."

ꝛ♠

Extract From: O.S.S. Cable [Bern Station Traffic]
To: Wild Duck 062 on 4 March 1945
Subject: Debriefing of Agent K

Summary in 39 Groups

Group 1:   Subject is 56 yr. white male born 22 November 1889

Group 2:   Lunen North Rhine Westphalia

Group 8:   In 1st Euro war, Commanded 4 Btty Field Artillery

Group 9:   States Counterpoint 720 [Adolf Hitler] served in Btty

Group 11: 8 Jan 1929 Assigned Consulate SF Calif.

Group 14: 24 September 1933 Assigned Adj. to Counterpoint 720

Group 15: Hard package en route detailing

Group 16: 20 Jan 1937 Assigned OKW OPS Ofc. of CG

Group 17: Hard package en route detailing

Group 18: Entered Swiss 16 Jan at point 27 Baker

Group 21: Passed to this ofc. 22 Jan

Group 24: Subject claims follow

Group 25: Point 1 Subject claims to rep a group of high ranking officials

Group 26: Point 2 Subject claims officials are known as Crystal Movement
Group 27: Point 3 Subject claims Crystal Movement is pro settlement
Group 28: Point 4 Subject claims Crystal Movement is prepared to come over
Group 29: Point 5 Subject claims Crystal Movement requires assistance in crossing
Group 30: Point 6 Subject claims Crystal Movement will surrender documentation on Reds
Group 31: Point 7 Subject claims documentation covers Reds post war intentions
Group 32: Point 8 Subject claims Crystal Movement requires assurance of amnesty
Group 33: Point 9 Subject claims offer expires at cessation of hostilities
Group 34: Confidence is high
Group 35: Subject is articulate self-assured but evasive
Group 37: Request instructions and authorizations
Group 38: Will report further
Group 39: Cloudburst 414

CHAPTER TEN

SHATTERED CRYSTAL

Constance Cadiz had joined the O.S.S. for excitement. All her life, she had been viewed as capable, competent, with a knack for languages. She'd had lots of friends when it came to doing group activities like hanging decorations for school dances, but she'd been on her own when it came time to dance.

With her thick red hair, large green eyes and pretty smile, she should have had lots of beaus. Somehow, though, the chubby child had grown into a chubby teenager and the final blow was her intelligence. Girls were just not expected to be that bright in the 20s and 30s, and most boys were put off by it.

Teaching seemed the natural choice for her, and after months of sending résumés and fighting misconceptions, she landed a position at a small eastern university. There, she was successful and relatively content.

When she was twenty-eight, Connie had the opportunity to go to work for the State Department. She had hoped that the move to the nation's capital would give her a fresh start among new people. But the story remained the same. Fifty years later, she would have been viewed in a much different light, but in prewar Washington, she was seen as odd or a threat.

Two years later, she was feeling fed up with the "boy's club" mentality that seemed to pervade official Washington. As a result, she agreed to go to a meeting with a girlfriend of hers to hear about a newly forming agency. At this meeting, she heard about the Office of Strategic Services. That had seemed much more glamorous than what she was doing.

When Allen Dulles came along with an offer to go to Switzerland, she felt as if this was a dream come true. This new group was very close knit, caring only about how good you were at your job, and Dulles was a true gentleman, to the manor born. Even the dangerous trip to Bern was wonderful.

She had a new life. She was valued, and really part of the team at last. She loved everything about the job, the strange country, the new people, the embassy life. Even routine felt good.

Four years later, she still enjoyed the job, the country, the life. But the O.S.S. team had come to be known as the "Oh So Social." She understood why they partied so hard, considering the stresses of their work. And they always tried to include her, but she never felt totally comfortable.

These last two months had been different and it was because of Wenger.

He was interesting, cultured, and he exuded Old World charm. She was glad she had gotten her master's in german literature. The one thing that made her uncomfortable was the undeniable fact that he was one of the enemy. Her job was simply to facilitate his processing, but she found herself looking forward to seeing him, being around him.

Thoughts of Wenger and her feelings about him were on her mind as she walked into E. George Williams' office. "Helen gave me your message."

"I'm glad you could come by." Williams offered her a chair. "I know it's Sunday and you probably had plans."

"That's all right."

Williams sat back. "You've done a good job with Wenger, so I was wondering about your taking on something a little different."

"What do you have in mind?" It sounded as if she wouldn't be working with Johann again and all of a sudden she felt a lead weight inside.

"There comes a point in working with these people when you have to start offering the carrot, not only the stick. We're going to be getting down to some tough decisions for him, and we thought it might help if his situation were eased a bit."

"What do you mean?"

"He's been cooped up pretty much. We thought we might permit him a little normalcy, an occasional stroll; a typical Bernese Sunday."

Connie nodded.

Williams continued. "Naturally, there will be special conditions and parameters involved. Obviously, we can't allow him on his own. We need one of our own people with him. Someone who is familiar with Bern, knows German, someone we can trust to see to it that he makes no inappropriate contacts."

Connie protested. "I'm not a field agent."

"But you have the advantage of having been in on this case almost from the beginning. You're intelligent, and you've been with us for years. I think you'd be able to spot any attempts he'd make to leave notes, signal someone, that kind of thing."

"What if he tries to get away?"

Williams laughed. "I don't think so. Maybe earlier on, but not at this point. The deal's too far along. What do you say?"

Connie was silent for a few moments, thinking. When she first came in, she thought she'd never see Johann again, and part of her felt this was the solution and it was out of her hands. Now, she was being offered an opportunity to see more of him, on an almost social level, but did she really want to? "When do I start?"

꿎

Wenger paced back and forth in the living room of the O.S.S. apartment. It had been two months since he first contacted them; two months of probing interrogations, and examinations, broken only by the occasional signal sent to Germany to let them know negotiations were progressing. He wasn't permitted to indicate more than that, nor did he want to. This was his show and the longer it took, the better the chance of it staying that way.

But he was tired of the four walls, the inactivity, the news of the war. He was bored. If it hadn't been for Constance, he wasn't sure he'd have gotten through it. There's nothing worse than constant repetition, the same place, same people, same everything. It could wear you down faster than torture.

Constance had been the one bright spot in all the drab days. She was young, so interested in everything about him. Not like Williams and Dulles. A genuine starry-eyed, awe-filled interest. His ego needed that. And he was grateful for her presence.

Just then, Constance walked into the living room, wearing her hat and coat and smiling broadly. "Good morning, Johann. It's such a lovely morning. Would you like to take a walk?"

Wenger was flabbergasted. "Constance, good morning. Where are we going? I wasn't informed of any meeting today."

Constance continued smiling. "No, no meeting. You have permission to take an occasional stroll, perhaps go to the park, watch the chess players, just have a change of scenery. Of course, I'd have to accompany you."

Now Wenger was the one to smile. "I'm delighted, my dear. Even more so to have your company."

As they left the building, a young man lounging across the street folded his newspaper, and began to follow them, remembering Williams' instructions. "Follow them. Discreetly. At a distance."

ða

It was a brilliant morning. General Rubschlager strode aggressively towards his transport. For the first time in weeks, he had gotten a good night's sleep. Heavy clouds overnight had kept the Allied bombers away. Now on this shining morning, he was preparing to fly out of the hell that Berlin was becoming to the relative safety of southern Germany near the Swiss border. Intelligence from the outposts there was becoming infrequent and he had assigned himself the job of finding out why.

He was content. The reports from Switzerland were good, and if everything continued on schedule, one day soon he would board another transport, this one not stopping at the Swiss border, and he would be free…and rich.

He settled into the plush seat of the Heinkel and opened the file on his lap. His aides also settled in for the long flight which would be made in stages to avoid Allied air patrols.

At 0815, they were airborne. Rubschlager had four hours and thirteen minutes left to live.

❧

At a forward Allied Air Base in France, the pilots sat around drinking coffee and being briefed by the squadron commander.

"The weather is clear along your flight path and bombing raids along the northern and central fronts should keep the Luftwaffe well away from your area of operations."

Captain Jerry Harris lightly tossed his cup into the trash. "No sweat, Colonel." He looked at the two junior pilots he would be training. "I'll keep their asses safe."

The squadron commander smiled. Harris was experienced and cautious. "Jerry, you and Earle will be in live ships. Ramos will fly the camera bird."

First Lieutenant Richie Ramos groaned. He had hoped to be the one to get to engage Captain Harris in the mock dogfight. The captain had beaten him badly last time and the entire squadron had laughed at the pictures.

"You have a problem, Lieutenant?"

"No sir!" He'd be sure to get good pictures of Earle being waxed by the captain. That would make it all worth it.

The squadron commander understood. With the fight in the air winding down, he could read the coiled tensions in his pilots. He knew that these "fights" helped some, but nothing could replace the real thing. That's why two of the planes always carried live ammo, on the off chance that they might encounter an errant fighter or something.

Captain Harris continued for the commander. "Our flight is designated Brigham One through Three. We'll be operating over the Lake of Constance near the Swiss border. Stay alert not to drift over Swiss territory or you'll spend the rest of the war behind some desk in a neutral country."

They all laughed.

"Take off is at 1145 hours."

❧

Rubschlager had been on the ground at the southern Aerodrome for twenty minutes, waiting for clearance to continue his flight. He wondered idly what he would be doing this time next year with a new name and a small fortune.

Perhaps he would go back to his first love, horses. A small horse ranch in Spain perhaps, maybe in the Pyrennes. He would count his money and watch his horses running and forget all about this abortion of a war. If the Allies came through, and Wenger seemed to think they would, his new name and money would let him live out his life in protected bliss.

His plane finally received the clearance to continue on to his final destination; a small intelligence center near the Bodensee (Lake of Constance).

He had perhaps twenty minutes left to live.

ટ&

"Come on, Earle, tighten up!"

"Copy, Brigham One."

"Brigham One from Brigham Three."

"Not now, Ramos."

"Uh, Brigham One, I think you need to see this."

"Brigham Three from Brigham One. See what?"

"Three o'clock, your position. I have an unidentified slow and low, circling,"

"Brigham Two from Brigham One. Break off exercise and tuck in on my wing. Brigham Three, climb to Angels Eight and observe."

"Brigham Two, roger."

"Brigham Three, roger."

"Brigham Flight from Brigham Leader. Come to Three Five Zero magnetic. Brigham Two, follow my pass in. Brigham Three, watch for bandits."

"Brigham Two, roger."

"Brigham Three. I'm watching skipper."

"Brigham One to Brigham Flight...Tallyho."

ટ&

Extract from:	Report on Whereabouts		
Subject:	Rubschlager, Hugo	Rank:	Lt. General
Listed Status:	Killed Body Not Recovered		
Declaration:	0335927 PGLM		

Investigation

Witnesses: Capt. Jerry Harris USAAC,
                1st Lt. Dick Earle USAAC
Evidence: Motion Picture footage
SHAEF Confirmation: Confidence is high

Remarks: According to Declaration of Status, General Rubschlager left Intelligence Headquarters in Berlin on the morning of 9 March 1945 bound for a refugee debriefing center across the border from Lake Constance, Switzerland. As he was trying to land, his transport allegedly was attacked and shot down by 3 P–51 fighters; crashing into Lake Constance on the Swiss side of the border.

The investigation of this office has established the following:

A. Rubschlager left from Zone 1 Aerodrome south of Berlin at 0812 on 9 March in Transport #74523, a twin engine transport with three horizontal green stripes on the tail assembly.

D. At 1223, Brigham 1 reported seeing a transport with German markings and 3 green horizontal stripes on the tail assembly. Brigham 1 and 2 immediately engaged the aircraft, making five passes at it.

E. Brigham 3 followed the transport as it banked south, heavily damaged. Brigham 3 then activated his starboard wing camera.

F. The footage of Brigham 3 clearly shows a Heinkel class transport with smoke billowing from the starboard engine. The port engine is not visible in the frame of the picture. The #745 are clearly visible on the vertical stabilizer.

G. Brigham 3 observed the transport crash into Lake Constance and break apart and sink rapidly. No parachutes were seen.

Conclusion

This office can confirm the shootdown of General Rubschlager's transport.

Submitted by: Greene, Bill
                Lt. Colonel
                USA JAGO

❧

E. George Williams' face was frozen in a grimace, perfectly reflecting his mood. It had been that way ever since Communications had delivered the paper he now held in his hand. It had been engraved more deeply when he'd had to set up this meeting.

Sitting opposite him was his prize, Johann Wenger, and he was about to give the man some news which could change the entire aspect of their negotiations. "Johann, please read this document and then hear me through before commenting." He almost winced as he passed the paper to Wenger who was beginning to wonder what dire turn of events had taken place.

Wenger started to read, and immediately the Wehrmacht Administrative File #033 leaped to his notice. "You seem to have excellent intelligence," this comment coming out involuntarily.

Williams grunted acknowledgment.

Wenger continued to read, his face impassive, but a myriad of thoughts tumbled through his mind. The first, almost reflexive, one *less for me to deal with later on.* Then, as the shock of what he was reading hit him, *Does this mean that the United States has changed its mind? Are they planning to kill them all? What's going to happen to me?* He felt like an animal caught in a trap with the hunter about to bear down on him. His mind raced, looking for a way to save himself. As he found and rejected ideas, the paper dropped from his hand to the desk automatically. He sat unmoving.

"This wasn't any of our doing," Williams began. "It was an unfortunate accident."

Wenger barely heard Williams. Were they toying with him? To what purpose?

"We'd begun keeping tabs on the whereabouts of the Crystal Movement officers in preparation for moving them out. That's when we came across this." Williams gestured at the paper. "Your General Rubschlager just happened to be in the wrong place at the wrong time. We didn't order it," Williams reiterated. "What I need to know from you, Johann, is just how much this impacts on Crystal Movement's information, and their willingness to come forward."

Wenger caught the note of embarrassment in Williams' voice, his use of the first name. He began to breathe easier. He thought for a moment before answering, mostly about how best to serve his own cause. "General Rubschlager was really only on the periphery of the group. I am deeply saddened by his death. Hugo was, after all, a friend." He sighed. "But as far as Crystal Movement is concerned, he only joined towards the end. The information will still be available, I assure you.

"General Reineke's disappearance or death; that was extremely upsetting. Kurt was involved almost from the beginning, but we knew we could go on with it. And, as you know, that led to my being sent here. The main people remain; Albrecht, von Streck, Minscel, and myself, of course."

"Of course." Williams smiled to himself. Amazing how Wenger had changed from "just a courier" to one of the "main people." It fit with his profile though. A self-serving man. Well, they'd just have to see how best to use that trait.

Allen Dulles had been monitoring the conversation from another room and now chose to join them. His entry made a still wary Wenger somewhat more so. "Under the circumstances, I think we need to contact your friends again, Mr. Wenger."

ঽঌ

"Kirche," the German word for church, was the codename for Hans Bader, a police prefect in Central Germany. In addition to his routine police work, he also served as a clearinghouse of information for OKW Operations Intelligence. He did his double duty well enough to receive the occasional bonus from his army masters, an extra ration of meat or cheese, the luxury of petrol for his car, and the promise of an early evacuation when the Allies drew near.

Each night he would faithfully sit by his secured phone and wait for three hours, from midnight to three A.M., and pass along any information to the appropriate parties. Tonight, there was no exception.

Due to a blackout, he was forced to sit in the dark this night, checking his watch occasionally by the light of a burning building across the street from his house. At precisely three A.M., he picked up the receiver and dialed a number in Berlin.

"Hello?"

"Kirche."

"One moment." There was a pause of over a minute and then a second voice came on the line. "Talk to me, Kirche."

"Nothing tonight, sir."

"You're sure?"

"I am sure, General."

"Thank you, Kirche." The line went dead.

&.

Albrecht hung up the phone and looked around. The Operations Center, now manned twenty-four hours a day, was bustling with activity but no senior officers were in evidence.

Damn, Albrecht thought to himself, Reineke gone, Rubschlager dead, no word from Wenger in over two weeks. Time is running out. Soon events will overrun plans and all could be ruined.

He paced through the 'pit' and angrily chewed out some junior officers for nothing in particular. He was feeling claustrophobic since he had moved into the Center full time on orders of Hitler. The end was near and the *Fuhrer* wanted his top commanders available around the clock. For Albrecht, it seemed almost like a sentence to prison.

Finally, he decided. He would give Kirche three more days, until the end of the week, then he would try to get to Switzerland himself. Deal or no deal.

&.

The delay was also a worry to Williams. They had planned to make the call the day after he briefed Wenger but the defector had mysteriously come down with a cold that night. At first, they had thought it was a suicide attempt but the Station Doctor assured them that the symptoms were not the same as cyanide poisoning. He also told them that Wenger was faking.

Williams had realized that the man had his own agenda, but now his delays and phony cold had brought the question directly to bear and Dulles had ordered that the call not be placed until they could be certain of Wenger's motives.

Another delay.

Williams had assigned Cadiz to look after the ill defector. She had given him soup, read to him, and generally kept his spirit up, but he never confided to her. Williams was getting desperate and he decided to try one last gambit. He went to see Wenger.

The man was wearing an expensive robe, scarf wrapped around his neck, hot water bottle nearby, and wrapped in an expensive blanket. The image of the country squire recovering from a cold. Williams shattered that image right away.

He chased Constance from the room, locked the door behind her and walked sternly up to Wenger. "You and I have business."

Wenger nodded. "Would you care for a sherry?"

Williams shook his head and pulled up a chair. "I would care for straight answers."

Wenger coughed feebly, "I'm not well."

Williams slowly opened his briefcase and pulled out two guns. With the allegedly sick man watching with great interest, he placed one gun by the hot water bottle and cocked the other one, aiming directly between Wenger's eyes.

Wenger straightened slowly and locked eyes with Williams, trying to read the man's thoughts. It was useless. "You have my attention, sir." He took a sip of sherry.

"You've been delaying. I want to know why. If you don't tell me, I'm going to kill you."

"In cold blood?" He seemed amused at the notion.

"It will be found that you were trying to escape, had hidden a gun, it was unfortunate but…"

Williams' eyes were cold and Wenger could see no clemency there. "What do you want?"

"Everything."

ðê

As they settled around the conference table, Dulles leaned over to Williams. "How'd you get him to stop delaying? What was the problem?"

Williams shrugged. "He was worried about the deal falling apart, about whether or not he would be included in the amnesty et cetera."

Dulles nodded and turned to Wenger. "You may place the call now." He turned to Connie. "Please give us a running translation." She nodded as Wenger picked up the phone.

"Hallo? Hier Zentrale. Geben sie mir bitte Hamburg zwo vier sechs null acht neun."

"He's asking for a phone number in Hamburg."

ðê

Translated transcript of Agent K phone call placed in presence of
Cloudburst 414 and Eyelid 612

Contact: Hello. Lehrter Train Station.
Agent K: Could you please see if anything is missing?
Contact: As far as I know only the shaving kit is gone.
Agent K: Have you heard of the train accident?
Contact: Well, I only hope our train won't derail.
Agent K: No.
Contact: Don't lean out the window.
Agent K: Okay.
Contact: You have to declare the contents and show the key.
          Connection terminated at other end.

ৰ

Dulles put down his earphone. "Okay Johann, what was that all about?"

Wenger smoothed back his hair. "I have been instructed to inform you that the information is ready to be brought to you if you are ready to bring out the generals."

Williams interrupted. "You promised us a sample."

He nodded. "If you go to the Hotel Strauss and ask at the main desk for a package under the name of Dulles, you will be given the sample."

"Dulles!"

"It seemed appropriate."

ৰ

"Hello?"

"Kirche."

"One moment."

"Talk to me, Kirche."

"The bag has been claimed."

ৰ

Life at Herrengasse 23 had taken on a subtle lightness. Dulles smiled a lot, complimented staffers. Williams was known to make jokes more and more often. The package sent by Crystal Movement, though not extensive, had very strong information, enough to give Bern Station high marks back in Washington.

For Connie and Johann, it meant that the regular Sunday walks were augmented by strolls during the week, dinners together, and a growing closeness. She talked about her home, her dreams; he turned out to be a very good listener. He talked about the places he'd been, his love of racing, his other interests and hobbies. They both tried to imagine what their lives would be like after the war.

Johann wondered where they'd send him. Connie hoped it would be the states. She started to tell him about the country until he reminded her that he'd lived there years ago. They laughed over it. They found themselves laughing over a lot of things together.

When the weather was too cold or wet, they stayed in. He started teaching her to play chess. She learned quickly and enjoyed the games.

The familiarity, the fondness, the total disappearance of Connie's Midwestern reserve and Johann's formality was not lost on Williams. Ordinarily, this would have set off alarm bells in his mind. Oddly, he turned a blind eye to it. When Dulles commented there might be some concerns there, Williams indicated that everything was fine, and if their guest was feeling relaxed, so much the better. The whole situation would be resolved soon, and then it would be Washington's headache.

The euphoric atmosphere blanketed the senses, and Dulles went along with it. The important thing was to protect the United States' interests, and on that, they were working very hard.

Everyone felt fired up. For Williams, it was agony waiting for all the I's to be dotted and T's crossed before they could pull out Crystal Movement. They had demonstrated that their information was good, and he knew in his bones that what they would have with them would be worth its weight in gold.

The warmth of the air was matched by Connie and Johann's feelings. Connie had stopped fighting herself inside, and enjoyed herself. She tried to ignore the small voice that said "He's married. He has a wife and children."

Johann, for his part, avoided all discussion of his family, as if that would make them disappear. He had given a lot of thought to his future. Chances were good that when the members of Crystal Movement were given new identities, the O.S.S. would want to keep things as simple as possible. The others, he felt sure, would want to stay in Europe, well maybe South America as an alternate. They'd insist on their families being brought out too.

As for himself, he'd always enjoyed the United States. A new name, some slight cosmetic surgery. It could be very pleasant. There were still friends there who would keep his true identity secret. He didn't want to encumber himself with his wife and children. It would be far too difficult to keep anonymous.

The diamonds, a new life. An American wife would be the perfect capper, and Connie was comfortable. Yes, it might all work out.

And so he daydreamed.

✿

For Minscel it was not a daydream, but a walking nightmare. Twice on this trip into Berlin, he had almost been captured by advanced patrols of American and British Commandos. Only luck had seen him through.

Now as he sat in the cubicle deep beneath the Chancellery, he contemplated the end.

The messages from Switzerland were vague as to the exact date when the Allied transport would come for them. It would be soon, but would it be soon enough? That was why he waited for Albrecht in this soon to be lost city. Waited, and for the first time in his life, prayed.

Albrecht entered, looking ten years older. "It's good to see you, Gerhard." For once, he meant it.

"Any news?"

Albrecht looked around. "They say they will come within a fortnight."

"So long?"

"Apparently."

Minscel leapt to his feet. "It may be all over by then!" He started to pace feverishly.

Albrecht walked over and put his hand on the man's shoulder. "Try and calm yourself. They have agreed to the rendezvous point and to the pick up procedure."

"When do we leave?"

Albrecht smiled for the first time. "Use your own judgment. As for myself, I feel a recurrence of my injury from the attack on the *Fuhrer* coming on. I think I shall leave for my home very soon."

Minscel nodded. "I agree. What about Streck?"

"I'm briefing him when he returns this afternoon."

"Where has he gone?"

"He is leading a patrol to gather intelligence."

"Leading it himself?"

Albrecht shrugged. "It's his way."

It had been a long patrol.

Von Streck felt every one of his sixty years boring in on him. Slogging through the mud along the deserted road with his kameraden, he thought longingly of the early days with the AKEF. The heady days of training, of parachuting, of floating soundlessly through the skies and landing among his men, men whom he loved as dearly as his own sons. But that was long ago.

Now, the war was almost over. He was convinced of that. This patrol, his way of actually seeing what was happening along the front, had proved to him that all was lost. Finally, and irrevocably.

Nowhere were they able to hold the line. Patton poured in on the Reich from the west, Montgomery from the south, and the Russians, God, the Russians would probably be in Berlin within the month. The situation was lost.

Again.

Where had the mistakes been made? Had they tried too much with too little? Had the fates been against them from the beginning? Or was it simply...no.

Nothing about what had happened was simple. It couldn't be reduced to one or two mistakes. They had been beaten, beaten soundly and that was all there was to it. He stopped his reflecting and resumed his role. He ordered the patrol towards Luckenwalde. They would rest there for an hour or so before proceeding on to Berlin.

The seven men marched, with weapons at the ready, silently moving down the road; but von Streck couldn't silence his mind.

He thought back to his University days in Cologne. Those days when the world was open to him for the taking. Those days when poetry and history were more important to him than gun emplacements. He thought about the choices he had made, right and wrong, and how he had come to be on this road at this time.

And always his mind drifted back to Africa.

Whatever would happen to him after the war, whether he fell into Russian or Allied hands, he didn't care. He knew that his punishment would come when he stood before the souls of the 1,071 men he had led to their deaths and had to explain to them why.

It was almost dawn as they approached the crossroads. Rest was only fifteen minutes away and every cell of his body ached for it.

Off in the distance, he could see another patrol coming out of Luckenwalde. They walked casually, seemingly more concerned with looking at the town they had just come from than watching where they were going. When they passed, he would discipline their leader.

Both patrols reached the crossroads at the same moment and froze.

Bernhard could not believe his eyes. American Commandos! A patrol of American Commandos! My God, here!

Apparently, the Americans were just as shocked at seeing the German patrol. They stood there for over thirty seconds, staring as though they couldn't believe. The shock wore off someone and a shot was fired. Reacting on instinct, both sides scattered, fell to the ground and the fight began.

Although outnumbered, von Streck's men maintained their discipline and fired slowly but effectively. They drove the Americans off the road proper and towards the field where von Streck knew mines awaited.

Using hand signals, he ordered his men to advance, to drive the Americans into the minefield. Four of his men responded and seemed about to succeed when an explosion ripped through the air and caught them mid chest. Bernhard knew they were dead before they fell.

The explosion seemed to energize the Americans and they started to move forward. Bernhard quickly surveyed his men. Only two were left and they were wounded.

'Enough'. Finally for Bernhard the war was over. He signaled to his men to lay down their arms. The three of them placed their hands on their heads and stepped out where they could be seen. In flawless English, he called out, "Stop your firing, we are done."

For the first time, he had a chance to look them over. His earlier impression had been correct. They were Commandos. He saw the patch of the 101st Airborne Division. He smiled inwardly as he thought 'at least I have been taken by my own kind'.

They looked good, these Airborne Commandos. They reminded him of his own beloved AKEF. These were men!

The Americans slowly came towards Bernhard and his men. As they came, with weapons leveled, Bernhard realized that he had been wounded. He felt the warm stickiness move down his left side and knew he had been shot. Still, he maintained his erectness.

Suddenly, a sharp click was heard through the eerie silence that had descended. Everybody froze and looked to the side of the road.

A young American was standing there with a look of panic on his face. He was standing on a pressure mine. His next move would be his last, and if he didn't move in ten seconds, he would be killed anyway.

Bernhard saw all this in a second. He saw the young, brave Commando standing there. Not American, not German, just a young brave Commando, like so many before him.

Like 1,071 before him.

He acted. He rushed forward and reached the young man in three strides. Bernhard threw the shocked man off to the side and allowed his own body to collapse over the mine as it exploded.

His body was thrown twenty feet into the air, landing in a culvert by the road. Broken and bleeding, he could feel his life draining away. The Americans gathered around him, but he didn't see them. He saw his men, his Commandos, unbroken, tall and strong, and able to beat the world.

He closed his eyes and joined them, the 1,072nd casualty.

&

A solitary car stood parked beneath the trees with its lights off but its engine running. The moonless night, the chill wind that had suddenly come up, and the innate tension of the occasion caused its driver and sole occupant Karl Albrecht to shudder slightly.

Several times over the last few hours, he had heard patrols in the area. Each time, he had braced for a quick escape. Each time, they had passed him by. Now as the time for the pickup grew nearer, the usually unflappable general was at the end of his rope. He could not survive another night like this one.

Something called his attention to the other end of the meadow he was parked by. A solitary figure in civilian clothes was walking towards him. He unholstered his Lugar and waited for the man to draw nearer. Just as he was about to fire on the man, he recognized Minscel, and relaxed.

"I thought you'd never make it."

Minscel climbed into the car's relative warmth. "God in heaven! It's cold." He held his hands by the car's heater. "I had to walk the last kilometer. Patrols are everywhere."

"Ours or theirs?" Albrecht asked.

"Do we still have an ours?" Minscel joked. For the first time, Albrecht noticed that Minscel was a little drunk. "Or are theirs now ours?" He was beginning to slur his speech.

"Get yourself together man!" Albrecht barked. "We have a difficult enough night ahead as it is."

As if in answer, Gerhard took out his flask, saluted, and took a deep drink. "I think perhaps you are no longer my superior." He took another drink. "We are equal, yes? Equality among thieves I believe they say."

Albrecht turned away angrily.

≥≈

The unmarked plane soared through the moonless sky at near maximum altitude. The pilot, copilot, and single passenger were on oxygen and spoke only through the intercom.

"How long?" Williams' voice sounded strange to him on the intercom. When he got no answer, he asked again. "Captain, how much longer?"

"Uh, Mr. Smith, if that is your name, I'm not going to descend until the last possible minute. In case you've forgotten, this bird we're in is unmarked. I'm not about to get shot down by our own boys."

"Understood, Captain," Williams began, "but how much longer?" These Air Corps guys could be difficult, he thought to himself.

"About fifteen minutes."

"Thank you, Captain." Fifteen minutes until the biggest triumph in Williams' career. He counted the seconds.

≥≈

Minscel was passing in and out of consciousness. Albrecht looked over at him and wondered vaguely how he had ever allowed a man like that to become part of Crystal Movement. He prayed to his private Gods that wherever the Allies put him, it would not be with this drunk.

The sound of a plane overhead stirred him from his reverie. Its engines were clearly throttled back and he could hear it make a low banking turn just above the meadow. Hoping desperately that he was right, Karl turned on the car's lights.

⢀

"Okay, Phil, give me five degrees flaps until touchdown. Then full flaps and reverse thrust." The pilot sounded nervous. He was right to be. The meadow was smaller than had been reported, and with no lights, the landing and subsequent takeoff would be a near thing.

Williams braced himself in the back of the plane. He checked that his rifle was loaded and the safety off. The plane seemed to nose straight down and he knew the landing was imminent.

⢀

Albrecht shoved Minscel brusquely in the ribs with his elbow. The man stirred and then came fully awake as he also heard the sound of the approaching plane. Both men watched the sky.

The plane appeared suddenly over the furthest row of trees on the far side of the meadow. It seemed to hover for a moment and then it touched down at the halfway point. It used the remainder of the meadow to slow and then turn to face the direction from which it came.

Albrecht and Minscel waited without breathing for the signal. After what seemed an eternity, actually only a few seconds, it came. Two short flashes followed by a pause and then two long flashes. The two men looked at each other as Albrecht returned the signal. They grinned like children, and then began walking towards the plane.

⢀

The car's flashing headlights were all Williams needed. He dropped unseen from the plane's hatch and lay the way Colonel Fairburn of the British Commandos had taught all O.S.S. operatives to lay. It was called sniper position. On your stomach, legs spread shoulder width, toes dug into the ground, propped up on your elbows, sighting along the barrel of the rifle.

The two figures quickly came into view. He spoke quietly to himself. "All right. Select your target, aim at your target's chest, take a deep breath, expel the breath, kill the target." He fired one shot and the first man fell.

"All right. Stay calm." He increased the pace of his chant. "Select your target, aim at your target, take a deep breath, expel the breath, kill the target." He fired again and again a man fell to the ground. He counted to five, and when no one moved, he got up and ran forward.

Shooting had never been his strong suit and he saw now that he had almost botched the job. The first one, he thought it must be Albrecht by the description, had been hit in the head. Williams had been lucky that he hadn't missed him altogether. The second one, he was sure it was Minscel, was hit in the upper chest. Neither man seemed to be breathing.

The pilot revved the engine preparing for takeoff so Williams cut his examination of the bodies short, grabbed their briefcases and suitcases, one each, and hurried back to the plane. He threw the bags inside and scurried in behind them. He rushed forward to the cockpit. "Hurry! Let's get the hell out of here!" The pilot needed no encouragement and moments later they were airborne, scraping the tops of some trees on the way.

"What happened back there? We thought we heard some shots." The pilot screamed to be heard over the engines.

Williams nodded. "I guess the Germans figured out what was going on. We were jumped by the Gestapo. Our passengers were killed."

The copilot frowned. "Then all this was for nothing?"

Williams shook his head. "Not quite. I managed to get their papers before I had to retreat."

"Good work."

"Thanks."

"You took a hell of a risk."

"It'll be worth it." Williams smiled and returned to the back of the airplane. It would all be worth it. Worth the promotion and possible medal he would get. Worth the reputation for bravery he would get. And most of all, worth the ten diamonds, half of all of Wenger's diamonds that he had promised him.

It was a good night's work.

&.

The German patrol was on its way back in, when they got the call to check a nearby field for reports of a mysterious aircraft. Dawn was just breaking as they fanned out across the field.

They found the tracks of the plane quickly enough and they followed it across the field to where it had apparently turned and took off again. There they made another discovery.

The sergeant was on the radio instantly. "Headquarters from first squad, urgent!"

"Go ahead, first squad."

"We are at point nine six seven. A plane landed and took off again. No sign of whose."

"Anything else, first squad?"

"Affirmative. We are bringing in General Gerhard Minscel." He has been shot in the collar bone. We are administering first aid. It does not appear serious."

"We will have an ambulance meet you at point nine five two. Proceed at once."

"Acknowledged."

"Any other wounded?"

"No. Nobody else around at all."

&.

He wandered through the underbrush for hours. Slowly, he regained his senses. He wasn't sure what had happened but he knew one thing for certain; it was time to disappear.

After a while, he came upon a small abandoned farmhouse. He found some old clothes and quickly changed out of his uniform which he willingly used to light the furnace.

As he watched the gold braid catch and begin to burn, he ceased to be his old self. From this time on, and for the foreseeable future, he was simply a displaced person, with memory loss due to wounds. He would wait and watch and be invisible. His time would come.

&.

Minscel regained consciousness to excruciating pain. His arm was in a sling and a cast covered the upper part of his body. He vaguely remembered what had happened, but his present circumstances prevented him from expressing the rage he felt.

For two days, he lay in that field hospital. He told those who asked that his car had broken down and he was walking for help when he had come across the mysterious plane. Soldiers, probably Russian, had fired on him from the plane and that was all he remembered. Germany was in chaos, and everyone seemed to believe this fiction.

On his second day of recovery, he was sent for by Admiral Doenitz. Paralyzed with fear that he had been discovered, he reluctantly went along with the S.S. guards.

On arrival at Doenitz' headquarters, he was ushered into the admiral's presence. The admiral wasted little time.

"Last night, the *Fuhrer* took his own life in his bunker in Berlin." Minscel gasped. "The war is lost. It has fallen to me to hold things together until a cease fire can be arranged."

Relief didn't begin to describe how Minscel felt. "I stand with you, Admiral. I am wounded," he opened his jacket to show the cast, "but whatever I can do to assist..."

Doenitz nodded and handed Minscel a list of operations. "Can you oversee the winding down of these? I don't have time to review them myself."

Minscel's attempt to scan the list stopped with the first item. Crystal Movement had been listed as an operation only to explain the radio and message traffic between the conspirators. Now it was number one on Doenitz' list. Luckily, no one had yet looked into it.

Minscel snapped to a painful attention. "I will personally see to them." Doenitz nodded, and Minscel limped from the room.

The next day, he personally oversaw the burning of every document he could find relating to Crystal Movement. Then he changed into civilian clothes, burned his own file, and disappeared.

ò•

To: **All Unit Commanders OB West**
From: **Supreme Commander OKW**
Date: **2 May 1945**

l. *You are hereby commanded to arrest and otherwise prevent any officers of staff rank from leaving their command positions without specific entitlement from this authority.*

2. *You are hereby instructed that General Karl Albrecht has forfeited all rank, privileges and honors due for the crime of desertion under fire on 30 April 1945.*

3. *You are hereby ordered to apprehend the criminal Albrecht and inform this office upon doing such. (Items 4–23 are repeats of the wording of 2 & 3 naming eleven other officers)*

24. *All operations involving aforementioned criminals are hereby under the direct command of this office, with the exception of Werewolf, Flotilla 6, Crystal Movement, Anvil, and Glow Worm.*

25. *Werewolf and Flotilla 6 operations are herein transferred to Gen. Geyr von Schweppenburg.*

26. *Crystal Movement, Anvil, and Glow Worm are herein transferred to Gen. Gerhard Minscel.*

Authorized by my hand,
Keitel from Doenitz

₰

As the war came to an end, there was universal rejoicing among the Allied nations. Even at O.S.S. Station Bern, a party started and continued for three days.

Most were celebrating victory.

Two men, who celebrated privately, celebrated a victory of a different sort.

CHAPTER ELEVEN

TRIALS

Germany was destroyed, completely and utterly. Whole towns ceased to exist. The once arrogant German people had been reduced to a rubble equal to the remnants of their cities. The anger of all of Europe was turned upon them with a ferocity born of years of repression and atrocities.

Revenge was uppermost in the minds of the people of Europe and their leaders agreed wholeheartedly. Churchill called for the immediate execution of all war criminals without trial, without chance of clemency, without mercy. Other leaders echoed the late American president's sentiments of "turning Germany into a potato field."

But there were other voices, too. Small voices, mostly American, who called for trials. A conference was called for and in June of 1945 the four powers met in London to settle the issue.

The Russians, however, were for show trials followed by certain convictions and, in their view, approximately 200,000 executions to follow. Into this bloodthirsty environment came the American representative, Robert Houghwout Jackson.

An associate justice of the United States Supreme Court,

Jackson was considered one of the most brilliant lawyers that FDR had brought into his administration. As Attorney General, he had defended New Deal policies in front of an opposing Supreme Court, and as an associate justice he had argued persuasively that judges should try to keep their judgments free from personal opinion.

A man of enormous energy and strong beliefs, Justice Jackson would never compromise on any details no matter how small if they involved principle. He joined in the negotiations with the tenaciousness and zeal that were his trademark. Quickly, he came to dominate the London Conference.

His position never wavered from that he had first set out in his report to President Truman before leaving for the conference: "Unless we write the record...we cannot blame the future if...it finds incredible the accusatory generalities uttered during the war. We must establish incredible events by credible evidence."

He bullied, bellowed, argued and antagonized but eventually emerged from London with an agreement for an International Military Tribunal.

He also emerged as the chief american prosecutor of that Tribunal. He returned to Washington to begin his briefings for the trials. Soon he would return to Europe, to write that record and right some wrongs.

There were dark days ahead.

>●

Spring had come to Bern and spring fever to those O.S.S. people not on urgent assignment. Parties were proliferating, and Connie was feeling a joyous restlessness.

She went to see Williams. "We'd like to go on a picnic."

Williams looked up from the pile of papers he was working on. "Whose idea is this?"

"Mine. Helen invited me but I thought it would be fun if Johann and I could have one of our own."

He considered this for a moment. Only this morning, he had received notification of Justice Jackson's pending arrival. It wouldn't hurt, he thought, to have Wenger relaxed and feeling at ease when we spring Jackson on him.

He looked up at the fresh-faced girl and wondered for the

hundredth time whether or not Wenger was sleeping with her. The surveillance tapes hadn't revealed anything but... "Same rules as the walks, agreed?"

"Agreed."

"I want to know the where and the when twenty-four hours in advance."

"Of course."

He returned to his papers and mumbled "Have fun." As he watched her virtually bounce from the room, he again speculated about whether Wenger was using her. He shrugged.

છ.

Connie had chosen the food, the place, her prettiest casual clothes with great care. It had been an absolutely delightful day. She packed the remains of the lunch and dishes back into the basket and smiled to herself as she remembered how surprised and pleased Johann had been when she broached the idea to him.

Now, he lay back on the blanket on the grass, completely content, watching her covertly. She's really quite pretty, and a surprisingly good cook. Educated, some culture. It was as if he was dispassionately checking off qualifications for a job, and he wasn't quite sure why. "That was delicious. You're too good a cook. I can hardly move." He patted the blanket next to him. "Come here."

Connie lay down and Johann was very much aware of the warm, voluptuous body beside him. He leaned over and kissed her on the cheek. When she didn't move away, he raised up slightly, took her in his arms, and kissed her on the lips. He felt her body move closer to him. But the warning bells sounded inside his head. She's O.S.S., and I can't trust them. He gently placed her back on the blanket and moved to her side. "A kiss for the cook."

She felt him take her hand in his. "The cook is pleased." What a stupid thing to say, she thought, but when I'm around him my IQ goes down to 10.

She looked at her watch and stood up. "We'd better get back." They packed up and, looking back regretfully, they headed home. He carried the basket with one hand, and held her hand tightly with the other.

છ.

Dulles hated the Embassy.

In World War I, while in the Consular Service, he had learned first hand of the lack of respect career diplomatic personnel paid to Intelligence. They saw it as impolite and therefore not worthy of their attention. At that time, leaks were plentiful and unapologized for.

Things had improved slightly but, in his estimation, the changes were, at best, cosmetic. Diplomats couldn't be trusted. Period.

The O.S.S. offices at the Embassy were limited to two rooms used primarily by the code breakers and the cipher clerks. Field personnel were advised to keep far away and do their business at the Herrengasse Headquarters.

But today was different.

He had borrowed the use of a small conference room at the Embassy for today's meeting with the prosecution team for the upcoming International Military Tribunal. It was what he often referred to as a "pro forma performance." He hoped it wouldn't take up much of his time.

Dulles and his "team" were set up on one side of the long conference table and were waiting. Across from them an equal number of chairs was set, each with a pad, a pen, a cut crystal glass, and a pitcher of ice water before it. Files had been carefully placed and the room painstakingly arranged. The O.S.S. on one side, the Prosecution team on the other. Almost, but not quite, confrontational.

He hoped that there were enough places for his guests at the table.

Five minutes after the appointed hour, the door to the room was opened by the Embassy's chief of protocol.

"Gentlemen, Mr. Justice Jackson."

The O.S.S. team stood as Jackson strode into the room. To Dulles' surprise, he was accompanied only by an Army colonel. After an embarrassing moment, while Jackson surveyed all the chairs that had been prepared for him, the two men sat.

"Are we expecting a banquet, Mr. Dulles?" Jackson smiled as he talked.

Dulles knew that smile. His own brother often wore that smile while giving Allen a rebuke for a violation of etiquette. He grit his teeth at the unpleasant memory. "We were expecting your full party,

Mr. Justice Jackson."

"This is my full party, Mr. Dulles," Jackson said as he fumbled in his briefcase for a folder.

Jackson was living up to his reputation as a straightforward man who depended little on aides. Dulles could see why Truman liked the man.

Jackson gestured at the colonel next to him. "This is Colonel John Amen, my chief interrogator." He looked up and down the table. "And which of these gentlemen is…" he checked one of his files, "Agent K?"

&

The room had been cleared of most of Dulles' staff leaving only Dulles and Williams on one side of the table, and Jackson and Amen on the other.

"I'm sure you understand the sensitivity of this matter," Dulles began. "Certain information needs to be restricted as much as possible."

Jackson nodded. "I wholeheartedly agree. That's why I was more than a little surprised to see the peanut gallery that you'd brought with you."

Dulles took a deep breath. Jackson even used the same phrases as John Foster, Allen's overbearing older brother. "I had assumed Mr. Justice Jackson that you were here to go over all the information we have for you." He gestured at the folders. "I had prepared a thorough briefing."

Jackson pushed his folder over to Colonel Amen who placed it in his briefcase. "And I'm sure it's fascinating reading," he said. "But I'm here for only one reason, to interview Agent K. As for the rest of this, you and I both know that if it reflects the information sent to Washington…" he paused.

"It does, sir," Dulles forced a smile.

"…then the bulk of it is fantasy or disinformation if you prefer."

Dulles was furious. "Sir! This is the product of five years of hard work by men and women putting their lives on the line and in many cases losing their lives. For you to call it fantasy is to spit on the unmarked graves of those dead heroes!"

Jackson sat quietly with his hands folded. "Are you done?" He waited, when he received no answer, he looked directly into Dulles' eyes with an intensity Dulles would never have expected. "Save your speeches for Congress. We both know that all stations of the O.S.S. have been sending false and misleading reports home almost from the beginning. In the intelligence business, that's to be expected. We'll go over your reports. We'll even use them if we can. But understand me clearly, this tribunal is going to write the record of all those atrocities committed in the name of the Nazis and it's going to write them with the truth." He paused and took a drink of water. "Good God man, don't you think the truth is damning enough?"

Jackson was impressive, even to Dulles. "Mr. Justice, I apologize for my outburst and I will do everything I can to ensure that you are given only carefully checked information." Jackson nodded. Dulles turned to Williams. "George, will you brief the gentlemen on the circumstances and actions taken regarding Agent K."

An hour later, they were finished.

Williams closed his file and sat waiting for the other shoe to drop. He had withheld, upon Dulles' orders, the most important piece of information.

Jackson reviewed his notes. "So you're saying he had unrestricted access to all of these leaders? Remarkable."

For the first time in the meeting, Colonel Amen spoke. "Can I get complete transcripts of all interrogations to date?"

Williams nodded. "You'll have them this afternoon."

"If you're the man who did the interrogating, I'll also need to meet with you."

"No problem."

For the first time since the beginning of the meeting, Jackson was smiling. "When can I meet your prize catch, Mr. Dulles?"

Dulles shifted uncomfortably in his chair. "There's a problem."

Again, Jackson fixed him with his stare. Slowly, he said, "What problem?"

"Agent K does not yet know that he will have to testify." Dulles expected an explosion from Jackson but none was coming. For five minutes, the four men sat in the oppressive silence. Finally, Jackson spoke clearly and firmly.

"Well, let's go inform the good colonel of the facts of life."

ॐ

The "Good Colonel" was pacing back and forth in his rooms. Ten minutes ago, he had been informed that he was to make himself available immediately for a "very important visitor." Something was happening and, from his perspective, it couldn't be good.

A knock at the door snapped him out of his thoughts. Before he could answer it, it was opened and four men walked in. Dulles and Williams he knew but they were accompanied by an Army colonel and a slightly balding man in his fifties. The balding man seemed to be in charge and Dulles and Williams seemed nervous. They walked over to him.

"Johann," Williams began, "I'd like you to meet Mr. Justice Robert Jackson, an associate justice of our Supreme Court, and Colonel John Amen."

Johann came to attention and extended his hand. All his defenses were at maximum. Something indeed was going on. "It is an honor to meet you, your excellency." They shook hands and Johann couldn't help but be surprised by the strength in the man's grip, that and the way he never took his eyes off of him.

"Colonel." Jackson sat on the couch.

Johann was slightly caught off guard by the use of his rank. It had been a long time since anyone had called him by his true name or rank. He sat in a chair across from Jackson. "You have the advantage of me, sir."

"And I hope to maintain it."

Johann noticed that Dulles and Williams were leaving the room. As he was about to shut the door behind him, Dulles looked back at Johann as if to warn him. But of what?

As if reading his thoughts, Jackson said "This will be just you, me, and Colonel Amen."

The door closed and for the first time since the day he had crossed the border, Johann felt completely alone.

Jackson began brusquely. "First, let's get a couple of things straight. I am not here in my capacity as a Supreme Court Justice. I'm here as the chief american prosecutor at the upcoming International Military Tribunal." Johann nodded. "Also, although people around you prefer to call you by your *Nome de guerre*, I will address you by your true name. Finally, I expect you to answer all of my questions clearly and completely. Do you understand?"

Johann nodded.

"You are Colonel Pieter Franz Konigsmann of the German High Command?"

"I am."

Jackson nodded at Amen who opened a file and began to question Franz.

"Why are you traveling under the name Wenger?"

"I considered it wiser."

"Who is Wenger?"

"Does Wenger exist?"

"Does anyone else know that you are using the name Wenger?"

It went on like this for the better part of two hours. Endless questions about his cover name, how he came to Switzerland, who knew about it, etc. He answered all their questions as thoroughly as he dared. Throughout, Jackson remained silent, watching, studying Franz. Finally, he interrupted the questioning.

"I think that's enough, John." Amen closed his file and walked from the room, leaving the two men alone.

Franz was tired but still wary. He tried to take the momentum away from the man across from him who he was already referring to, in his mind, as "the enemy."

"May I get you something, your excellency?" He started to rise.

"Sit down, Colonel." It was more a command than a request. "We have much to do this evening."

Franz sat.

"Colonel, how were you placed in the chain of command and what were the types of documents that were likely to pass through your hands?"

Now Franz was beginning to understand. "I fail to see what that has to do with the Soviets' post war intentions?"

"At the moment, Colonel, I don't give a rat's ass about the Reds. Answer my question."

Franz jumped to his feet. "My agreement called only for my cooperation on intelligence regarding the Russians. I have lived up to this agreement. You received documentation and that is all that you will get from me."

Jackson wiped his eyes with the heels of his palms and then slowly, as if completely exhausted, rose to his feet. "Colonel, I'm tired, hungry, and fed up to here with your Nazi arrogance. My God, your people must be the most bellicose people in the world. I am sick and tired of your posturing and pretending. You lost the war, Colonel, and you have to answer for what you did."

He paused and took a deep breath. "Now sit down and start cooperating or by God you'll be on the next train for Spandau Prison. And I'll personally make it my business to see that your comrades already there know of your cooperation with us."

Slowly, like a tire losing its air, Franz dropped into the chair. In a weak voice, he said, "But we had an agreement."

Jackson sat down and began flipping through a file. "I'm modifying it."

ﻬ

Over the next several hours, Jackson slowly pried the information he needed from Franz. Also slowly, Franz' arrogance returned until at the end, he was strutting around the room as he recounted conversations and meetings.

"It was in 1938 when I had tea with President Roosevelt, at his home in Hyde Park. Did you know that?"

They were in the home stretch and Jackson was willing him home. "So I understand. You are sure there is no chance whatever that internal OKW documents might have been signed for by secretaries or aides?"

Franz looked at him with disdain. "We were a disciplined organization. We followed procedures and they called for each officer to sign for the documents himself." He paused. "It was a delicious Earl Grey I believe and Mrs. Roosevelt served it in the most delicate china."

Jackson continued to ignore the posturing. "I'll bring the specific documents for you to look over before your testimony." He rose to leave.

Franz walked him to the door. With his arms clasped behind his back and his head down, he spoke softly. "And I must testify?"

"Yes."

"But after that, I mean after the trials, you will keep your promises?"

Jackson stopped and turned to face him. "You have my word you will receive a new identity, relocation to the city of your choice in the United States, worthwhile employment, and most importantly, complete amnesty."

"I have heard that before."

Jackson looked at him solemnly. "I know you have." He wanted to say something but couldn't think of what. He shook Franz' hand and walked out of the room.

In the hallway beyond, Williams and Dulles came up to meet him. He saw Amen sitting in an alcove reading documents. He turned to Dulles. "A most extraordinary man." He signaled to Amen and they started down the hall, leaving the others behind.

He got about halfway when he suddenly stopped and came back to Dulles.

"I want him watched very closely, around the clock. There've been enough suicides." He turned and walked purposefully from sight.

In the room behind him, for the first time that he could remember, Franz Konigsmann also known as Johann Wenger, collapsed on the couch, his head buried in his hands.

It had all been for nothing.

For hours, he sat in this position, unaware of the day passing into night, movement in other rooms, street sounds. It was as if he were a creature in a box closed off from the living world. Gradually, he became more aware, and he wondered, when the box would open, which creature would emerge, Colonel K, Consul Franz Konigsmann, Johann Wenger, or...?

After the conversation in the hallway, Williams quietly looked in on Konigsmann and decided to leave him alone with his thoughts for a short while. Then, heeding Mr. Justice Jackson's warning, he went to his office and called Connie. He explained only that Johann had been through a difficult interrogation, and he, Williams felt it would be helpful if she kept an eye on the man and reported later.

"The room is so dark, Johann." Connie entered the room with misgivings, and turned on a lamp. Johann lifted his head, wanting to respond but unable to break through the box. He simply looked at her. The weak light of the single lamp showed the face of a man in hell. It was as if he had aged twice his lifetime, and his eyes were those of a man who had surveyed the ravages of all his deeds and misdeeds.

"My God, what's happened?" She sat down beside him and took his hand in both of hers.

Her touch revitalized him somewhat. With a sigh that was like a moan from the depths of his soul, he began, slowly at first, and then letting it all pour out. She remained quiet, unmoving except to squeeze his hand from time to time.

He told her, in vague generalities, of the meeting with Jackson. Then "they want me to go back to Germany, to testify...against Keitel, Jodl, Albrecht, against men I respect, men who trust and respect me. I've been given no choice. All the promises...meaningless...I can't face them. I can't do it. I can't go back to Germany, not this way."

He withdrew his hand from hers and turned away, "I don't have the strength," his voice broke and trailed off. They'll kill me, if not the Allies then certainly my old friends, he thought to himself.

Constance had never seen him like this. Even during the long arduous interrogations when he first arrived. He'd always remained strong, proud, never faltering. She couldn't bear to see him this way. Her heart went out to him. He needed her. She had to be there for him.

Resolutely, she stood, took his hands and turned him to face her. Gently, she tugged, and he stood up and put his arms around her. She looked up at him with concern and love. "We'll get through it together, Johann."

"It's not Johann anymore, it's..."

"Shh. No more talking." She kissed him for a long time, and then together they went into the bedroom.

≈

Later, they lay in each other's arms, content, having taken what they needed most from each other. He took the strength to put himself back together, be the old arrogant, self-assured Franz; she, the warmth of being needed, being cared about, belonging. With lazy reluctance, Connie finally rose. He lay in bed, watching her dress, comb the luxuriant red hair. He was relaxed, more comfortable about being able to deal with the future, but strangely, he felt he had to justify himself to her. "I'm not a traitor. I'm not a monster."

Connie chose her words carefully. She was in love, but she was also a realist. "The war's over. Whatever happened, whatever you did, that's the past. You're not a monster. You're my love." She smiled. "You'll get past this and you'll make a new life soon."

At the phrase 'new life', Johann once again felt the betrayal, and the rage within him began to grow. "They haven't kept their word. I don't know when, if ever, they will."

"They will. Jackson is an honorable man."

"And Dulles? Another honorable man? You know, I'm really no different than your Mr. Dulles. Whatever I did was for my country, my people, perhaps more honestly than your Dulles or Williams. From my view, it was honorable, from theirs immoral."

"A question of perspective?"

He nodded. "I am, I was an officer in my country's service."

"You don't need to explain to me."

"I need someone to understand. I need you."

She came and sat beside him. He sat up. "I kept my part of the bargain, and your honorable Mr. Dulles reneged. They send me to my end."

"No, it won't be that way. I know it seems bleak now but just give it time. It'll work out, and I'll be here to help you through it."

"Will you help me?"

"You know I will, every way I can."

They fell back into each other's arms.

ॐ

The next weeks were filled with debriefings, visits by Amen and Jackson, and sorting through hundreds of documents. The lovers had little time to themselves, but found solace in stolen moments and hidden pleasures. Finally, the day for departure arrived.

Franz had followed the beginnings of the trials with an almost detached air, even laughing aloud when shown newsreel footage of Goering swaggering about the Prisoners Dock. "Can you imagine that obese addict seeing himself as the leader of the Fatherland?" Towards the other defendants, he showed uniform distaste, "they were people of the most inferior type, lackeys and bootlickers all of them." Only towards Jodl did he express any regrets, "A thoroughly adequate mind and a fair man."

On the train to Germany, dressed in an expensive tailored suit, and once again using his Wenger papers, he reviewed the documents he would be asked about.

He shook his head and turned to his escort, an American captain from the Judge Advocate General's office. "These really are in the most shabby condition. I can barely make out some of the signatures."

The captain looked over his shoulder. "Isn't that Jodl's signature?"

Franz smiled and nodded. He had won the moment that he hoped to use to save at least one of the men on trial. Perhaps he would not be a complete traitor after all.

After crossing the German border, he was whisked away by an Army staff car to a waiting airplane which immediately took off. The charade had been played. The train trip would make it appear that he had returned voluntarily to testify. Now he closed his eyes and napped.

The captain nudged him awake after several hours. Franz looked out the window and saw that they were descending through the clouds. He waited and watched and then suddenly there it was spread out before him.

Franz remembered the beautiful old city of Nuremberg. In happier days, he had been here many times; sometimes with family and friends, sometimes as part of Hitler's entourage. Looking around as he arrived, he could see the city had suffered from the war as much as the people. Allied bombers had destroyed a large portion of the city.

As they transferred to another waiting staff car, he turned to one of his escorts. "Did you know that for centuries this city was known as a cultural center of Europe?"

The man turned to him. "And in this century, the birthplace of Hitler's Nuremberg Laws. The cradle of fine art and music, and the cradle of the spirit of genocide. Interesting what you and your friends have done, isn't it?" They traveled the rest of the way in silence.

Then they were there. Looming ahead was the massive compound that housed the International Military Tribunal, the prison, and the Nuremberg Palace of Justice.

It was still early in the day but as they quickly drove past the main entrance, Franz saw the huge crowds gathered, the reporters and the photographers. Though the trials had been going on for weeks, the excitement remained palpable, even felt in the enclosed car. A circus of the macabre, Franz thought.

The Palace of Justice itself had needed extensive repairs before trials began. The Allied bombings had done tremendous damage. Franz had been briefed on what to expect in terms of the physical set up. In order to accommodate the large number of prisoners, defense counsel, and prosecution staff, a wall had been removed between adjoining courtrooms. Publicity was both expected and zealously courted to achieve one of the goals of the trials. Therefore, a large press section and visitors gallery were created on the northern side. In front of them were placed four large tables for the prosecution.

The judges were seated along the western side of the high-ceilinged expansive room. On the eastern side was the Prisoners' Dock with defense counsel in front of it, and a special elevator behind it to facilitate moving the prisoners from the prison area to the dock.

There were camera booths, and sound booths in various corners of the room. Translators, who provided simultaneous translation, were located near the Prisoner's Dock. Court reporters and clerks were seated in front of the judges, just to the right of the chief prosecutor. There were facilities for display panels and a movie screen on the southern wall, behind and to the left of the witness box.

Security was extraordinarily tight. The American military guards with their gleaming white helmets were everywhere. The judges were all bareheaded, most dressed in simple black robes, though the Russian judges preferred wearing their military uniforms. The four national flags, United States, U.S.S.R., France, and Great Britain were displayed behind the judges. All in all, it was a pageant, a panorama to impress or intimidate as the case might be.

Franz was neither impressed nor intimidated as he was escorted into the witness waiting area. It had been specially cleared in order to preserve his anonymity. He settled down on the uncomfortable sofa and waited. After about fifteen minutes, Jackson came in.

"How are you feeling?"

"I'm ready."

Jackson noticed the tightness around the jaw and how he kept clenching and unclenching his right fist. He sat down next to Franz and patted him on the shoulder.

"I just want to assure you that we have taken all precautions to protect your identity." Franz nodded. "A temporary partition has been erected between the witness dock and the defendant's dock. They will be unable to see you at all. All counsel will refer to you only as Colonel K. No names or ID numbers will be used."

"You must think that they are imbeciles," Franz snapped. "They will know it is me the moment I begin to talk."

Jackson smiled. "We've taken care of that. Your voice will be electronically distorted except to the translators, and they are our men."

"But the lawyers will see me." It was a statement of despair.

Jackson nodded solemnly. "That's true. They have to be allowed to see you during their cross examination. But they are under strict instructions not to convey to their clients any details of your appearance. If they violate any of the terms of the agreement, they can and will be jailed themselves."

Franz just shrugged and said bitterly, "I am deeply reassured, Mr. Justice."

For the first time, Jackson seemed concerned about Franz' attitude. "You understand that if you don't cooperate our deal is off." No answer. "You are to testify honestly and completely." Again no answer. Jackson finally sighed and patted Franz on the shoulder. "It'll only be a few minutes." He walked from the room.

Franz got up and started to pace. Having no faith in any of the measures taken to protect his identity, he sought desperately for a way to hedge, to soften, to shape his testimony. If he had to defend himself later, to his friends, he wanted to be able to point to something concrete that he had said that helped someone.

The loudspeaker in the room blared a harsh tone and then a sexless voice came on. "Witness 281, Witness 281, we are ready for you."

Two immaculately clean and pressed guards came for him and escorted him into the hall.

೩

Nuremberg Trial Transcript Morning Session

P = American Prosecution Team

W = Witness 281 (Identity withheld per Directive 24 of the Tribunal)

P: Per Directive 24 of this Tribunal, I summon Witness 281 to be referred to as Colonel K.

Clerk: Will you take a traditional or civil oath?

W: Civil.

Clerk: Do you solemnly affirm that the testimony you are about to give before this tribunal is true in all parts, omitting nothing of bearing, based upon your personal experiences and recollections?

W: I do so affirm.

Dr. Krost: Your honors, I renew my objections to the guidelines established for this witness's testimony.

Justice Ignachenko: Objection is overruled but noted.

P: Colonel K, for the bulk of the war, that is sir, from 1942 until 1945 where were you assigned?

W: I served in the Office of the Chief of the Operations Staff of the High Command of the Armed Forces.

P: In the course of your duties, did you ever come in contact with Generals Jodl and Keitel?

W: Yes. Many times each day.

P: You are shown now Prosecution Exhibit labeled Block B. Have you ever seen this before?

W: Yes. I was shown these in the past days.

P: Would you describe to the Tribunal the contents of Block B?

W: Papers.

P: Would you be more specific?

W: Printed papers.

P: I remind you sir of the terms of your testimony.

W: I remember them.

P: Would you then please describe the contents of Block B?

W: It consists of internal memorandum of the operations staff.

P: And can you personally identify any of this memoranda?

W: Yes.

P: How?

W: Appended to each document is the list of circulation. It was required for an officer to initial this list upon reading the attached document.

P: Could not a secretary or an aide have initialed the circulation list on behalf of an officer?

W: No.

P: Why not?

W: That would have been a court-martialable offense. For the officer who allowed it as well.

P: So if initials appear on a circulation list, it means the officer who initialed it must have read it?

W: Yes.

P: You are shown document 7,636. Did you initial this document?

W: Yes.

P: Did General Jodl?

W: Yes.

P: Did General Keitel?

W: Yes.

P: You are shown document 41,862. Did you initial this document?

W: Yes.

P: Did General Jodl?

W: Yes.

P: Did General Keitel?

W: Yes.

P: And to the best of your knowledge, have any of these twenty-four documents been altered in any way?

W: They did not appear to have been, based on the short time I was allowed to examine them.

P: Would you like more time for examination?

W: No.

P: You are shown document 57,386, would you read its title?

W: Minutes of conference on defense logistical problems May 6, 1944.

P: And the subject of this conference?

W: The subject appears to have been the delays in establishing defensive fortifications along the French coastlines.

P: And was the conclusion of this conference that more slave labor would be sent to the area?

W: Apparently.

P: Did you initial this document?

W: Yes.

P: Did General Jodl?

W: It appears so.

P: Did General Keitel?

W: Yes.

P: Nothing further.

Dr. Krost: Did you ever see General Keitel initial any of these documents?

W: No.

Dr. Krost: So he might have violated regulations and had an aide initial them for him?

W: They were his regulations. He enforced them quite ruthlessly, but it is possible, he was not a thorough man.

Dr. Krost: So he might have?

W: The chances are remote in the extreme, but yes he might have.

Dr. Krost: Did you ever hear General Keitel say that the slave labor problem was an appalling problem and of deep concern to him?

W: He said it often.

Dr. Krost: Nothing further.

P: What did you take as General Keitel's meaning when he made the statement you just confirmed?

W: He used the phrase whenever a field commander would complain about the lack of slave labor in his operational area.

P: So it was not a condemnation?

W: The *Fuhrer* approved of and supported the slave labor program completely. General Keitel never to my knowledge ever condemned any of those programs. It was not in his nature.

P: Nothing further.

Dr. Bentasy: Sir, a few questions only. You worked for General Albrecht who worked for General Jodl. Is that correct?

W: Yes.

Dr. Bentasy: Were you an intimate of General Jodl?

W: I knew him through my functions as a staff officer only. No, we were not close.

Dr. Bentasy: Did he ever express any personal opinions to you?

W: Never.

Dr. Bentasy: You have been very forceful and sure in your testimony. However, when you were asked to identify General Jodl's initials on document 24,714 you said "It appears so." Why?

W: The initials are smudged but the letters are clear. As I said they appear to be in his hand but I cannot be sure.

Dr. Bentasy: Referring to document 57,386, you were quite sure of your own and General Keitel's initials but not General Jodl's, are they also illegible?

W: Almost. I was told by an American captain that it was Jodl's initials and I repeat they appear to be, but I cannot be sure.

Dr. Bentasy: An American captain told you to identify these initials as General Jodl's?

W: Essentially.

Dr. Bentasy: You are currently a guest of the Americans are you not?

W: I am in their custody.

Dr. Bentasy: And they tell you what to say?

P: Objection. Terms.

Dr. Bentasy: I humbly withdraw the question. Sir, during your time on the operations staff did you ever hear of, or witness General Jodl oppose positions taken by the *Fuhrer*?

W: Yes. Many times.

Dr. Bentasy: On what issues?

W: I do not recall specifically but I believe the abuses of civilians was a particular concern of his. Also the bombing of nonmilitary targets.

Dr. Bentasy: And why is there no record of this in the memorandum?

W: Considering the climate of distrust and paranoia that often swept through headquarters, to object on the record would have been suicidal.

Dr. Bentasy: He would have been killed for objecting?

W: Yes.

Dr. Bentasy: Nothing further.

P: Did anybody tell you to identify initials as other than you specifically believed them to be?

W: No.

P: No one told you what to say?

W: No.

P: Finally, what are the Imperial Articles of Conduct?

W: They are the rules which govern how an officer should comport himself.

P: You are shown a copy of the Imperial Articles of Conduct. Have you ever seen this before?

W: Yes.

P: Do you know of anyone else who possessed a copy?

W: Every officer was issued a copy.

P: Would you read Article Sixteen?

W: It is the responsibility of each officer to prevent, or cause to end any mistreatment of noncombatants or wounded enemy personnel; even unto the sacrifice of his career or his life.

P: And to whom was that copy of the Articles issued? You will find it inside the back cover.

W: Alfred Jodl.

P: Would you read the line that appears beneath the name?

W: I do hereby swear upon God on highest to live by these Articles.

P: Is it signed?

W: It is.

P: Read the signature please.

W: Lieutenant Alfred Jodl, April 1919.

P: Nothing further pending recall at a future date.
Justice Ignachenko: Would the witness care to make a statement?
W: No.
Clerk: The witness is dismissed pending recall with notice.

ఽ

The attic room was dimly lit, the windows covered by heavy curtains and only a single hanging bulb for light. Musty and damp, it often felt oppressively small and depressing. But not this afternoon. This afternoon, all was forgotten as the room's sole occupant listened intently, through a pair of earphones clamped to his head. Listened and seethed.

The trials, broadcast on the radio were, to the listener, obscene. The men in the dock had merely followed orders. An honorable man could do no less. Now the victorious Allies were holding up these men to ridicule, scorn, and hatred. And what was worse, what was unpardonable, was that one of their own was helping.

The changed voice, the use of another name, all the precautions meant nothing to the listener for he knew who Witness 281 must be. The listener knew that only one man was placed in such a position to know all that he was testifying about.

He listened carefully as the testimony shifted from Jodl and Keitel days before, to the invasion of Austria and other countries.

ఽ

Nuremberg Trial Transcript

Afternoon session

P: It is one of the qualities of a man of honor to keep his word?
W: Yes.
P: Then you knew, did you not, that Germany had given her word to respect the neutrality of other nations?
W: I suppose so.
P: Was a protest raised by any men of honor against the breaking of Germany's given word?
W: It was not possible for anyone to speak at all. A discussion did not take place and was not permitted by Hitler.
P: You mean it was impossible for men of honor to defend their honor?

ఽ

The listener grabbed the headphones from his head and flung them across the room.

"Swine!" he yelled, shocking himself. The man on the stand had been trusted! Trusted with State secrets and trusted with the listener's private secrets. Silently, he made a pledge to himself.

One day, somehow, accounts would be settled. The listener would, he promised himself, be avenged on the traitor.

But for now, he would wait. He recovered the earphones and once again settled in to his listening.

Listening for the name he hoped not to hear.

Albrecht!

&.

Back in Bern after the last of his testimony, Franz analyzed the last few weeks. He had tried to walk a tightrope between minimally incriminating his fellow officers and yet keeping enough of his part of the bargain to induce Jackson and Dulles to keep theirs. It had been difficult in the extreme. Sometimes being so physically close to some of the German officers had been frightening. How could they help but know it was him? Had he said enough to ensure his new life? Had he equivocated too much?

Finally, he made up his mind to lay it to rest. He would work on the assumption that everything was fine. It was time to tip the scales in his favor. He'd remind Williams of the private pact between them. Better to have the lure along, the payoff. But that could be a problem.

Connie was delighted to have him back. Each time he left, she worried about how it would go, if he'd come back, back to her. Now it was over. She could hardly contain her joy. All of this was very evident to him and so he decided to take a calculated risk.

They were out for their usual Sunday walk. Franz, as always, was aware of the surveillance at a distance. He never mentioned it to Connie, wasn't sure she knew. Nevertheless, he felt safer talking out here than inside. "My dearest Constance," he began, "it's so good to be with you again." She beamed. "I imagine we'll know pretty soon when and where I'll be going. I'll miss these strolls."

"There must be some way we can see each other once you're in the States."

"I'm sure there is. Even with a new identity, it's certainly all right for you to know. I promise I'll find a way for us to be together. Trust me."

"I do."

"There is something that might help." He paused. "I hesitate to ask you."

"Anything, anything at all."

"Well, I've been keeping something, an insurance policy I think you call it."

"Yes?"

"The O.S.S. knows nothing about it. I arranged to put it away for safekeeping before I presented myself here."

"What is it?"

"I'm sorry, my darling. It's very sensitive material. I thought I might use it if the negotiations ran into a snag. I think now I might use the...material to help us, but unfortunately I'm not in a position to get it myself."

"Let me get it for you."

"I don't know. If your bosses knew..."

"Don't worry. Just tell me what to do."

"All right, dear. It'll be our secret."

"Of course." She nestled against his shoulder.

"One thing though. For your own protection, it's better you don't know anything about it. I'd never forgive myself if you were hurt."

Connie laughed. "I sneaked into Switzerland during the war and made it all right. I'll be fine."

"Nevertheless, promise you'll follow my instructions and neither tell anyone else nor look at the packets yourself. I'll feel better about it. Please, give me your word."

He looked so solemn and concerned, she relented. "You have my word. Just tell me how to get it, and I'll bring it right to you."

He nodded.

⁂

The imposing lobby with its dark woods and conservative furnishings was as quiet as a church. Indeed, the Credit Suisse was the financial Mecca for many after the war. But for this visitor it was a frightening place, peopled by unknown enemies.

She had made her way there carefully, using a pretext for leaving very early. First, a bus to the old quarter, then some shopping where, among other things, she purchased a large shopping bag; then a bus for the "clock tower" where she took pictures of the wooden rooster, the man in armor, the dancing bears and the man on the throne as they each appeared as the hour was struck. She mixed with the ever present tourists and finally made her way back towards the Old Quarter and the bank.

Many times, she stopped to check behind her, using store window reflections and her compact mirror. Finally assured of her safety, she entered the bank.

At first, she was confused just where to go. She approached a man in uniform who directed her to an older woman at one of the desks nearest the door.

"Excuse me," she said in halting German. She spoke the language fluently but Johann had instructed her to appear to struggle with it. "I am trying to get to a safety deposit box."

The woman behind the desk smiled and asked for the account number. Constance wrote it exactly as Johann had instructed. The woman took it, spoke quietly into a telephone and waited for an answer.

To Constance, the wait seemed like hours. Every smile, every glance from a stranger, seemed somehow sinister and threatening. For the first time, she understood the pressures and fears that O.S.S. field operators must feel. Finally the clerk put down the phone.

"If you will accompany this gentleman," she pointed at an approaching young man, "he will assist you."

Constance thanked her in broken German and walked in silence with the man one flight up of thickly carpeted stairs, where she was shown into a small office. On the table was a metal box. The young man left her alone in the office.

"Ring when you are through, madam." She was through in minutes.

She hurried from the bank, certain that everybody was staring at the large bulge in her shopping bag. Again she took her time heading back. When finally she arrived at the two bedroom flat that she shared, she collapsed from the tension.

She put the shopping bag under her bed and climbed in. All that night she never slept, worried about exactly what was in those two odd pouches hidden in the bag.

But she never looked.

ᘍ

Franz walked into the office, looking very much the man in control. Shoes mirror polished, pants creased razor sharp, manner confident. He had requested this meeting, and it had George wondering.

"Come in, Franz. You did well in Nuremberg. A couple of false starts, but that's understandable."

Franz sat down without being asked. "I did my part."

"Yes. You wanted to see me about something?"

"I did my part. We had a bargain. You and I, George, had a particular bargain."

E. George Williams was feeling a little uncomfortable. He was used to being in control, and determined to take back that control. "I haven't forgotten. You know we're winding down here. You're on the list. I'll let you know when we're ready."

Franz' face was impassive. He reached into an inside pocket of his jacket and pulled out the packet he had prepared the night before. He placed it on the desk exactly midway between them. "It's time, George. I've done everything you've asked. I've been here for months. I want, I need a home, a life."

Williams ignored the packet, and looked straight into Franz' eyes. "Not here, not now."

Franz looked right back at him. "You've called the shots. Remember, we have a mutual interest. Now I'm calling this shot."

Williams laughed but there was little humor in his eyes. "Do you really think you can pressure me? There are still charges outstanding on you." He stood, walked around the desk and perched on a corner. "You'll get what I give, when and if I give it."

Franz was not surprised by the attitude, but decided to be only slightly more conciliatory. "You have the power here; no question. And I have," he patted the packet of diamonds. "Perhaps I am mistaken for asking you for what was promised. I realize how busy you are these days. It might be better for me to discuss this with Mr. Dulles, or Justice Jackson."

"Don't threaten me."

"Don't dismiss me."

They stared at each other for a moment, coming to the same

conclusion. Williams walked to a side table, picked up a folder, and returned to his seat behind the desk. He opened the file and scanned the top sheet.

Franz, long practiced at the espionage art of reading upside down, recognized the letterhead of the United States Justice Department, and the title of the document which was "Actions regarding disposition of Colonel K." George handed the document across to Franz, who read it, smiled and nodded at Williams.

 è

Excerpt from Justice Department Document:
Actions regarding disposition of Colonel K

...therefore, it is my opinion, based on the fullness of his testimony, degree of risk in his giving said testimony, and cooperation on other issues, that Colonel K should be immediately enrolled in Project Masquerade.

è

Franz looked out across the terrace at the magnificent Bernese Alps. Freedom was almost within his grasp. He would get a new identity, a new life, and he had always enjoyed America. There were few details left and he'd be on his way.

The question had come up about his family in Germany. He felt that for his own preservation, it would be better to start fresh. His wife would never understand what he had done to get this amnesty. And even if she did, if she and the children came along, he felt certain he'd be recognized in the States, O.S.S. efforts not withstanding. He couldn't say all this, merely indicating that, with the extensive bombing, he, regretfully, felt he no longer had a family.

Williams read between the lines, seized on this, and hastened to agree. He did indicate, however, that he had thought a quiet family in the States might be a fine cover.

Despite their occasionally adversarial relationship, Franz respected Williams' judgment. So now he stood on the terrace, a fine wine and a bouquet of roses (both acquired with Williams' help) waiting in the living room for Constance's appearance.

The sun was just setting when she arrived. The warm glow over the old buildings and the vineyards added the perfect touch. Franz was prepared to be at his most charming.

Several days had passed since she'd given Franz the pouches.

He had seemed quite agitated at the time, and she'd worried about him ever since. She was delighted when Williams told her that Franz wanted very much to see her. "Consider this a special invitation," Williams had said, and she was still wondering about that odd phrase.

Franz thought he heard her footsteps on the cobblestone road and turned back to the living room. There she stood in the middle of the room, beaming. She had found the flowers on the table and was cradling them in her arms as she read the card: "My Angel, I look at these roses, these beauties of nature and see only your face. You've given me light in my darkest moments and enwrapped my soul in love greater than I deserve. Wherever I wander, my heart will only be at home in your arms." There were tears in her eyes.

Franz had planned the evening with great care, but when he saw how she had been affected by the note he had so carefully crafted, he decided this was the moment.

Slowly, he walked up to Connie, took the roses from her, and placed them on the table again. Then very gently, he lifted her face to him and said, "I'm leaving here soon and I cannot abandon my heart. Will you come with me and be my wife?"

ঽ৶

After months of inaction and waiting, suddenly events came at a breakneck pace.

Coded Communication
From: Cloudburst 414 Bern Station
To: O.S.S. Headquarters
Subject: Confirmation of previous orders

Message: Agent K agrees to terms of new identity. Send immediately papers in the name of Jack Donald King for his use.

Cloudburst

ঽ৶

The intensive practice of the last six weeks was about to get its most severe test.

He had worked with a voice coach, with Connie on their improvised honeymoon, and even with Williams, at toning down his accent and trying to blur it into a slight inflection that could be mistaken for Irish long living in America. His fluency in English helped, but still he practiced "Americanisms" with Connie every night. His knowledge of the country helped but he studied history books and maps until they were second nature to him.

He cleared his head with a deep breath and strode towards the customs agent. If anything went wrong, there was an O.S.S. agent nearby, but he was determined to make it on his own. After all, he had been one of Germany's premier spies in the late thirties and crossing borders under false IDs was nothing new to him.

The immigration and customs agent looked up and routinely held out his hand for the man's passport.

Franz handed it over. The man flipped through it randomly, finally stopping on the next to the last page. "Name and place of birth?"

"Jack Donald King. Boston."

"You were away for a long time."

Franz nodded. "The war," he said solemnly.

The agent looked him over. "Medical Certificate."

Franz handed over the document that had been signed by the O.S.S. Doctor in Bern. After reading the certificate, the agent handed it back, looked Franz over once and then indicated the suitcase. "Anything to declare?"

"Just personal property."

A brief inspection of the suitcase revealed nothing and the agent marked it accordingly. He paused and then stamped the passport with an entry seal.

Franz took his bag and began to walk through the gate. As he was about to pass through, the agent's voice rang out.

"Mr. King?"

Franz turned slowly, trying to suppress the tremor that raced through his body. This was the moment that all agents feared when crossing borders.

The agent looked sternly at him, and then suddenly broke into a smile.

"Welcome home, sir."

PART THREE

SLEEPING DOGS

"Do not desire to seek who once we were, or where we did, or what, or in whose name."

—*Steven Vincent Benet*

CHAPTER TWELVE

CHASING PHANTOMS

Day drifted into night and the automatic lighting in the safe house clicked on, but the trio around the computer didn't notice. For hours, they sat, watched, and read as Rudy poured forth the story of Konigsmann cum Wenger cum King. Only once, when Rudy signaled for a break, did they leave their seats. The rest of the time, they appeared as statues.

Much, Rudy had had to fill in; the documents told only so much. But being an experienced historian, Rudy had taken educated guesses and Robby knew enough to trust those.

Finally, it was over. Robby took the phone off the modem and flicked on the speaker box.

"You're on with all of us, now."

Robby's voice, speaking to Rudy, was the first sound to break the long silence. It was as if they were all coming out of a prolonged sleep. At first, voices were hushed, gradually strengthening as they all wrenched their minds back to the present.

Eve was the first to speak. "My God, someone's trying to kill me because of things that happened fifty years ago, because I'm writing a history? It doesn't make sense."

Rudy's disembodied voice on the speaker broke in. "What you've done, child, is conjure up the ghosts of greed and deception. People generally like to keep those matters concealed. What do you think, *Momzer*?"

Robby played with his pocket watch, thinking. "Pretty powerful ghosts. Fifty years is a long time."

Rudy added, "Obviously, someone doesn't think it's long enough."

Robby looked up. "He'd have to have one hell of a lot of money to mount this operation. Besides, if he's still alive, he's in his nineties."

Eve desperately needed to put a name to her enemy. "If what you've been telling us is correct, Franz Konigsmann had all those diamonds. He'd have the money."

Robby shook his head. "It doesn't feel right. Something's missing."

"Good boy," the speaker crackled, "I always knew I was an excellent teacher." They could almost see Rudy smiling.

Robby began flipping through some of the printouts of Rudy's research. "What happened to him after New York?"

There was a long silence at the other end of the line. "I don't know...not for sure."

"Guess."

They could hear pages being turned in Washington. "He went to work for one of the agencies formed to wind down from the war effort. Beyond that, I'll have to keep looking."

Robby frowned. "Do it." Then something occurred to him. "You might try the New York Police Department's Alien Squad. They should have some sort of record on him."

"I'll leave immediately."

"Then get your butt back here. I'll need you to coordinate."

Rudy sounded puzzled. "Coordinate what?"

"A scavenger hunt."

&

It was early morning when Robby finally caught up with Seymour. He had traced him from the hotel to the Desert Inn Pro Shop and finally out onto the Championship Level course. It was early, but the course was becoming crowded.

Robby went up to a course steward whom he knew. "Have you seen Gale?"

"He should be somewhere around eight or nine by now," the man said.

"What's he wearing?"

"You'll recognize him, all right." The man laughed.

Robby was walking towards the tenth tee when he spotted Seymour. It would've been hard to miss him. Granted, in the last few years, golfers had become less sedate in their clothes, but Seymour frequently outdid them all. Today, he was resplendent in bright red slacks and equally bright red shirt with slashes of Kelly green, white, and blue on the collar and sleeves.

Danny, who was playing the round with his father, waved as Robby approached. "What're you doing up before noon?"

"I've got to talk to your dad."

Danny grimaced. "Bad timing. He's three over on the front nine."

Seymour, who had been studying the hole dimensions from a chart his caddie held, looked up and saw Robby. "Now, my misery is complete."

Robby shrugged and walked up to him. "We have to talk."

Seymour immediately looked concerned. "Is something wrong? Or can it wait until I'm through?"

"Let's walk and talk."

Danny teed off on the tenth. A beautiful shot right on the green to the right of the hole. Seymour took another look at Robby and then teed off. The ball hooked badly to the right. He looked back at Robby as he handed his club to the caddie. "Why don't you just shoot me now and get it over with?"

As they walked to the ball, Robby began to brief him on all that Rudy had found out. The news distracted him and he played his next shot into the sand.

Looking daggers at Robby, he continued to hack away until he completed the tenth with a double bogey 5. He threw his club to the ground and saw Danny laughing behind his hand. "Not a word. Not a sound or you're out of the will."

For the next few holes, Robby talked and Seymour listened. As he grew more intent on the story Robby was weaving, he forgot about his game and just went through the shots as if by rote.

"Hey Dad," Danny said as they approached the sixteenth, "You're back to par." Seymour just nodded as he continued to listen to Robby.

"Bottom line," Robby was saying, "is that whoever is behind the attacks, is somehow involved with Konigsmann and the diamonds." Seymour didn't even realize that he had just birdied the last hole as he teed off on seventeen.

"We're dealing with heavyweights here, Robert. Are you sure of your ground?"

"As sure as I can be." He paused to let Seymour take his second shot. Neither man noticed as the ball bit on the green and rolled into the hole. "I have Rudy checking out some things in New York."

They walked to the eighteenth tee. "Hey Dad," Danny said just before his father teed off.

"Not now." Seymour snapped. He teed off and then listened intently as Robby began to lay out his plan of action. Again, just before he played his second shot, Danny tried to interrupt but a look from Seymour closed out the opportunity.

He played the shot and was only vaguely aware of it falling just short of the green. He turned back to Robby. "And I foot the bill?" Robby nodded.

He chipped his approach shot and turned to Robby even before the ball landed. "Besides helping the girl, what do I get for my trouble?"

Robby smiled. "The knowledge that you did a mitzvah?'

Seymour stared at him. *"A gantze metziah,"* he said sarcastically. Danny was trying to get his attention but he held up a hand to stop him.

Robby laughed. "Okay, your investment plus an eighth of the diamonds."

"Of the carat weight." Robby nodded. "Such a deal," Seymour said. He turned to walk up on to the green. He looked all around but didn't see his ball. He looked at Danny. "Where's my ball?"

"In the hole."

"What?"

"It's in the hole."

Seymour looked shocked and slowly walked over to the flag and looked down at his ball. As the realization of his Eagle sank in on him, he stuttered "That gives me a..."

Danny was openly laughing now. "A sixty-seven. Five under." Seymour was stunned. "But I shot a thirty-nine on the front nine." Danny checked the scorecard. "And a twenty-eight on the back nine." "Jesus Christ!"

Robby was starting to walk away as Seymour began his celebration. Seymour called after him. "Hey, *macher*." Robby stopped and turned back. "Take care of yourself. This is a lousy time for me to have a new vacancy."

☙

"The committee will come to order." The chairman monotonously banged his gavel on the table before him as the crowd slowly settled into their seats. "The media will please return behind the bar." As the room became quiet, he banged the gavel once more for effect and then nodded at the men at the witness table. "The Chair recognizes our esteemed colleague from Rhode Island."

The two men at the table sat erect and looked serious. The smaller of the two, Senator Nathaniel Larson shuffled his papers as the other man smiled at friends in the crowd and then turned to face the committee.

Larson cleared his throat and began. "Mr. Chairman, members of the committee, it is with a deep sense of personal pleasure that I place before you the name of the president's nominee to be the next director of central intelligence..."

The nominee sat quietly, studying the committee. At the moment, he reckoned that the vote would be eight for, eight against, with two undecided. When he spoke, he would concentrate on those two. He refocused on Senator Larson's voice.

"...You have before you the skeletal record, but that only gives you the cold facts. Allow me to flesh out that skeleton.

"As a young man, only twenty-five years old, just out of the service, he joined the office of strategic services, the forerunner of today's central intelligence. He was assigned to Bern, Switzerland, to the human intelligence desk at a time when the world, and that part of it in particular, was rife with danger and espionage activities.

He persevered and acquitted himself well, making decisions, judgments in personalities, always measured against what was best for America."

Larson continued to drone on as the nominee remembered the time in Bern. It was a memory that was particularly current to him.

"After the war, he was coopted by state department intelligence division. Then in 1950, like most young men fresh from their country's defense, he looked to build a life for himself and his family. He joined IBM and within a short time, his intelligence, ability to make decisions, and excellence of character led him to the position of vice president of their far eastern division."

A note was passed to the nominee from his administrative aide. It said "Found." He read it and then scribbled a short reply on the same sheet of paper. As he passed it back to his aide, he listened to the senator continue to extol his virtues.

"His honesty, dedication to his work, and clear evaluations of difficult situations did not go unnoticed and in 1962, a year of great national and international crisis, he returned to his country's service in the dangerous world of Spy vs. Spy. He returned to the CIA.

"In a short time, he rose to become the director of the directorate of Intelligence where his accomplishments are so well spoken of in the classified testimonials before you.

"In 1965 in recognition of his skill, patriotism, intelligence, and years of service, the president appointed him, and this body confirmed him as director of the National Security Agency."

The administrative aide rose and quietly left the room. Only when he had reached the steps outside did he glance at the note. It said, directly under his note, "Lose it."

❧

The van sat alone in the parking lot opposite the Empress. Slightly beaten up, with primer spots showing on the sides, it blended perfectly with the other cars around it. It was just after six in the morning and no one was around. It was one of those rare periods in Las Vegas of quiet and rest. Except in the van.

Three men sat in the back, watching a battery powered TV showing the confirmation hearings. Senator Larson was continuing to extol the virtues of the nominee.

"Most men in their fifties would settle in at their jobs and plan for retirement. But when he was asked to become our ambassador to the Philippines, once more he answered his country's call.

"Then he 1977, he was offered the post of president of American University here in our nation's capital. He has been there as a beacon for our youth ever since. He has influenced our youth for the better, imbuing in them a sense of value of government service and pride in country."

The cellular phone at their feet rang twice, and one of them answered it as another turned down the set's volume.

"Hello?"

"Gemstone."

"Go ahead, Gemstone."

"I have new instructions for you."

"Standing by to copy."

The man on the phone gestured to the others. They both picked up pads from the floor of the van and prepared to write.

"Two, eight, seven, five."

The man in the van repeated aloud, "Two, eight, seven, five. Copy." The other men wrote as he spoke.

"Three, nine, twenty-four, sixteen."

"Three, nine, twenty-four, sixteen. Copy." The men copied rapidly.

"Thirty-seven, twelve. End message."

"Thirty-seven, twelve. End message. Copy."

"God Bless." The line went dead.

As he hung up the phone, he saw that his two companions had already taken small spiral notebooks from their pockets and were comparing the numbers they had written with words in the books. The one by the television looked up first. "I have a valid message."

A moment later, the other looked up. "I concur." They both handed their translations of the code to the man by the phone.

Both papers read the same. "Terminate the threat." He took out a disposable lighter and soon the papers were burning in the van's ash tray.

❧

Robby walked beside her as they emerged from the First Street entrance of the Empress. It was a cold morning and he wore his heavy McCloud over a sweater and jeans. She was bundled up in a trench style raincoat, scarf, and sunglasses. But wisps of her blonde hair could be seen beneath the scarf.

On the street, Robby looked around and motioned towards Fremont. They walked slowly but deliberately on, with Robby always on the watch.

The men in the van, having been alerted by an accomplice in the hotel, started the engine and watched the couple walk down the deserted street. In the background, they could still hear Senator Larson.

"At seventy-one, this is still a vibrant man of honor, integrity and valor." They pulled out of the lot and onto the street. "His credentials are impeccable. He has seen the intelligence community from many different perspectives." The van pulled slightly ahead of Robby and then turned right, onto Fremont.

Robby noted the van but seemed to relax when it turned down the street away from them. He led her across First Street and down towards the Union Plaza, the opposite direction the van had taken. He didn't see the van take a U-turn at Fremont and Casino Center Blvd. and head back towards him.

In the van, the man who had been on the phone was driving. The two others checked their Ingram machine guns. Larson's voice filled the cargo area as the van slowly approached the couple. "He understands the necessities of maintaining responsible, accountable behavior towards the Congress and the people of this country."

The van began to pick up speed. The men in the back silently slid open the door and prepared to cut down the couple.

Robby had stopped them in front of the Las Vegas Club. The woman seemed to be adjusting her scarf. The van moved closer and closer. The street was empty and their fate seemed sealed.

Someone else was also watching the scene. On the roof of the Union Plaza, looking directly down Fremont, Barker settled the crosshairs of his rifle on the driver in the van. Beside him on the roof, Ernie DiNofrio held a walkie-talkie and was speaking quietly into it.

"Fifty yards...forty yards...thirty yards..." On the street below, Robby listened to the monotone voice through an earphone. He started them walking towards the Union Plaza again.

"Twenty yards…ten yards…NOW, NOW, NOW!!!"

Barker squeezed the trigger twice and watched as the windshield of the van exploded into slivers. It careened to the left and narrowly missed two parked cars, ending up jumping the curb and dangling on the retaining wall of the Golden Gate Casino's parking lot. There was no movement from inside.

At the cry of warning from Ernie, Robby threw himself to his right, knocking down Jenna, sending her blonde wig and sunglasses flying. He stayed down, on top of her, until he heard the van hit the parking lot wall. Then he was up and racing across the street. He reached the van just as its remaining live occupants were coming to their senses.

They were piled up in the rear of the van and were both woozy from the accident. The driver was slumped over the steering wheel with the upper half of his head missing from the force of Barker's .762 steel jacketed shells.

As Robby climbed in, one of the men regained his senses enough to recognize Robby, and to pull his gun, but it was a futile action. Robby's .380 flashed and the man died. He grabbed the other man, the sole survivor of the assassination attempt, and pulled him from the van.

From behind, he could already hear sirens. Metro was one of the most efficient police departments in the country and Robby had no desire to stick around and answer questions. He threw the man's gun back into the van, and then looked down Fremont to see a Cadillac Eldorado driven by Danny Gale come racing up.

It screeched to a stop at the scene of the accident. Robby threw the man into the trunk that Danny had opened from the inside and then slammed down the lid. Danny was out now, standing by the open driver's door.

Robby nodded at him as he rushed in, behind the wheel, pausing only to make sure that Jenna had gotten in on the passenger's side, and then left smoking rubber in his wake as he headed down Fremont to Main Street. Then a right, and in two minutes he was leaving downtown behind him as he accelerated on the 95–515 Freeway.

Danny walked over to the crashed van as a crowd began to

gather and the first police cruiser pulled up. He thought it odd that inside a small television set was on, and on it Senator Larson was finishing his introduction speech.

"His life has been dedicated to preserving the values for which our country stands. This is the man America needs at this time, for this job.

"On behalf of the President of the United States, it is my privilege to present to the committee for consideration as Director of Central Intelligence, E. George Williams."

&

Rudy stepped out of the Hotel Pierre onto East 61st Street, turned left to Fifth Avenue, and crossed to Central Park. The once magnificent expanse of green now exuded the stench of rotting trash. He ducked a menacing bum demanding money and a fellow hawking watches from a folding cart at the curb. Now I know I'm back in New York, he thought.

Taking courage in hand, he walked purposefully a little way into the park and found a bench. The limp was at minimum. No sense looking like a victim. He checked terrain, neighbors, and the mounted policeman close by. Then he sat to review the morning's work.

Earlier, he had made a point of checking in at the New York Police Department Archives just before a shift change. Lots of people in a hurry to go home, watching the clock and the door for their replacements. Rudy and the limp, then at Olympian proportions, approached the man at the desk. "I'm Professor Rudolph Ehrencoles. I have an appointment this morning to go over some old New York Alien Squad files."

"Some what? What appointment?" The harassed officer was trying to complete his shift report. A little old confused man was not what he needed with ten minutes to go.

Rudy tried to look crestfallen. "I have my credentials right here." He fumbled awkwardly in his briefcase and found them. "My colleagues at New York University and Columbia assured me all arrangements had been made with the Mayor and Police Commission."

"Hold it a minute, Professor..." he looked at the ID. "Ehrencoles.

What's it all about?" The officer had resigned himself to never finishing the report.

"I don't understand the problem. I'm here all the way from Nevada. It's a very important monograph on America, the Melting Pot, with all the socioeconomic factors clearly delineated. Let me explain it to you." Rudy started rummaging in his briefcase again.

"Uh, never mind, Professor. Just a fuckup, I'm sure." He called out to another officer passing the desk. "Martinez, get a pass for the professor here and explain the rules to him." Under his breath, he murmured, "In ten minutes, he's somebody else's problem."

Rudy was escorted to a small cubicle with old books and new microfiche. After an hour of filling out forms and waiting for documents, and a half hour or so of reviewing material he already knew quite well, he clicked off the microfiche reader and shut the books. Nothing new there except for the increasingly strong threads of the oft repeated phrase "Suspicion of Espionage" and eventually just "Espionage." He was depressed. It had taken him more time to get into the Archives than it did to review them.

As a last resort, he glanced through the "chit list," a collection of onion skins listing individuals and agencies who had requested the file or received copies of parts therein. Even that had nothing unusual. He was about to give up when one of the last few listings caught his attention. A complete copy of the file had been sent, at the request of J. Edgar Hoover, to one Perry Sloane, Special Agent In Charge of the New York Field Office of the FBI. The date was November 15th, 1947. At least that moved him forward a few months. He resumed what he thought of as his Oscar winning performance and left Police Headquarters pleased with himself.

Now sitting in the sun on the bench in Central Park, the nefarious intrigues of Konigsmann and company, and Eve's mysterious adversaries seemed almost unreal to Rudy.

Rousing himself, he left the park and hailed a cab. "Fifth Avenue and 42nd Street," he directed.

"The library?" the cabby inquired. Rudy nodded and the cab took off.

A few minutes later, thanks to light traffic and maniacal driving, Rudy found himself deposited in front of the New York Public

Library. He stood at the bottom of the steps, admiring the famous lions guarding the entrance to the white marble building, one of the largest library systems in the country, a researcher's dream. Rudy felt he was entering paradise as he passed under the lofty arches at the top of the stairs.

Inside, he wrapped himself in the comforting quiet and soft lighting of a world apart. Following the directions of the young woman at the front desk, he wound his way down to what surely must be the bowels of the building. There were more books and fewer people the lower he went. At last, there was only a tall, slim woman with long, straight blonde hair and the pallor of the denizens of the deep. Her face was ageless and blank, as if, having no human contact, it required no human expression.

She looked up from the book in her hand as he approached. "Rudy Ehrencoles, or are you an apparition?" She appeared surprised and wary.

"Vera. I went to a lot of trouble to track you down." Rudy came up to her, smiling from ear to ear.

She scowled at him. "When you show up, it means lots of work and grief for me, you old bastard."

"Only a modicum of work and no grief, I promise, my Goddess. It's been three years. Surely, you've recovered since then!" He reached up and hugged her. Then pulling up a chair next to her desk, he asked softly, "Anyone else around?"

She remained standing. "No, it's very quiet today. Probably stay that way for another couple of hours. What God awful thing do you want?"

Rudy leaned forward and started to relate the story, but Vera stopped him.

"I don't want to know. Just tell me what's necessary."

"All right. Just the facts, ma'am." He backed up and gave her a very brief and sanitized version of past events. He concluded with "Now, I need to see what interest this FBI type has in all this."

"Rudy, you know how to use the Freedom of Information Act as well as I do. What's the problem?"

"No problem. Just a question of time. I need all the information I can get and as quickly as possible; the FBI and any other agency material. You know the kind of stuff I'm looking for."

"I knew it. You're not just a voracious researcher. If it's extralegal or sleazy, so much the better."

Rudy feigned pain. "It's for a good cause."

She hesitated, then picked up a legal size pad from her desk and a ring of keys. "Okay, grab a shovel and let's start digging." Motioning Rudy to follow, she headed through increasingly dark and narrow aisles to an almost hidden door in back. She unlocked it, and they moved through it into the darkness.

ॐ

"Wake up, Moffatt." Robby gently slapped the man he had pulled from the van until he was completely awake. The man looked around in a panic as he remembered the crash, and looked at Robby.

Robby stood about three feet in front of him. Moffatt tried to rise but realized with a start that he was firmly tied to a stenographic chair. He sat back and tried to calm himself. He had been trained for exactly this type of situation.

Robby smiled as he read Moffatt's thoughts. He held up the man's wallet. "Let's get down to it." He opened the wallet and read the contents. "Maryland driver's license in the name of Harry Moffatt, corporate ID card in the same name for something called forecast research," he looked through the rest. "And that's about it." He looked puzzled. "No Social Security Card, no credit cards, no personal notes, no pictures...?" He threw the wallet aside and walked up to Moffatt. "You wouldn't be a spy, would you?"

Moffatt remained silent.

Robby shrugged. "Makes no difference to me. All I need to know is that you tried to kill me. Now we could play a lot of games and shit like that, but frankly I'm not in the mood." He pulled a chair in front of Moffatt and sat down. "Did they tell you about me?"

They had indeed told him all about Robby, his record, and his reputation, but only now, for the first time, was he beginning to believe it.

Robby began polishing his pocket watch with his shirt as he spoke in a friendly tone. "Your bosses consider me unstable because I won't do stupid shit like trying to gun down someone in downtown Vegas." He looked at Moffatt. He waited for some response, but when none came, he continued on in a conversational tone. "You're going to tell me everything I want to know, and you're going to do it quickly and completely. Understand?"

Something in Robby's relaxed attitude was unsettling. They had told Moffatt that Robby was as good as they came, deadly, devious, and exactly as he had said…unbalanced. But more than that, it was Robby's complete relaxation that sent a clear signal to Moffatt. This was a man in complete control of the situation with no concerns about being interrupted by the authorities.

Moffatt mustered his fading courage. "Fuck you!" He spit it out with all the anger he could muster. To his surprise, Robby began laughing.

"I'd say that if I were you." Still laughing, he pulled his gun and pointed it at the floor between them. "An object lesson." He fired the gun once into the cement floor. The noise bounced around the room, echoing for several minutes. The bullet tore loose several pieces of flooring and sent them as splinters flying into Moffatt's legs. The pain was not severe but the lesson was learned; the gun was loaded.

The smile vanished from Robby's face and was replaced by a hardness and sense of removal. It was as if Robby had absented himself and been replaced by a robot. The gun was leveled at Moffatt's eyes.

"I'm going to ask you some questions and if I even think that you're lying, I'm going to kill you. So think very carefully before answering."

Moffatt looked for even a trace of humanity in the face that had been laughing a moment before. He saw none. His bosses were right, Moss was crazy.

Robby extended his arm and touched the still warm barrel to Moffatt's head. "First question, who do you work for?"

ôª

"That was horrid. Simply horrid!" Eve couldn't believe the scene that had just played out in front of her. "You were going to kill him, weren't you?"

"Yup."

"You terrorized him! It was, it was," her emotions overcame her as she searched for the words. "It was exactly what they were doing to me. There's no difference!"

Robby continued typing his account of the interrogation. "There's one difference."

"What's that?" she said angrily.

"I'm doing it to help you."

Eve was momentarily silent. Then she collapsed into a big chair. "Great. Now it's my fault." She flipped on the TV and tried to ignore Robby as he finished his typing.

They had returned to the safe house right after the interrogation, leaving Barker alone with Moffatt. She tried to concentrate on some show but her mind kept floating back to the sight of the terrified man tied to the chair with the gun at his head. What was worse was she kept imagining what had happened to Moffatt after they had left. Finally, she could stand it no longer and she turned to Robby, who was now Xeroxing his work.

"What happens now, I mean to that man?" Her voice was quiet now that her anger and fear was exhausted.

Robby smiled reassuringly. "He's fine. Barker's storing him right now. We'll let him go when it's safe for you."

"Storing him?"

"Don't ask," he laughed, "but I promise you he'll be safe." He walked over to the refrigerator and began making himself an ice cream soda. Eve shut the TV and walked over to him. Something had been bothering her from the beginning and now she had to get an answer.

"Robby," he turned to her, "why? Why this? Why are you doing all this? You don't know me. Hadn't even met me before a little over a week ago. And since then because of me," she ticked off the events on her fingers "you've been shot at twice, chased, almost kidnapped, and broken so many laws that I've lost track! So why?"

"The diamonds aren't a bad incentive."

She shook her head. "Not good enough. You started all this before you ever knew about the damned diamonds."

Robby sat down in a chair by her. He reached into the nearby cabinet and pulled out a small plaque and lightly tossed it to her. As she read it, he recited.

"At such times as this, there are many dangerous things to be done which nobody else will do, and therefore I cannot help attempting them." He paused and looked into his soda. "John Adams, 1775."

They were both quiet for a long time. Robby sipped his soda and Eve looked from the plaque to Robby and then into space. Finally, she broke the silence.

"It doesn't make sense."

Robby stood and started for the office. "Neither does betting the double zero."

&

Night was falling over Washington as E. George Williams' limousine moved down Pennsylvania Avenue towards the Beltway. He blankly stared out the window at the lights on the marble official buildings. He allowed his mind to wander over the events of the day.

The first day of hearings was largely a blur to him. It had been consumed with speeches, introductions, and more speeches. What dominated his thoughts were the events taking place across the country, in a city that he had never seen, to people he didn't know.

He had thought that he had it under control. The woman should have been a little problem. Routine. But now a man, who in some ways reminded him of himself, had placed himself between Williams and his long worked for reward. And if that man were not stopped...

For the third time, he read through Robby's file. And for the third time, he stopped at the section of the personality profile that troubled him.

&

Excerpt from the Personnel File of Boulder 683 (Moss, Robert P.)

Q: **What would you say were your best and worst attributes?**
A: **My mind set.**
Q: **Which one is that?**
A: **Both.**
Q: **In three words, describe your personality.**
A: **Arrogant. Obnoxious. Relentless.**

&

Williams closed the file and slid it into his briefcase. He settled back on the seat and tried to fall asleep, for he still had the better part of a two hour drive before he was home. As he drifted off, one word kept repeating in his head over and over again.

Relentless.

ءۛ

Barker came to the safe house to relieve Robby around two A.M. Without comment, he walked past Robby, into the main area to check on Eve. He found her sound asleep in the back of the house and after checking the rest of the area, he silently returned to the outer office, where Robby was pulling on his McCloud and hat.

"You set for the night?" Robby asked. In answer, Barker picked up the gym bag that he had deposited by the front door. From it, he extracted a large foil wrapped sandwich and an old, thick book with a worn leather cover.

Robby eyed the sandwich. "Meatball?"

"With cheese. Enough for two."

For a moment, Robby wavered between his need for sleep and his love of Barker's meatball sandwich. Sleep won out. Reluctantly, he turned towards the door.

Barker called after him, "Where do I reach you?"

"Home," Robby said, "till seven. Then I pick up the nutty professor at McCarren and bring him back here. Count on an eight A.M. breakfast meeting."

"Jenna coming?" Barker unwrapped the sandwich, which Robby eyed lustfully.

"Uh, don't know. Let you know." With a wave, he forced himself out of the office and away from temptation.

The car was where he expected it to be. For security reasons, they used only one car, Barker's. It was a restored 1974 AMC Javelin. Its low profile roof, sleek lines and special suspension made it the envy of many a collector in Vegas, but Barker would never part with it. It was his pride and joy, and the only other person he allowed to drive it was Robby.

Robby climbed in, adjusted the seat and mirror, and fired up the big 440 cubic inch engine. He tuned the radio to a classical music station, slipped the car smoothly into gear and was off.

The car was responsive, more so than even Robby's Mustang and driving it was effortless. He relaxed as he allowed the car to find its own way to the Empress. He relaxed and allowed his mind to wander.

Eve was right, more than she knew. What Robby had done, or would have done, was just as wrong as what 'they' were doing to her. It bothered him how easily he could slip into the old ways that he thought he had left long behind him.

He had never accepted the argument that whatever you do to defeat an evil thing was justified. It was simply too easy. Too easy to justify something you didn't like as evil and thereby feel no restraints upon your actions.

And so he thought, as he drove down the nearly deserted highway, If I become evil in order to combat evil. He let the thought disappear.

❦

The conference room was slowly filling up. The men came in, got some coffee or doughnuts, socialized and eventually found their way to the folding chairs arranged in a semicircle. The group leader, Sam, stood and spoke softly.

"Everyone want to take his place so we can get started."

The room settled and then was still. Sam smiled. "I want to welcome all of you to the meeting. My name's Sam."

"Hi, Sam," the men responded.

"My name's Sam, and I have a problem with violence." The men watched him. Some intently, some bored, others in between. "After five years in the Teams, I discovered that the only way I knew to solve conflicts was to react violently. I got into fights constantly. Lost my job, my wife, my kids, my life. But I can honestly say that I haven't committed a violent act in three years."

Most of the men applauded and shouted words of support. All of them were now paying rapt attention.

"I want to encourage all of you to get up whenever you feel like it and tell us your situation. We make no judgments here. We've all been there, in the military, law enforcement, intelligence. Whatever." He paused and looked over the room.

"All right, we have some business we can take care of now. Jason. Will you come up here?"

A tall, heavy set man stood and walked slowly to the front of the room. He turned and faced the group. "Hello. My name is Jason, and I have a problem with violence."

"Hi, Jason."

"I'm a deputy sheriff and I'm currently on a six month suspension for excessive force. I did it, I was wrong. I know that. But I've come to understand, through therapy and coming here that I've got to find other ways to deal with these impulses. I haven't committed a violent act in a month. It's been a bitch." There was nervous laughter around the room. "But I'm hanging in."

The men applauded and Sam stepped forward. He handed Jason a small white poker chip. Everyone knew what it meant. One month without a violent act. For six months you got a green one, and for every year a blue one.

Sam looked out across the room. The first few speakers always required encouragement. After that the meeting would pick up a momentum of its own. Now he looked around and was astonished to see a man who had long ago abandoned these meetings. He nodded at him.

The man stood up slowly. His voice was soft but choked with emotion. "My name's Robby and I have a problem with violence."

"Hi, Robby."

*

Three o'clock in the morning in Las Vegas is a busy time. The final shows have played out, and the people, mostly dressed to the nines, are taking one last chance at the tables before heading to bed. As he walked through this late crowd, he realized that he was too wound up to sleep. He headed for the roulette tables.

Jack Bragdon was the oldest croupier at the Empress, he had started with Seymour at the beginning. Although he had been retired for over five years, he was still allowed, when the urge struck him, to come back and spin the wheel. This night, his table was empty and he spun the wheel lazily, waiting for a player.

"Two hundred in twenties, please."

Jack turned and saw Robby settling himself at the table. He slid the credit pad across to Robby who signed it and slid it back. "How you doing, Jack?"

"Got to be better than you." Robby looked more tired than Jack had ever seen him. There was always an air of excitement around Robby, but tonight Jack sensed only exhaustion. And he didn't think it was physical.

Robby played forty dollars on nine. Jack spun the wheel, "Eighteen, no winner." He scooped up Robby's bet. "Place your bets." Robby gambled in a desultory way for about fifteen minutes without saying a word. Finally, Jack broke the silence.

"What's wrong, kid?"

"Nothing."

Jack laughed. "Your nothing must be one helluva something. I've never seen you this…" he searched for the word, "I don't know, this wrung out."

Robby smiled bitterly. "Good choice of words."

Casually, Jack pressed a button on the floor by his right foot. This activated a camera above his table and set off a beeper in Seymour's office. Robby played twenty-one and the ball came up nine.

"That figures."

&

In his office, Seymour turned up the volume and listened to Jack and Robby as he watched them on his monitor.

"The problem is," Robby was saying, "that this time I may have gotten in too deep, too fast."

Jack smiled warmly. "They don't call you the Plunger for nothing."

For the first time, Robby laughed, but Seymour didn't like the look on his face. He picked up his telephone and spoke quietly into it. Then he watched as the pit boss walked over and handed Robby a note. Robby looked up at the hidden camera, nodded, and then put all his chips on the double zero.

Jack spun the wheel as Sy adjusted the camera to see the results better. For a moment, the ball seemed to linger above the green double zero slot and then at the last possible moment, it bounced away. Robby shrugged, tossed a chip that he had saved to Jack for a tip and walked away silently.

Sy called room service and ordered an ice cream soda. It was waiting for Robby when he arrived.

&

They sat silently together for half an hour, the only sound Robby drinking his soda. At last, Sy spoke up. "When I first opened the Empress, I put everything I had into it. I don't mean just money, although God knows I begged, borrowed, and stole everything I could get my hands on. I also invested every fiber of my being into it.

"About a month before opening night, there was a fire. I was in L.A. at the time but I took the first train and rushed back. When I got here, it was early morning. I stood before the smoking ruins of my dream, looked at the devastation, and felt like I was a dead man."

Robby stared into his soda, but Sy knew him well enough to know that he was listening.

"Not only was the joint destroyed, but somebody, probably the firemen, had gone through the gift shops and the jewelry store and helped themselves to whatever they wanted."

Robby looked up. "Robert, however you feel right now, I guarantee you I felt worse. I stood in the wreckage all day, just wandering through it. Completely stunned. One thought kept running through my mind What had I done to deserve this?"

For a moment, the memory returned a little too clearly to Sy and he had to stop. He pulled himself together and continued.

"Anyway, as the sun was setting, the last of the fire officials left and I thought I was alone. Then I heard a sound of hammering. It took me a minute but then I found Jack Bragdon, deep in the standing water and ashes, doing his best to save a roulette table. I walked over and silently we began salvaging everything we could. Eventually," he gestured at the casino, "we succeeded."

Robby seemed disappointed. "What's the moral then," he asked. "Hard work is its own reward?" He sounded bitter.

Sy took a deep breath. "No *schmuck*. No moral. I'm just telling you that I know the difference between letting things overwhelm you and fighting back. I always fight back." He fixed Robby with a hard stare. "And so do you."

Robby got angry. "Why, goddamn it! Why do I have to always fight back? Especially against things that aren't any of my goddamn business! Why!"

Sy smiled. "Because you're a fighter. And one more thing."

"What?"

Sy stood up and walked to his bookcase. It took him a minute to find the volume he wanted. He opened it to the passage he was looking for and handed it to Robby.

It was a copy of Thomas Jefferson's first Inaugural Address. A passage was underlined. Robby slammed the book shut without reading it. He knew what it said. He had given the book to Sy for his birthday several years earlier. "What's the point?"

Sy smiled and took the book from Robby. He reopened it to that section and began to read. "Let's see. Jefferson lists the principles that he believes our country is based on and then he says," he paused to put on his glasses.

&

Excerpt from the First Inaugural Address of Thomas Jefferson

March 4, 1801

> ...these principles form the bright constellation which has gone before us and guided our steps through an age of revolution and reformation. The wisdom of our sages and the blood of our heroes have been devoted to their attainment. They should be the creed of our political faith, the text of civic instruction, the touchstone by which to try the services of those we trust; and should we wander from them in moments of error or of alarm, let us hasten to retrace our steps and to regain the road which alone leads to peace, liberty, and safety.

&

Robby took the book and reread the words. Sy watched as the anger drained from his face and was replaced by a determination. "The problem is, Robert," he paused and Robby looked up at him, "you still believe."

CHAPTER THIRTEEN

THEORIES

The passenger terminal at McCarran Airport, like Las Vegas itself, was relatively quiet at seven A.M. Rudy padded softly through the carpeted arrival area, glancing at the chairs all around. Most were empty but there were a couple of sleepy looking faces who had probably stayed up all night to be on time to meet people.

There is a distinctive look about McCarran. Unlike most big city airports, it mirrors the town you're about to enter, like a preparation chamber. There are a myriad of slot machines arranged in little islands, leading into a corridor whose walls are filled with backlit posters hawking the pleasures of the major hotels and casinos.

Not seeing a familiar face, Rudy moved into the corridor. Hurrying to one of the pay phones in the recessed areas at its side, he stopped suddenly, spotting a serious-looking Robby coming towards him. They met at the end of the corridor where it opened into an area of shops like a mini-mall. Rudy began staggering as if under a great weight, his limp at comic proportions.

"I get the message." Robby grinned at him. "I'll get your luggage." The grin disappeared, replaced by the solemn look once more.

"What's the matter? Something happen?" Rudy dispensed with games and looked sharply at Robby.

"We'll talk in the car. You have a productive trip?"

"Very." Rudy patted the briefcase he carried.

Robby grunted and they moved silently through the luggage area to the car where Robby deployed Rudy and luggage quickly and efficiently. Robby got in on the driver's side and they took off.

As they left the airport and headed east on Russell Road, Robby filled Rudy in on the assassination attempt and the follow up. As Robby talked, Rudy listened more to the tone than the words. He thought about what Robby said, and more importantly, what was left unspoken, in light of what he had learned in New York.

"*Momzer*," Rudy tried to lighten the heavy silence that descended, "you're allowed an occasional fall from grace. Only the Gods and Ehrencoles are impervious." He was genuinely concerned about Robby, Eve and their whole 'mob', particularly Jenna.

The trip continued in silence as they detoured up Hobble Creek Drive and crisscrossed side streets, driving generally north until they picked up Nellis Boulevard, regularly checking for a tail.

At Maslow Park, they slowed almost to a stop and checked once more. Then, satisfied they weren't being followed, proceeded up Boulder Highway to the safe house.

ಜ

Eve was still wiping the sleep out of her eyes when Jenna arrived. Barker had just been relieved by one of his men and joined Jenna in the dining room.

After the shoot out, Robby had left Jenna at her apartment for a return to relative normalcy. She had been in on a few 'incidents' with Robby before and had developed her own routine for dealing with the adrenaline rush, fear, and the need to maintain sanity.

She'd let her feelings out, confront the incident, and come to terms with her part in it. Then after a reasonable night's sleep and a luxurious shower, she was usually ready to face the world again.

Eve, however, had slept fitfully, pictures of the preceding day's events constantly intruding on her rest. It showed in her slow, lethargic movements.

Jenna made coffee, set the table, and put out on a platter the croissants she had picked up on the way in. Eve fell into a chair at the table as Jenna poured coffee and gave Barker the chocolate doughnuts he particularly favored and which she had brought just for him.

Suddenly, Barker pushed his chair aside abruptly and stood up, facing the door, completely alert. The two women stared at him as an air of danger and expectancy filled the room. "They're here," he said.

The office door opened a minute later and Robby strode into the room. Jenna and Eve relaxed and sat down, but Barker remained standing, his eyes locked on Robby's.

"I don't like that look in your eyes," he said. "You get that look and I usually end up bleeding."

"Could happen," Robby said flatly. His expression was determinedly set. "We're going up against pros this time."

"We?"

Robby smiled in a bitter way. "You don't want to miss this one." He reached out and patted the tattoo on Barker's left arm. A parachute with two large feathered wings coming out of the sides and a five pointed star on top. "Hell, you might even know them." He left Barker looking down at his tattoo and walked over to Jenna.

"Where's Dad?" she asked.

"He'll be along. He's making some copies." He motioned at Eve who was fixing her makeup. "How is she?"

Jenna shrugged. "Hanging in. Scared. You name it." She waved at Rudy as he came in. "Do you have any good news for her?"

Rudy walked up to Jenna and gave her a brief hug. "I thought I told you never to volunteer." He paused. "Are you all right?" She smiled and kissed him on the cheek.

Robby walked into the living room area, sat down on the couch, and gestured to the group. "Everybody might as well get comfortable. This is going to take awhile."

Barker remained standing near the table, but Eve came and sat in a chair across from Robby. Jenna sat next to Robby, and Rudy settled himself into a deeply cushioned recliner which he extended fully back.

Eve was visibly nervous. "I'm tired of just sitting here. I feel so useless."

Rudy smiled and handed her a sheaf of Xeroxed pages. "You

won't feel that way long." He handed out copies to the rest of the group. "Shall I begin?" He waited for a dissent, hearing none, he began.

"Let's see, when we last left the redoubtable Colonel Konigsmann, he had arrived in the U.S. under the name of King, yes?" He paused for effect.

"Now, let's talk about what happened to our debonair Colonel, a man used to surroundings of glamour and wealth. To keep it relatively uncomplicated, my children, let's call him King from this point on.

"King went to work for a government agency charged with interviewing German prisoners of war who didn't want to be sent back to Germany. He handled some debriefing and made recommendations as to whether or not they'd be granted asylum."

"I remember running across the ECD a couple of times," Eve interjected.

Rudy nodded, and continued. "He started there about two weeks after he arrived and continued at this rather bland job for ten months; six days a week.

"His personal life wasn't much more exciting. He and Constance lived in an apartment in a converted Brownstone in midtown Manhattan; not very large, and covered with a not too fresh coat of paint hiding old construction. In this dismal environment, Constance gave birth to their son on July 25th, 1947."

Jenna interrupted. "That would make him in his mid forties now."

"Do we know where he is?" Robby asked. Rudy shook his head. Robby looked over at Barker, who nodded.

Rudy went on. "They shared their small apartment with a certain Otto Streck who I believe to be the son of the General who brought the diamonds to Crystal Movement. King had run across him when the young man was being interviewed at ECD. King obviously persuaded his wife to join him in accepting young Otto into their crowded apartment. He was paroled to their custody and went to work at ECD with King."

The group had been going through documents as Rudy spoke, but more than the papers, they hung on his words. Occasionally,

Robby would push some papers aside, and polish his watch, but he listened carefully.

Pulling a table a little closer, Rudy rested his bad leg on it. "On November 12th, King called the CIA."

Robby looked up. "How do we know this?"

"Several sources," Rudy said. "We don't know who he talked to or what he talked about but there's clear evidence that the call took place." Rudy shuffled some papers. "On November 13th, he went to work as usual. Investigators were able to document his movements on the afternoon of the 14th."

Jenna asked "What investigators?"

"Patience, child. All will be revealed in…," Rudy counted document pages, "in good time."

ₔ

Excerpt from Federal Bureau of Investigation

Incident Appendix to Case #47–93779

November 14, 1947

> **3:00 P.M.**—Jack Donald King stops by his landlady's apartment to ask her to turn the heat on. He indicates that he will be back that evening.

> **6:00 P.M.**—A mounted police officer spots King on the Grand Lawn in Central Park talking to another man. The officer thinks nothing of it.

> **8:30 to 9:00 P.M.**—The same mounted police officer again sees King in the same spot, this time standing alone. The officer makes a note of it without noting the exact time.

> **10:10 P.M.**—The same mounted police officer once again spots King in the same spot, this time with the man from earlier in the evening. He overhears King say to the man, "The rink at the Center in about thirty." The Officer makes a note in his memo book about all three meetings "Just in case something happened, I wanted to be covered."

> **11:45 P.M.**—The same officer, now off duty, sees the other man from the park at the skating rink at Rockefeller Center, looking anxious and nervous. The officer thinks he sees a gun in the man's waistband, but before the officer can take any action, the man disappears. The officer calls

the incident in to his desk sergeant who notes it in the official log.

᧞

"On November 14th," Rudy continued, "Citizen King neä Konigsmann AKA Wenger AKA Colonel K disappeared off the face of the earth. The disappearance prompted one of the FBI's larger manhunts of the Forties. King's lifestyle at the time certainly did not reflect the ownership of millions of dollars in diamonds. Was he playing it close to the vest? Waiting till he was no longer under close scrutiny? Had he become fed up with the dull, quiet life of Mr. Everyman? Or was there a more sinister reason for his disappearance? Here's where the fun begins."

᧞

FBI Teletype To: SAC NYFO Sloane, Perry J. 186–07341
From: Assistant Director Tolson, Clyde S. 106–07489
Date: 15 November 47
As Pertains to: NYPD Disappearance Investigation
Status: Urgent

Individual associated with National Security disappeared between 2235 and 0035 this morning in West Fifties section of Manhattan Island. NYPD inquiries currently unaware National Security Implications. This office informed 0430 this date by XXXXXXXXXX NYFO to make maximum effort to locate and/or ascertain circumstances of disappearance. Agents from XXXXXXXXXX will contact NYFO this date with further.

Tolson

᧞

"What do all those X marks in the document mean," Jenna asked.

"They indicate the work of some ham handed censor on a power trip, my dear." Rudy went on. "Obviously, someone was concerned enough about King's 'no show' to call the assistant director of the FBI at four in the morning. Sloane promptly put eight agents on the case. Their bosses burned up the wires with concern.

᧞

Extract from: FBI Teletype
To: SAC NYFO Sloane, Perry J. 186–07341
From: Director Hoover, John E. 100–00149
Date: 15 November 47
As Pertains To: NYPD Disappearance Investigation

Status: Urgent

King disappearance has gravest implications on national security. Imperative all areas of inquiry be delved. Secondarily, NYPD must be discouraged from pursuing investigative leads that would lead to links between King and XXXXXXXXXXXXX.

ੋ▰

Extract from: U.S. Government Memorandum
From: Perry J. Sloane SAC NYFO 186–07341
Date: 15 November 47
To: Assistant Director Tolson 106–07489
Condition: Urgent
Subject: King Investigation

There have been developments at the site which I believe require immediate transmission to the director. S.A. Bass and S.A. Reilly have developed information from the site that XXXXXXXXXX and two (2) other individuals were seen in the area of the disappearance within an hour of the event.

Further, XXXXXXX has been out of touch with "the friends" for some time.

Sloane

ੋ▰

"A cover up?" Jenna asked.

"No," Barker laughed, "typical paranoid reaction."

Rudy smiled. "Let's go on. It continues to get interesting, my boy." They continued reading as Rudy continued his story.

"As you can see, Hoover responded the next day in typical fashion. He ordered electronic surveillance on young Streck and reinforced to Sloane that the incident was to be covered up at all costs." He checked his notes. "Actually he said…"

ੋ▰

Extract from: FBI Teletype
To: SAC NYFO Sloane, Perry J. 186–07341
From: Director Hoover, John E. 100–00149
Date: 16 November 47
As Pertains To: King Disappearance Investigation
Status: Urgent

…Suggest to other agencies including NYPD that Bureau interest is strictly due to Federal employment of King…

JEH

ੋ▰

"Let me jump ahead here," Rudy said.

"Thank God," Barker said under his breath.

Rudy turned to him and snarled. Then he returned his attention to his notes. "The investigators began to focus on a man named Martin Planschke. An internee, where King worked, released on King's recommendation."

Robby looked up. "Do we know where he is?"

For the first time Rudy looked solemn. "Unfortunately, yes. I'll be getting to that." Robby returned to polishing his watch.

Rudy took a drink of coffee and continued. "The relevant document is dated December 6, 1947." They all turned to it. "The first part is simply a summary of the case." He began to gesture rapidly. "For reasons best known to themselves, they became convinced that Mr. Planschke knew more than he was telling. They tapped his phone, put him and his family under full surveillance, the whole nine yards.

"Finally, in the middle of the document we find the transcript of what they considered to be a threatening phone call. Most of the rest of the document is heavily censored, but the final paragraph indicates that they no longer consider King just to be missing.

☙

Extract from:	**FBI Memorandum to the Director**
Date:	**December 6, 1947**
Case #:	**47–93779**
SAC:	**Perry J. Sloane 186–07341/NYFO**
	Charles E. Biggars 189–43101/DCFO
	Div. 5 SAC
CIO:	**Clyde S. Tolson 106–07489**

Recommendations

Immediate action seems necessary. Firstly to XXXXXXXXX XXXXXXXX XXXXXXX. Secondly consideration should be given to conducting an investigation into why XXXXXXXXX was interested in King AKA XXXXXXXXXXXXX. Finally it must be examined whether or not this has changed from a case of disappearance to a case of homicide.

Sloane/Biggars

☙

The room was silent as they read the words "case of homicide." Rudy closed his copy of the notes and finished from memory.

"Things happened quickly after that. Hoover got Streck deported without a hearing…"

Eve interrupted. "That's illegal!"

Robby continued reading. "That's Hoover."

"Regardless," Rudy continued, "it happened."

"Maybe we should try to get in touch with Streck," Eve suggested.

"That won't be easy." Rudy said. "He died of pneumonia in Leipzig, Germany in 1953."

"Pity," Barker said.

"He also died pathetically poor. Anyway, fewer than two months after King disappeared, and this huge manhunt launched, it ended with all files taken from the New York Field Office and sent to the personal supervision of Hoover and Tolson."

"That leaves us up against a blank wall." Eve was disconsolate again.

"I'm not so sure," Jenna interjected. "It seems to me there are a couple of possibilities. We can't simply take it for granted that Konigsmann was murdered. Maybe he disappeared himself. Or…" she paused, thinking aloud, "maybe, if he was killed, the guy who did it is the one after us."

Eve and Robby smiled at Jenna's use of the word 'us'.

"You mean because we might find out who killed him?" Eve perked up.

"Possibly. A lot would depend on the reasons for killing him," Rudy added. "If it was revenge, then chances are the killer wouldn't be too concerned."

"On the other hand, if they were to get at the diamonds…well, maybe the killer never got his hands on it."

"And they think we might find it first?" Jenna was getting excited.

"If he really was murdered." Barker broke in. "It seems to me that if I had that kind of money available to me, and had to live the way," he looked at Rudy, "the expert," Rudy sneered, "described, I'd look for a way out…fast."

"Not everyone's as avaricious as you are," Jenna laughed.

"Not everyone would admit it." Barker took a half hearted

swipe at her.

The discussion was making all of them concentrate on a puzzle rather than the danger. They were feeling relaxed for a change.

Robby spoke up, his voice cold and flat. So cold, in fact, that everybody stopped talking and looked at him.

"This isn't some college debating society. This is life and death." He looked at Rudy. "Get together later with Eve on this stuff, see if you can get something solid for us to go on. In the meantime, we have something else to discuss."

Eve looked scared and spoke in barely audible tones. "You mean that man who tried to kill us."

He nodded. "The men who jumped us worked for a company called Forecast Research." He looked over at Barker.

"It's a private think tank," Barker began, "owned by a dummy corporation called Cloudburst Ltd. I'm still working on who owns them."

"Anyway," Robby interrupted, "they do private intelligence work for corporate America. Also, they seem to hire a lot of ex-intelligence types."

"Like our friends from the van?" Jenna asked.

"Like our friends from the van." He turned to the rest. "I persuaded the survivor to answer a few questions." Eve flinched, while Rudy looked at him disapprovingly. "He was well briefed and well prepared. His orders came from a series of cutouts, and high tech relays. Very slick, very elegant. Too elegant for corporate."

"So who was pulling his chain?" Barker was getting anxious. He was a doer, not a waiter.

"He doesn't know." When Barker looked at him skeptically, he shook his head. "Trust me. He wasn't lying. Not at the end anyway. More to the point, he's the kind that wouldn't want to know."

Jenna shook her head. "So that leaves us exactly where we were before. Somebody may or may not have a fortune in stolen diamonds. That same someone may or may not be responsible for the disappearance of a Nazi war criminal who may or may not be the reason for the attacks on Eve and us." She shook her head. "It could drive you nuts!"

Robby smiled. "We're not quite where we were. For one thing, we now have three directions to go in." He looked at Eve. "Like I said before, you and Rudy stay on top of the King lead. See if you can track down the FBI agents that worked the case. Any of them. Find out what's not in the files."

He looked at Jenna. "Go see Danny Gale. Use his and his Dad's contacts to get everything you can on the eminent Mr. Williams, the future CIA Director."

He looked at Barker. "Up for a trip?"

"Forecast Research?"

Robby nodded. "Psychic, positively psychic."

"Psychotic is more like it, when I go with you."

"Probably true. In any case, can you find anyone to watch over Eve while we're gone."

"Calendar Dan, Louie Gross, Bobby Petronelli?"

Robby thought for a moment. "Louie Gross, if not him then Calendar."

Barker nodded and went to the phone. After a minute or two he turned to Robby and mouthed the word "Louie."

Robby stood and stretched. "Any questions?"

Rudy nodded. "We really should check the German Archives."

Robby thought about it. "Okay, sounds right. If everything stays calm, I'll meet you in Berlin in four days."

"Not Berlin," Rudy said authoritatively. "Freiburg. That's where the German Military Archives are."

"*Ja Wohl*, Herr Professor."

ᨀ

Forecast Research sat off by itself in a park-like setting that contained several office buildings. Its gleaming white walls and huge picture windows gave it an air of a library or museum. Not of the largest private intelligence company in the country.

Now, at three in the morning with a light mist falling, and multicolored flood lights bathing the building, it seemed more like a piece of modern sculpture than a building.

Guards in blazers, not uniforms, casually patrolled the grounds. Actually, they were unnecessary. Hundreds of sensors constantly monitored the area around the building, sending their electronic messages back to a state of the art security system. It was thought to be unpenetrable.

Robby sat in the rented car, half a block from the complex and waited for Barker to start the show. Timing was everything and the timing was dependent on Barker. So Robby sat, and waited and watched.

Barker, meanwhile, was moving quietly towards the floodlit lawn. Dressed in black, and moving with a stealth and grace that belied his size, he closed on his target...a guard lounging against a nearby tree.

The guard, unaware of the danger nearby, was watching an upper window of a building nearby, where he could see a woman sitting at her desk. He had watched her every night for the last week, fantasizing about her, trying to work up his courage to meet her. He never saw Barker rise up out of the shadows, and he never felt the blow that knocked him unconscious.

Barker worked quickly. Making sure the young man was alive and uninjured, he quickly tied him, took his blazer and radio, and casually strolled out into the light.

Ten minutes later, all hell broke loose.

Every alarm in the building seemed to be ringing at the same time. Lights flashed on and off, shouts could be heard, and, for the moment, confusion reigned. Guards rushed out onto the lawn, spotlights came on and swept the area, and in the distance, police cars could be seen speeding to the scene.

Robby waited for the cars to pass him before he started his car and pulled in behind. He followed them through the gate and up to the front door. Cops mixed with security as they tried to sort out the situation. Robby got out and mixed with the crowd. Dressed in jeans and a sweatshirt, he pulled out a badge and clipped it to his collar, as some of the plain clothes officers were doing. As long as they don't look too close, he thought.

As things began to get sorted out, an older police sergeant started to walk over to him. Just then, they were all knocked to their knees by a large explosion that shook the ground and was immediately followed by a fireball on the lawn to the south of the building.

When everyone got back to their feet, Robby was gone.

He moved quickly and silently through the nearly deserted

building. He had gotten a brief look at an overall map of the complex when he entered and he flawlessly navigated by memory. Suddenly, a man appeared in his path.

Robby froze. The armed security guard immediately pulled his gun. "Freeze!" For a moment, they stood staring at each other, then the guard started to reach for his radio.

Robby moved. Throwing himself to one side to dodge the shot that would never come, he simultaneously kicked up with his right foot catching the guard flushly under the chin. The man was catapulted backward and onto the floor by the blow. Quickly, Robby was on him and delivered a smash with the heel of his hand to the man's forehead.

Without moving from the fallen guard's chest, Robby looked around. Silently, he went through his automatic checklist. Cameras? None. Witnesses? None. Decision? Continue ingress. He placed the fingers of his left hand against the guard's throat and felt for a pulse. It was strong and regular. He would be all right. Robby dragged the guard into a nearby service closet and moved on. Less than a minute had passed.

Robby began jogging through the halls. His time was now limited to the time the guard would be unconscious, and that could not be guessed accurately. He figured fifteen minutes. His inner clock began a countdown.

Finally, he came to the room he was searching for. The comptroller's office. A moment to manipulate the lock and he was in. He made his way to the inner office and to the computer terminal within. He worked quickly but without hurry. He opened drawers, checked shelves, examined every small piece of paper stuck to the desk or the wall. Just as he was about to give up hope, he found what he was looking for.

Most people, contrary to advice, write down the access codes to their computers, and keep it hidden nearby their terminal. Luckily for Robby, the operator of this terminal was no different. On the back of a copy stand, scotch taped, was the code. He typed in the number and was in.

Scanning down the menu, he quickly punched up the records of the parent company, Cloudburst Ltd.

Normally, this information would be unavailable to Forecast employees, but Robby hoped that the comptroller's office would be exempted from that kind of in-house security.

He printed out the information without reading it. Waiting nervously, he checked the hall, and listened to the radio. The search was spreading from the outside to inside the building. He was almost out of time. As the printing stopped, he grabbed it and ran to get out of the building.

In the vast open areas of the grounds, he could safely operate without endangering the guards; but here in these narrow corridors he might be forced to kill some if he was cornered. And he desperately hoped to avoid that.

He raced through the corridors, changing directions whenever he detected a sound or from the corner of his eye caught a movement that he didn't like. He almost made it.

As he turned into the final corridor that led to the loading docks, the alarm sounded. He felt, more than saw, the huge iron door start to slide down to cut off his escape. He dived forward, flattened himself and rolled, just barely passing beneath the door as it clanged shut.

He jumped to his feet and grabbed the radio that he had taken off the guard. "Double zero to double one."

A voice he didn't recognize came on the radio. "Who's using this frequency? This is a privately licensed frequency."

Robby ignored it and listened. After the voice cleared, about thirty seconds, he heard Barker's voice come crackling through.

"Double one to double zero. Five seconds after visual."

Robby smiled as he dashed down the corridor. He threw the radio away as he reached the door. He paused to catch his breath, and then burst through the door out into the flood lit night.

"Southeast entrance!" Several guards yelled at the same time. Robby raced in a zigzag towards the cover of the trees. Three police officers moved to cut him off.

From the trees, Barker watched Robby run. He saw the cops cut him off and he saw Robby brace himself for defense. Without taking his eyes off the scene before him, he reached down and pushed the button on the detonator by his feet.

Explosions ripped through the air as hastily planted flares and smoke bombs went off. The cops were distracted long enough for Robby to dart to his left into the lights and smoke. By the time they recovered, he was gone. They heard a car start and speed off, but were too late to get a plate.

As more cops and security rushed to where Robby was, nobody noticed Barker casually walk up to Robby's rental. One minute later, he was gone, leaving confused security people and cops in his wake.

૨૦

"So what you're saying, George," Senator Larson intoned, "is that the majority of our intelligence failures in the last ten years is due to invoicing?"

Williams laughed. He was in his element. The cocktail party was in its final hours, and the people gathered around him were being enraptured by his every word.

"Not exactly, Senator. But you have to concede that with our reliance on contract operators, we have to improve our bill paying procedure. We can't keep top people if we only offer ninety or one hundred twenty day billing."

"And I always thought it was about spies."

Williams took a drink. "Someday soon, I predict," everybody leaned closer, "accountants will run the world." Everybody laughed.

As he was reveling in the attention, an aide leaned close and whispered in his ear. The smile froze on his face as the aide talked. He put down his drink and stood.

"You'll have to excuse me, ladies and gentlemen, but affairs of State call."

Senator Larson moved to Williams' seat and continued the conversation as he watched the aide lead Williams away. "It's probably his accountant calling." As he listened to the laughter and looked at the expression on Williams' face, he privately hoped this wasn't the beginning of some bad news.

Williams sat behind the big desk in the study. "What happened?" he demanded angrily.

The aide shifted nervously. "There's been an incident over at Forecast. Explosions, lots of smoke, flares, and we think a break in."

"You think!"

"A man was seen running from the scene, but the security

people and the police were unable to identify him."

Williams bit the end off of a cigar angrily. "With all we spend on electronic security, somebody tries to blow up the place and then breaks in? And gets away clean?" He was quiet while he lit his cigar, then he threw the lighter across the room, narrowly missing his aide. "Is that what you're trying to tell me?"

Quietly, the aide said, "There's more."

Williams' anger was barely contained. "Of course there is," he said in a low guttural voice.

"There was a break in on the computer in the comptroller's office. Someone accessed the Cloudburst file." He braced himself for the reaction.

Before Williams could articulate the rage that was written on his face, a low buzzer sounded. The aide went to a wall cabinet, unlocked it and picked up the scrambled direct link to Forecast Research that was kept there. He listened for a minute, said a few quiet words, and then hung up.

"They've got a picture of the man." He walked to the computer console beside the desk and punched some codes. A moment later the printer began to hum and a picture began to emerge.

"How many cameras do we have out there?" Williams asked.

"I think about thirty." He stood over the printer almost willing out the print.

"And we got one picture? I don't fucking believe it!!"

The aide pulled the picture from the printer and looked it over. He was stunned. "It's not possible, it's not!"

Williams grabbed the picture from the young man's hand and stared hard and long at it. It couldn't be, it couldn't. He had ordered the man killed, and his men didn't miss. Ever. And yet the evidence was here in his hand. Not only was the man alive, but he had effortlessly gotten past all of the elaborate security that protected Forecast Research.

That protected him.

He collapsed into his chair, and for the first time since 1947 felt afraid, insecure, and vulnerable. Quietly, he murmured the name and the thought.

"Moss. Relentless."

ঽ▲

In Europe, it was early morning. The old man sat dozing on his patio that looked out across lush fields. He was ninety and in ill health, but still was one of the most feared men in the back alleys of the world. The power he wielded, and would soon pass on, could strike out anywhere, anytime, and the results were uniformly devastating.

"Herr Schlussel?" The young man was tall, blonde, and erect; as one would expect him to be in this world. He gently touched the old man's shoulder.

He opened his eyes, looked at the young man, and reached down for his sunglasses. "*Ja?*"

The young man talked for about ten minutes. As he talked, the old man leaned closer and closer to him. The conversation was in German, but even a casual listener would have recognized the one name that kept coming up.

"Moss!"

ঽ▲

It had taken Jenna most of a day to find Danny Gale. However, it took less than half an hour to convince him to help. Danny immediately took over an office in the executive suite of the Empress and made a few phone calls, called in some favors, and finally was directed to the home of a recently retired agent from the Las Vegas FBI field office. Harold McIntyre was with the FBI for more than twenty years, and had ties with assorted intelligence types for a decade longer. He stood at the entrance to his living room, assessing Danny and Jenna. He had been urged to see them, but considering the strained relations he'd had with the Bureau since before his retirement, he was cautious.

"I'm probably out of my mind talking to the two of you," he said as they entered, "but what the hell, it might make a good chapter in my book." As Danny shook hands with him, he noticed the gun in the man's belt.

"Your book?" Danny asked.

McIntyre shrugged as he led them into his living room. "Didn't you know? Every ex-agent thinks he's got a book in him. Unfortunately, most publishers don't think so." He laughed. "Okay, what do you want, that I either don't know or won't tell you? And," he raised his hand before Danny began, "exactly why do you want to know?"

Danny took a deep breath. "Mr. McIntyre, this is strictly between us. We've been told that you're," he searched for the word, "not exactly enamored of certain elements of our government." McIntyre was stone faced. "We'd like all the background we can get on the nominee for CIA Director."

"Williams? That's a tall order. He's one slippery character. Not much on him that he doesn't want known. Maybe you heard the committee hearings? Senator Larson gave a pretty good picture of the guy's professional life. Mr. Squeaky Clean." Acting as if this were a huge joke, McIntyre laughed loud and long. "What do you want the info for?"

Danny looked at Jenna and nodded. She began, "Mr. McIntyre..."

"It's Mac, honey," he interjected.

"Okay, Mac. We have reason to believe that Williams has something to do with, uh, some attempts on the life of an associate of ours."

The first thought that went through his mind was that he was looking at two plants from the Bureau; but he had done some work for Seymour Gale and had been dealt with fairly. He decided to cooperate, to a point. "I wouldn't be surprised." He turned to Danny. "My kids and their in-laws are coming to visit next month. What are the chances of a great suite at the Empress?"

"I think a good suite could be arranged."

"A great suite?"

"A very good suite."

"Fair enough."

He settled himself still deeper into the thickly cushioned chair and thought for a moment before beginning. "This Williams. I had some dealings with him back in the 60s and 70s. I did a little contract work for the company before settling in at FBI. He's the kind of guy who'll do whatever it takes to accomplish his goals. Legality, morality, those words don't mean shit to him.

"The appearance of things, now that's another story. Anyway, he was recruiting guys to do some private stuff for him then. I don't know exactly what. There were a lot of rumors flying around, but nobody dared to ask too many questions. The feeling was that it was more than a question of getting into trouble with the big shots, more like getting your throat slit in some quiet little alley."

"Anything concrete?" Jenna asked.

"Rumors aren't concrete. I may have been young, but I wasn't totally stupid. The pay was good but I figured I'd live long enough to spend it only if I had a little insurance."

"Like?" Danny was getting impatient. "Come on, Mac, what've you got?"

He hesitated. "You got to remember, I only dealt with the man briefly in the mid-sixties. I can only tell you about then."

Danny was anxious. "So tell us."

"I'll answer anything you want to know, that I can of course."

"Stop playing games." Danny was exasperated, but Jenna seemed to sense something.

"Mac," she said sweetly, "when in the mid-sixties?"

He smiled. "From January 1965 to early January 1966, I was assigned to a task force called 'Burnish Group'."

Jenna continued smiling while Danny, who had finally caught on to the method, quietly took notes. "And what was 'Burnish Group'?"

"The directorate of intelligence at CIA thought there was going to be an attempt by Sov. Block to slander some of our top people with disinformation and carefully fabricated stories. 'Burnish Group' was supposed to prevent that."

"And Williams?"

"He was in charge of the directorate and personal head of the task force."

Jenna looked blank, but Danny picked up the slack. "This private stuff you talked about him recruiting people for, did this have anything to do with the task force?"

McIntyre got up and turned on his stereo and television. Then he walked to his front door and checked the street. When he was satisfied, he returned to them, and motioned for them to lean close. When he spoke, it was in a bare whisper.

"I've got to know something before we go on. I worked this

town eleven years and," he looked at Danny, "no offense, but this kind of stuff is beyond you. Even beyond your father." Danny started to speak but Mac held up a hand for silence. "If it's just you asking the question, you've got all I'm gonna give; but if it's for someone else...." He poured some ashes from an ashtray onto his coffee table and traced out the letters M-O-S-S-?

Danny and Jenna looked at each other and then nodded to him.

He wiped the ashes from the table. "If you want to know about Williams, ask yourself one question." He hesitated, then seemed to reach a decision. "What was 'Burnish Group's' interest in two calamities in February and November 1965?" He got up and shut the stereo and TV and opened his living room door.

"Time for you to leave."

All the way back to the Empress, Danny and Jenna kept throwing questions at each other excitedly, but got nowhere fast. Arriving at the executive suite again, they were about to plan next moves, when Seymour's secretary came in.

"This came just after you left. Your father said to wait for you to open it." She put a large Federal Express package on the desk in front of Danny. "Anything else?"

"No, thanks, Laura. Oh yeah, any messages from Robby Moss or the professor?"

"Nothing yet. Mr. Gale said to tell you the staff's at your disposal but don't push your luck."

"I get the message. Thanks again."

As the door closed behind Laura, Danny and Jenna rushed at the package. "It's addressed to both of us." Jenna tore at the tape. There was a bulky stack of computer printouts and a brief handwritten note from Robby, indicating the printouts came from F.R. Inc. "I guess he made it into Forecast Research," Jenna said.

"I never doubted it," Danny responded, "but what the hell do we have here?" They both began thumbing through the papers. "It looks like payroll records, accounts payable, bookkeeping records."

"Hey, here's Moffatt's payroll record." Jenna pointed to the middle of a page.

Danny looked and shook his head. "I don't know. I personally don't think he's paid enough to go up against Robby."

Jenna kept sorting through the papers. "Here we go." She started pulling out individual papers and putting them aside. Then she pushed the others away from her, gathered the new pile, began showing them to Danny. "These are copies of material sent to the Securities Exchange Commission. You can't fool with them. Lists of stockholders in Forecast, for one thing."

"And E. George Williams is one of them?"

"Give the man a cigar. Not just one of them. The major one. Actually, Cloudburst Ltd. is the major stockholder, but E. George is Cloudburst Ltd. Nice little cut out, just not enough of them. You're getting sloppy in your old age, mister."

"Let's hope he stays that way. Anything else?"

"I think we'll have to wait on Robby to see. In the meantime, what about Mac's clues?"

"Calamities, right?" Danny thought a minute. "I guess we'll have to start at the newspaper morgues for 1965."

"Maybe, but we don't know where those calamities took place, here in Las Vegas, the U.S. at large, or maybe even in Europe. Also, Mac called them calamities, but was that just his point of view or the way the rest of the world might view them?"

"You don't make it easy, Jenna. All right, I guess the first stop is the library, *New York Times* files, or *L.A. Times*. That should take care of the U.S., both coasts, and anything major in Europe or the Pacific."

Jenna seemed not to hear him. "That could take a lot of time."

"So?"

"Do you have a key to Robby's?"

Danny laughed. "My Dad owns the hotel."

"Follow me." Jenna led him out of the office.

Robby was a self-admitted "history junkie." His living room contained bookcases full of magazines, books and clipping files dealing with everything from the Revolutionary War to modern times.

The centerpiece of this collection was the World Book Encyclopedia Year Books from 1961 to the present. These books dealt, in encyclopedia form, with the events of note for each year. Everything from politics and world events to who won the World

Series and the Academy Awards. They were a gift from Rudy and his favorite reading material.

Once in, Jenna headed for the World Book for 1966. When Danny objected, she pointed out that '66 would have the events of the past year '65. Thumbing through, she quickly found first the section on the Chronology of Important Events of the year, and then the section on Disasters.

Danny shook his head. "You're really your father's daughter."

"I've had some practice with this kind of thing," Jenna admitted. "I'm going to go with what feels right at first. I'm hoping we can cut through quickly to what we're looking for. If not, it's going to be a long, slow process."

Danny joined her, pouring over the text. "We can probably eliminate natural disasters. Williams isn't that good."

Jenna nodded. "Let's see. In February '65, there were two major plane crashes, a couple of bus accidents in Mexico, a mail train caught fire in Spain, and a mine explosion in France."

"Why don't we start with the plane crashes? They look like the biggest catastrophes; eighty-seven people killed in the Andes Mountains and eighty-four killed in the Atlantic off Jones Beach." Danny pulled a small pad out of his shirt pocket and started taking notes.

"We're going to need details of the crashes, and a list of the dead as well as survivors. And, hopefully, fast. Any ideas, Danny?"

"Well, if it's fast you need, we'd better call Dad. He knows a helluva lot of people. What about November?"

"In November, we have a cruise ship that burned and sank in the Atlantic on its way from Miami, a bus cut in two by a train in Mexico—remind me never to take a bus in Mexico—another bus accident in Egypt, and four plane crashes. Take your pick." Jenna took a page from Danny's pad and scribbled some notes.

Danny looked at her notes, and copied the rest of the list for himself. They looked at each other, nodded, and left the suite.

❧

Seymour Gale sat at the bar in a neighboring hotel, waiting. For the last day and a half, he had made phone calls, talked to friends, business associates, and some people he preferred not to classify; all to get the information Danny and Jenna had asked for. The calls had clearly caused waves because this morning he had received a phone call from a member of the Gaming Commission. An unexpected phone call from one of those august gentlemen could easily cause angina in many a hotel owner, but as his life flashed before his eyes, Seymour decided he was relatively pure, and breathed deeply. John Chasen claimed it was purely social, and suggested they meet at another hotel. "Neutral territory" was the thought that ran through Seymour's mind. He sipped his drink, nodding to passing acquaintances, and watching the entrance.

"How're you doing, Sy?" Chasen greeted him in a booming, voice. "Sorry to keep you waiting, but this town keeps us hopping." He looked around, spotted an empty booth, and signaled to Seymour to join him.

"Far be it from me to keep you busy, John. I like it best when you're relaxing. What's up?"

"Always right to the point. I like that about you, Sy. No bullshitting. It's really not a big deal."

He took a drink, and then looked deadly serious. "It's just that some people wanted me to talk to you." Sy was listening closely. "They know you're close to Robby Moss, and they thought maybe you could talk to him."

"Somebody need a bodyguard?" The joke was strained.

"Not yet. But people can get into a lot of trouble when they get into places they don't belong. You should talk to him, explain the facts of life. There's no reason for him to be involved in...whatever it is he's involved in. And he's dragging you in. He can't be a very good friend if he puts you at risk."

"What do you mean 'risk', John. I run a clean...no, very clean place. And you know it."

"Sure, I know it, and you know it. But those calls you've been making. Some people might think you're getting tied up with the wrong people. The Gaming Commission gets very nervous about hotel owners being involved with 'bad guys'. You could be implicated in some very shady doings. It could cost you your license. Nobody wants to see that happen."

"And all I have to do is convince Robby to be a good boy. Is that it?" He was getting angry and he didn't care if Chasen knew it. "Then all of a sudden, I'm not associating with any of the 'bad guys'. Your nervous friends must be real heavyweights. You're usually reasonably straight." Seymour's voice grew deeper and slower as he spoke, a sure sign to those who knew him that he was about to explode.

"Sy, take it easy. I don't like this any more than you do. But you're obviously rocking somebody's boat. I don't even know who. Except that whoever it is, even the Gaming Commission is small potatoes to him. Be cool, Sy. Just talk to Robby. He'll listen to you." The man was almost pleading. "Please. Don't do anything foolish, either one of you." He was acting very unlike himself.

Seymour was impressed with John's upset. He'd never seen him like that before. Anyway, he'd already received the information he'd gone after so he'd try to keep John peaceful.

"I'll do what I can. No more phone calls, for now. But Robby Moss is his own man. I'll see what I can do." The roles were now reversed. Seymour patted Chasen on the shoulder as if to comfort him, and Chasen left the bar.

Seymour finished his drink, overtipped the waitress, and walked out into the harsh noonday Vegas sun. As he waited for his car in the crushing heat, he could think of only one thing.

As he drove back to the Empress, he thought only of the coming storm.

CHAPTER FOURTEEN

DESPERATE MEASURES

Louie Gross was unhappy. There were two things in life he took very seriously; food (he weighed 235 lbs. on a 5' 8" frame), and his assignments. Barker had been explicit about the security for Eve, including the fact that she was not to have access to a telephone.

Rudy had spent the better part of an hour arguing with Louie about the two telephones he wanted to bring in. He explained at length about the further research they needed to do, but Louie was adamant. Ultimately, a compromise was reached, but only after Barker was tracked down and gave approval. Louie would watch the proceedings, and only Rudy would use the phone.

The living room area was strewn with documents, mostly FBI teletypes and memoranda. Eve made lists of every FBI agent mentioned in those documents. Wherever possible, she and Rudy made efforts to contact them. Frustration was mirrored on both their faces. It was all so long ago, most of them were either retired or transferred to other areas. Rudy had borrowed the extensive phone book collection from Laura's office, and he and Eve poured over it. A couple of times, Eve had reached for the phone, inadvertently, but Louie, despite his bulk, was immediately at her side, putting his hand on the telephone. Whenever Rudy did get current status on someone, he passed the information to Eve, who noted it next to the agent's name. Several of the agents in whom they were interested had died years ago, and Eve noted this with discouragement. "We're not going to get anything from anyone," Eve said. "Even if we do locate someone, nobody's willing to talk to us about anything."

"Let's not give up," Rudy said. "We knew this wasn't going to be easy. Let's take a break and come back fresh."

Eve made coffee, and they sat drinking. She scanned the lists randomly. "Rudy, we're not doing this as thoroughly as we should."

"What do you mean?"

"Well, take that last call you made. They told you that Howard had died years ago. How?"

Rudy looked at his notes. "He and his wife and another couple, the Murreys I think, died while on a cruise to Kingston."

"Right, and so we indicated on our list that Howard and Murrey had died. But we didn't check on exactly when or how. And we just accepted it, and put 'dead' next to Murrey's name."

Rudy hit his head. "Don't ever let Robby know I'm getting senile. He'd never let me live it down. I'd never be that haphazard in my regular research."

"We're both getting a little batty," Eve said. "Why not call back and see if you can't get more details?"

"Those people won't talk to me again. They're positively hostile."

"You can't blame them. You're probably bringing up painful memories."

"Yes, but I can call the Murrey family." Rudy went back to the phone and Eve listened as he reached a younger brother of Agent Murrey.

From listening to Rudy's side of the conversation, she could tell it was rough going. But he persevered.

"Mr. Murrey, I understand your reluctance. I assure you I'm only interested in working up statistics for a study I'm doing. Please feel free to check my credentials. If you like, I can call you back after you've checked." Rudy was trying very hard to sound patient and non-threatening, a difficult task for him.

"Yes, Mr. Murrey. Anything at all will be appreciated. You said it was November 1965?" Rudy wrote as they talked. "Right. Very sad. A cruise to Kingston. Other agents? How many?"

He listened closely. "No, of course you couldn't know for certain. Just your best guess. That would be fine." He listened again and took notes. "The cruise ship caught fire. A terrible, terrible thing. And it sank. What was the name of the ship?" Rudy wrote down *The Windsor*. "Is there anything else you can add? No? Well, I do truly appreciate your help. Should the study come out in book form, I'll be pleased to send you a copy. Thank you again." Rudy hung up.

He sighed deeply. "I wish you could take over this part of it. I'd like to grab them by the neck and shake some of them."

Eve chuckled. "I know how hard it is for you to be humane when you're looking for research answers."

He glared at her, then smiled. "Back to work, young woman." They went back to the list, clarifying and amplifying wherever possible. It became increasingly clear they were not going to be able to interview any agents. As an alternative, they looked over their lists again, looking for anything that might be helpful.

Eve, growing as tired as Rudy, was about to give up when something jumped out at her. "Rudy, look at this. There were four agents that we know of that died in that freak sinking of the cruise ship."

"So? Men who work together decide to vacation together."

"But they didn't work together. Not for twenty years. Not since the King disappearance. They were all living in different parts of the country."

Rudy looked at the lists again. "Very good." He grew excited. "There is something to be said for youth after all," he said as he looked at Eve admiringly. "Are there any other oddities?"

The only other one they could find dealt with a plane crash near New York City. Three agents died in that one, as far as they could tell. All the other agents on the list were now retired, not talking, spread all over the country, or otherwise unavailable to them.

"I guess there's not a lot we'll be able to tell Robby when he gets back," Eve said.

"Don't be too sure," Rudy responded. "Remember, my dear, sometimes no information can be as valuable as a fund of information. Anyway, let's not make judgments until we all put our findings together." He yawned, elaborately. "All in all, it's been an interesting experience. A good day's work." He nodded approvingly at her, and began to gather up the documents.

꽃

Freiburg, Germany is a city of about 175,000 people. Located in the southeastern corner of the country, it lies virtually on the borders of France, Switzerland and Germany in the state of Baden-Wurttemberg.

Not a major tourist attraction, and with little heavy industry, it is a quiet place with museums, libraries, parks, and a dirty little secret.

On a long wide street, that sweeps from the far north of the city in a long gentle arc to the large park at the Merzhauser Stralle, sits a tall narrow building. When the citizens of Freiburg walk this street and pass this building, they look away and hurry by.

The street is the Wiesentalstrasse, named after famed Nazi hunter Simon Wiesenthal, and the building is the Bundesarchiv—Militararchiv, the home of all of the records of the Nazi war machine from World War II.

Robby stood in front of number ten Wiesentalstrasse, the main entrance to the archives, and checked his watch. He had been waiting twenty minutes, and was preparing to go in by himself, when he took one last look around. At last, he saw Rudy, limping down the street, with a big grin on his face and carrying a thick briefcase.

"You're late," Robby said as he took Rudy's case.

"The impatience of youth," he growled. "My plane was late arriving in Zurich, if you must know. Then I missed the train and had to take another."

"Bitch, bitch, bitch. You just like to make an entrance," Robby laughed. As they walked into the building and cleared through security, Robby and Rudy caught up on all that had happened.

"When we finish here, get back with the others and try to

organize your findings with theirs. I need a direct link between," an Archive worker escorted them to a table so Robby chose his words carefully. "A direct link between Cloudburst and our friend's research. That's primary."

Rudy nodded and took out a pad and pen. He spoke in flawless German to the worker and shortly, two bulky accordion files were brought to the table.

Robby's German was not as good as Rudy's but he managed to wade through some of the clearer files. Every time he looked up, however, Rudy was furiously writing and cross referencing documents. After thirty minutes, Robby began to burn out but Rudy was still going great guns.

"I've got nothing we didn't have before," Robby yawned. "What about you?"

Rudy never looked up. "I've got everything." He handed Robby a document. "Read this."

ぎ▲

Excerpt from Communications Logs Army Group B Headquarters

December 1944

ITEM	AUTHORIZED	MESSAGE	TIME
44/526	Litke	Unit Movement OK'd	0134
44/527	Becker	Reporting Duty Sta.	0145
44/528	Rubschlager/van Eyck	Contact re: Crystal Movement	0245
44/529	Schmidt	Intell Report	0530

ぎ▲

Robby repeated what he was starting to think of as the magic words "Crystal Movement."

Rudy pounded his finger on item 44/528. "Van Eyck, I'd bet your last dollar that he's Dutch, and that he's the one they went to, to cut the diamonds. We've got to find him!"

Robby thought for a moment. There seemed to be no end to the research on this mess. And instinctively, he felt that time was running out. Still, he trusted his friend's instincts also.

"All right. But I'll go to Amsterdam, not you. You're better with this stuff than I am. Get everything you can out of it, then get back to Vegas and coordinate the research. We need to act soon, and right now," he paused and took a deep breath, "I don't know in what direction or against whom." Rudy started to interrupt, but Robby stopped him. "Williams, right now anyway, is just our best suspect, not our only suspect."

Rudy nodded. "When do you leave for Amsterdam?"

Robby stood. "Right now!"

&

Alexandra Rapoport swept down the staircase into the ornate lobby of the Empress Amsterdam as if she owned the place, which in fact she did; or at least thirty percent of it. A long time partner of Seymour Gale's, she served as the general manager of the hotel and as Seymour's personal representative in Europe.

They had met thirty years ago when Seymour was vacationing in Europe looking for hotels to buy and new challenges to conquer. Alexandra had provided both.

He had been interested in a large but faltering hotel in Amsterdam. Before he could make an offer, Alexandra had grabbed it from under his nose and then sold it to him in a partnership deal. It had made her a fortune and secured her place as the leading hostess in Holland.

Rather than being angry, Seymour had been enthralled at Alexandra's bravado and business skills. There were few people who could best Seymour in a deal. He fell in love on the spot.

She knew that they would never marry. He would never leave his beloved desert for more than a few weeks at a time, and she loved Europe. So they continued their long distance love affair irregularly but happily.

She waved and smiled at guests as she moved through the lobby. Her favorite part of the job was caring for her guests as if each was her own personal house guest. She frowned as she noticed a full ashtray. She walked over, picked it up and carried it to the concierge desk.

"Sorry, Madame Rapoport." The concierge stood and emptied it. Alexandra took it back and replaced it. Perhaps other general managers would have had someone else do it, but the personal touch was Alexandra's style.

The bell captain walked up to her, and bowed formally. "Madame, the gentleman you have been expecting has arrived. He is waiting in your office."

"Thank you, Vincent." She turned and walked across the lobby to her office. As she passed her secretary, she smiled and held up two fingers. Within minutes, Robby and Alexandra were enjoying hot cups of coffee and engaging in small talk.

Robby liked what he saw. Alexandra was smart, attractive, and charming.

"So, Mr. Moss, Seymour speaks very highly of you. He explained to me the basics of the issue. How can I be of help?"

Robby liked her style. "I need to find a diamond cutter. He'd be in his seventies or eighties, and probably lived here during the German occupation. His name is van Eyck."

Alexandra pulled a small directory from her desk. "I don't recognize the name, still..." She flipped through the book, shaking her head. "None listed." She thought for a moment. "Let me try a friend." She picked up the phone and dialed a number.

"Mr. Wester, please...Nicholas, Alexandra Rapoport, thank you. I was wondering if you could help me. A friend of mine is looking for a cutter who worked during the occupation...van Eyck." There was a long pause. "Yes?" She took some notes, exchanged a promise to be in touch soon and hung up.

"There is a man, much younger than the man you're looking for, but he might be able to help." She handed Robby the paper. "His name is Willem van Eyck. Perhaps he is related to your man."

Robby smiled. "Thank you, very much. Where do I find," he read the note she had given him, "the corner of Paulus and Potterstraat?"

She picked up the phone and spoke a few words in Dutch, then turned to Robby. "It is just behind the Rijksmuseum, but never mind, a car is at your disposal as long as you need. Also," she took an envelope from a drawer and handed it to him. "Seymour suggested that you might need some funds." Robby opened the envelope and looked at her in surprise. She said, "Five thousand Guilders, a little over twenty-six hundred dollars American. Also, a suite has been set aside for your use." She handed him a key.

Robby stood and she extended her hand. He took it lightly, kissed it, looked at her and said, "Sy has exceptional taste." He turned and left the office.

She watched him for a moment, then picked up her intercom and spoke in Dutch. As Robby's limo pulled away, a small Saab fell in behind at a discreet distance.

ᘒ

The diamond industry settled in Amsterdam in the mid 1700's when most of the many diamond cutters, who were among the victims of the Spanish Inquisition in what is now Belgium, came to the Netherlands. In about 1750, the industry employed only about six hundred people, but the discovery of diamonds in South Africa saw an unexpected upturn in their fortunes.

During the Second World War, tens of thousands of Jewish citizens of Amsterdam, including about two thousand diamond cutters, were deported and never returned.

Today, Amsterdam has at least a dozen firms of diamond cutters and over sixty diamond processors. Some, like A van Moppes and Zoon are large and international. With their own museums, and in some cases restaurants, they give guided tours of the process. Others are strictly four or five man operations, too busy to cater to the public.

It was to one of these that the limo took Robby.

It looked more like a small mansion, than a place of business. A tiny yard, with trees, manicured bushes, and brightly colored flowers, was behind the wrought iron fence. Only the bronze plaque on the wall beside the door gave an indication that a business resided within. It read "van Eyck."

Robby walked to the door and pressed the buzzer on the intercom.

"*Ja?*"

"My name is Moss. I was referred to Willem van Eyck by the director of," he paused, "Holshuysen-Stoeltie."

There was a long pause. "One moment please, Mr. Moss." Robby waited, and after five minutes, he could hear the bolts being thrown, and a moment later the door was opened.

A short, elderly woman motioned Robby in. She closed and locked the door behind him. She smiled up at him. "My English," she shrugged, "not good. You wait here." She pointed into a small den. Robby smiled and walked into the room.

It was elegantly, but sparingly furnished. A fragile looking antique desk sat at one end, with two gilt chairs in front of it. A small sofa was in front of the fireplace and the coffee table had a decanter of cut crystal, with glasses.

Robby felt distinctly uncomfortable.

Willem van Eyck entered the room. He was short, barrel-chested, and prematurely gray. In his fifties, he had the appearance of quiet elegance, and walked with the spring of a gymnast.

"Mr. Moss, I am Willem van Eyck. May I be of some assistance?" He seated himself behind the desk and indicated a chair for Robby. "I spoke with Mr. Koest of Holshuysen-Stoeltie." He looked puzzled. "What may I do for you?"

Robby thought for a moment. He could either take a chance with the truth, or fabricate a plausible story. He decided to take the risk.

"Sir, I am on a somewhat unusual mission, and it could involve you somewhat indirectly."

Van Eyck nodded. "How so?"

For the next fifteen minutes, Robby detailed what he knew of the history of the diamonds, culminating with the discovery of van Eyck's name in the German records.

When he finished, van Eyck stood, walked to the window and looked out. He was silent for a long time. "And you think that I may be related to the man you seek?"

"I don't know."

Van Eyck turned back to Robby. "Frankly, I am not fully informed as to all of my relations. And during the war..." he shrugged "a great many were lost."

Robby nodded. "I fully understand."

The telephone rang and the older man answered it. He spoke in Dutch for a few moments and then hung up. "Mr. Moss, how long will you be in Amsterdam?"

"No more than a day or two."

He started to escort Robby to the door. "If I can find the man before you go, I will be in touch with you."

Robby stood in the open door and turned to van Eyck. "I'm staying at the Empress. I'll await your call." They shook hands and

Robby left.

Willem closed the door and returned to the den. He walked to the window and watched as Robby signaled for his limo. As the long black car started to pull up, two men across the street, at a sidewalk cafe, suddenly stood and began walking towards Robby.

Willem watched as Robby started to react. Robby threw himself towards the curb as the men pulled odd looking guns and fired. Robby fell, almost at Willem's feet, just outside the window. Willem could see two small darts in Robby's back. Something about the sight snapped him out of his trance and he turned and rushed from the window to call for help.

On the street, a van raced down the Potterstraat and screeched to a stop in front of van Eyck's window. Two more men jumped out, one pointing a machine gun at Robby's limo, while the other three began to load the unconscious man into the van.

Willem hung up the phone and started to race for his door when he heard the shots. One long burst of machine gun fire, followed by two smaller bursts. He froze. A moment later, he threw open the door and, followed by his staff security guard, ran out onto the street.

Four bodies lay sprawled across the pavement, blood running in rivers of gore into the gutter. In the distance, sirens could be heard approaching, and a crowd was starting to gather. Van Eyck looked over the dead men, looked in the van. He ran to the limo. The limo driver lay dead, half his head taken off by the slugs that had ripped through the windshield.

But there was no sign of Robby.

ða

Vondel Park is the largest of the many parks in Central Amsterdam. With several small lakes, brightly blooming flowers, and with its proximity to the Rijksmuseum, it is a favorite of both tourists and natives. In the spring and summer months, it is constantly crowded around the clock. It was, therefore, the perfect place for a covert meeting.

No one took any notice of the young man pushing the elderly man leisurely through the park in a wheelchair. And no one noticed a third man drop into step beside them.

"My respects, Herr…Schlussel," the third man began. "It is an honor for us to have you in our area."

Schlussel adjusted the blanket on his lap. "What happened?" he demanded in a weak voice.

The third man leaned close. "You have to understand, there was not much time. Much had to be improvised." The old man just stared up at him. The third man began to sweat. "And as we were led to believe, his reactions were very good."

"What happened?" This time the voice was not so weak, it was in fact chilling.

"It appears that," he was beginning to sweat heavily, "someone interfered with my men." He waited for the furious reaction. When none came, he relaxed, slightly.

They stopped at a bench and the young man sat, as did the third man. The wheelchair was in front of them both.

"This is the last time I will ask. What happened! No more evasions!" Schlussel's expression reinforced his statement and the third man began to talk.

"We know Moss was hit by the darts. The tranquilizer must have worked in seconds because the transport was immediately sent for. Then, it seems someone, I don't know who, suddenly appeared. When I arrived, my men were dead and there was no sign of Moss." He waited nervously.

Schlussel was quiet for a long time. It almost seemed as if he had drifted off, so distant was the expression on his face. "He will go to New York next."

The third man straightened. "I will contact the appropriate cell immediately, Herr General." He caught himself and quickly looked around to see if he had been overheard. There was no one within earshot.

For the first time, the old man smiled. "No, no. You have done quite enough. It is time you received your compensation."

"I ask nothing but to serve the cause," the third man said proudly.

Schlussel shook his head. "But I insist." The man started to smile, and then his face contorted with pain, as the young man slipped an ice pick easily through the man's shirt, under his rib cage, and into his heart. He died instantly. It took but a moment to arrange the man as if he was slouching, deep in a nap. The ice pick was quickly pocketed.

As the young man pushed the wheelchair out of the park, toward the waiting limo, the old man mumbled to himself.

"Franz, ah Franz. After half a century, another postponement. Well, our rendezvous is nearly at hand." He drifted off to sleep on the ride to the airport.

⋟

The Saab approached the building in the old section of Amsterdam with its lights out. When it got within half a block, the driver shut his engine and allowed the car to coast to a stop noiselessly in front of the door he wanted.

A man got out on the passenger side after whispering instructions to the driver. He stood in the lightly falling mist for a full minute, looking up at the one light burning in an upstairs window. Then he approached and rang the bell.

The building was a converted apartment building that had been transformed into a comfortable home. The man watched the progression of lights move downward toward the door, as the occupant was roused from his sleep. It was three A.M. and the street was deserted.

A glint of light shot through the peephole as it was opened for the occupant to examine the unexpected visitor. The man stood stock still. After a long moment, the light disappeared and he could hear the locks being turned.

Willem van Eyck threw the door open and stared at the man with a mixture of surprise and fear. "Mr. Moss, I, I thought you had been…"

Robby interrupted. "May I come in?" His voice was flat and cold, and van Eyck knew he had no choice.

"Please."

He escorted Robby to a sitting room down a long hall. He then excused himself to reassure his wife. On his way back, he briefly considered calling the police. He wasn't sure why, but he didn't.

He returned to find Robby standing by a fireplace, examining the engraving on the bricks of the wall. Robby turned to face him. "I need some straight answers. Is the cutter van Eyck I'm looking for any relation to you or not?"

To Willem, Robby's eyes seemed to have lost their color and become almost grey. His manner was formal and threatening.

Van Eyck sat down. "Why do you want to know?" Robby didn't answer. "Sir," Willem began, "I heard your history of the diamonds, but, considering the business of this afternoon, I need to know why." He was scared, but this was the one secret he had, and he had years before taken an oath to protect it. To the death, if necessary.

Robby seemed to be considering. Willem watched as he drew a chair close to the older man. "Two young, innocent boys are dead, there have been several attempts on an innocent woman's life. And I would be dead now, if a friend had not provided that gentleman outside. You, yourself witnessed the attack on me. And the only possible connection is the diamonds."

Willem still held his secret close. "Who is doing this? I must know!"

Robby spoke quietly. "There's an important man in the States who has a lot to answer for, but I don't think he was responsible for this afternoon."

"Then who?"

"The four men who died this afternoon were members of a Neo-Nazi organization called 'The Rhine League'."

Willem seemed electrified. "Nazis!" He stood and started pacing rapidly. Robby watched him for five minutes before the man calmed. Finally, he sat and leaned very close to Robby.

"The man you seek was my father. He was considered a collaborator during the war. Only my mother and I knew better and for our protection have kept the secret these many years."

He gestured at the room. "This room was his, our apartment when the Nazis came. I bought it ten years ago and converted the building." For a moment he was lost in memory, then snapped out of it. "He was murdered in this room."

Over the next hour, Willem related the story of how his father had come to work for the Nazis. Of how he and his mother were smuggled out of the country in exchange for his father's coopera-tion. And of his father's letter they had found hidden in with their belongings, telling them to flee to England and forget him because he was sure that his captors intended to kill him when he had completed his job.

They had fled to England, but Willem would never forget. That was why he had bought this building.

He gestured at the fireplace wall engravings that Robby had been looking at. "Each of those was carved by hand, by my father." He pointed at one brick after another. "This one is the Hebrew for 'shalom', this one Dutch for 'The Hope', this one is my name."

Robby looked at the wall. Twenty-three bricks in all had some kind of carving on them. Names, phrases, prayers…He stopped suddenly and concentrated on one brick in particular. One near the bottom of the wall. One which merged with all of the others, but to his mind stood out like a flashing neon sign on the Las Vegas Strip. Hoping van Eyck hadn't noticed his attention, Robby turned back to the man.

"Did your father leave anything that might indicate who exactly he was being forced to work for?"

Willem noticed that the threat had gone from Robby's voice and been replaced by an excitement. He walked to a side table and picked up a picture frame. After gazing at it lovingly for long moments, he handed it to Robby.

It was a letter, carefully preserved under glass. With Willem's help, Robby began to read.

ૐ

My Dearest Willem,

Although you are only seven, you are now the man of the family. You must resolve yourself that you will not see me again in this life.

Evil men have come, and I have bought your life, and your mother's by making a Devil's pact with them. I will delay as long as I can, but I know, in the end, I must submit.

I love you dearly, more than I can say in these few hurried words. Be strong. Protect your mother and honor our faith. And do not think too harshly of me for my collaboration. In the end, all they will have from me is my life. I will deny them their prize.

Rest Peacefully,
Papa

ૐ

"He was killed in late 1944 by the Gestapo." There was a tear in Willem's voice.

Once again, Robby stole a look at the brick that had caught his attention. He was surer now, more than ever. He returned the letter to Willem. "And you don't know what it was the Nazis wanted him to do?"

"From what you have told me, I have no doubt they asked him to cut the diamonds. At the time, he was considered one of the best in Amsterdam."

"Did your father keep a safe in the house."

"He did, but when we returned, after the war, the house was an empty shambles."

Robby didn't seem upset by the news. "Thank you, thank you very much Mr. van Eyck. You've been of great help." Robby turned and started to leave.

Van Eyck walked him to the door. "I cannot see how." He opened the door. "Mr. Moss?" Robby turned to him. "Will you find these men, these Nazis?"

"Yes." Robby answered firmly and without any doubt.

"And what will you do when you find them?"

Robby paused. "Collect long overdue payment." He turned and walked to the Saab which started its engine as he got in. It was halfway down the block before its lights came on.

ès

Willem tried to get some sleep before morning. As he slept, he dreamed for the thousandth time of his father.

And for the first time, his father was smiling.

ès

It was early evening in Las Vegas. Locals were at dinner, tourists were making preparations for an evening on the town. Jenna and Danny stopped at the Empress kitchen and loaded up their car with dinner for five. Danny, knowing Louie Gross's appetite, added an additional dinner. Then, armed with their notes and printouts, they headed out.

Eve was talking with Rudy as they arrived. After laying out the food, they all exchanged nervous small talk as they ate. Finally, they got down to business.

In the living room area, Rudy had set up a large chalk board on which he was busily drawing a series of diagrams. As the group exchanged information, Rudy constantly changed and redrew his chart, making entries in the appropriate columns.

One column listed the direct chain, as far as they knew, from the finding of the diamonds to the disappearance of King nee Konigsmann. A second column listed only those people who had had direct contact with Konigsmann. Other columns listed the names of the known FBI agents and others who were involved with the case either during the war or immediately after it.

Rudy and Eve led off. Conspicuously, no one asked about Rudy's recent trip to Germany. Rudy began with professorial deliberateness. "We made extensive efforts to contact every FBI agent listed in the documents I obtained in New York."

Eve added, "Like the famous three monkeys, nobody knew anything. Most of the agents have scattered throughout the country or are dead or we simply couldn't find them. However, we were able to get hold of some relatives. I think we've come up with some fascinating coincidences.

"Of the many agents involved, those who came up with solid leads were uniformly transferred out to the sticks almost immediately. There is a consistent pattern of cover-up, probably emanating directly from Hoover's office."

"We did find," Rudy said, "a small hole in the cover-up. It may be simply a series of bizarre coincidences or something far more diabolic."

Jenna interrupted. "Dad, don't be so melodramatic. What actually happened?"

Rudy looked at his daughter disdainfully and continued. "Back in 1947, six agents were assigned to intensive investigation of the initial disappearance, specifically the involvement of a man called Martin Planscke. Two of those agents we've been unable to account for, but the other four," he checked his notes, "Kalen, Moore, Howard, and Murrey all died at the same time in the same place, in the same peculiar manner in 1965."

He looked over his audience and was pleased at their rapt attention. "They were on a cruise ship out of Miami bound for Kingston."

"So they were vacationing together," Danny said.

"*Schmuck.* We thought of that," Rudy commented. He noticed Jenna checking out some of her own notes intently all of a sudden. He continued. "They were all living in different parts of the country, Florida, Michigan, New York, and Pennsylvania. Also we believe that at least two or more of them had been retired from the Bureau for a period of time prior to their deaths."

"What was the name of their ship?" Jenna asked.

Eve checked the file. "*The Windsor* owned by the Grand Cayman Cruise Company in Miami."

Jenna picked up the story. "We know about that ship." Danny handed her a file. "Our source led us to it. Williams was responsible for a group that may have been behind it. The circumstances certainly are mysterious."

Rudy focused on her. "Expand, expound, explain." Louie groaned and went back to his meal in the front office.

Jenna read from the file. "It happened on November 13, 1965. Uh, a fire was discovered in the forward staircase area which rapidly spread, and enveloped the midship passenger section and the bridge. The ship sank about five hours later. About thirteen miles from Great Stirrup Cay, that's near the Bahamas. eighty-five passengers and two crew were missing, presumed dead, and three passengers were known dead.

"The weather at the time was good, the sea smooth, the sky clear and visibility excellent. Uh, the last examination of the vessel by the Coast Guard Marine Inspection Office was about a month before. They found three minor violations but they made sure that they were corrected before it sailed."

Danny had gotten up and taken a piece of paper into the front office while she was talking. Now, he returned and distributed the copies he had made.

"These," he said, "are copies of the official Coast Guard investigation of the sinking. The bracketed areas are our comments."

ã

Extract From: **United States Coast Guard**
                    Findings of Fact on Sinking and Loss of Life
Re: **The Windsor**

Conclusions

1. That the fire originated in room 610, on the main deck...The fire smoldered and increased in intensity for an unknown period of time. [This is the deck on which the dead agents had their cabins]
2. That the source of the ignition of the fire could not be determined, but could be attributed to any one or a combination of the following:
    A. Malfunction of the lighting circuit in room 610 which had been jury rigged.
        [Letter B is omitted because it is a technical explanation which is highly unlikely.]
    C. ...Acts of persons entering room 610 during the evening of November 12, 1965,...placing of mattresses so that they came in contact with the jury rigged lighting circuit etc. [Like sabotage.]
6. That the General Alarm did not ring during the casualty.
11. That with the possible exception of the sliding Fire Screen Door in the Port passageway aft of room 610, there is no evidence that any fire doors in the vessel were closed. [A Vegas Fire Marshall who owed us a favor says that the effect of that door being closed, was to force the fire into a flash down the corridor directly at the cabins the agents were staying in.]
21. That over half of the persons who are missing and presumed dead were assigned staterooms on the boat deck and their loss is attributed to the rapid rise of smoke, heat and fire in the forward staircase reaching the closed overhead of the staircase on the boat deck and rapidly spreading...preventing passengers exiting through the passageways. [This jibes with our expert's opinions.]

"Can we definitely lay this at Williams' door?" Eve asked.

Danny looked unusually serious. "I wish we could. Even if we're ninety-nine percent sure, we can't prove it, at least not legally."

A voice boomed out from behind them, causing them all to turn. "Legal niceties don't interest me," Barker said. He carried his overnight bag and was followed by Louie.

Rudy stood and walked over to him. They spoke in hushed tones for a moment, and then Rudy returned to the group. "Our young dragon slayer is in Amsterdam. He wants us to meet him in New York, day after tomorrow."

Barker had borrowed Danny's copy of the document and was

being brought up to date on all that had happened. He perched on the arm of the couch.

Jenna looked up at him. "How's Robby?"

"Robby."

She was about to ask him something else, when Louie entered in a hurry. He walked up to Barker. "We've got a problem."

"Go."

"Two cars, one pulled in ten minutes after the first. Parked either end of the block. Four men in each."

Barker turned to the group. "Everybody up."

ва

They approached the building in three groups. Three men from the north, three from the south, and two covering the door. They walked casually, cradling their Ingram submachine guns under their coats. Each had a headphone/microphone set on his head. They spoke quietly.

"Three from one. Clear. Advance to edge of lot."

"One from three. Wilco."

"Two from one. Watch the roof to your right."

"One from two. We see it."

They reached the corners of the building and stopped. They removed their jackets and held their guns openly. One, from the group to the north, took a satchel charge and stealthily approached the door. He pulled the activation cord and raced back to his group. Five seconds passed before the explosion.

The ear shattering sound split the air and sent clouds of dirt, dust, and smoke into the late night sky. As it lifted, the men held their positions. The leader of the coverage group looked through his night vision glasses at the gaping hole where the door had been. Inside nothing moved.

"Three from one. Go for entry."

"One from three. Going in."

The group from the south entered the building and vanished from sight, followed a moment later by the group from the north.

The office had been badly ripped up. The desk lay on its side and a file cabinet had been forced into the wall by the explosion. The door to the living area was jammed into the frame and wouldn't budge when they tried it.

One of the men handed his gun to another and stepped in front of the door. He took a deep breath and then kicked at the door with all his strength. It exploded backward into the room followed only an instant later by three blasts from Barker's sawed off.

The shots caught the man full in the chest, lifted him from his feet, and threw him against the far wall. His chest had a hole clean through it and he died before he hit the floor.

The men returned fire. They were disciplined and fired short bursts blindly into the room, always holding their guns in front of the open door and never exposing themselves. No return fire was heard.

After a moment, they tried to enter again. Three men leapt inside, expecting to be shot as they hit the floor. Nothing happened. A minute passed. Nothing. The other two men crouched and entered at a run.

The distinctive chatter of a Kalishnikov broke the silence and cut one of the crouching men almost in half. The other dived just as Louie threw down on him and unleashed another burst. It caught the man low on his left side and stitched a crimson seam from beneath his rib cage through his groin.

The men on the floor finally reacted and fired their Ingrams. Louie dived back towards the sleeping area and was hit in the back and propelled through the partition.

The men began to advance on the rear. Firing alternately as they crawled, they moved closer and closer. As they reached the couch area, five shot gun blasts resounded through the room. The back of the couch seemed to explode outwards towards the men as Barker's shotgun tore up two of the remaining intruders.

The left arm of one landed back by the door, and the other's face was turned to goo. The last man was stunned and his discipline vanished. He stood and ran for the door. He never made it.

He was hit twice, once from a shotgun and once from a burst from a Kalishnikov as the double hammer blow lifted him and threw him out onto the street.

Amidst the stench of the cordite, smoke, and dead men, Barker looked at Louie, who stood bleeding at the edge of the partition.

Outside, the cover men looked closely at the body of their associate laying in the front door frame.

"Three from one...three from one...two from one...two from one..."

They looked at each other. This wasn't supposed to happen. Now they were left with no choice.

They opened the case they had brought with them. Each pulled the pin that released the cover from the Light Antitank Weapon, and they extended the tube's barrels. Sighting into the door frame, they slowly pushed the firing buttons, one after the other.

They saw the high explosive rockets hurtle into the building and then were knocked to their knees as the explosions shook the ground. When they looked up, secondary explosions could be heard coming from within the building, and the roof was slowly collapsing in on itself.

They left just ahead of the first police and fire units. Total time elapsed...three minutes.

PART FOUR

REQUIESCAT

"There is nothing so melancholy as a battle lost;
Save perhaps, a battle won."

—*Alfred Lord Tennyson*

CHAPTER FIFTEEN

TIME TRAVEL

The decor of Senator Larson's office reflected its occupant to the nth degree. Gaudy and overbearing. One wall was nothing but awards, certificates, and trophies he had been presented during his career. Another was floor to ceiling photographs of Larson with Presidents, politicians, movie stars, and fund raisers. The carpet was a bright yellow, the desk a gleaming chrome and glass affair, and the draperies a noxious Kelly green and yellow plaid.

Williams always had a headache by the time he left. He gave the office half the credit. The other half belonged to Larson himself. The man's pomposity knew no bounds. Still, he was useful.

He had been waiting for twenty minutes before the Senator made his entrance.

"George." Larson exclaimed as he burst through the door, "how is the next director of central intelligence?"

"Fine, Senator."

Larson poured himself a glass of bourbon and one half the size for Williams. He brought the drink to Williams. "Whenever I leave the Senate floor, I always feel the need to imbibe." He settled behind his desk, loosened his belt, and put his feet up. "What can I do for you?"

George came right to the point. "How do you read the confirmation hearings so far?"

"Slightly better than average. Nobody's laid a glove on you yet."

"And the vote breakdown?"

Larson looked his visitor over carefully. "Eight for, five against, five on the fence." He paused. "Why?"

George phrased the next part very carefully. Larson's antennae were finely attuned to danger signals, and were even now starting to probe.

"I met with the president this afternoon."

"So I understand."

"Considering the current state of affairs in the world, the Man felt that perhaps we might find some way to expedite the process."

Larson was wary. "It's still damn early in the hearings. What's going on?"

George was evasive. "Just passing along the president's message."

Larson laughed bitterly. "Shit, George. Don't try to sidestep me, I wrote the book on slipperiness. What's happening?"

George took a deep breath and then smiled. "I never could get anything past you." Larson wasn't smiling. George moved his chair closer to Larson's desk. "There was a book in the works."

"Was?"

"The woman who was working on it had some kind of an accident, and as a result the project's dead." He waited for a reaction. It wasn't long in coming.

Larson immediately pulled out a legal pad and began taking notes. "What's the book about?"

"World War Two intelligence operations."

"And your involvement?"

"Minor, really. She was looking into some of the operations of the Bern Station of O.S.S. As you know, I was Director of Human Intelligence there."

Larson seemed to relax some. "And you didn't always play by the rules?" George nodded. "It was war." Both men smiled knowingly. "And you say the woman writing it had an accident?"

George relaxed. It was going to be all right. "Yeah. I don't know exactly what happened, but I can assure you she's no longer working on it."

"So what's the problem? If she stopped writing it, you're off the hook."

"Notes, manuscript, you never know what my opponents might try to come up with. Especially if it shapes up as a close vote."

Larson thought it over. Obviously, there was something else here. And just as obviously, it had to do with something from Williams' espionage past. If the problem was from World War Two, no problem. Any mistake from fifty years ago could be dealt with, but somehow, he sensed something else.

"Is there anything she could have that would be considered," he searched for the word, "criminal?"

George was ready for this. He spoke emphatically. "Clearly not! We may not have been Boy Scouts in the O.S.S. but we were definitely not criminals." He smiled reassuringly. "At worst, there might be some embarrassing actions. Nothing more."

The senator's mind raced. He had known E. George Williams for many years, and while he considered the man a close friend, he couldn't really say he knew the man. He doubted that anyone could.

"Damn it, George, embarrassing actions are just that. If I'm going to be able to help, you've got to be more up front with me."

There was no question in Larson's mind that Williams was the right man for the CIA. The president wanted him, he was politically correct, and Larson could always count on access to him. But there was something inherently shifty about the man, always something just beneath the surface hidden away from view.

George sat silently for a moment, assessing his options. He sighed deeply as if about to share something against his better judgment. "Neal, it was, and still is a matter of national security. We sometimes had to do unpopular things, things ordered by the president, himself. It was all perfectly legal, but you know how it is. The public is exceedingly naive. We can't afford to be." Larson made his decision. He was publicly committed to the man, had laid his own prestige on the line. He picked up the phone and dialed a number. As it rang on the other end, he turned to George. "I think we can work something out." He switched on the speaker phone as it was answered on the other end.

"Select Committee on Intelligence."

&

Jenna stepped cautiously, keeping the flashlight beam well ahead of her. She could feel Eve's hand on her shoulder, and hear Rudy's voice, softly, urgently exhorting them forward.

It was only moments ago that Louie had informed Barker of the suspicious cars outside, only minutes since their emotions had changed from relaxed puzzle solving to near panic.

Barker had immediately shepherded the group into the bedroom at the back of the safe house. In moments, he had shoved the bed aside, revealing the trap door underneath. Jenna pulled at the flashlight taped to the door, as Barker opened it. Before rational thought could set in, he pushed her towards the steps revealed below. "Go. Hands on shoulders in front of you. Quick, quiet. Jenna, you know where."

She nodded as she was half way down. By the time she reached the tunnel, Danny had helped Rudy down, and the door was shut.

They moved forward for a few seconds, not knowing where or why. Then they stopped as a series of tremors went through the tunnel. They didn't know it, but the explosions above had flattened the house.

Jenna had been through this before, but always in practice sessions with Robby. Now, feeling the shock waves, she thought Oh my God! What's happening up there? She picked up the pace, forcing herself not to dwell on the probable fate of Louie and Barker. She whispered a quick prayer for their safety, patted the trembling hand of Eve on her shoulder and moved on.

After a few minutes under the streets of Las Vegas, Jenna saw a slightly widened alcove in the wall. There was a stool, and a first aid kit with another flashlight and a key on a shelf above it. She stopped and turned. "Everyone holding up all right?" She turned the beam towards them but lowered it slightly. In the eerie light, Rudy and Eve nodded solemnly, and Danny tossed her a halfhearted salute.

Jenna handed the first aid kit to Eve, and gave the additional flashlight to Danny. "It won't be much longer now. Robby always prepares for emergencies." She turned and they continued the trek. The air, which had smelled stale and musty, seemed to get fresher. There were now weak pinpoints of light up ahead.

As they drew closer, they saw another flight of stairs and a real door with two small holes punched in it. The light came from those holes. Jenna stopped again. "I'm going up first. If there's a problem, I'll lock the door." She saw the fear in Eve's face. "Don't worry. It's just a precaution. We always do these things by the numbers." She hoped she sounded more assured than she felt. After all, nobody had expected the security of the safe house to be breached.

Danny signaled that he would go first, but Jenna waved him off. She padded up the stairs quickly and quietly, and stopped and listened at the door briefly. Then, taking a deep breath, she unlocked the door, and entered the room.

It was an oversized storage garage a few blocks from the safe house. Robby had always believed in backups, and this was one of them. He had converted it into emergency living quarters. The two lights that lit the room dimly were on automatic timers, but were also triggered to turn on when items were removed from the shelf in the tunnel.

Jenna threw the door open wide and helped Eve in. Danny did the same for Rudy, with Jenna quickly reaching behind and closing and locking the door after them. She pulled down a screen to cover the door, and shut the flashlight. "Welcome to the Way Station."

Eve laughed nervously. "Our new home?"

"No, just a temporary rest stop. There's a not too comfortable cot in the corner and a slightly more comfortable but decrepit couch across from it. Also a small refrigerator with cold soda behind the couch. Ignore the two old cars. They're window dressing, although they're in a lot better condition than they look."

Jenna stepped behind the couch and took out cans of soda for everybody. She pressed her own cold, wet can to her forehead to steady herself. Trembling is the last thing I need right now, she thought.

As their eyes became accustomed to the semi-gloom, the group scattered about the room, sipping their sodas and looking around, doing what each needed to do to achieve normalcy once more.

Once again, Jenna took charge. "We'll be here for a little while, not too long. We need to get help, to arrange to get out of here, to find out what happened back there," she nodded towards the now screened door, "to pick up the pieces and go on from there."

There was a slightly harder edge to her voice now. She knew Eve had to be held together, and that Danny and Rudy were worried about Barker and Louie. Robby had long ago taught her that there was a time for that kind of concern, but not until the immediate situation was covered.

"I'll call my Dad," Danny volunteered.

"I don't see a phone anywhere." Eve was trying hard to function in the present.

"I think we'll find everything we need here." Jenna lifted off the top tray of a large metal tool box from under the cot, and pulled out a burlap covered package, handing it to Rudy.

He uncovered it, exposing a leather briefcase. "I hesitate pulling Mr. Gale into this."

Jenna nodded agreement. "For the moment, I think we need someone with a little more..."

"Survivability." Barker stood framed in the tunnel doorway. "And nobody's making any calls." He was bleeding above the left eye, his shirt was not only torn but actually smoldering. He looked like the monster from some bad late night movie that nothing could stop.

Eve and Jenna rushed to embrace him.

꙰

Calendar Dan Fuselli was one of the best dressed men in Las Vegas year in, year out. So, when Barker let him into the safe house an hour later, he stood out like a sore thumb. He looked around at the disheveled group with distaste.

"You do run with a grubby crowd, Barker."

Barker looked at him through his one good eye. "Everything ready?"

Dan looked offended. "I'll pretend I didn't hear that." His gaze lingered on Eve for a second. "Everybody ready to go?"

They followed him out to a stretch white limousine with a driver in full livery. Barker looked at him and shook his head. "I said low key."

Dan opened the rear door and helped Eve and Jenna in. "In Vegas, this is low key."

They drove seemingly randomly at first. Then Jenna realized where they were going. Twenty minutes later, they slowed near the Rancho Drive exit to North Las Vegas Airport. As they approached the gate for BiCoastal Aviation, Dan turned around from the front passenger seat. "Everybody down, please. Security seems to have done a disappearing act." He spoke quietly and calmly.

Barker helped everybody to the floor of the car and a moment later it started forward again.

In the parking lot closest to the tie down area for the Empress Corporate Jet, two men stood, checking out the limo carefully. It parked near the gate to the field and Dan got out.

The men approached him. "Who's in the car?" Dan smiled at them. The men looked him over and laughed. "All right, faggot, we'll look for ourselves." One of the men advanced on the car, while the other pulled a gun and casually pointed it in Dan's direction.

Dan's reaction was so sudden that even his driver, who was covering him from the car, had no time to react. Dan spun to his left, throwing the heel of his hand out, breaking the bridge of the nose of the man with the gun and sending fragments flying into his brain. At the same time, he lashed out with his left leg, causing the other man to go tumbling to the ground. Completing his 180, he walked over and drove the heel of his boot into the man's throat, crushing his windpipe. Both men were dead or dying within seconds of the attack.

Barker opened the door of the car and hurried the passengers out. He looked down at the men and shook his head. "Fucking amateurs!"

Dan walked the group to the foot of the plane's steps. "What do you expect, they were wearing double knit." He turned and walked back to his car.

Five minutes later, Empress One was airborne. All except Barker were shocked by what they had seen. But one more shock was yet to come. The door to the cockpit opened and Seymour

Gale walked out.

"Mind if I hitch a ride?"

ঽ৶

The car pulled into the darkened warehouse guided by a man with a flashlight. After it disappeared into the cavernous interior, the large shipping door was quickly rolled down and locked. Only then were the lights turned on.

Twenty men, standing in rows of five, stood in front of the car at attention. They were all in their thirties and forties, dressed in good suits, and had short cropped hair. They were expressionless, waiting.

The driver got out and spoke briefly to the man who had led them in. They nodded, and the driver went to the driver's side passenger door. The other man, clearly the leader of the group, returned to them and stood in front and to the side. He was ramrod stiff at attention.

The car door opened. Schlussel's aide stepped out and looked the group over. The driver got a wheel chair out of the trunk and brought it around to the door. Together, the two men helped Schlussel out of the car and into the chair.

"Attention!" The leader shouted out the order. The men snapped to an even stiffer attention than they had been at previously.

Schlussel was wheeled over. About ten feet in front of them, he signaled for a stop. His aide locked the chair's wheels, and slowly, tenderly, helped Schlussel to his feet.

Despite their discipline, a buzz could be heard from the men. This was the man who embodied what they believed in, a man who had actually had unrestricted access to Hitler.

One hard look from their leader silenced them. Schlussel approached slowly, with short faltering steps. With his aide standing close by, he pulled himself to attention and extended his arm in the Fascist salute. Instantly, the men responded in kind.

"HEIL DER VIERTE REICH!!"

The leader of the men came over and saluted. "Herr General, allow me to present to you Detachment Three, North American Schicksal Brigade."

Slowly, Schlussel walked down the row of men. Each tried to

straighten just a little bit more as he passed. Finally, he was done. He returned to the front and for the first time addressed them.

His voice was weak, but with an underlying strength. They hung on his words.

"Kameraden! It does these dried, old bones good to see such young, strong men carrying on the struggle against the Bolshevik Conspiracy and the Jewish menace to the purity of our blood. I hope that before my time here is finished, I can meet all of you individually and shake the hands of the next leaders of our immortal Reich. But for now, I need only a few. Thank you."

He sat down in the wheel chair. He handed a sheet of paper to his aide, and the driver wheeled him off to a nearby office. The aide turned to the leader. They held a brief, quiet discussion and then the aide joined Schlussel in the office.

The leader turned to his men. "After I have summoned the specialists required for this mission, the rest of you will be dismissed." He paused and looked them over. "On your blood oaths, at the cost of your lives and the lives of your families, you will not reveal the contents of this meeting or the fact of this meeting."

They all snapped the salute. The leader returned the salute. "The general will require two police officers; Dennis and Leary, I think. A surveillance team, Donahue and Peterson. And a strike team, Kintzler, Weber, and Shapper. The rest, dismissed."

The others left quickly and quietly. The seven men and their leader stood alone on the warehouse floor. After a moment, their leader led them to the office and to the bitter, almost insane old man who would use them.

Schlussel now sat behind a desk, with the wheelchair folded and up against a wall. The office was bare, but there was no need for chairs, no one dared to sit. The men stood at attention in front of the desk. Schlussel looked them over.

"Take out your daggers," he ordered. Each man pulled out a small eighteenth century German dagger. "With your blood, swear your allegiance to our sacred cause and to this mission!"

One by one, each man pricked his thumb with the tip of his dagger, drawing a drop of blood. The leader also drew blood. "Join your bloods," Schlussel ordered. The men extended their arms and held the tips of their daggers touching in the center of the semicircle they had formed. The leader added his dagger to the circle and solemnly intoned the oath by which they lived their lives.

In the words of the monster that they had deified, they pledged their fidelity to Schlussel and his mission.

"I am ready to undertake responsibility at the bar of history for the time in which the bitterest decisions of my life are made, in which fate has taught me to hold fast to the dearest thing that has been given us in this world, the Aryan people and the Fourth Reich."

"Who is the strike team?" Schlussel's aide asked.

The three men stepped forward. The aide looked down at Schlussel who nodded approvingly. The aide looked back at them. "For the moment, your job is the personal protection of the general. Later, you will be briefed on other aspects of your mission. Arm yourselves, and report back here within the hour." The men saluted and left.

The aide looked at the leader. "The police officers?"

The men stepped forward. The aide handed them each an envelope. "We need to know everything you can find out about the people described within. As quickly as possible." The men saluted and left.

Now, Schlussel spoke. "You are the surveillance team?" The two men stepped forward and saluted. He returned the salute with effort. "Your mission will be the most difficult. You must find a man," he paused as a coughing fit shook his entire body. When it passed, he continued, with his voice so low the men had to lean forward to hear.

"He is a trained intelligence agent and very resourceful. When you find him, you must not lose him." He started to drift off. "You must not, must not…"

Schlussel's aide hurried the men from the office. "The general needs his rest. He walked the three men out to Schlussel's car. He reached into the car and took out a briefcase. He spun the combination locks and took out two photographs, giving one to each of the Surveillance men.

"The target's name is Robert Moss."

❧

Metro Police Lieutenant Jesus Molina stood in front of the still smoking ruins of the safe house. It looked like a giant had come along and stepped on it. The roof had caved in on the interior of the building, but somehow, the exterior walls remained standing.

A path was being cleared to the interior by a small skip loader and fire fighters sprayed a fine mist over the wreckage to keep down the dust and prevent any flare ups. They were into the office area now.

Four bodies had been cleared from the debris so far, and from the yelping of the search dogs, there would be more to come. Even now, Molina could see a rescue crew working feverishly on the far corner of the building.

A young patrolman came running up. "We've got a survivor!" Molina nodded but didn't move. "I'm not surprised."

The patrolman looked at him as if he had lost his mind. How could anyone expect survivors at a scene like this? Molina seemed to sense his thoughts.

"Have you seen the bodies we've gotten so far?" he asked. The patrolman nodded. Molina continued. "Well, look again." He walked over to what had once been the doorway to the building. A body lay covered by a green tarp. He pulled back the tarp.

The patrolman had seen some dead bodies before, but none quite like this one. A large part of the left upper torso was missing and along the visible back were three neatly spaced bullet holes.

"I saw that he'd been shot."

Molina shook his head as if exasperated by a young child. "Look under his head." The patrolman bent down and looked closer.

Crumbled beneath the man's head was a radio headset. "Now look under that chunk of wall over there," Molina said pointing directly to the man's left. The patrolman turned his head and could just see the end of a gun peeking out from under the slab of cement.

Molina started walking over to where the firemen were working feverishly and the dogs were barking. "Who owns this building?"

"The Empress Hotel," came the reply from the patrolman.

They stopped right on the edge of the rescue effort. Firemen were using a small crane to move one last huge piece of roof.

"You think the Gales are involved? Maybe mob activity?"

Again Molina looked irritated. "We've got multiple bodies, sophisticated communications equipment, automatic weapons, and a mysterious explosion, all on Empress property." The piece of roof gave way and revealed the top of a sturdily built metal desk. The firemen began cutting through it. "And judging by those shotgun strikes and, unless I'm very mistaken, Kalishnikov hits, we've got either Barker or..."

The firemen lifted off the desk top, revealing a large man jammed into a tiny space beneath. Molina leaned over the hole and smiled. "Hello Louie, I'm going to want to talk to Robby about this."

Louie smiled weakly and gestured at his wounded shoulder. "You mind if I stop bleeding first?"

In the ambulance, on the way to Valley Hospital, Louie and Molina talked.

๛

For Immediate Release
For Further Information: Lieutenant Jesus Molina
                               Detective Division
                               Las Vegas Metropolitan Police Department

At 0230 this morning, a natural gas explosion swept through a storage warehouse belonging to the Empress Hotel. Ten persons working in the warehouse at the time were either killed or are among the missing.

Further details when available.

๛

The sight of Seymour broke the unspoken tension. Everybody started talking at once. The relief was palpable. It was as if their father had joined them and now everything would be all right. Even Barker relaxed.

Seymour walked over to Danny and looked at him closely. "Okay?" Danny nodded, and Seymour hugged him. Then he went over to Jenna and patted her cheek. "Robby would never forgive me if I didn't take care of you." He smiled at her. He moved to each member of the party, smiling, checking, and, in Eve's case, doing his best to project massive reassurance. Finally, he turned to the group at large.

"You're a motley looking crew but you're alive and relatively undamaged. That's the bottom line. I don't know if you got the word, but Louie is fine. They're patching him up as we speak, and I've left word that his convalescence be hedonistic and suitably gluttonous. I've also been on the phone with Robby. You'll be pleased to know that we're on the home stretch. Which, by the way, is why I'm coming along."

"Where are we headed now?" Eve asked, a little plaintively.

"New York." They all immediately looked at their clothes, and put their hands to their hair.

Anticipating their questions, Seymour continued. "I've arranged for change of clothes for everyone. You'll find suitable necessities of life in your rooms on arrival. In the meantime, the stewards will help you remove some of the debris of the last few hours. We'll be arriving at Teterboro Airport where I have a car waiting."

"Are we staying at the Atlantic City Empress, Dad?" Danny asked.

Seymour flinched involuntarily. "It's not practical. I've arranged things with another hotel in New York City, since that's going to be our base of operations. But don't get any ideas, Danny. This is not a precedent." He took a long pause. "I hate giving money to the competition."

"What about Robby?" Rudy had been sitting quietly, recovering his usual sangfroid. "What's happening with the *Momzer*?"

For the first time since he joined them, he turned serious. "Things haven't been...boring." He seemed about to go into details but thought better of it. Rudy understood. There were some things best left to Robby to explain.

Rudy quickly changed the subject. "So where are we staying? Not some 42nd Street hovel I trust."

Seymour smiled. "Only you, Professor. For the rest of us, I've engaged a floor at the Cadastré." He turned to Barker. "A man named Goorland is providing security."

Barker nodded. He now realized that, even without knowing of the attack on the safe house, Robby recognized the severity of the threat they were facing. Still, he wondered why Robby had chosen a security firm run by ex-Israeli Mossad agents.

As the sun rose off to the jet's right, he relaxed. Knowing Robby, this might be his last chance to rest for quite a while.

&

Myor Goorland did not look like a man to be reckoned with. At seventy-one, he stood or rather slouched some 5'4", with a rather spare frame, and a face that had developed striking lines, but still remained cheerful. His grandfatherly appearance belied the fundamental toughness that lay just beneath the surface.

A veteran of virtually all of Israel's covert wars since 1948, he had chosen to take his "retirement" in New York. His pension had been the seed money for him to form a high risk security firm which, during slow times, still did favors for "the boys."

At the moment, he wandered along the L shaped corridor of the top floor of the Cadastré, checking on his people.

The corridor seemed deserted, but each time Myor passed a stairwell door, it opened and a casually dressed young man or woman appeared, with gun drawn. Myor would nod or smile at them and then move on. At the elevator bank, he stopped and addressed the two huge men standing there.

"*Nu?*"

"Everything's cool."

"Keep it that way. And…" Myor took a few steps away and called over his shoulder. "Get a haircut, or a dress." The men laughed as he moved off on his never-ending rounds.

There should have been a revolving door to Seymour's suite. It had become the nexus of all activity of what they had all begun referring to as the Research Group. Rudy lay on the couch reading Xeroxed documents from Freiburg, Danny was on the phone conducting Empress business at Sy's directions, and Jenna was constantly in and out, ferrying messages from Eve whose computer had been set up in another suite.

Barker felt uneasy. At the moment, there was nothing directly for him to do, so he spent his time refamiliarizing himself with a Manhattan street map and waiting for a delivery that Myor had arranged.

Eve joined the Group and plopped down into an overstuffed

chair near Rudy. "There is absolutely no trace, in any way, shape, or form of any Jack Donald King after 1947."

Rudy smiled. "I didn't think there would be, but we had to know for sure."

Sy strolled over to them. "A friend of mine in Washington says he will arrange a meeting with the right people, if we have anything to tell them. Do we?"

Before anyone could answer, a familiar voice called from the doorway. "Any number of things." Robby walked in.

"You really do like your entrances, don't you." Danny said as Robby slapped him on the back.

"What's happening?"

It took just over an hour for Robby to bring everyone up to speed on what had occurred on the European trip. He told them everything, except about the brick which dominated his thoughts.

Then Rudy took the floor. He reviewed, for Robby's benefit as well as the Group, the material they'd been discussing about the sinking of the *Windsor* when the safe house had been invaded. "It seems someone considers FBI agents expendable," Seymour commented.

Robby was polishing his watch again, a sure sign of intense concentration. Without looking up, he asked, "One series of arguably coincidental deaths does not a conspiracy make, and concrete proof is something we don't have, or do we?"

"There's more than one series of deaths," Eve shuffled some papers to find a specific set. "While checking on the various agents involved in the case, and cross-referencing them against suspected Burnish Group activities, we found another interesting set of coincidences."

Robby looked at her. "What's Burnish Group?"

Rudy answered. "Not germane at the moment. I'll explain after you all hear what else we found."

Eve took it up at this point. "As you know, we had a great deal of difficulty reaching anyone who would tell us anything. What we did find, aside from the Windsor deaths, was the so called coincidental deaths of three other agents…"

"Harper, Timmons, and Lyons," Danny said as he handed Robby a copy of the official report.

Rudy looked up, almost gleefully. "You found something on the airplane crash, I'll bet."

"Trans-Atlantic Air Lines, Flight 366, known as TAL 366," Jenna said.

Danny continued. "TAL 366 was a DC–7B en route from Kennedy Airport to Richmond, Virginia. It crashed in the Atlantic near Jones Beach, around six-thirty in the evening, shortly after taking off." He checked his copy of the report. "Eighty-four people died, no survivors. Uh, the CAB Report blamed a near collision with a Aerolinas Blanco flight for the crash."

Jenna interrupted. "Basically, they decided that the Trans-Atlantic Flight had to make such an extreme evasive maneuver that they couldn't pull out, and crashed into Jamaica Bay."

Robby looked at her. "But you don't think so."

Jenna and Danny nodded. Jenna said, "From what we read in the report, they just about ignored what the Aerolinas Blanco crew said, and created a scenario they thought would fit the situation." She handed Robby an annotated copy of the CAB report.

ও৯

Excerpt from:	Civil Aeronautics Board
	Aircraft Accident Report
Adopted:	November 14, 1966
Released:	November 17, 1966
Section 2.2	Conclusions

1. **There is no evidence of any malfunction of the aircraft, its engines, or components.**
[They weren't able to recover most of the plane.]
4. **Weather was not a factor in the accident.**
5. **The crew was properly qualified and they were not incapacitated prior to the crash.**
[According to CAB's own report, the cockpit recorder wasn't functioning during that flight, so how could they know?]
7. **The Captain was unable to see ABA 212 during its approach turn.**
[This, despite the statements of the Aerolinas Blanco crew that they were able to see the Trans-Atlantic plane very clearly and that therefore the Trans-Atlantic crew should have been able to see them just as easily.]
15. **The evasive maneuver of TAL 366 placed it in a vertical bank at an altitude from which recovery was virtually impossible.**

Probable Cause: The Board determines that the probable cause of this accident was the evasive action taken by TAL 366 to avoid an apparent collision with ABA 212. The evasive maneuver, prompted by illusion, placed the aircraft in an unusual attitude from which recovery was not effected.

[One wonders how the TAL flight crew could have an illusion while seeing exactly what the ABA flight crew saw. Also, how did the Board come up with the flight path they indicated when to do so would mean totally discounting what the Aerolinas Blanco crew and Flight Controllers told them? To add to all of this, eyewitnesses reported seeing "a ball of fire fall into the sea" and hearing "something that sounded like a thud or small firecracker" before the ball of fire fell into the sea.]

à

"Fascinating," Rudy observed. "The eye witnesses all saw the ball of fire before the crash, and the radar records and Aerolinas Blanco flight crew both say that the two planes were elsewhere. But of course, the CAB knows better. Incredible!"

"That makes two incidents, hardly coincidental now, don't you think so?" Danny looked at Robby.

Robby asked questions; the Research Group did what it could to answer. Burnish Group, *The Windsor*, the TAL disaster all were discussed. Finally, three and a half hours later, they were finished.

A silence fell over the suite as all faces turned to Robby. Danny, speaking for the Group, turned to Robby. "So, what do we do now?"

Robby stood, opened the door of the suite, and beckoned Myor in. "Now, we start getting even."

à

Two guards patrolled the lawn and the grounds. Floodlights illuminated every square inch of the outside, and all doors and windows were heavily armored and alarmed. While not a fortress, it was certainly the Virginia countryside's version.

Oak Lawn Manor had been George Williams' home for over fifteen years. Even when his career took him to the other end of the world, he would count the days until a vacation would bring him home. His wife even joked that he loved wandering the private woods more than he loved her. The twenty room mansion was his fortress against the world.

Since the confirmation hearings had started, he had had little opportunity to spend time here. But ever since the events at

Forecast, he had retreated here at the end of every day. After dinner and a teleconferenced staff meeting, he would retire to his bedroom and read position papers and briefings until he fell asleep, usually long after midnight. Tonight was no different. After kissing his wife goodnight, they no longer slept together, he had read press accounts of his hearings until he dropped off an hour ago. It was now two A.M.

Outside, Robby and Barker looked at the house intently. They had been there since just after eight P.M., watching, timing, planning. Still, they waited another hour before they acted. A guard stopped and looked in their direction. On instinct more than anything else, he walked towards them. He came within thirty feet. Robby jumped from the bushes and the guard, momentarily surprised, turned towards him. A moment later, his body convulsed from the fifty thousand volts that Barker's Taser shot into him.

The clicking of the stun gun filled the night for about ten seconds before Barker took his finger off the button. The guard collapsed to the ground, all his muscles flaccid. Robby was on him instantly. He pulled a syringe packet from his jacket pocket, swabbed the guard's arm, and injected him with a light pentothal solution. He would be out for two hours. Barker hid the unconscious man in the bushes and he and Robby moved towards the house.

They crouched among the rose bushes near the house and waited. Ten minutes later, the other guard approached and the procedure was repeated. After hiding him, they moved to the front door.

It took them twenty minutes of taking sensor readings before they tried to disable the alarm. Barker held his breath. Electronics were never his thing. Finally, Robby nodded and Barker picked the lock gently, and they entered the darkened home.

In the foyer, they put on their night vision glasses. The darkness was transformed into a greenish daylight, and they moved easily through the house. They silently climbed the stairs and began checking the house room by room. No one in the first two. In the third, Williams' wife. Across the hall from her, they found who they were looking for.

Barker closed the door behind them and moved to the opposite side of the bed from the sleeping man. Robby put down his back pack and approached Williams as he turned in his sleep.

The phone was on its third ring before Williams answered it. He rolled over and checked the clock radio on his night table, four thirty-five in the morning. "It better be good," he growled as he picked up the phone.

"Acting Director Williams?" The voice was muffled but clear.

"Who is this?"

"Cloudburst 414?"

Williams felt as if he was as filled with electricity as his slowly recovering guards were. "Who is this?" he said slowly.

"What happens to Eve Palmer happens to you." The voice was now low and menacing.

"I don't know what you're talking about."

"Remember anyway." There was a click and the line went dead.

Williams was now fully awake. Damn, he thought, how could they have gotten this number? He started to get up, but remembered his glasses were on the other night table. He turned to get them and stopped dead.

The color drained from his face and sweat poured off of him, dripping onto the sheet as he looked at the black double zero painted on a green field on the pillow next to where his head had been.

His first reaction was to run from the room. As he reached for the door, the cold metal knob in his hand brought him back to reality. He raced back to the night table, held his breath as he reached for his gun. Yes, it was still there. He took it in hand, checked that it was loaded. Only then, after a couple of deep breaths, did he start moving slowly, deliberately, with careful thought. Williams listened at the door before opening it. Moving from room to room quietly, he turned on lights as he went. Suddenly, he realized what had been bothering him at the back of his mind. Where were the guards? Certainly, they would react if they saw the lights going on if for no other reason than that it was highly unusual. How had they been eliminated?

He slowly walked downstairs and was about to go through the same procedure there, when he heard a sound from above. His wife. He'd completely forgotten about her. "George, what's going on? Are you all right?" His wife appeared at the top of the stairs, closing her robe about her.

"It's nothing, Emily. I couldn't sleep. Just a slight disturbance. Nothing important. Go back to sleep. And lock your door." He tried to sound natural.

"Lock my door? Something is going on." Emily Williams came downstairs. "George, you don't have your robe on. Where are the guards. I won't be lied to. Now, tell me."

Williams was close to panic, and he felt exasperated at having to deal with his wife. "It would be more helpful if you'd make some coffee. I'm going to have to deal with some, delicate matters. Make the coffee and then, for God's sake, go to bed and let me be." He was on the edge of screaming from the effort to remain composed.

Emily went into the kitchen, started coffee brewing. He waited tensely for her to finish her ministrations. When she went back upstairs, he waited till he heard her door slam shut. Then he drew his gun, and gingerly opened the front door.

The bright lights on the lawn blinded him for a moment. He heard groaning, and then saw one of the guards staggering towards him. "What happened, Henry? What the hell do I pay you guys for? I might as well sleep in the Capitol Rotunda for all the protection I get. Where the fuck is Carlisle?"

Carlisle could be heard groaning, and staggered up and vomited on Williams.

Williams started to laugh, slowly at first. The tension, the fear and the guilt rose in him until the laughter gradually turned to hysterics.

Somewhere deep within him, he knew his time was running out.

ᴥ

It was after ten o'clock at night when they trooped down to the passenger vans that Myor had arranged. Led by Barker, they piled in and headed out for Central Park. Robby had sent Barker to get them. His only message… "It's time to time travel." Their puzzled looks had been answered by a blank stare from Barker.

It was ten-thirty when the van turned onto Transverse Road #2 near 5th Avenue and E. 79th Street. They turned right onto East Drive and a few moments later stopped. Barker got out first and looked towards the Great Lawn. He could make out a figure standing alone. He took out a flashlight and turned it on and off quickly. Instantly, the signal was returned. Barker turned to the van and signaled for the group to follow as he walked out to meet Robby.

Robby was standing alone, looking pensive. Something was different tonight, and Jenna in particular noticed. They all stood quietly.

Robby looked around and began to talk. "This is where King slash Konigsmann was last seen. Right here." They all started looking around. "And here is where we start to find him again."

He had them transfixed now. He turned to Seymour and Danny. "Sy, you know New York," Sy nodded, "you're King. Danny, you're the man the mounted policeman saw talking to him." He moved Danny and Seymour off to the side of the group. "Danny, when I say now, I want you to walk over to Fifth, get a cab, and go to the skating rink at Rockefeller Center. Understand?"

A mood was descending on all of them. Danny, swept up in this almost religious mood, said nothing but nodded his assent.

"Go."

Danny started for the street followed by one of Myor's men who had accompanied them. Rudy had taken out a small pad and was making notes. Eve whispered something to him but he just nodded in return. After about five or six minutes, with Danny gone from sight, they returned their attention to Robby.

Before he could begin again, they were interrupted by four young thugs on the prowl for victims. They started to advance towards the Group, but Barker went to meet them.

"You need a tourist guide, motherfucker?" the biggest of the thugs said menacingly.

Barker casually opened his overcoat. All four punks took a step backwards at the same moment. Under the coat, Barker was wearing two .45's, one under each shoulder, and a sawed off ten gauge on a sling around his neck.

He lightly fingered the shotgun. When he spoke, it was in quiet, non-threatening tones. "Not tonight, okay?" They were gone a minute later.

Robby began again. "All right, Sy, you're Franz. What do you do now?"

"That depends. I get the feeling that I'm going some place first, before making my meeting. Some place close by."

"You have to be at the rink in thirty minutes."

Seymour started walking, crossing East Drive and cutting across the Metropolitan Museum of Art lawn to Fifth Ave. The group, led by Robby and followed by Barker, began to follow close behind.

Sy stood on Fifth Avenue, looking around. He spoke almost to himself. "If I'm going to make the rink on time, my immediate destination is within a block or two here. Say between 77th and 82nd." He paused. "But if I've been followed, I could have been picked up right about here just before leaving the museum grounds."

Robby shook his head. "Strike one. If he was picked up, he could have been taken anywhere, and we're wasting our time. Try again."

"Okay, if he's headed for his girlfriend, the Countess, he's going to be cutting it awful close."

It was Rudy's turn. "She was long gone by then. Kicked out of the country in early '41."

Robby's face was grim. "Strike two."

Seymour's eyes suddenly lit up. "I've been going about this all wrong. He's headed for the rink at Rockefeller Center, right?" Robby nodded. "It's only logical that if he set up a meeting there, it was because it was close to where he had to go first."

Eve shook her head. "This is pointless. We could talk ourselves into anything."

Robby turned to her. "Not true. Sy's about the same age as King was when he disappeared. Also, he lived in New York in 1947. And finally, he's one of the best abstract thinkers I know."

Seymour ignored all this and was deep in thought. "There are a lot of places in this town where people can meet unnoticed. He chose the rink, because it was close to Saint Patrick's Cathedral!"

Robby smiled ear to ear. "Lead on, MacDuff."

Seymour started down Fifth Avenue with the rest trailing behind. Rudy followed in the van. This strange late night parade continued down the street. Now, Robby set the pace. Like a blood hound on the scent, he pressed ahead relentlessly. It was cold and they had walked over twenty blocks already. One by one the group started to fall out. Almost like in a marathon, they would stop, and be picked up by the van. Seymour, the long time golfer, was one of the last to give up and take the ride. Jenna and Barker were left and Jenna was fading fast. She reached out and touched Robby on the shoulder.

"Robby, slow down."

He didn't even break stride. Jenna looked at Barker who shrugged and kept pace. She gave up and got in the van.

Barker knew Robby best of all, so he understood and said nothing. He knew, without looking, that the eyes had gone from blue to gray and that the expression was set and hard. Barker watched the back of Robby's head and knew that they were fast approaching a critical moment. Silently, he prepared himself.

At last, they were there. The van parked and they all piled out. Jenna walked up to Robby and looked at him. However, he was staring across the street at the huge cathedral.

Even at night, it was an impressive sight. An enormous gothic building which just by its nearness transports you back to medieval times.

For a moment they were all swept up by the sight. But Robby was not swept back hundreds of years. Only around forty-five years. He stepped forward, wove his way around the relatively light traffic and crossed to the cathedral side of the street.

The group walked to the corner of 50th and 5th, crossed and eventually caught up with him. Robby turned as they approached and beckoned to Rudy. They stepped off to the side and talked intensely for a few minutes.

So engrossed were they, that they failed to notice the two men watching them closely from across the street. Donahue checked the photograph for the third time. "That's him."

Peterson nodded and picked up the cellular phone. He dialed a number and waited. "Tickets."

Peterson checked his code book and gave the appropriate reply. "Two on the aisle." There was a long pause, and finally Peterson heard a beep. He counted to five silently and then spoke clearly and slowly.

"Exhuming Crystal Movement."

CHAPTER SIXTEEN

SEPULCHER

They stood outside the great cathedral and listened as Rudy instructed.

"We're going to fan out around the building in teams. Eve, Barker and I will move around clockwise. Robby, Jenna, and Sy will move counterclockwise. I want you to examine the masonry carefully."

Barker spoke up. "What are we looking for?"

"Hand tooled marks, made to appear as if they are accidental or part of the natural contour of the building."

"What will they look like?" Eve asked

"We'll know that when we find them, child." Rudy was smiling. "Discount anything new, anything that shows the lighter color of the interior of the stone. Remember, what we're looking for is at least forty-five years old." And with that, they fanned out and began the search.

To the casual observer, this group of people must have looked quite mad. They circled Saint Patrick's, checking every stone, every brick, for the telltale signs of a mark, of anything that might indicate the spot they looked for.

Several times, they thought they had found it. All turned out to be either natural wear on the building or some juvenile graffiti far more current than what they wanted. Once, on the 50th Street side of the church, Rudy stopped and looked hard and long at a seemingly random series of slashes in the stone near the bottom of the wall. But nothing proved out.

After two complete circuits of the building, the group met again on Fifth Ave.

They were exhausted and disappointed. Over a radio that Barker carried, Danny had been called and soon arrived with coffee and doughnuts.

They sat in and around the van which was parked on 50th Street across from Saks and ate, drank and commiserated. Rudy and Seymour particularly seemed frustrated.

"Maybe what we're looking for is inside," Seymour ventured.

Rudy shook his head. "Not likely. First, he would have hidden his diamonds someplace where he could gain access to them at any hour of the day or night; and second, the cathedral closes and is locked up tight every night at eight forty-five."

"Maybe I was wrong."

Robby was staring up into the dark at the Middle European spires of the church and shook his head. "You weren't wrong." He turned back to Rudy. "Where are your notes?"

As Rudy walked back to the van to get his briefcase, Eve came up to Robby. "What notes?"

"Before I left Rudy in Freiburg, I asked him to find out what he could about the way the Nazis handled their dead drops." Eve looked blank. "Dead drops are places that messages or packages can be left to be picked up by someone else at a later date."

Rudy returned and handed Robby the pages. With the others reading over his shoulder, Robby scanned the pages.

ë

INTELLIGENCE DETACHMENT INSTRUCTIONS
COVERT OPERATIONS
COMMIT TO MEMORY
[Translation from original German; document in bad condition]
Intelligence Department Regulations
The agent must remember three rules:

1. Access.
2. Control.
3. Malignant Fate.

Access—the agent must be able to gain the package at all times.

Control—the agent must be able to [unreadable] [unreadable] that the package will remain in friendly possession at all times and not accidentally fall into enemy hands.

Malignant Fate—precautionary measures must be taken to guarantee that mistakes are reduced in accurate selection of dead drops that are remote yet easily accessible with a minimum of civilian traffic. Each dead drop must be marked with one of five marks by a [unreadable] visible plain level surface within seventy meters of the dead drop. The marks must be by a durable or permanent object so that future agents may be able to find [unreadable] easily.

The Marks are: Canaris' Mark;
                Abewehr Mark;
                Frisch's Mark;
                Operation Sea Gull Mark;
                Kohler's Mark.

The marks must also be permanent so that marks by brick, tile, or stone are [unreadable].

                     ❧

While the "instructions" were passed around, Robby turned back to Saint Patrick's. Beneath his breath, he repeated three words as if in a mantra. "Access, control, malignant fate. Access, control, malignant fate. Access, control, malignant…" He stopped suddenly and raced to the corner.

The group caught up to him, but he ignored them and continued talking to himself. "Access…I have to be able to get to it whenever I want! It has to be outside!"

Danny shrugged. "We figured that out already."

Robby turned to him with fire in his eyes. "Shut the fuck up!" He ran to the front entrance. Jenna began to worry that he had lost control, but Barker hung back, mentally shadowing Robby's actions.

"Control…it has to be somewhere where it won't be found by accident, somewhere out of normal reach; but still accessible." He thought for a moment. Suddenly, he raced towards 51st Street and went around the corner.

When they caught up with him, he was intently studying the rows of stained glass windows and muttering to himself. "Malignant Fate...remote but accessible, minimal civilian traffic, with a mark clearly visible within seventy meters of the dead drop. Where?" He looked all around him. A desperation seemed to creep in on him. Everybody was clearly worried about him now, and Jenna started to go to him, but Barker grabbed her shoulder.

"Let him be."

Robby began pacing distances down 51st Street towards Madison Avenue. Seventy paces, then he stopped and turned back to the group. The guard in front of the Venezuelan Mission to the United Nations, across the street, looked at him strangely. When Robby got down on his hands and knees, the guard looked away. After all, this was New York and he had seen stranger things.

After crawling around in circles for about five minutes, Robby leapt to his feet and ran out into 51st Street. It was well after two A.M. and traffic was light to nonexistent. Just in case, Barker walked out into the street to direct cars around him.

After looking at the asphalt and cursing a particularly foul obscenity, Robby ran to the far curb and once again dropped to his hands and knees and began crawling around. He took his hand and rubbed street grime from the curb and the gutter. Finally, he stopped and sat back on his haunches, looking down at the curb, a huge grin spreading across his entire face.

Barker wandered over and looked down and also smiled. Slowly, the rest of the group crossed over.

There in front of them, partially covered with God knows what, encrusted with mold, they could clearly see three slanted lines with a horizontal line going through it.

"What are we looking at?" Eve asked.

Rudy's voice was hushed as if he couldn't believe his own words. "That, Professor Palmer, is the last Will and Testament of Pieter Franz Konigsmann."

They all stared quietly and intently at the marks. With all they had researched, and all they had been through, these four old lines, more than anything else, made Franz real for them.

Danny was the first to break the spell. "The diamonds. This means the diamonds must be around here somewhere. Right?"

Robby shook himself as if to clear his head. The more he learned, the less sure of himself he became. It was an uneasy feeling. "I hope you're right. There must be something he left that he felt was of importance or value."

"Maybe we can finally nail Williams with what we find." Jenna was feeling absolutely euphoric, and it was contagious for the rest of them.

Eve hugged Jenna. "Where do we start?"

Robby stood up, turned around and faced Saint Patrick's Cathedral. "Seventy meters from this mark, we should find some answers." He didn't sound as enthusiastic as the rest. "Fan out. Our goal is somewhere in the vicinity."

Seymour was eager to start. "Exactly what are we looking for now?"

Rudy stepped forward. "The same mark, only this time with the horizontal line underneath the slanted lines, not through them." They immediately set off on the search.

a

The cellular connection was fuzzy but audible.

"I say again, they seem to be searching around Saint Patrick's on 51st."

"Do you think they've found what they're looking for?"

"No, sir. But based on their activity, I would say that they are very close."

There was a long pause, and the message could be heard being passed on. "The strike team is en route to you. ETA of twenty minutes. They have new instructions for you."

"Understood."

"Make sure that there are no interruptions. Either to us or them."

"Understood." The line went dead. He waited a moment, then dialed another number.

"Manhattan Central."

"This is Peterson and Donahue, Car 23 King."

"Yeah, Rich."

"We got a stake out in progress on 51st by the Cathedral. Will you notify the blues?"

"You got it, buddy."

"Thanks, man." He hung up and turned to his long time partner. "Now we wait."

"And watch," Donahue chimed in.

ֶ֑

They had been looking for a half hour and their enthusiasm had waned. They now moved around in a desultory fashion. They were tired, cold and hungry. Rudy walked up to Robby slowly, this time not faking his limp.

"Robert, it's been almost fifty years. It could be gone. Found, covered over, destroyed. We could look forever and not find it."

Robby ignored him. He was busy drawing on a small pocket pad. Rudy looked over his shoulder. His sketch showed the street, the stores, the Cathedral, and the location of the marks. Lines were drawn and distances noted. Right now, he seemed to be working on a line that stretched directly from the marks on the curb to the Cathedral wall. The distance noted was well under 70 meters.

Robby smiled for only the second time that evening. "Danny!" Danny walked over. The others stopped their searching and looked on. "Stand on the sidewalk, directly above the marks." He handed him his flashlight. "Face the Cathedral and shine this straight ahead." Mystified, but trusting, Danny did as he was asked.

Robby crossed the street and was joined by the rest of the team. He was barely breathing and quite the opposite of the man who had, not one hour earlier, been crawling around in the gutter searching in the ooze.

He stood stock still, looking back and forth from Danny's flashlight, to the faint light it cast on the wall of the Cathedral. After five minutes of study, he stepped into a line with Danny's light.

Keeping his eye on Danny, he started to pace slowly backward, talking all the while.

"It's twenty meters from that curb to this one. Another twelve from this curb to the wall." He was now standing about six paces back from the curb. He stopped and beckoned Danny over. "That makes thirty-two meters. Sixty-four round trip, marks to wall to marks. If you count off six more meters…"

Barker spoke up. "That'd put you in the middle of the street. Helluva place for a drop."

Robby knelt down and started to examine the area of sidewalk he was standing on. "Correct. So we improvise. We adapt." He paused. "We overcome." They hung on his every word. "If we start counting again, not from the street but from this side of the street, we end up here."

Eve shook her head. "That's an awfully big leap of faith. It could be anywhere. You're just guessing."

Robby never looked up. "Sometimes you've got to ride the double zero." He paused. "This piece of sidewalk is different from the rest."

Suddenly, all the flashlights turned on the spot. In fact that square of sidewalk was clearly newer, lighter in color than the rest.

"They must have resurfaced it after they put in that tree," Eve commented pointing at a nearby planter.

Seymour nodded. He pointed a little way down 51st Street. "Look over there. All the planters are in line up to this point, then they move into line again, only this time ten feet further back."

They all understood instantly. At some time in the past, perhaps 45 years in the past, a planter had stood here, and perhaps beneath it…

Nobody had noticed but Barker had slipped away. Now, he returned. He carried with him two heavy sledge hammers and a pry bar.

Jenna looked at him as Robby took off his coat. "That's gonna make one hell of a lot of noise."

"This, I can handle," Seymour said happily. Five minutes later, they started pounding the pavement to gravel.

Danny stood on the corner of Madison Avenue and Seymour stood on the corner of Fifth. Whenever they saw no cars coming, they flashed their lights and Robby and Barker pounded away. When cars were coming, they flashed them again and the hammering stopped. Working like this, it took them a little over twenty-five minutes. Finally, they broke through to the original pavement and the sentries were recalled.

All lights shone down as Rudy, on his hands and knees, with the care of an archeologist, brushed the fragments and dirt away to reveal the yellowed original sidewalk. It only took a few seconds to find the marks.

"It's a miracle they didn't move the flagstone when they repaved," Eve said.

"Keep praying," Robby grunted and held his breath. He replaced Rudy and knelt by the stone. Tenderly, he pushed one corner of it. Nothing. He tried again, harder this time. Still nothing.

"It's been a long time, man," Barker said. He knelt beside Robby and together they pushed.

It moved!

As Barker inserted the pry bar and they started to slide the stone still farther, Rudy observed, "It probably slid quite easily onto the grass of the old planter." The opening was now about eight inches across. Robby stuck his hand in and burrowed in the earth. Suddenly, he stiffened.

"I have something."

That's when the world exploded around him.

᠄᠄

The three man strike force, along with the two cops, had watched Robby and company for a long time. When they saw the hammering begin, they called in for instructions. The answer came quickly and concisely.

"When they find what they're looking for, pick them up."

The concern of the strike team, all along, was Robby and Barker. When they saw the two men concentrating solely on their labor, they decided not to wait any longer.

The strike team left the stake out location in Donahue's car and drove around to Madison Avenue. Donahue and Peterson got in the strike team's van and waited for the signal. After five minutes, their cellular rang.

"Yes?"

"We go in thirty seconds."

Peterson hung up and turned to Donahue. "Here we go."

They could see that the entire group was bending over, looking down into a hole. They could see the strike team start to walk around the corner towards the Group. They watched as one of the strike team pulled a stun grenade from his overcoat pocket and casually tossed it towards the group.

The blinding flash of light was followed almost instantly by an ear shattering blast. Peterson started the van and quickly pulled up just as the strike team ran up. The blast had thrown the group onto the ground. They lay sprawled around the hole they had created, shaking their heads, trying to regain their senses. Seymour and Jenna had been blown forward landing on top of Robby. Danny was spread-eagled against a nearby tree, and Eve and Rudy had been thrown into the street. Barker lay on the sidewalk next to Robby.

"We'll cuff them in the van," Donahue said. He bent to pick up Rudy.

Barker, still blinded, responded to the sound. He sat up quickly and fired his shotgun in the direction of the voice. The first shot missed Donahue, but blew a hole in the wall of the van.

"Look out!" Shapper called. They were his last words as Barker fired three shots in his direction, the second of which caught the man full in the chest, killing him instantly.

Quickly, the other men opened fire and Barker was hit three times. He fell limply to the ground.

The Nazis worked quickly now. They literally threw the remaining members of the group into the van, where Peterson handcuffed each with plastic flex cuffs. When they got to Robby, they paused only long enough to search him for weapons, then he too was thrown in. Peterson not only cuffed Robby's hands, but also his ankles.

Four minutes after the explosion, they were gone. The only signs of the attack were spent cartridges and Barker's motionless, bleeding body.

Almost as they were pulling away, the man Goorland had assigned to drive came running around the corner. He stopped as he saw Barker's body lying on the sidewalk. Quickly, he ran back to the van.

Ten minutes later, a car pulled up to the curb and two men got out. They pulled out Uzi machine guns and looked all around carefully, then they nodded to the van.

Myor Goorland got out and walked over to Barker's body. He looked down at it and then motioned to his men. "Take him and let's get out of here." As his men struggled Barker into the back of the car, Myor methodically picked up the spent cartridge cases. He took one last look around and stopped. Just beneath his toe, where some digging had been going on, his flashlight picked up the shine of oilskin. He bent and pulled up a thick packet. He brushed the loose dirt off, and decided to take it along just in case it turned out to be important.

"Stupid," he said as he walked to the car. He shook his head. "Stupid." He got in and they drove away into the early morning.

As his mind cleared, Robby heard rather than saw the man leaning over him. "Don't be foolish. No brave moves." The man, later referred to as Kintzler, spoke softly, deliberately, with just a trace of German accent. "You don't want to do anything stupid, because then we would have to kill your friends."

They all heard the man. Fear, the plastic cuffs, and the close quarters kept them all subdued and unmoving. Robby had been thrown in face down, and now attempted to turn his head to see the man's face, but felt a boot pressing his head back in place. After driving for what Robby estimated as fifteen minutes, with three rights, and two lefts, the van stopped. Kintzler spoke again. "When you're taken from the van, you will be inside a secure, soundproofed building. Any attempt to escape or resist will result in considerable pain, so be cooperative."

Two of the men helped each member of the group out of the van, and to a chair where they were tied securely in place. Kintzler and Robby were the last to leave the van.

Robby was taken to a small office, past the other prisoners, where Kintzler tied him in a chair. Kintzler and Weber stood on either side of him, guns drawn. Peterson and Donahue kept guard over the rest of the group.

Robby heard a car drive in, muffled conversation, and another sound. In another minute, he was able to identify the sound as he saw a very old, frail looking man being brought in in a wheelchair. The guards stiffened at attention. The wheelchair was positioned in back of the office desk, facing Robby.

"Herr Moss, I am very glad to meet you at last. You have given us considerable trouble, but that is over now." The old man spoke very slowly, with a heavy German accent. From time to time, his voice faded to a whisper or ended in a coughing fit. The young man who had wheeled him in, clearly his aide, would get him a drink, and he would continue.

"Who are you?"

"The most important person in your life." The old man beckoned to his aide and whispered to him.

The young man addressed himself to Kintzler and Weber. "You have the parcel Moss was digging for?"

The men blanched. Kintzler spoke. "We were busy picking them up. We didn't see anything."

"What about the others?"

"Maybe they picked it up." Kintzler did not sound hopeful.

The aide went into the other room. Schlussel just sat quietly looking at Robby who studied him in turn. After a few minutes, the aide returned.

"The fools didn't take anything. I've sent the surveillance team to get it," the aide said.

Schlussel shrugged. "I've waited almost half a century, I can wait a few more minutes."

It was beginning to make sense to Robby. He needed only a few more details to fill the holes. "You mind if I ask some simple, childlike questions, Pops?"

The aide walked over and struck Robby across the face with the barrel of his pistol. The blow opened a cut from just below his right ear to the corner of his mouth. For a moment, Robby's head hung down limply, then he slowly raised it and shook his head to clear it. "Is that a yes or a no?" he rasped out between clenched teeth.

The aide pulled back his hand to deliver another blow, but Schlussel intervened. "No! Let him talk. We have time to..." he smiled, "to kill."

Robby turned to the aide. He grimaced through his broken face and said in a low voice, "I'll talk with you later." He turned back to Schlussel. "I've got to call you something."

Schlussel shrugged. "Whatever you wish, I have many names."

"How about Karl?"

Schlussel half rose out of the wheelchair and then sank back. He looked as if he had seen a ghost. "How do you know that name?"

Again Robby smiled painfully. "It seemed appropriate." The aide looked at Schlussel who waved him away. He walked to the doorway, after checking Robby's bindings, and then walked outside, shutting the door behind him. The two men were left alone.

"You live up to your reputation, Herr Moss."

"Thanks, Karl." Robby studied the expression on the old man's face. Somewhere between fear and confidence. "So can I ask my questions?"

Hesitatingly, Schlussel nodded.

"How'd you know I was onto the diamonds?"

"I was informed."

"May I guess?" No answer, so Robby continued. "Professor Palmer's research into a German diplomat sets off some alarm bells in some archive or other and eventually the ringing reaches your ears.

"Now, let's say that this diplomat was something more than everyone thought, and that he disappeared carrying something that belonged to you," he paused, "sort of. And let's say that you've spent the bulk of your life in search of this diplomat and when you hear that this professor in California is looking into him, you figure what the hell. Maybe she can find him when you never could. How'm I doing so far?"

"Excellent. Please continue." His expression belied the confidence in his voice.

"Here's where it gets a bit confusing. I can't figure out why you killed her assistants before going after her."

Schlussel took the bait. "We did not touch the boy in New York. What happened to the one in Los Angeles was an accident. Not all of my associates are as efficient as," he gestured at the door, "these men. And we never attempted to abduct the professor before this evening."

Robby was quiet for a moment. It was all falling into place. "And when she became associated with me?"

"You were the perfect stalking horse."

"Of course." Robby paused. "So after Amsterdam failed, you decided to let me lead you right to the diamonds."

"It was most convenient."

Robby stopped smiling. "One last question. Did you kill Konigsmann?"

Schlussel was quiet and when he finally spoke, his voice was low and weak. "Would that I had."

"Who did?"

"Until tonight, I believed that he had disappeared himself; changed his identity again and run off with my diamonds. But your find changes all of that. Now I assume he was killed by the Americans. His ultimate contact, a most unpleasant man, rose to some prominence. Even now."

Robby closed his eyes for a moment. "Thank you."

A door could be heard slamming shut from somewhere in the building. Schlussel looked at his office door. "It seems my men have returned. For your sake, I hope they have brought me what I want. Otherwise, I shall ask the questions. And your friends will suffer for any obstinacy. Most painfully, I assure you."

They waited in silence. Suddenly, strange sounds could be heard coming from the other room. Sounds like sacks of wet cement hitting the floor. Just as Schlussel's expression was changing from confidence to concern, his aide burst through the door with his gun drawn.

"ISRAELIS!!"

The aide started to turn his gun on Robby but he was too late. Robby raised his feet together and planted them deep into the man's groin. As he let out a withering scream and fell to the ground, Robby brought them down hard onto the man's chest. There was a sickening, cracking sound and the man's body started to quiver. After a moment, he lay still.

As Schlussel recovered and started to reach for a gun under his blanket, two young men dressed in black stormed into the office and pinned his arms painfully behind his back. A moment later, Myor walked in.

As one of his men was untying Robby, Myor looked from the

wound on the side of Robby's face to the old man in the wheelchair. Suddenly, he froze.

He walked slowly behind the desk, and stared closely into the man's face. When he spoke, it was in quiet, almost reverential tones.

"Karl Albrecht." He took off his glasses, put them inside his jacket pocket, and suddenly reached out and slapped the old man in the wheelchair. "If you are a religious man, pray that there is no hell!"

⹊

The bodies of Albrecht's men were being carried off to one corner of the large room as Robby came out of the office. He looked around at the young men, all dressed in black, all carrying silenced .45s. He turned to Myor. "Your men work quiet," he said.

"Why advertise." Myor turned back to supervise one of his men wheeling Albrecht out of the office. "Strip him, and search him good. His type likes to keep a false tooth with cyanide, or a small vial of the stuff taped behind the testicles." The man nodded and wheeled Albrecht off. Albrecht looked like a deflated balloon. He was wheezing, and muttering obscenities in German under his breath. As he was being wheeled off, he turned and spat at Myor and turned a vicious glare on Robby. Then he was gone, off to meet his just fate.

Myor looked at Robby's wound. "We better get that taken care of." He signaled to one of his men, who quickly came over with a first aid kit and began to work.

Robby winced as Jenna came over, looking pale. "How's your father?" he asked.

"Recovering." She looked at the nasty cut that Myor's man was in the process of sewing shut. "My God! What happened to you?" She looked away quickly as the needle threaded through Robby's cheek.

Robby grit his teeth. "Minor disagreement." He looked around. He could see Eve looking none the worse for wear, being ministered to by two of Myor's men, Danny and Seymour off to one side rubbing their wrists, and Rudy off by himself looking through some papers.

Robby took another look around the room and then turned back to Jenna, just as Myor's man was placing a large bandage on the side of his face. "Where's Barker?"

Jenna looked pale. "I, I thought you knew." She turned away. "He's dead." Her voice was filled with pain. "They shot him when they took us."

Seymour and Danny had come over and caught the last part of Jenna's answer. Seymour put his hand on Robby's shoulder. "I'm sorry."

Robby looked up at him blankly. "Don't be." He got up and walked over to Myor. "How's Barker?"

The old man chuckled. "Pissed off and resting uncomfortably at Mount Sinai Hospital. He took two in his vest and one just beneath his collarbone."

Robby walked over to Rudy, who looked up at the blood stained bandage. "What happened?" Rudy asked.

"Some people have no sense of humor." He looked down at the pile that Rudy was going through. "What've you got?"

Rudy smiled. "The nice thing about Nazis is that they keep such scrupulous records. These," he indicated the papers in front of him, "are a Who's Who of the American Nazi movement."

"I'm sure Myor can find a good home for them." As he spoke, he suddenly felt as if the world was melting away from him. He never remembered passing out.

He came to slowly. It felt like a sledge hammer was pounding against his cheek and another pounding away inside his skull. Slowly, he opened his eyes.

He was back in his suite at the Cadastré. Jenna was sitting by his bed reading a magazine, and he could hear the others in the next room talking in low voices. Jenna noticed him stirring.

"Welcome back."

"How long have I been out?"

"About eight hours, more or less." She stroked his forehead. "Everything's going to be all right." She spoke soothingly. Robby sat up. "Tell them I'll be right there." Jenna started to protest, but one look at his face made her think better of it.

Robby dressed quickly and staggered out to the living room. They were all gathered around the coffee table, talking when he walked in. He sat down in a comfortable chair. "What's happened since I've been out?"

Rudy picked up a brown paper wrapped package and brought it over to him. "This came from Goorland a couple of hours ago. I saw Barker, he's fine and gets out of the hospital tomorrow. Otherwise, everything's been quiet."

Robby started to unwrap the package. He put the paper aside and looked at the two leather pouches it had contained. Taped to one of the pouches was a note. Robby read it out loud.

"Here is what you left behind last night in your hole. My package is safely on its way to the promised land. *Shalom*. Myor."

They gathered round as Robby opened one of the pouches. Carefully, he reached inside and pulled out a bunch of small square packets, each wrapped in tissue paper. He felt around inside, making sure it was empty, before he went on to the other pouch.

From this one, he took out still more packets and a small notebook wrapped with several wide strips of elastic. He set the notebook aside and picked up one of the packets.

Slowly, he unwrapped the paper. When it was completely open, he poured the gleaming contents onto Rudy's scarf which lay on the table.

They all gasped. "The diamonds," Eve whispered.

It was as if they were all frozen as Robby methodically unwrapped each of the packets and the pile of gems grew. Jenna took her index finger and spread them out on the scarf. Under the bright light of a nearby lamp, all the colors of the rainbow were reflected in them.

Jenna was the first to snap out of the trance. "Dad, let me have your glasses." She picked up one of the larger stones, about the size of her thumb nail, and held it up to the light. She peered at it through her father's glasses.

"Somebody give me blank white paper and a pencil." Jenna commanded. Eve pushed them towards her. Quickly, Jenna drew a straight line on the paper, took off her father's glasses, and placed the stone, table down, centered on the line. "I'm not exactly an expert, but diamonds are one of my favorite things. A jeweler once showed me this trick, if I needed to check something quickly. It's not perfect, but a pretty good start until we get to a jeweler." Jenna looked down at the stone. "Everybody, take turns looking at the line through the stone." Something in Jenna's voice made Robby look at her curiously.

He looked at the stone, and then moved away, smiling. The rest of the group took turns viewing, returning to their seats, puzzled.

"Just what are we looking for?" Eve asked.

"How many lines did you see?" Jenna wanted to know.

"Two!" It was almost a chorus. Eve was trying to be quite precise. "Actually, I saw a line to the side. I think, to each side of the center."

"Exactly! If that was a diamond," Jenna explained, "you would not have seen the line or at best lightly through the center. But you'd have seen only one line which was what I drew. This stone is probably a beautifully cut zircon!"

"Are you sure?" Danny asked.

"Pretty sure. At least enough to raise a question. I thought something didn't look right when I looked through Dad's glasses."

Everybody seemed crestfallen except Robby who continued smiling.

After a moment, everyone was reaching in, drawing lines, and testing the stones. They were all talking at once, bewildered by the turn of events, hoping that only a couple of the stones were not diamonds. Finally, it became clear. There was no point in continuing. There wasn't a single diamond in the pile.

Before the group could become too despondent, Robby reached out for the small notebook which had been neglected until now. He carefully removed the elastic bands holding it closed. Though well protected, it was obviously quite old, and he didn't want to take the chance of destroying whatever was inside. Everybody turned towards him as he opened it, and began skimming through the pages. He went back and forth in the book as they watched in silence. Then, closing the book and placing it back on the table almost reverently, Robby looked up. He turned to Eve. "I think we've just found the ending to your book."

ᨆ

It was early Sunday morning in Washington, DC. The corridors of the Hart Senate Office Building were relatively deserted, as was his office when Senator Martenson ushered in his two visitors.

"Thank you for seeing us on such short notice, Senator." Eve said.

"Mr. Gale called and explained the situation. I'm more than happy to help in any way I can, Professor Palmer, Professor Ehrencoles." A young man came to the door of the inner office. "I'd like you to meet Steven Michaels. He's an assistant Minority Counsel. You'll be talking with him today."

As introductions were being made, the senator was gathering some papers and placing them in his attaché case. "Under the circumstances Sy stated, I thought it best that you meet in the privacy of my office. I leave you in good hands, I assure you."

The senator left hurriedly. He was willing to do a favor for Seymour but Williams was both prominent and powerful. Martenson would rather not be known as his opponent until the Committee rejected him. A hasty retreat now would still afford him some deniability if needed.

"Before we begin, I must explain that I can't discuss anything with you until Claire Barnes arrives. She's my opposite number on the Majority side of the aisle."

As if on cue, there was a knock on the door. Michaels opened it, greeting a short, slim, conservatively dressed woman, slightly greying, obviously somewhat older than Michaels. She stood in the doorway for a moment, surveying the group.

"All right, Steven, what's this all about? Some of us have a life on the weekend."

"I'm sorry to inconvenience you, Claire, but this is Committee business. I know your people are anxious to get this over with quickly, but something's come up, and I thought if we handled this together informally, we could expedite matters."

"And these people are...?"

"Professor Rudolph Ehrencoles, Assistant Chairman of the Department of History at the University of Nevada at Las Vegas, and Associate Professor Eve Palmer from UCLA." Barnes nodded in their direction. "They have indicated they have information relevant to the hearings regarding Williams' confirmation."

"I see." Barnes found a seat and took a legal pad out of her briefcase. For the next half hour, Michaels carefully brought out Rudy's and Eve's educational background, emphasizing their degrees, academic achievements, and especially in Rudy's case, papers published and awards received. Claire asked few questions and then only to bring out whether or not they had any strong political motives.

When Michaels felt this had been covered to everyone's satisfaction, he sat back. "Professor Palmer, I understand you have some very serious allegations to make concerning E. George Williams."

Eve nodded.

"Without getting into any specifics, can you tell me whether or not we're dealing with allegations of criminal, civil, or personal misconduct?"

"I am absolutely certain of the criminal and personal misconduct. But I'm a history professor, not a lawyer. I'm not quite certain what constitutes civil misconduct." Eve replied.

"Completely understandable," Barnes said. "We don't expect you to make legal judgments. Strictly from the viewpoint of a lay person and an academician, how would you characterize the misconduct?"

"Gross criminal conduct," Eve answered, "attempted kidnapping, attempted murder..."

"Don't forget bribery, and actual murder." Rudy interposed.

The room was silent for several minutes, and then Barnes turned to Rudy. "Those are very serious charges, not to be made casually. You understand that?"

"There is nothing casual about the events we're talking about," Rudy said.

Michaels and Barnes conferred quietly for a moment, then they turned back to Rudy and Eve. Barnes led the questioning.

"I'd like to ask you both some yes or no questions. Wherever possible, please try to confine your answers to that." They nodded. "Are you eyewitnesses to any of these crimes? Specifically, the attempted murder and murder."

"Yes."

"Did any of these crimes, specifically the murder and attempted murder, take place under government sanction?"

"No."

"Have either of you personally met or been in the presence of Mr. Williams?"

"No."

Barnes looked at Michaels who continued the questioning. "Professor Ehrencoles, please be specific without recounting specific events, how you could have personally witnessed Mr. Williams commit any of the alleged crimes, since you admit you've never been in his presence?"

Rudy was angry. "When an attempt is made to kill me by Williams' agent, at his direction, on more than one occasion, and attempts made simultaneously on my associates...well, is that good enough for you?"

Barnes leaned in towards Rudy. "Professor, do you have any physical or documentary evidence which in any way, any way at all, can connect Director Designate Williams to any of the charges," she paused and then emphasized her next point, "from bribery to murder."

"Yes, oh yes." Rudy reached into his briefcase, and pulled out the notebook that Robby had found. "Let me tell you a story."

❧

The restaurant was mostly empty. The lunch crowd had emptied back onto the crowded streets of Washington, and the dinner mob would not begin arriving for another two hours. It was a time for the staff to clean up, rest, and prepare.

In the back of the restaurant, in a plushly appointed booth, Williams sat sipping a coffee and waiting for his guests. He appeared outwardly calm, but inside his stomach churned and his heart pounded.

He had never been truly afraid of anyone in his life. He had always had the power or the angles to hold off any threat. But this man that he had come to meet was different. He was like some natural force. Like thunder, lightning, fire or flood. The Israelis had a word for it. Barak. He could never be completely controlled. Maybe, he could be reasoned with.

They were late, probably intentionally so. Still, he waited

calmly, the only outward signs of tension, tiny beads of sweat on his forehead. He looked towards the door and saw them come in.

It took Robby and Seymour a moment to adjust to the relative darkness of the restaurant interior, then Seymour gestured towards Williams and they walked over. Williams stood to greet them.

"It's a great pleasure to meet you, Mr. Gale. I've stayed at your hotels many times and always enjoyed myself immensely." They shook hands. Williams held out his hand to Robby. "And you must be Moss."

Robby sat down without shaking hands. His face was a blank. The other men also sat. The tension at the table was enormous. Williams tried to break it as the waiter came over.

"Would you like anything?"

Seymour ordered a cup of coffee and Robby said nothing. They sat in silence until after the waiter returned and left. Seymour took a drink of his coffee and then turned to Williams.

"I appreciate your seeing us on such short notice," he said.

Williams nodded. "I thought it was time we talked."

Seymour continued. "We are both in vulnerable positions, Mr. Williams. Me, through my hotels, you on the Senate floor. I thought we might reach some kind of accord."

"I'm not sure what you're talking about," Williams began, "but if I can be of any help, it would be my pleasure." He looked at Robby who remained silent and blank.

"I want nothing else to happen to my family or friends," Seymour said.

Williams was not used to bluntness. "Please continue."

Seymour took another drink of coffee. "I want three things. One, I want your guarantee of no more attacks on my people. Two, you will remove whatever pressure you are putting on the Gaming Commission."

He was interrupted. "I don't have any idea what you're talking about, Mr. Gale. But I'd be happy to make some calls on your behalf."

"Three," Seymour said ignoring him. "I want you to withdraw your name from consideration for CIA Director."

Williams laughed. "And why would I do that?" he asked. He

lowered his voice. "You have nothing concrete, and with Ms. Palmer's unfortunate accident..." His voice trailed off.

Seymour stood up. "I've said my piece." He turned and walked away.

Williams watched him go and then turned back to his coffee. With a start, he realized that Robby was still at the table. His blank expression was gone, replaced by a cold fury.

For the first time in his life, he thought he might not be able to slide out from under this problem. He glanced at the only other diners in the restaurant, his undercover bodyguards.

Robby spoke slowly and quietly. "Look under the table." Williams looked and saw Robby cradling a small automatic in his lap. It was pointing directly at Williams. "Tell your men to leave."

For a moment, he thought about signaling for help, but the look in Robby's eyes made him think again. He nodded with his head towards the door, and his men rose and left the dining room.

He turned back to Robby. "What now?"

"Gale told you what to do. I'm going to tell you what happens if you don't." He paused as the waiter came over and refilled Williams' coffee. "If any harm comes to Gale, his family or his friends...you die." He slid over and pushed the gun into Williams' ribs. "If anything happens to any of Gale's businesses...you die." He thumbed down the hammer of the gun. He could feel the man begin to tremble. "And within a month of your becoming CIA Director...they'll bury you. Guaranteed."

Robby rose to leave. He holstered the gun and looked down at the shaking man.

"By the way, Eve Palmer is alive."

CHAPTER SEVENTEEN

THE TRAITOROUS INNOVATOR

Desperate men do desperate things. So the axiom goes. E. George Williams was a desperate man and he knew it. One chance and one chance only remained for him to salvage the situation and win the day. One chance for him to survive.

He had met through the night with his closest, most trusted advisors. As they laid their plans, the news got progressively worse. CNN was reporting that the Israelis had captured former Nazi Deputy Director of Operations General Karl Albrecht and were, at this moment, interrogating him somewhere in a military prison in Israel.

Just as Williams was recovering from the shock, and trying to figure out what, if anything, Albrecht could or would say about him, information was received from a source on the Intelligence Committee that Eve Palmer would testify in open session the next day. This news was further worsened by the fact that Senator Larson would no longer take any calls from Williams.

And always looming just on the edge of Williams' mind, was Robby's threat.

Every time the phone rang, Williams jumped. The White House was seemingly oblivious to what was happening, but that could change at any time and the call that he dreaded could come.

Finally, the plan was set. One bold master stroke that, if successful, would not only eliminate the threats of Palmer, Gale and Moss, but would divert attention elsewhere and allow him to be confirmed quietly.

Desperate men do desperate things and Williams was a desperate man.

ॐ

Dawn over Washington.

Pagetts Corner, Maryland is a tiny community just outside the Capital Beltway. With only a few hundred residents, it is quiet, sleepy and relaxed. Except this morning.

At a small motel on the Temple Hill Road, three long black limousines were pulling up. Calendar Dan came out of one of the rooms and talked to the drivers. Two minutes later, each car pulled up to the door of a motel room. A moment after that, the doors to both cars and rooms opened and people hurried from the rooms into the cars. The drivers slammed the doors shut and got in behind their wheels.

Dan climbed into the front passenger seat of the lead car and picked up his walkie-talkie. "One ready," he said.

His answers came crackling back.

"Two ready."

"Three ready."

He turned to his driver. "Let's do it."

The limousines pulled out behind the lead car and headed north on Temple Hill. The plan was to avoid the usual routes (the Beltway, Pennsylvania Avenue etc.) and proceed by side roads to the Committee room. Only at the last moment would the convoy turn onto a main road.

In the back seat, Eve turned to Rudy. "I'm scared."

Rudy smiled comfortingly. "Nothing to fear. The senators want to hear what you have to say."

"That's not what I meant."

"I know," he said. "But Robby's plans, no matter how brazen they may seem, have a way of coming out all right." He squeezed her hand. "Have faith."

The limos were now headed west on Brinkley Road. Shortly, they turned northeast on St. Barnabas Road. Quick turns and changes of direction were critical and every few miles they made them. Northwest on Wheeler Road, east on Alabama Avenue, then north on 25th Street to Kenilworth Ave.

Kenilworth is a wide highway and the limos fanned out in an inverted V formation. Finally the turn west, straight in to the Capitol, on Benning Road and then a short run southwest on Maryland Avenue.

Danny looked out the window at the passing monuments. "You know, I just realized I've never been here before." He turned to his father. "You think we'll be able to get in some sight seeing while we're here?"

Seymour gave him a dirty look. "Funny, you ain't."

The attack came as the cars prepared for their turn onto Maryland.

A cement truck suddenly pulled out in front of the convoy as they approached the narrow turn, forcing the cars to skid to a halt just in time. From both sides of the road, men opened fire on the convoy with Schmeisser machine pistols.

The nonstop firing continued for just under a minute. It riddled the sides of all three limos with holes. The windows spider webbed but didn't give in. The armor in the cars held out against the assault. Quickly, the men firing saw this and halted their shooting.

One man stepped forward from each side of the road, armed with German made Mannheim antitank weapons. They extended the barrels and sighted in, but before they could fire, a roar filled their ears, as a helicopter swooped down upon them.

At the last moment, the chopper pulled out of its dive, and as it did, three satchel sized packets were released from its underbelly. They fell quickly and on impact with the asphalt exploded with a massive sound and huge blue clouds of smoke.

The attackers were stunned but not wounded, and quickly began to regroup. Too late.

Heavily armed men poured from the limos. With disciplined and superior firepower, they began to cut down the attackers. By the time the helicopter came in for another pass, it was all over. The attackers were either dead or in custody, and the FBI Special Reaction Team was beginning to clean up the scene.

The airport van with Seymour, Danny, Eve and Rudy pulled into the underground garage of the Rayburn House Office building and was met by Capital Police. They escorted them to a security elevator and, in less than five minutes, the four sat in the Committee room waiting for the procedures to begin.

Back out at the scene of the attack, the Special Agent in Charge walked over to Dan and asked for his radio. Dan smiled and handed it to him.

"High Cover, this is Lead."

In the helicopter, Robby answered. "Go ahead, Lead."

"Thanks for the assist and the tip. We can handle it from here."

"Roger, Lead. Anytime."

"Hey, Robby?"

"Yeah, Mike."

The agent spoke softly. "This makes up for the San Juan fiasco."

Robby winced at the reference to an old adventure. "Thanks, man."

❧

The Committee room was packed. The word had gotten out that there was going to be something sensational happening, and the media was preparing for a feeding frenzy.

Eve sat at the green felt covered table with Rudy beside her. They had decided, in consultation with Seymour, not to have a lawyer with them. They felt they could handle whatever came up, and that the perception to the Committee and the public would be one of truthfulness and sincerity. Seymour, Danny and Jenna sat behind them. On the table in front of them were the documents and notes they felt they would need.

The buzz of the room quieted as the chairman pounded his gavel and called the hearing back to order. "Copies of the exhibits referred to have now been furnished to all members of the Committee." He gestured towards Rudy. "Professor Ehrencoles, you may continue your statement."

Rudy took a drink of water and began. "As I was saying, the O.S.S., FBI, and SHAEF documents before you lay out the chain of events leading up to the disappearance of the man known as Jack Donald King. It is our contention that this King person was in fact Pieter Konigsmann, a senior officer in the Nazi High Command.

"We further allege that Director Designate Williams, either on his own, or with the tacit approval of Government officials, conspired to subvert justice by concealing Colonel Konigsmann's true identity from the Congress as the law required. And finally, in this time frame, we contend that Director Designate Williams entered into an illegal relationship with Colonel Konigsmann that resulted in the payment of a substantial sum to Mr. Williams in exchange for services that included an illegal use of grants of immunity and acts of murder. Further, we allege that these actions of perfidy continue to this day in light of the recent attacks which we have detailed to this committee earlier."

The reaction of the Committee and the media was instantaneous. The noise exploded through the room and it took the chairman several minutes to restore order.

❧

Since he had heard of the failure of the attack earlier that morning, Williams had been in a growing panic. He sat stunned, in front of the television, watching the proceedings.

He held one last hope. That the Committee would understand that everything he had done, then, as well as now, was for the good of the country, and only of the country.

❧

Rudy was responding to a question from Senator Martenson. "We anticipate that Mr. Williams will invoke love of country and the flag in the defense of his actions. However, what patriotism or noble effort can account for the murders of seven FBI agents and their wives. Not to mention the deaths of nearly two hundred additional innocents, under the guise of yet another illegally constituted government operation called Burnish Group."

❧

Williams blanched. His world was crumbling rapidly. He grabbed a phone and tried for the thirtieth time to reach Larson.

Once again, he couldn't get through.

He put down the phone as he watched Larson begin his

questioning. Maybe, just maybe at least one of them could be discredited.

❧

Senator Larson had been wavering in his mind as to which was the greater evil; allowing Williams' confirmation or not allowing it. Certainly he wasn't going to accept these statements at face value.

"Professor Palmer, in reviewing your background, I am struck by two things. First, allow me to congratulate you on the achievements you have made at such a young and relatively inexperienced age. They must have come at a great personal price."

Eve nodded and braced herself for what Seymour had told her to expect.

"The second issue that concerns me is particularly relevant to today's proceedings. It is my understanding that you are being sought by the authorities in Los Angeles concerning your recent, I don't know any gentle way to say this, your recent escape from a psychiatric ward in that fine city."

"Senator," Eve began, "the basis for my appearance here today is that Mr. Williams, through his agents, have for the better part of the last month, subjected me to an increasingly severe series of attacks. As a result of which, I did in fact enter a facility. However, I did not," she sneered the word, "escape. I was the victim of an attempted abduction by Mr. Williams' agents." She paused for effect. "In effect, I am living proof of the saying, just because you're paranoid does not mean that people are not after you." There was light laughter from the audience.

Larson spoke gently and appeared grandfatherly all of a sudden. "Miss Palmer, you mentioned proof. Isn't that really why we're here?"

Rudy interrupted. "Senator, you have to bear in mind that you cannot consider the actions of this month individually, but you must view the events as a whole. I believe that we would all be better served if Professor Palmer and I were allowed to present these events in chronological order. I call your attention to the exhibit which I believe has been marked Ehrencoles One. The personal diary of Pieter Konigsmann."

❧

Excerpts From Diary of Pieter Franz Konigsmann

January 1947

Back in New York, but how different. I'm exhilarated, and terrified. For my own protection, I need to think through, set down something of the past few months. I do not trust anyone. I am my own security.

Nuremberg, I still shake when I remember. I survived, and I'll continue to do so. Williams has guaranteed it. None of my old associates will be able to find me. Even if they survive the trials and somehow find a way to get here. Williams. I certainly paid him enough. It's a good thing he didn't know how many diamonds I really have. He's a greedy bastard. But he did kill Albrecht and Minscel and falsified the record. It was worth some of the stones for that. I had to give the O.S.S. some material but it was only against the Communists. Albrecht and Minscel were expendable. It was my life or theirs.

My honor remains intact, but Williams cannot pretend. He thought he could decide when and where I would be pushed around. But his greed was his undoing. When he took those ten diamonds from me and then, almost immediately, arranged for me and my Constance to come to New York, I knew he was mine.

I'm going to wait. I think in a few months, when the situation has stabilized, I shall make my move.

July 1947

My son, Pieter Franz was born on the 25th. This complicates my plans. Working at the ECD is dangerous. I'm always afraid someone will recognize me. I've gone along with the job, marking time.

Now that we are in the States, and Constance has become a *hausfrau*, life has become more mundane and stultifying than ever. I have more than 290 diamonds waiting for me. I can make a new life. The government will look after Constance and the child. Eventually, I can make provision for my son, or perhaps, when he is older, I'll make myself known to him.

September 1947

It finally happened. Otto Streck, Bernhard's son came through the ECD process, and recognized me. I was lucky it was him. I have explained to him that I am working secretly for our cause, and that he must be silent. He believes me. But to play safe, I've arranged for him to come live with Constance and me. He will work with me at ECD. It is so crowded and miserable at home but for the moment, it will have to do. I don't know how much longer I can wait.

November 1947

I think I have been recognized again. A man named Planscke came through the processing. He kept staring at me. Clearly, he remembers me. I have been through too much. If any of my old friends should discover me, they would not be kind with me. I'm sure they could not understand the pressures put on me at Nuremberg. I have not gone through all this to be destroyed by vengeful fools.

I know the FBI keeps track of me, but they can't help. I tried calling the CIA. Williams is no longer there. He owes me. I gave him a considerable value in diamonds. He must help me get away. I told the CIA liaison I had urgent information but would only speak with Williams. We have arranged to meet in two days. This goes back in my hiding place again. For the last time. The next time I pick this up, the diamonds and I will have begun a new life.

Senator Larson had just about decided which way the wind was blowing, but before definitely deserting Williams, he thought he'd better check a few more things. "Professor Ehrencoles. Let's go back to your Exhibit One, for a moment. We have only your word that this was written by Colonel Konigsmann."

"Senator, if you will examine exhibits Palmer One through Four," Eve said, "you'll find other documents which contain the handwriting of Colonel Konigsmann. These documents are certified copies taken from National Archives Records. I believe this Committee has the resources to compare them with the diary."

The chairman turned to Larson. "Senator," he said, "the reason we asked them to provide originals, as you well know, was to confirm the authenticity of the diary. It would be extremely helpful if you would confine yourself to those areas with which we can deal today. After all, it was your side of the aisle that requested the expediting of these hearings."

Larson thought carefully. He was coming perilously close to being viewed as a defender of Williams. It was time to sell short. "Mr. Chairman, I would only add that I would appreciate being informed of the scientific findings as soon as possible so that those of us on this side can join with the Chair in a thorough investigation of the truth of this matter." He stood. "I regret that I must absent myself at this time to tend to constituent affairs." He started to leave the room.

"Senator Larson?" Larson stopped and turned to face the Chair. "Senator, I thought that's exactly what we were doing here, searching for the truth."

‏‮♠‬

Williams had had enough. Half way through the exchange, he threw an ashtray at the television set. It missed, and he walked over and shut the set, laughing to himself, "I can't seem to do anything right." It was the last time he would laugh. All the years of effort, the danger, walking a fine line, the diplomacy, everything, everything. It was all disappearing. It wasn't fair. Well, he wasn't going down. Maybe he couldn't stay in the States. But he could still have a good life. He deserved it. It was important to think clearly, deliberately.

Williams picked up the phone and called his lawyer. "Jed, no, no, I know you're watching the hearings. To hell with that. That's not why I'm calling. Shut up and listen. I pay you enough." He paused, thought for a minute. "I'm writing out the necessary documents so you can handle transfer of all stock, etc. from Forecast and Cloudburst to Emily."

There was a pause as he listened to his lawyer. "Don't be ridiculous, Jed. I'm not going to do anything foolish. Far from it. I just want to be unencumbered, that's all. Emily can do whatever she wants to with them. And no, you don't need to know what my next steps will be. You've always said you didn't want to know, anyway. I'll be in touch."

He slammed down the phone, and hurriedly scribbled the obligatory notes. At the end, he added a brief one to Emily. Poor Emily, she never really did understand what he was all about, but she came from a good family and had done right by him for a long time.

When he finished, he walked to a corner of the room, moved a chair, and pushed back the rug. Underneath was a floor safe, rarely opened. He was certain Emily had forgotten it even existed since together they had always used the wall safe in the library. He removed several thick envelopes of cash and bearer bonds. He used to think of the contents as "my parachute," funds acquired in somewhat less than conventional ways, waiting patiently, "just in case." He had never really expected to need them. It was almost a game, collecting it all. Now, he was glad he had it.

Some of the cash went into his pockets. He did not plan to use credit cards, too easily traced. The rest went into his attaché case. Then he composed himself, sat down at his desk, and buzzed for his aide, who appeared almost immediately.

"Ryan, a strategic retreat is in order. Suggestions?"

Ryan had been with Williams a number of years, a graduate of Forecast Research. He was accustomed to strange requests, at unusual times. He was generally unflappable, and totally amoral, the perfect aide to Williams. "Permanent or temporary, sir?"

"I'm not sure. But to be on the safe side, let's say permanent."

"I assume out of the country."

"Correct."

Ryan thought for a moment. "There are a number of places where extradition would not be a problem, but it seems to me that the whole possibility of extradition should be avoided."

"Exactly."

"That means we have to go either to South America, where we can buy sanctuary or," he paused, "Switzerland."

"Why Switzerland?" Williams asked.

Ryan was precise. "We have enough deposits in various Swiss banks to guarantee a positive reaction to any plea for sanctuary."

Williams was beginning to feel better. Choose good men, pay them well, ensure their loyalty. It pays off.

"Switzerland," he said firmly.

"Sir, if memory serves, we used an acceptable place just outside Bern some time ago. Thirty room mansion, twenty acres of land-scaped grounds with an advanced security system already installed."

"That's perfect. Make the necessary arrangements."

"How quickly?"

"Immediately, within the hour, if possible."

"Of course. Any other requirements?"

"There should be no way of tracing our route, or even the fact that we've left. Also," Williams paused, and shuddered as he spoke, "I want the absolutely complete security package for the estate.

Beef it up, I don't care where you get the men so long as you are completely certain of their reliability. And the technical aspects. Upgrade the hardware, both personal and estate to top level and beyond. I don't want a flea to be able to penetrate."

"Understood, Sir. Is there anything else?"

"No. Just get to it."

Ryan left and Williams hurriedly gathered the last things he would need from his desk. As he was making a last survey of the room, the phone rang. After a moment of uncertainty, he answered it.

"Williams."

"George, I thought you'd like to know that the Committee is considering issuing a subpoena for all your records."

"Thanks."

"I owed you that much at least."

"Thank you, Senator." He paused. "It was the very least you could do." He slammed the phone down.

Twenty minutes later, the chartered Gulfstream cleared American airspace and Williams was a free man.

At least, physically.

*

The VIP suite at the Empress Atlantic City was filled with a party atmosphere. Music played from the expensive stereo, a lavish buffet was being attacked by Louie Gross, who didn't let a little thing like a sling bother him, even Barker was smiling despite the cast that covered his chest.

Rudy and Eve were dancing, possibly two different dances at the same time. Their appearance before the Intelligence Committee had been overwhelmingly successful and they were both besieged by offers for interviews, appearances, and in Eve's case, a movie and an indecent proposal.

Seymour walked across the room, patted his semi-drunk son on the head, and sat down next to Robby.

"All in all, a successful conclusion to an unpleasant episode," he said.

Robby stared down into his ice cream soda. "It's not over yet."

Seymour turned serious and looked him in the eye. "Let it go."

"I can't."

Seymour shook his head. "Williams will get his."

"You got that right."

Barker painfully came over and slowly sat beside Robby. "Lighten up. So we didn't find the diamonds. Seymour's the one out God knows how much."

Seymour took a deep slug from his JB. "Not only God knows. You should see the bills."

Robby looked up for the first time. "Who says I didn't find the diamonds."

Through the music, the partying, and Louie's chewing, everybody stopped instantly and yelled, "WHAT!!!"

"I was going to tell you after I got Williams."

Louie came over and looked deeply into Robby's eyes. He frowned. "That's bad thinking. You cannot, I repeat cannot, go after Williams. He's probably surrounded by a fucking army!"

Jenna came over and put her hands around Robby's throat. "What was that about the diamonds," she batted her eyes in a mock seduction. Everyone laughed.

Robby appreciated her point. "We'll get the diamonds. But I have something to do first."

"Your priorities are all screwed up, my friend," Danny slurred. "Williams will keep. If you know where the diamonds are, why are we sitting here?"

Rudy spoke up from the other side of the room. "Robby's right. Williams remains a threat to all of us until he's dealt with."

The argument shifted over to Rudy. Seymour seemed to come down on both sides at once. Barker and Louie, while being supportive of Robby, thought they had all been through enough. Eve and Jenna both wanted to go after the diamonds immediately.

Danny, who had been arguing the pros and cons with his champagne glass, suddenly announced to the group that "if the diamonds have any respect for any of us, they'll bring themselves here." He then quietly slipped to the floor. The group looked at him for a moment and then turned back to their argument.

Robby walked over to Danny and dropped a piece of paper on his head.

The argument raged and waned for the next half hour. Finally,

Seymour went to get himself another drink. It didn't register at first, but then it became clear to him. "Where's Robby?"

Calls downstairs and a search of the adjoining suites were fruitless. In exasperation, Jenna went to rouse Danny to see if he had seen Robby go. She discovered the paper hanging half out of his mouth.

She called everybody together and read it aloud to the silenced group.

"Sometimes, you have to do what's right. Robby."

か

Williams had been on the estate just outside of Bern for four days now. After the jet lag, and checking things out, he finally let go, and allowed himself to feel the exhaustion and the stress of the last week. He had slept for almost twenty-four hours, and began feeling like his old self.

He was pleased with the staff Ryan had assembled, and all the arrangements that had been made. He felt safe at last.

He wandered about the grounds, and then about the manor itself. He watched television briefly but was always brought back when the news came on. The media just wouldn't let go of the story.

"This is Bobbie Batista for the CNN International Report. The search continues for missing CIA Director Designate E. George Williams who disappeared last week after startling testimony was heard by the Senate Select Committee on Intelligence. We go to Christianne Amanpour for the report."

"To hell with them." Williams shut the television set. "They'll never find me. They might as well quit and save themselves the expense."

He decided to read for a while, but the newspapers were equally full of the story, and he couldn't concentrate on any book.

か

Empress One was at 37,000 feet and cruising towards Europe. Robby was burning up the satellite links with computer traces of every Williams' owned or controlled company he could think of. He was confident that Williams would run to Europe or Asia. He had spent many years in both, but Robby gambled that he would find a more sophisticated acceptance in Europe. Right now, technically, the jet's destination was Paris. His computer search to this point hadn't yielded anything he could use. But Robby was patient and undaunted. He decided to try another approach. Over the years, Williams often had to travel covertly. He used standard CIA techniques; and Robby was also ex-CIA. He checked, through the computer, all flight plans filed for private jets bound for Western Europe since the day before Williams had disappeared. He then had the computer cross-check those against flight plans that had been altered in mid Atlantic.

It would take time, but they were still four hours out of Paris. Robby was prepared to wait.

ﻙﺎ

Williams now found himself wandering aimlessly about the house and grounds. He couldn't sit still, and he couldn't find anything to hold his interest. He began rechecking the security set up. First, he turned on all the television sets in the house to the security channel so that he could see all the areas being surveyed.

He repeatedly called Ryan in, and would interrogate him at length as to the background of each and every guard and staff member. Then, he'd call him back in, and together, they would go over the entire estate, checking the specialized equipment that had been installed throughout.

Periodically, he would sit down and try to organize his defense. He worked intently, for short periods, on a letter that he intended to send to the president that he believed would exonerate him. At the very least, he would remind the president how much he, the president, owed him. The first part of that letter was revealing of just how far he had slipped. Once, when he had left the letter on a table, and gone off to check some equipment, Ryan had glanced at it.

"My Dear Mr. President," it said, "I believe it imperative that you understand just how far my enemies will go to silence what they consider to be the true voice of America. They understand, perhaps better than the craven, pusillanimous, weak-hearted politicians and reporters who are their tools..." The rest of the letter devolved into an illegible scrawl.

Ryan covertly ordered that all sharp objects, including Williams' razor be stored under lock and key.

ﻙﺎ

On the ground at Le Bourget, Robby went over the three possibilities that the computer had kicked out. The first was a corporate Lear bound Washington for London, that had changed its flight plan to Liverpool. He discounted that one.

Next, he examined a private Gulfstream bound Washington for Barcelona that had diverted to Tenerife. This was a strong possibility. Tenerife was a playground for the world's rich and useless from Robby's viewpoint. It was the third flight plan that he was betting on. This was a Gulfstream that had left Baltimore headed for Florence, Italy. While refueling in Valencia, the plan had been altered for Antwerp, and then altered again mid-flight for Bern, Switzerland.

Robby understood Williams and the obvious appeal that Bern would have for him. After checking that the jet had landed at Bern, Robby ordered Empress One into the air again. It would arrive late that afternoon.

ᴥ

The "special" guards from Forecast Research and elsewhere were all over the property. With high tech communications and detection devices, they covered the Bernese estate to effectively prevent any unauthorized entry. In addition, every square inch of the grounds were floodlit.

Still, Williams knew that "he" would come.

Guards patrolled the outside of the high stone wall in special jeeps with ammonia sniffing detection devices that could sniff out a man at over one hundred meters. Every entrance was heavily guarded and secured by double steel gates, each of which could not be opened unless the other was closed.

Still, Williams knew that "he" would come.

Sharpshooters were on the roof with night vision sights, and state-of-the-art rifles capable of accurately sighting and killing a man almost a mile off.

But Robby came anyway.

He came alone, unassisted by any of his friends and associates. He came alone, because this final act was to be a *pas de deux*. Just him and Williams. To the death.

At one in the morning, a rocket screeched through the air and blew out a large section of the north wall. The guards scrambled to repel an attack…that never came.

At two in the morning, a rocket tore out both of the gates on the south side of the estate. Again the guards scrambled to react, again nothing more happened.

At a quarter after three, the guards discovered a message spray painted on the east wall.

"Any security forces left inside these walls as of 0400 this morning will be considered hard targets." The message was signed with a double zero.

The men were disciplined but, by the appointed hour, four had left. The remainder braced for an attack.

Four o'clock. Four-fifteen. Four-thirty. The time passed slowly, agonizingly. The tension was a living thing that wandered among the security men, tapping them on the shoulder, causing sweats and dry heaves.

Four thirty-eight. Three rockets, fired in rapid succession, came screaming through the hole in the north wall. They exploded against vehicles or the ground. But these were different than the earlier ones.

Large white fragments, trailing smoke, exploded out from the warheads and drifted gracefully to the ground, instantly causing whatever they hit to burst into flames. "Phosphorous!" several men screamed at once. Three men were dead, two others were on fire. They scrambled to save themselves and the property from the growing inferno.

Amidst all of this chaos, no one noticed the alarm trigger on the west wall, or the solitary figure lightly drop onto the grounds from it. He vanished into the smoke and flame.

The guards inside the mansion were watching the carnage outside when all of the interior alarms sounded at once. Momentarily panicked, they quickly recovered and raced to their alert positions. A group of three guards raced for the control room. Two made it. The last of them was grabbed from behind and jerked into a side room so quickly that the other two never noticed.

The guards on the staircase never heard the shots that cut them down. The guards outside Williams' office had time to start to point their weapons before they died.

Inside, Williams crouched behind his desk. He had heard the men fall to the floor and he knew that the inevitable was coming through the door any minute. One word kept repeating in his mind. Relentless! He pointed his gun and waited.

Suddenly, the wall to his right exploded. He tried desperately to turn but flying plaster and wood slowed him. The next thing he knew, Robby was standing in front of him, with his gun pointed at Williams' left eye.

Williams let his gun drop from his hand.

"Get up." Robby's voice was cold and his intent clear. His eyes had gone gray and the wound on the side of his face was bleeding slightly. He motioned at a chair behind the desk. "Sit."

Williams slowly moved to the chair and sat down. He looked Robby in the eye, and in as steady a voice as he could muster, he spoke. "Is there anything I can do to save my life?"

"Maybe."

"Anything," he begged.

"We don't have much time before your guards come." Robby moved to a love seat against the wall from which he could watch both Williams and the door. "Tell me about November 14, 1947."

For a moment, Williams seemed disoriented. Then, as if a cloud was lifting, he remembered the date. "It was very cold that night."

New York City, November 14, 1947...

The night was filled with a heavy mist that occasionally coalesced into a wispy fog. Williams pulled his overcoat tightly around him as he walked across the vast expanse of lawn at the center of Central Park. He saw the man he was looking for standing in the distance. He had hoped never to see him again. Yet this was the second time tonight.

King stood stock still as Williams approached. "So," he began, "are my terms satisfactory?"

Williams nodded. "Conditionally."

"What does that mean?"

"It means that I have terms of my own." Williams was angry and he let King know it. "First of all, you don't ever call me again. Not directly and not through the agency! Do you understand?"

King nodded, barely.

Williams continued, scarcely restraining his anger. "And secondly, what happened during the war is an isolated incident. If you ever bring it up again, I'll make it my business to tell your old 'beer buddies' exactly where you are and exactly what you did."

King sneered at him. "Information is a two edged sword. I also can tell many things." He paused. "At least ten things. Gems of information you might call them."

Williams seemed to relax. "All right. As long as we understand each other. I've been told to tell you that we are prepared to convert your," he searched for a word, "your pension into cash. Where do you want to meet?"

King thought for a moment. "The rink at the center in thirty."

Williams nodded. He turned and walked away.

King watched until he disappeared beyond a stand of trees. Then he started out. He walked quickly for he had a long way to go. He didn't want to take a cab, there was no telling who might be driving it. He decided to walk down Fifth Avenue. That would take him past the cathedral and his *tote graben.*

He took a short cut through a group of trees that were near the Fifth Avenue wall. Suddenly, he froze. The cold barrel of Williams' pistol was pressed against his neck.

"Where are they?" Williams hissed. King remained silent. "You have ten seconds left to live if you don't tell me." King still refused to talk. "I'm not bluffing!"

"You will not kill me, I think," King said, his German accent more pronounced. "Without me, you have nothing." King thought he felt the gun waver. Slowly, he turned around to face Williams. Despite the cold, Williams was sweating. "What do you propose?" he asked through clenched teeth.

King shrugged. "Exactly what we agreed to before. Nothing more. You arrange for me to convert the diamonds to hard currency and I give you ten percent."

"You have them on you, don't you?"

"Don't be stupid." The old arrogance was back. King squared his shoulders, turned his back on Williams, and started to walk away. "Shoot or don't. I have more important things to do," he called over his shoulder.

He got about ten feet away when his arrogance betrayed him for the first and last time. A single shot rang out. King stumbled forward two steps, righted himself, and turned slowly around. Stiffly, he lurched towards Williams, his face chalk white, his expression stunned.

Williams backed away, firing his gun until it clicked on empty chambers. Then he threw the gun at the walking dead man. Two feet from his murderer, King collapsed to the ground.

Panic overcame Williams. Nearby, he had seen an area that had been cleared and leveled for new walking paths. The tools were still there. Quickly, he stripped King and threw his clothes, contents and all, into the remnants of a shopping bag he found in a nearby garbage can.

It took him over an hour to dig the hole and roll King into it. Another hour and a half to bury him and level the area. All the time, he was sure that millions of people had seen him at work. He was terrified. He hurried from the scene.

The next day, he discovered how wrong he had been. On one hand, he discovered that King had told the truth. He didn't have the diamonds on him, nor was there any indication of where they were. On the other hand, when he gambled and returned to the scene of the crime later that morning to assist the FBI in their investigation, he happily noticed that workmen were smoothing heavy slabs of concrete onto the final resting place of King.

"That's all of it," Williams whimpered. He was starting to fall apart physically and mentally.

Robby heard footsteps in the hall and jumped to his feet. He stood behind Williams with his gun in the crying man's ear. The guards kicked in the door and aimed their rifles at Robby.

"DON'T SHOOT!!" Williams yelled. They held their fire. It was a standoff, for the moment.

Robby knew that the impasse couldn't last, and that even if he killed Williams, the guards would kill him. Slowly, keeping his eyes on the guards, he bent down and whispered in Williams' ear.

The guards couldn't hear anything but the last thing Robby said. "This isn't over." With an unexpected burst of speed, he pushed Williams towards the guards and simultaneously threw himself threw the window behind him.

Glass flew everywhere. Shots were heard, but Williams knew, somehow, that Robby had gotten away. He began to mumble.

Ryan turned from the window and went to help Williams off the floor. The man was mumbling something over and over. As he leaned over to help him up, he understood what Williams was repeating.

"It can't be. Fakes. The stones are fakes! All for nothing! Nothing."

He helped Williams to a chair and then turned back to the window. Suddenly, a shot rang out behind him. He whirled just in time to see the gun drop from Williams' dead hand and the grievous damage that the .45 had done to the old man's head.

≈

Two hours later, Robby limped aboard Empress One, and five minutes later, they were airborne. He picked up the on board satellite phone and punched a four digit code. It took two minutes for the connection to be made.

"Empress Atlantic City, Executive Offices."

"Moss."

"One moment, please."

Seymour came on the line. "Are you all right?"

Robby sighed. "Yeah."

There was a long pause. "Williams is dead, is it over?" Seymour asked.

This time the pause was on Robby's end. He took a deep breath and then whispered his reply.

"One last spin of the wheel to go."

CHAPTER EIGHTEEN

FINAL SPIN

Seymour arrived in Amsterdam and since that time, there was rarely a minute when he and Alexandra weren't together. Only this time, instead of hotel business intruding on their romance, it was the "Quest" as Alexandra had come to refer to the machinations and intrigues of the Research Group.

"Alexandra, my dear," Seymour began awkwardly, "I hate to do this to you, but I really need your help in this."

"You always do. For almost a year now, our affair has been strictly long distance. Now, you're here, and what do we do? We put ourselves on hold again. I'll never have you to myself until this is settled. What do you have in mind?"

"I thought perhaps we could take the van Eycks out somewhere tonight, and then a late dinner here at the hotel, something simple but quite elegant. It's positively essential that we keep them entertained all evening."

"I know better than to ask why. There's a wonderful concert this evening. Tickets are all but impossible to get. However, I do have a few helpful friends. I'll call and arrange things."

So now, the four of them sat in surroundings that were elegant,

374

with the music subdued and pleasant, the ambiance luxurious. The van Eycks were having a delightful evening at the invitation of Seymour and Alexandra.

"I can't tell you how much I appreciate your understanding," Seymour was saying to the van Eycks, "about your recent encounter with my associate. I hope this evening can in some small way make up for any unpleasantness you suffered because of him." Seymour was at his smoothest.

"He's young but his heart is definitely in the right place," van Eyck said. The wine and company were making him generous and expansive. "He is impulsive, and certainly lives on the edge, as you Americans say. I can tell. In my youth, I too had leanings that way."

Alexandra agreed that it was a characteristic of youth, and then turned the talk to the economy, what it was doing to the hotel, and business in general.

The waiter arrived, and they all turned their attention to the important business at hand, the main course.

ब

The street was dark and the Saab, driven by Alexandra's bodyguard, was parked down the block from van Eyck's home. Robby strolled down the street casually. He listened for the sound of the Saab's horn, which would warn him if anyone came by.

He reached the door and walked up and rang the bell. When no one answered, he tried the door. If anybody was watching, they would have seen him look frustrated, bend over to try and look through the door's window, and then straighten up when it opened. They wouldn't have seen him pick the lock and let himself in.

He quickly closed the door behind him, and listened for the telltale sound of an alarm buzzer. Hearing none, he went straight for the living room.

He didn't dare turn on a light, so he used a pen light to examine the brick wall around the fireplace. Slowly, he went over each of the inscriptions. He was sure he knew which one he needed, but he would be methodical. He had to be certain. All the inscriptions were very personal to the family. Names, favorite quotations from the Old Testament in Hebrew, and Yiddish sayings. At last, he settled on the one he had seen days before.

It was near the bottom, half hidden and long ignored in the corner, three bricks from the end and two from the bottom.

"*Requiescat.*" Robby quietly said to himself. The first part of the Latin phrase *Requiescat en pace*, rest in peace.

It was so jarring to find this Latin/Catholic phrase among all the rest of the inscriptions, that Robby had known its meaning instantly. Abraham van Eyck's letter to his son was the final proof. "I will deny them their prize. Rest peacefully, Papa."

Rest peacefully. *Requiescat en pace.*

Robby pushed the brick in all four directions. It wouldn't move. He didn't want to use the hammer that he had brought, so he stopped and thought. He examined it closely, but could see nothing that made it stand out from the other bricks. Except the inscription. He must be right.

He tried again, this time pushing in on each corner. When he pressed on the lower right corner, to his surprise, it rotated in. It was no brick, but just a facing of brick. He pulled it out from the wall.

Behind it was a small metal box. He pulled it out and opened it. Inside were several small felt bags, and by their feel Robby knew what they contained. All of them were black, except for one at the bottom, which was green. And beneath all the bags was a yellowed, dried out envelope. Carefully, Robby opened it and by penlight read the letter within.

ॐ

Seymour, Alexandra, and the van Eycks were up in Seymour's suite, having coffee. It had been a marvelous night of Opera and good companionship. Alexandra was regaling the group with the story of how she and Seymour had met.

"And then he announced that he intended either to ruin me financially or marry me. Of course, he didn't do either!" They all laughed.

The doorbell rang and Sy got up to open it. "I was afraid to. Still am." He opened the door and Robby walked in. Seymour looked at him questioningly, and thought he saw Robby nod.

Robby walked over to the group and sat down. Alexandra excused herself after introducing him to Mrs. van Eyck. Robby turned to Willem. "I have something for you." He handed him the yellowed envelope.

With a quizzical expression, Willem opened the letter and began to read.

❧

December 24, 1944

Gentle Stranger,

My name was Abraham van Eyck. If you are reading this, then I have been murdered this evening.

Gentle Stranger, I rely upon your humanity for my last request of any man.

Find my son, Willem van Eyck. I pray that he is alive and well away from the monsters who have murdered me. Give to him the pouch in green. The rest shall be yours.

The riches they contain were stolen by the monsters. I know not where. I would not have my family profit from the misery attached to them, beyond that amount which I believe I would have been able to provide for had the world been different.

Finally, if you can find it in your heart, find a Rabbi and ask him to say Kaddish for my poor unfortunate soul.

Gentle Stranger, I commend to you the last of me.

> **Signed,**
> **Abraham Solomon van Eyck**

❧

Van Eyck was crying as Robby handed him the green felt pouch. He took it and put it into his pocket without looking. He would do that later, when he was alone. Robby reached out and touched Willem's shoulder.

"If you say the diamonds are yours," he said quietly, "then they're yours. Here, now."

Willem looked up into Robby's eyes. "Thank you for giving my father back to me." Followed by his wife, he walked from the room.

❧

Two weeks later, Danny Gale walked out of a Midwest airport, to a waiting car. "I'm Danny Gale. You ready to roll?"

"Sure thing." The driver was a friend of Louie's, and could well have been his brother. "How's Vegas treating Louie?"

"He's living off the fat of the land."

The driver laughed. "If I know Louie, he is the fat of the land." He laughed uproariously at his own joke. "I don't usually take a client so damned far from the airport. It's a helluva ride. But Louie said this was special."

"It's appreciated." Danny handed him an envelope. "As agreed."

The driver took the envelope without checking the contents and placed it in the glove compartment, locking it securely. Then they took off.

Two hours later, they pulled up to a small shopping center, in the heart of a lower middle class residential area. Danny got out and checked the building numbers. At #138, he saw a large painted sign on the store window that proclaimed "Real Estate," and in smaller letters "Tax Accountant."

Inside, a teenage girl was struggling with a recalcitrant typewriter. "Can I help you?" she asked without looking up.

"I'm looking for Pete King." Danny said.

"Mr. King's office is the last one in back. Do you have an appointment?" Before Danny could answer, the girl called back, "A client, Mr. King."

Danny walked back, and was greeted at the office door by a short, slightly pudgy man in his 40's, with thinning red hair and green eyes. "Mr. King, I need to be sure I'm talking to the right man. I have a package to deliver."

King led him into the office, sat behind the desk. "What do you want to know? And what's in the package?"

"First, I need a couple of simple answers." Danny smiled to put the man at ease. "What was your mother's maiden name, and when and where were you born?"

"That's easy. Constance Cadiz. And I was born in New York, July 25th, 1947. So, do I win the jackpot?"

"You're the winner, all right." Danny took a small box out of his pocket. It was wrapped in tissue and tied with a gold cord. "This belongs to you. Sort of an inheritance, you might say." Danny put the package on the desk, turned and walked rapidly out of the building before King had time to react.

His driver was waiting, and started the engine the moment he saw Danny. King rushed to the door, package in hand. As he watched the car drive away, he pulled the cord on the package absentmindedly. The tissue fell away exposing a black velvet box.

King looked down, lifted the lid, and his mouth fell open. He was looking at the largest, finest diamond he'd ever seen in his life.

ॐ

It had been a month since Amsterdam, and this was Robby's first day out of the hospital since the surgery on his face. He wandered the Empress Casino happily. Barker and Louie had completely recovered and had received their shares of the diamonds. Eve was back teaching at UCLA and co-writing a book on the experience with Rudy. And in the lobby of the Empress was a display of some of the nicer large stones with a plaque that read "The Empress's Crown Jewels." Seymour was a happy man.

Robby wandered over to the roulette table that Jenna was working at, and handed across five one hundred dollar bills. She took them with the hand that displayed an absolutely gorgeous three carat diamond ring. Robby bet two hundred on the double zero.

"No more bets, please." Jenna spun the wheel. It came up seven. Robby shrugged and bet the other three hundred.

"I've been lucky lately," he said.

Jenna laughed. "You don't have to tell me. No more bets." The wheel spun, and the ball fell into the 16 slot.

Robby shrugged and turned to Jenna. "One day." He started to walk away as an elderly man walked up to the table. For some reason, he stepped aside to make room for him, and then froze in his track as he heard Jenna say, "Double Zero, green, a winner!"

Slowly, he turned around and walked back to the table. The old man was ecstatic. As she piled the chips on the man's bet, Jenna turned to Robby, almost laughing.

"Sorry, Robby. You almost got it."

He smiled and looked down at his right hand. On his index finger was a large gold ring with a green enamel inlay and diamonds forming the number double zero. "That's okay. I've already got mine."

ॐ

The temple was quiet and cool. Refreshing, considering the ninety degree heat outside. The sanctuary was half full and the Rabbi seemed half awake. Morning services were held only three days a week, and in Las Vegas, morning was always the slow time.

"Be not afraid of sudden fear," the young Rabbi intoned, "neither of the desolation of the wicked, when it cometh. Take counsel together and it shall come to naught; speak the word, and it shall not stand; for God is with us. And even to your old age I am he; and even to hoar hair will I carry you; I have made, and I will bear; even I will carry, and will deliver you."

In the back of the sanctuary, sitting by himself, Robby stood along with the others who had come to mourn. He thought of Abraham van Eyck, of the victims of the *Windsor* and the Trans-Atlantic flight, and all of the other victims of the obscenity that he had just been immersed in.

He thought of them and slowly began to pray. *"Yisgadal v'yiskadash, shme raboh."*

Afterwards, he walked out into the parking lot, took off his tie and jacket and climbed into his Mustang. He threw a Gerry Mulligan disc into the player and set off down Interstate 15.

❧

"There are but two creatures in this world who matter.
Those with a commitment,
And those who require a commitment of others."

—*John Adams 1774*

AUTHORS' NOTE

Just for the record...Requiescat sprung from rumors, shrouded stories, and clouded truths. Whether or not it is true or sprung whole from our imaginations is not the point. The point is, that the actions depicted in it happened many times throughout World War II and the years after.

Lives *were* taken freely and without thought by amoral men who believed they were preserving their own morality...on both sides.

Loyal officers and brave men of the German military *were* betrayed by their leaders. Many became bitter and sought escape, and some of those *were* helped by the U.S. Government with new identities and new lives in America. One has only to read the newspapers about Artukovic, von Braun and others like them, or look at those scientists who helped destroy London during the war, and put an American on the moon after it. We take no position, we merely acknowledge the facts.

Fortunes *were* stolen during the war and disappeared never to be seen again, much as the men who stole them.

This is a novel set across the panorama of what is perhaps history's most notorious years. Throughout this book, you have encountered a number of documents representative of various national and international sources. As presented herein, they are composites or similitudes of such documents.

Where real names of public men were used, we have taken great pains to ensure that their actions conform with both the public and private record. We harbor no grudges, have no axes to grind, we merely present them for you, the reader, to judge.

This book would not have been possible without the help and guidance of a great many people, both in and out of the government.

For their help in understanding the often shadowy and obscure world of international espionage both today and a half century ago, we would like to thank John H. Wright of the Central Intelligence Agency; Rosemary Melendy of the U.S. Department of State; and Milton O. Gustafson of the Diplomatic Branch of the National Archives.

For helping to explain some of the more obscure chapters of the Second World War, as well as assisting us in our seemingly endless searches of German Military records, we would like to acknowledge Bob Wolfe of the Modern Military Branch of the National Archives; Christine M. DePellegrini of Colt Manufacturing; and Aaron Breitbar of the Simon Wiesenthal Center; as well as Dr. Diane R. Spielman of the Leo Baeck Institute.

For the sections set in New York in the late forties, our gratitude is extended to Kathleen Roche and the Hagstrom Map Company; and the New York City Archives staff.

Perhaps nothing was so important as our understanding of the world of diamonds, diamond mining, diamond cutting etc. For their assistance in these areas we thank Joe Waldmann; Matt Fein of Ambel; the Gemological Institute of America; and especially, Sy and Gail Messing of Galleria Jewelers.

We are also indebted to the headache easing assistance of S. Maurizio & G. Sontgerath of the Credit Suisse in Bern, Switzerland; Lt. Cmdr. Paul R. von Protz of the United States Coast Guard; Susan Stevenson of the National Transportation Safety Board; and for lunches, mind clearing conversations, insights and unqualified friendship, Evelyn Krumbholz, and Phil Pearl.

And to the staffs at Martin Luther King Jr. Medical Center,

Glendale Urgent Care, and the UCLA Medical Center, without whom neither we, nor this book, would have had a chance to exist...Thank You.

Finally, if some basic truth shines through our story, if you recognize a familiar face or perhaps see yourself reflected in it, consider it *pentimento*, sketch lines showing through the finished portrait, and remember the lines of Stephen Vincent Benet:

"This is for you who are to come with time,
And gaze upon our ruins with strange eyes."

Requiescat en pace. Rest in peace.

Richard B. Steinberg
&
Gloria Usiskin Steinberg
Glendale, California
February, 1993